Praise for Aw C. Hope Clark

Hope Clark's books have been honored as winners of the Epic Award, Silver Falchion Award, and the Daphne du Maurier Award.

"Ms. Clark delivers a riveting ride, with her irrepressible characters set squarely in the driver's seat."

—*Dish Magazine* on *Echoes of Edisto*

"Page-turning . . . [and] edge-of-your-seat action. . . . Prepare to be absorbed by Clark's crisp writing and compelling storytelling. This is one you don't want to miss!"

—Carolyn Haines,
USA Today bestselling author on *Dying on Edisto*

"I am a big fan!"

—former Mayor Jane Darby,
Town of Edisto Beach, SC

"Entertaining and compelling start of a new series."

—Anna Maria Giacomasso,
NetGalley Reviewer on *Murdered in Craven*

The Novels of
C. Hope Clark

The Carolina Slade Mysteries

Lowcountry Bribe

Tidewater Murder

Palmetto Poison

Newberry Sin

Salkehatchie Secret

The Edisto Island Mysteries

Murder on Edisto

Edisto Jinx

Echoes of Edisto

Edisto Stranger

Dying on Edisto

Edisto Tidings

Reunion on Edisto

Edisto Heat

The Craven County Mysteries

Murdered in Craven

Burned in Craven

Edisto Heat

The Edisto Island Mysteries
Book 8

by

C. Hope Clark

Bell Bridge Books

Bell Bridge Books
PO BOX 300921
Memphis, TN 38130
Print ISBN: 978-1-61026-177-7

Bell Bridge Books is an Imprint of BelleBooks, Inc.

We at BelleBooks enjoy hearing from readers.
Visit our websites
BelleBooks.com
BellBridgeBooks.com
ImaJinnBooks.com

10 9 8 7 6 5 4 3 2 1

Cover design: Debra Dixon
Interior design: Hank Smith
Photocredits: C. Hope Clark

:Lhed:01:

Dedication

This book is devoted to the dedicated, die-hard Edistonians, who fight to keep Charleston out of its business and development outside its town limits.

Thanks for fighting to keep Edisto Beach's personality intact.

Chapter 1

SHE WALKED IN her front door, and the air-conditioning penetrated her sticky uniform, sending a quick shiver up her back. Edisto Beach Police Chief Callie Morgan wondered if she should shed right there in her entry hall to avoid contaminating the house. Every second counted before the odor turned into a stench that would invade every inch of her home.

Stiff and robotlike, she locked the front door and dropped her keys in the bowl on the credenza. Swallowing, she tried hard not to breathe through her nose. The warm beer, cheese, and shrimp mixture had dried in some spots but wedged thick in seams, buttonholes, and collar. She couldn't identify a good place to drop the nasty clothes without contemplating how to sterilize where she did. The uniform and all its accouterment didn't shed quickly, so gingerly she moved off the rug, not wanting to leave a presence, and made her way across the wooden floor to her bedroom.

Her weapon went on the nightstand. Clean, thank God. The utility belt appeared unscathed except for small spots near the buckle. Still, she laid it on the floor until she could wipe it down properly. Off came the badge, mic, etc. Leaving shoes on the bathroom tile, she stepped fully clothed into the hot shower, way too hot for a July day, but son of a biscuit, cold water wouldn't cut this crud.

Callie received the call from Marie at two in the afternoon, taking her to Point Street, not on the oceanfront but across the road from it. The ocean met St. Helena Sound at that part of the town, and the water held less ferocity. One would think the calmer surf would lead to tamer tenants, but eighteen people had crammed into a house designed for twelve, which, per the brochure, already meant people sleeping on pull-out sofas and day beds on the porch. Clearly, the party had turned semi-orgy, people half-clothed due to sex and sunburn.

Few could remember details of what set them off, but the full-on sun had driven everyone to double their booze. A husband taste-tested his sister-in-law, sending a few of them over the edge, including the scorned, screaming, red-faced wife who had become the barf culprit.

The impromptu spew across the police chief quieted the entire crew. Chagrinned and fearful of lockup, they'd apologized, laid trash bags in her patrol car, and promised on assorted grandmotherly graves and firstborns' lives that Edisto Beach PD would never need to visit again.

Which meant Callie took one for the team. The results beat arresting someone or writing tickets. Tourists were golden to the community, and better they leave beholden to Edisto than resentful.

She'd taken the time to light a candle she kept on the bathroom counter, to semi-mask the odorous task, and had muted her phone for calls and set it on the toilet tank, speaker facing the shower door, and turned on some Neil Diamond, her go-to relaxation music. The shuffled playlist hit "Sweet Caroline," a rather worn-out song of his, in her opinion, but a singsong moment couldn't hurt. Her two officers on duty, Thomas Gage and Cobb LaRoache, vowed to cover the beach the rest of the day. So, on she sang.

"So good! So good! So good!" Her eyes closed to ignore what flushed off her and down the drain past her clothes puddled in the bottom of the shower. Sterilized and scalded, she toned down the temperature to something more tepid.

There. Better.

"Sweet Caroline" slowed to "Hello Again." The romantic ballad washed over her as intimately as the rose suds covering her head to toe. She rested hands on the wall, sank into her thoughts, and let the water rinse the back of her neck and upper back, taking her to the last time she stood in the shower this lathered up.

She hadn't been alone.

A smile crept in.

She still caught herself coming to grips with thoughts of him, especially when he wasn't there, because when he was there, all rationality went out the window. Baby steps, he'd told her in the beginning. Nothing they did had permanence inscribed on them.

But Callie dated one man at a time, and she dated nobody without some reflection about a potential future. Nothing conscious, really. She couldn't help the straight and narrow of the logic in her. To be honest, she guessed Mark felt the same. He dated no one else. He was awfully good at understanding what she needed to hear, though, and their times together had proven so effortless that she welcomed the uncomplicated nature of their relationship.

Thank goodness her day was through. She might find her way to El Marko's for dinner, the Mexican restaurant her fella owned and ran. Nobody seemed to notice he wore Hawaiian shirts and came from Cajun heritage.

She shut off the water. As her neighbor and yoga friend Sophie Bianchi taught her, whose advice Callie ever pretended to ignore, she sucked in a breath to her navel to relax . . . and immediately regretted it, catching a whiff of the day's activities, now scented by a lavender candle.

She squeezed the water out of her hair, then paused. What happened to the music?

Opening the shower door, she reached for the towel on the counter and stepped out— "What—?"

Water. All over the floor. Outside the shower.

Immediately, she looked back into the stall, like she'd missed something, the message not quite sticking in her brain as to what was going on. Water off, drain worked, her clothes still trickled from their wadded pile. However, on the outside, an inch covered the entire bathroom floor.

Listening hard, she tried to sense the location. High-stepping through the water, then realizing the silliness of doing so, she opened the cabinets. All dry inside. For now but not for long. A sheen of moisture coated the room.

A Palmetto bug floated past, coming from the toilet direction. Guess she hadn't cleaned back there in a while.

Still naked, she threw the useless towel on the counter and followed the movement and the faint noise of a soft flow. *There!* Her phone lay underwater, behind the toilet, below an open pipe.

Are you kidding me?

In some incredible alignment of physics, Callie's phone had vibrated off the toilet, down the back, shearing off the turn-off valve en route to what Callie prayed wasn't its final grave. She lifted the phone, shook it, hoping to breathe life into the black screen. No such luck.

Then it hit her. With the valve gone, there was no way to stop the water! At least not inside the house.

Splashing, Callie grabbed a face cloth and attempted to plug the pipe. The raw edge slit the pad of her index finger, but she continued to force the terry cloth. The diverted sprays re-wet her head to toe, dowsed the sheetrock, and coated the glass wall of her shower. She spat, running a hand over her face. *Screw this!*

She spun and rummaged through her makeup drawer. Nothing shaped right to be a plug.

The speed in which she wasted time increased the odds that the catastrophe would reach her bedroom carpet, so she ran out, snaring bathrobe off a hook, and headed to the back door. The master shutoff was inside the meter box near the road . . . outside.

Hair dripping, bare-footed, and robe gripped around her, the tie left somewhere in her closet, she took two-step jumps down her two dozen stairs to ground level then scurried to the edge of her back property line on Jungle Shores Road. Brushing debris off the surface, she jammed a finger into the box's opening to pry it open. Of course it would not budge.

"Callie!"

Callie didn't even bother looking up. "Can't talk now, Soph." The lid shouldn't be this stuck.

Sophie reached her, in a kerfuffle and overly eager to be heard. "But it's important. I tried calling you—"

Callie gave a one-handed yank, still clutching her robe. What the hell was wrong with this box? "Help me," she pleaded. "I've got water gushing everywhere inside!"

Sophie fisted her nails, freshly done in a coral red each and every morning, and held balled hands against her chest. "Don't you have a tool or something?"

To hell with this. Callie straddled the box, her robe askew in front, the satin material clinging in the back. She slid two fingers of each hand into the slot and wrenched. The top flew off. She fell onto her butt in the grass, her front exposed.

"Oh my God!" Sophie yelled, dancing back ten feet.

Callie scrabbled her robe together, threw the lid down, and leaped up for the valve, only to retreat hastily from the edge.

A snake sat inside, coiled and none too happy at the disturbance.

"Is it poisonous?" Sophie squealed.

"Honestly, I do not care," Callie said, totally frosted at the day. She headed across the street to where landscapers sodded a refurbished marsh home. Or had been, rather. They'd long quit working to watch the show.

"Hey, you." Callie motioned, feet muddying up in the silt road, trying to recover herself. "Any of you carry a handgun?"

Three sets of eyes widened white against suntanned faces. They shook stunned heads, no longer humored at the crazy woman.

"Hand me one of your shovels, then."

One of them did, holding it outstretched, keeping distance between them. She returned to the box. The snake remained poised, judging.

"Let it escape," Sophie said. "It can't help that you're pissed. His eyes are round, not slitted. He's not poisonous."

At any moment, water would come tumbling down her steps, and in that instant Callie vowed that this nasty son-of-a-bitch creature, slitted eyes or not, wasn't going to cost her five figures of damage. She stood on Sophie's side of the box and slapped the ground next to the box with the shovel. The snake recoiled and stood his ground.

"Get out!" She lifted the shovel, struggling with how to aim the tool at the snake without doing what had already been done in her bathroom, shearing off the valve. She popped the ground again beside the box. The snake tightened further, owning its turf.

Laughing, the landscapers had ventured roadside. One of them whistled. Another spoke Spanish. Apparently, they hadn't been around Edisto long enough to know who they were whistling at, but in an instant of rationalization, Callie decided this not the moment to tout the badge.

"Callie," Sophie whispered. "Close your robe."

Callie looked down. The silk had parted, clinging at her nipples where the material hung wide enough to show her other assets. She dropped the shovel and groped for the tie that wasn't there.

Seeing its opportunity, the snake made a dash toward the marsh . . . and toward the men.

Officer Thomas Gage rolled up in his cruiser and stopped, window down. "Why aren't you answering your . . .?" He did a double take at Callie's half-nude dilemma. "Um . . . why aren't you answering your phone, chief?" He opened his door and got out. "What's going on?"

Sophie yelled, "Snake! Under your car!"

Thomas leaped knees high, hand on his weapon. "Where? Where?"

Laughter erupted from the other side of the cruiser. One of the landscapers came around, hand held high. Three feet of reptile hung down, curling around his arm. "Here is your monster!" The three men guffawed. "Flash us some more, lady!"

Thomas turned on him. "She's the chief of police, dude. Take your snake and get gone."

Callie could rue Thomas's exposé of her later. She reached into the meter box, turned the valve, and bolted back to the stairs. Thomas ran behind her, Sophie behind him.

At the bedroom door, Callie apprehensively scanned for damage. The water had stopped. Her bedroom carpet, however, squished under her feet. She heaved a long, disappointed sigh.

"Chief?" Thomas reached her. "You're bleeding. That snake didn't bite you, did he?"

"No." She was surprised he hadn't, though, at the way this day's events spun out. Thomas disappeared toward the kitchen.

She didn't feel the cut, but it bled with vigor. Blood smeared her soggy robe, wet silt spotted up the sagging hem. She crunched the finger up in a handful of the ruined robe to avoid it dripping onto the carpet, then wondered why bother. "I have no words for this," she said, blowing out hard. Then she remembered Sophie. "So what is your emergency exactly?"

"They were looking for you and worried you weren't answering. I called and you wouldn't answer. So I came to get you."

"Well, my phone drowned," Callie said, pointing through the doorway at the bathroom counter.

Thomas reappeared, Callie's kitchen first aid kit at the ready. He'd been to her house enough times to remember. "I tried calling, too. So did Marie."

"I'm sure you did." She held out her digit, letting the junior officer feel useful bandaging her up while she held her garment shut. He'd already seen enough of her . . . hoped he would keep it to himself. "What's the problem?"

"A car ran into the Island Ice Shack," he said, doing a way neater job at the bandaging than she expected. "Moved it four feet back from its foundation."

"Well, how about that?" she said.

Sophie looked questioning at Thomas who raised a brow back in warning to remain quiet. Two years had been long enough for him to read his chief.

Any other day, Callie'd rush to the accident. They were a six-person police force, expected at all the major incidents. The Island Ice Shack sat right where everyone had to pass, in front of Bi-Lo's parking lot and right off Highway 174. The small, almost portable shed was practically iconic. "And they asked for me?"

Thomas nodded, trepidation creeping into his expression. "Everyone. Then we got worried, and they sent me, and so I left LaRoache alone handling things especially after we called Sophie, and she couldn't get you—"

"Okay, okay. Let me put some clothes on." Guess a call to her insurance agent would have to wait.

As she sponged her way across carpet to the closet and dresser, she struggled with the fact her body image had been seared into young Thomas's mind. Shaking off the thought, she grabbed clothes and found dry shoes not on the floor. That's when she spotted her utility belt where she'd let it fall. So much for the radio. Thomas followed her stare and went over to lift it up. "Let me work on this tonight for you, Chief."

Well, at least she had her badge and her gun. Her license and keys. "Thanks, Thomas."

"I'll work on your phone, too," he added. "Might be salvageable."

"I'll mop all this up," Sophie added.

Callie walked around them to her guest room. "Soph, I don't own enough towels to mop this up. What I could really use is—"

"A place to stay," she added. "My home is open. You already have the key. I'll stay and work on this mess. You got any extra blankets and quilts you don't care about anymore?"

Callie was going to say she needed a phone. While the gesture was sweet, Callie wasn't sure bunking with her buddy at *Hatha Heaven* would work, but that could be addressed later.

Callie changed into jeans and hooked her paddle holster and badge on a plain nylon belt. No radio now with the belt wet, and she didn't have time to go by the station for the walkie or back-up work phone. She headed the lone mile up to the entrance of town, finding roadblocks a stone's throw from the accident. Took her a few *whoop-whoops* to get through the gawkers, but she found a place in the grocery store parking lot.

The Ice Shack sat super wonky off its base, a small Hyundai nosed into its side. She spotted the business owner. He seemed okay. She soon identified the driver, his cheeks rosy from more than the sun. Nobody mad, nobody hurt, but confusion still reigned thanks to the steady stream of rubberneckers expanding the crowd. Being late afternoon, cars full of day-trippers struggled to leave the beach. They weren't sure how, however, because Monty Bartow stood in the middle of the road attempting to direct traffic. "Hey, Chief," he shouted over heads.

Callie thought she spotted his baby-blue moped in front of the Bi-Lo. She smiled wanly and took in the accident situation. Thomas had not yet arrived, and LaRoache had his hands full with the incident report, so Callie waded through the sea of people, not an easy task at five foot two and lacking her uniform.

Monty, however, had donned his best dress. A button-up shirt from a past temporary job as a stocker in a hardware store and cargo pants to match the Edisto PD. The cargos presented much better than the striped pants he used to wear, the ones from the Colleton County jail where he'd done a short stint about ten years ago for shoplifting. The badge hanging on a chain around his neck came from Amazon, way too authentic for Callie's liking, and someone, some time ago, had given him a name tag for over his pocket that read *Officer Monty*. Again, not her choice. There was humoring the man, then there was feeding an obsession that interfered with real policing . . . regardless of how sincere the man was.

"Monty?" she called, pushing through the last line of tourists to reach him standing all braced and firm on the road's center line. "We appreciate what you've done." She redirected one car, then another. "But I need you to step aside and let me take over."

"Got this, Chief. They could not find you."

His voice was deep but not as thick as one might envision a thirty-year-old man with mental deficits from birth. One had to hold a conversation with the attractive young man for a minute or two to recognize his fifth-grade mentality. He used to trot to and from the beach, hunting ways to help on Edisto Beach which kept him fairly fit, but some good Samaritan donated the used moped a year ago after seeing him walking in ninety-five-degree heat. Now he was everywhere.

Monty lived with his mother, Minnie, a tax preparer who did mostly short forms for people across the island and operated out of their small home back up an inlet road. At sixteen she gave birth to Monty, the father unspoken of, and the story varied about Monty's limitations and their origins. Rumors tinkered with who her own father was, as well, her mother never having married either. Minnie claimed he died young, shortly after her parents' intense, brief romance, though nobody from the island could ever put a name to him. Monty's grandmother saw him into this world then died from cancer. It had been Minnie and Monty

Bartow for twenty-nine years, with the exception of the short time he went to jail. Edisto Island sort of took care of the boy/man here and there.

"But I'm here now," Callie said, touching his elbow. "Let me do my job before I get in trouble."

Monty didn't hug, and he particularly didn't like being told what to do, but he could take directions from women way better than he could from men since he'd never lived in a home with the latter. Callie had learned to manage him with a fairly deft hand.

He gave her a sideways glance. "But I like helping. You go do something more important."

She moved between him and the outgoing traffic to distract him while waving one confused family around. "Brice LeGrand and the rest of town council will think I'm slacking off. I don't need them mad at me. You can help keep people out of the street, though."

He puffed up. "I don't want to."

God, not here. Not now. "An officer follows orders, Monty."

A horn honked, then another. Some days Monty was six years old, other times twenty. Right now she read him about thirteen and obstinate. That's when she played the Chief card, calling on his deep-seeded dream of being a cop.

"We have a situation, sir. Please, do as you are ordered."

Monty hesitated. "Yes, ma'am." Then he dragged himself over toward the crowd, out of the road.

"Chief!"

She studied the crowd, hunting for the familiar voice.

"Over here by the Ice Shack."

She spotted Thomas pushing through.

"We have a fire on Dock Site Road," he said, almost to her. "Where do you want me?"

A fire. Her heart flipped then assumed a skipped beat rhythm. "How bad?"

"No idea," he said, holding out a palm for a car to stop, letting another by.

He was six foot and fully uniformed. Admittedly, he would make quicker time of this traffic uproar than her petite civilian-clad self.

"Do this," she said. "I'll head to the fire. What's the address?"

"Brice LeGrand's place," he said.

She froze. "Seriously?"

Sheepishly, he winced. "Sorry, Chief."

Brice was head of town council and the man she'd saved from jail six months ago, not that he felt beholden nor considered it a favor. In her two-year tenure, Callie had become a heroine around Edisto to some, but to Brice and his ilk, that only made her a bigger target. He'd dropkick her out of the job in a heartbeat.

But fire. *Jesus.* She didn't do fire. She had nightmares about fire.

Fire had consumed her husband. Fire had consumed her life with the Boston PD. Fire had left the eight-inch scar on her right forearm.

And while it took confronting her husband's killer to make sense of her phobia, it was a phobia, nonetheless. Lesser than before, but still.

Only very few on Edisto knew it.

She turned back to Thomas. "Watch Monty."

"Where'd he go?"

She gazed around for the wannabe, but he was gone, his moped not in its normal place against the Bi-Lo ice machine. Probably went off to pout.

She wedged through people to her cruiser and headed out. Two miles to Brice's place. Two miles to get a grip on what would meet her as she rounded the turn on Lybrand Street.

She rubbed the long ropey scar on her forearm.

Two miles to do breathing exercises and convince herself she could handle fire. Most Edistonians had seen her scar. Few of them could say how she got it.

Chapter 2

CALLIE ROLLED toward Dock Site Road trying to ignore a hammering pulse. *How stupid.* She breathed deep, reaching for normal. There should be no déjà vu this time. She should be past this.

Back in Boston, a counselor had warned her about triggers, but that was so long ago. And she hadn't had any triggers in a long time. This was the first time a fire at dusk had crossed her path since that horrible night four years ago, except for Papa Beach's place next door to hers, but that hadn't been at dusk. Sure, that fire had seized her, and her son had worried long and hard about her afterward, but she thought she'd come a long way since then.

She rubbed her sternum, a trick to refocus . . . a measure of how hard she could feel her heart trying to bust through. It beat pretty damn fast.

No, absolutely not. She rubbed harder. She refused to regress now.

She arrived on Edisto two years ago, mentally broken from the loss of husband, infant daughter, and career, and had commenced to losing herself deep in the bottle, which she had justified by arguing her past would've crushed the average person. But with her son Jeb to raise, her sweet daddy handed her the keys to the family place on Edisto Beach where she'd spent weeks as a child, deeding it to her with orders for her to get her act together.

She moved, reluctantly, the bold sunsets and their fiery reflections on the water immediately driving her indoors in the evenings, reminding her of her Boston home going up in flames, right at dusk . . . with her husband inside.

Sure, she'd evolved with as many scorching, blinding sunsets that occurred out here. She lived on an island, for God's sake, connected to a bigger island by one lone road. People came here in droves for these medicinal sunsets.

She, however, willed herself to do little more than accept them. Admittedly, on some days, she managed to enjoy the more subtle ones. She coped for Jeb, who had postponed college a year because of her flaws, their roles of protector and the protected reversed for a time.

These days, when she was out and about and dusk crept up on her . . . when a casual glance registered as fire instead of reflection on the water, she reminded herself she'd healed and instructed herself to recall how far she'd come. Ordered herself to remain strong. Between that mindset and getting a grip on her gin consumption, she'd conquered that quest. She was eight months sober now.

Still, her chest galloped like a greyhound on a treadmill. She hadn't seen this coming. Sunset was one thing. A genuine fire was quite another.

In for ten, out for ten. She breathed as she rounded the curve. The marsh side of the beach town was a different style of beauty than that of the active Atlantic, though similarly in high demand, as sales showed. She could see the marsh from her own back door, across the empty lot across the street . . . whenever she left those blinds up.

The back of Brice's place faced Big Bay Creek and incredible sunsets, one of which would happen in another hour per the cloudless sky. She expected that. This time it wasn't only about the sun.

The fire engine caught her eye first, and she sent up a prayer that no plumes of smoke or dancing flame fingers reached into the dusk sky.

She pulled up behind the truck. Two firefighters worked the storage room under Brice's house, but the open door blocked her view of the damage. Traffic cooperated in spite of the one-lane issue, so she strode to the front where Brice stood beside her counterpart with the fire department . . . and put on her game face.

"Chief."

"Chief."

"About time," said Brice, his five o'clock cocktail having come and gone . . . and then some. His cheeks and forehead were smudged, an old t-shirt as well where he'd touched something to do with the mishap. His hands lay palms against his pot belly. He looked mean, though his nature sported a perpetual frown since losing his wife, which worsened his drinking problem, a fact the whole island endured.

She let his sarcasm slide off like everyone else usually did. "You okay, Brice?"

He scowled deeper.

"He has some minor burns on his hands where he tried to put it out himself," the fire chief said. "Won't let us treat him, but he'll be okay. Nothing structural done to the storage room, but it'll be a job cleaning it up, maybe replacing some wood. Repainting. He called us in time."

"Someone set this fire," Brice spouted. "I'm telling you, someone intentionally did this." He looked at Callie, his go-to person to condemn for all things wrong on the beach. "This is unacceptable. The safety of this beach is waning, Chief Morgan, and as head of town council, this will be a topic on next week's agenda."

Chief Morgan, not Callie. Spoken toward an audience.

Chief Leon Hightower threw a subtle smirk at Callie. He hadn't lived on Edisto Beach for much more than Callie, a little under three years, but he'd readily grasped the dynamics of its people. First-responder leaders had to learn the dance early to survive the politics, but when it came to fire versus police, Callie usually took the heat.

Because fires were few on Edisto Beach, the fire department spent a lot of time on fire prevention, education, fundraising, and inspections. They assisted in any sort of rescue, with raccoons in the attic more the norm than cats in trees. They sold t-shirts and managed the beach wheelchair checkout for the differently-abled tourist or two.

Three full-time staff and a cadre of volunteers. Folks loved Leon and his people.

But out-of-sight, out-of-mind factored in big time with Brice. The police department performed a more visual, everyday job. Brice LeGrand had raised an *I'll-try-to-fire-you* issue at just about every town council meeting since Callie'd accepted the badge, and thank goodness, the rest of the council took his threats with more than a grain of salt and voted accordingly. Today's politics between police and town thrived in a way better environment, attendees often tongue in cheek at hers and his exchanges, than in those early days when Brice's word trumped hers. Even better since Brice and ex-wife Aberdeen displayed so much of their private lives to the residents at Christmas. Thanks to Aberdeen and Twitter, everyone knew Brice was broke. Everyone knew she'd screwed his best friend for months. And everyone knew Brice had been a suspect in his best friend's murder.

Callie had investigated Brice during that mess, forced to consider him as a suspect in the death of Aberdeen's lover who had, coincidentally, been Callie's stepfather, whom she'd barely known. She'd learned only a year ago that his wife was her birth mother. There hadn't been the time or the will to forge much of a relationship before he'd been killed.

Brice had escaped both jail and alimony in that domestic humiliation, but he remained pitifully alone in that house. Took him a couple months to show himself around town, finally lured out of isolation by a political event he couldn't pass up. Folks gave him far more forgiveness than he deserved. Some days Callie was among them.

The tourists had zero clue about Edisto Beach drama behind the curtain.

Chief Leon silently watched his two firefighters, a man and a woman. "So . . . what's the cause?" Callie finally asked when nobody said.

Brice acted like he hadn't heard, his scowl deepening.

"A hobby accident," Leon replied.

"Never got dangerous?" she asked.

"Nah."

Callie looked at Brice, like he ought to be contributing something to the conversation, but his attention was riveted on the firefighters emptying his storage room, strewing his belongings across the parking area and yard.

Beach houses were required a twelve- to fourteen-feet elevation in case of hurricane surges. Building code only allowed storage rooms under the main floor, between the heavy stilt supports, constructed in a fashion to break away in case of storm.

"A bucket of assorted rags started it," Leon said. "It was found outside the storage room, propping the door open. Inside, we found a spilled can of linseed oil on its side. Brice was fortunate that bucket fire didn't take a leap and do serious damage."

"My door's burned," Brice said. "My lawn chairs and hurricane shutters ruined."

"The door, yes, but those other things can be scrubbed, Brice," Leon said.

Callie peered around Leon at Brice. "Linseed oil, huh? Making soap, painting still lifes, or cleaning a gun stock?" She was familiar with the latter, having watched her father oil down his shotgun and twenty-two rifle stocks, maintaining that showcase gloss.

She swore he reddened, though his cheeks and nose held a perpetual sunburn appearance from a combination of fishing and bourbon. With Aberdeen gone, he entertained both way more than before. The local liquor store had a way of noticing drinking habits and tended to drop a comment or two to the customer stepping up to the counter about the one that just left. The reason Callie had bought her liquor in Charleston . . . before she quit.

"She made soap," Brice said.

Was he blaming Aberdeen or missing her? "She's been gone since Christmas, Brice."

His mouthed worked like he had dentures . . . or chewed on what to say. Callie almost felt sorry for him.

She did a mental backstep in the name of mercy. "Nobody blames you for taking up her hobby, Brice. I'd love a piece of homemade soap when you finish. What scents do you have?"

"I'm not making soap," he grumbled.

Maybe she shouldn't have mentioned Aberdeen. "Never mind," she said. "Sorry." She turned to Leon to finalize things and move on. She had an insurance agent to call and a flooded house to deal with.

Brice blurted out, "If you must know, I'm painting seascapes."

She and Leon glanced at each other, unsure how to address the revelation of their drunken councilman turning artist. Callie couldn't quite see past the absurd image of Brice at an easel, his horse-hair brush teasing whitecaps on the tips of waves.

"Kudos to you," she managed to say.

The silence turned awkward.

The volunteer firefighters put the finishing touches to the fire incident, a smidge comical with them being fully decked out over a five-gallon bucket fire. Chaise chairs, tools, a cheap charcoal grill, old paint buckets, assorted lumber and hurricane shutters lay scattered around the grounds to ensure they'd done a thorough job of uncovering any spark. Left Brice with a mess to clean up, though.

Callie's heart had returned to its normal rhythm the moment she'd realized the fire call was a simple one, without serious injury. This was the depth and breadth of fires in the town of Edisto Beach, to which Callie thanked the heavens. Grills caught fire mainly with little damage, but the potential was always there. Houses stood close, and fire was no respecter of property or life, thus the quick response. That and only two and a half square miles of properties to cover.

One could almost run to these fires, one of the reasons for the use of volunteers with the exception of the chief, an admin type, and an assistant chief. The town budget wasn't as padded as a tourist might think.

Movement caught her eye on the other side of the neighbor's latticework privacy fence. She had no need to go over, though she let her curiosity dwell a bit at the person's movements. She'd about decided against the need to interview the neighbors to protect Brice from additional humiliation.

Everyone wrapping up brought Brice back to life. "I didn't start that fire, and I want that put in both your reports, with a copy to me pronto."

"You used the linseed oil, right?" she asked.

"I closed the can."

"But you smoke, right?" Leon asked.

"Used to. Don't anymore. Haven't in months."

Callie had doubts about that, but this was not the time.

Brice began using his hands to pontificate. Callie noted their redness.

"I was upstairs, smelled the smoke, and ran down to find that bucket lit up," he said. "Someone set it, I say. Yes, I put those paint rags in that bucket. Yes, I use linseed oil, but I set it downstairs outside the storage until I could deal with it proper."

"How long before you put it there and you noticed the fire?" Leon asked.

"Ninety minutes, maybe less, but some hoodlum set it afire, I'm telling you. Your job. . . ." He pointed at the two of them, one at a time. "Both your jobs . . . is to nail the bastard."

Callie stared quizzically at Leon. She thought they'd pretty much already labeled the cause as an accidental spinoff of Brice's attempts at a Van Gogh.

"Do you have cameras on your house?" she asked, not seeing any from her vantage, but she could hope. At her place, such a culprit would've been recorded from six different angles.

Brice's head shook in spastic impatience. "No need out here."

Everyplace had a need, in her opinion, but now was not the time to debate security preferences.

"I take it you don't lock your storage then?" she asked.

"Neither do you, and neither do half the people out here," he accused back, pointing, his jowls and index finger both bobbing with emphasis.

Actually, Callie did lock her storage, but she wanted this to play out as a minimal accident, forgiven and forgotten.

Leon wasn't too terribly eager to help her.

"If someone did this to you," she started, hoping she wouldn't regret an attempt to meet Brice in the middle, "who do you think might have done it?"

His grunt reeked of cynicism. "You say that like I made it up."

"No, Brice," she said, trying again. "I state the facts as you have presented them. If someone did this to you, who should we suspect?"

He thought about it, watching as the two firemen started toward them, done with their work. Brice's audience was about to double. "Who should we suspect?" he repeated, louder, staring not at Callie but at the two approaching. "Why . . . one of my political enemies, of course."

The firefighters looked to their chief for direction . . . meaning permission to keep walking. His almost imperceptible nod allowed them to continue around the truck to put their equipment away.

"Did you hear me?" Brice said louder. "Had to be a rival."

Taking Brice by the arm, Callie moved him a few steps away before he embarrassed himself further. "Brice," she said up close and low, "you don't even have an election coming up. And since when has anyone seriously run against you? Fella, you are your own worst enemy. Close up your linseed oil and handle your rags properly."

"I want a full investigation!" he shouted, his hot breath taking hers away. Fried fish and beer, unless she was mistaken.

Brice . . . was back to being Brice.

Leon came over. "All is taken care of. I suggest you lock your storage room in the future, and if you seriously feel someone sabotaged your place, then quit giving them the tools to do it with. Lay your rags out to dry in the sun or put them in soapy water. Don't wad them up like that to gather heat and combust. Don't leave an oil can open."

Brice raised gray brows in sore need of a trim. "That's all you've got?" He jerked a wave back at the damage. "And that's your conclusion? Hell, you destroyed any evidence of wrong-doing with all that mess. Is that how you do investigations, Chief? Maybe I need to go after your job, too. A lot of people would love both your jobs for the privilege of living out here."

Leon didn't exactly blanch, but he looked to Callie for help. This type of threat usually had her name on it, not his.

"Don't want to step on your jurisdiction, Chief," she said, neatly sidestepping his entreaty to join him in the glare of Brice's anger. He needed the experience. "So I'll leave you to it."

Rubbing a hand through his hair, Leon gave her a gentle humph. "Appreciate that, Chief."

"We can stand trial together," she said with a half grin, saluting him before turning to leave.

Callie headed back to her car, settled. Her trepidation coming there had been for naught. That onset of fear bothered her, though, and a wariness set into her bones at the fact she still could be triggered like that.

Maybe she could deal with her own personal disaster now. In an afterthought, she glanced back at the latticework fence. Whoever had been watching wasn't there now. Probably went back in the house.

Chapter 3

IN AN AFTERTHOUGHT, Callie drove to the Ice Shack for a status check. With the crowd dispersed, LaRoache had finished his shift and gone home to his family, leaving crime scene tape encircling the off-kilter building, ticket issued, and hazard addressed.

Thomas still hung around, though, probably ensuring the dwindling traffic didn't stop and analyze the damage. He was the complete opposite of LaRoache, who worked per the clock, not that he didn't do his job. Thomas pulled extra shifts, begged for work, and loved the public. As a single guy, being alone in his trailer further up the island didn't sit well with him, so if he wasn't working, he was fishing, and if he wasn't fishing, he was begging for overtime to save for the boat of his dreams. He stood talking to a middle-aged couple and their teenage daughters, coy smiles on the latter. The family laughed at something he said.

Wait for it . . . there it was. He winked at the girls, sending them into titters and giggles.

In addition to being the best people person, Thomas also claimed the role of the department's token eye candy, making him one of the most effective ambassadors for the Edisto Beach PD. Almost thirty, dark, fit, a dimple in his cheek that melted mothers and beckoned their daughters, he used his assets strategically, and Callie had to admit he got results. She'd chosen him for specific duties because of those very assets.

She had no idea what she would do without him, and he seemed to favor her as well. She served as his chief, mentor, and quasi-mother with their decade-and-a-half difference in ages, but he had a maturity about him. He'd saved her life twice. He'd saved her reputation more times than she could count before she'd left the gin.

With the sun giving up the day, Callie flipped on her lights and waved at her young officer in passing, not wanting to interrupt his conversation. Then she second-guessed leaving when Monty pulled up on his moped.

Callie eased over toward Monty as he methodically parked his scooter up against Bi-Lo and turned toward the Ice Shack. It was dark. He had no business nosing around the messed-up shack, either. He should've been home by now.

"Monty?" she called. "Everything's done here. I appreciate your help earlier, though."

"Thought I'd hang around in case citizens had questions," he said. "Or if the traffic gets worse." He waved his hand around. "We can't afford a jam here."

He was still on his high. Let him do the least little part of any incident, and the boy-man thrived on it for days, repeating the details of his role over and over, seeking that inevitable pat on the back.

Monty never was much of an issue, but the day was done, and his driving a moped up Highway 174 to his momma's place was an accident waiting to happen for not only him but the tourists zipping around him. An impatient driver had driven Monty off the road and then sped off only last year, barely a month into his owning the moped. A local gave him a ride home. Another local paid for his moped repairs.

The residents made sure Monty did all right for himself.

"Come on," she said, motioning toward his transportation. "I'll follow you home and make sure nobody hits you."

He walked around the Ice Shack, inspecting. "Everything does appear to be in order."

She smiled. "Good deal then. Hop on your bike. You get a police escort tonight for all your help."

God forbid anyone call it a moped . . . or a scooter. It was a bike, as in motorcycle. Sounded more official that way. Monty beamed big at the escort idea.

She waited for him to get going then motioned at a driver to hold up while she eased behind the bike. She followed Monty out of town, but once they crossed Scott Creek, however, night fell like a blanket, and the moped's little light barely cut through the pitch.

He sped up, probably showing off, and while the dated bike couldn't quite reach thirty miles per hour, it was thirty too fast if oncoming traffic wasn't paying attention. Callie flipped on her blue lights, and a thrilled Monty pumped a fist in the air, with only the slightest of a swerve.

A little more than three miles out, they turned left on Oyster Factory Road, then two miles down the dark two-lane until reaching a reflector hung by a nail on a rusted mailbox, marking the dirt drive. Monty pulled in, dismounted, and opened an old cattle-gate affair.

Callie shut off her blue lights, her headlights trained on the drive. "Go on in, Monty. Leave it open for me, too."

He shook his head. "It's late. Momma doesn't want to see you."

"Maybe I want to see her," she said. "It's been a while. I'd be rude not to say hello."

"She won't like it," he grumbled but did as he was told.

Fishing Creek ran across the back of the property, but one couldn't see it from the road, much less at night. In the daylight, however, one detected the faintest sense of Forrest Gump's rutted drive where he shed his leg braces running through lines of ancient oaks to his run-down antebellum home in Greenbow, Alabama. The real movie locale, however, had actually been forty-five minutes away near Beaufort, South Carolina.

The gate was metal versus the eroded brick in the movie, and there wasn't nearly as many lush live oaks dangling yards of Spanish moss. Four oaks was more like it, two rather straggly, the ground covered more with batches of wax myrtle bushes and a few Palmetto trees that had never seen a trim. Five acres of rustic, backwoods, coastal living.

No white antebellum house either. At the end of this road was a thousand-square-foot brick template seen across hundreds of acres around the South. Hard-lived-in sort of homes with soffits rotted in places, the yards long overtaken with whatever scrub grew by choice. This was the kind of house they called a federal Farmers Home house, the subsidized mortgage paid off ages ago by Monty's great grand-mother. A power-company pole wanly shined, the thick darkness swallowing up the light.

Night didn't get much blacker than out on a dirt road on Edisto Island.

Arms crossed and feet spread apart on a tiny porch not big enough to handle two people and still open the door, Minnie Bartow waited none too pleased. "You're late," she said to her son, in a Lowcountry accent hanging somewhere between Geechee and redneck.

Callie approached first as Monty, head tucked, locked up his bike in a lean-to carport to the side of the house. "Hey, Minnie. I wanted to make sure Monty got home okay. How y'all doing?"

"We're all right."

The tiny porch lamp had a bug light in it, the yellow giving Monty's mother a tired expression with Frankenstein shadows under her eyes. Her hair needed washing, her dress holding little shape. She was almost as wide as she was tall, her feet slippered in mules too small, heels running over the back.

She looked cleaner on the days she did taxes.

Her age was indeterminate, her features not yet old, but she seemed as worn as her twenty-year-old faded Saturn under the carport . . . color tan. Callie knew Minnie to be forty-six, give or take on either side.

Minnie stared her son down as he reached the porch. "What's he done?"

Smiling to temper the moment for Monty, Callie replied, "Nothing, Minnie. It got dark on him, and I wanted to make sure he got home all right."

Monty disappeared inside. Minnie gave Callie a somber nod of thanks.

Callie hoped her presence hadn't gotten the guy in trouble. For her own peace of mind, she stood there a moment, listening. The windows were open to let in the cooler night air, the wooden door ajar for circulation, the screen door giving a miniscule semblance of security. A window unit hung precariously on the east side of the house, turned off for the evening.

Callie didn't think of these two often, but the sight of either tugged at her heart. There was no fixing this. Minnie owned the house, and in truth, mother and son showed pride at owning their real estate, so theoretically there was nothing to fix.

They understood how much their land might be worth sitting on that creek because many contractors and tourists had shamelessly knocked on their door begging them to sell. Minnie refused any and all offers. Sometimes it wasn't about price.

Though many affluent folks thought otherwise, the more disenfranchised people fully understood the value of land, leading them to hold on to it even more than most. After all, where would they move to, even if they got a good price? Most of them had deep family roots in that sandy ground.

Talking between the two carried out the living room window, but Callie couldn't quite make out the words. Nobody sounded happy.

Poor Minnie, though you better not call her that to her face because she was tough as nails. Word was that women in the Bartow family didn't live past fifty. Word had it that their family tree consisted of only women, with the unnamed men being no more than seed to perpetuate the women's Bartow name. Callie didn't believe most of the stories, but those who did only fed the rumor that Minnie's boy child was likely cursed and that Monty's days were numbered, too.

Callie listened harder. Minnie was crying.

Callie started to go up and knock, to ask if everything was all right.

"It's okay, Momma. I came home," Monty said, soothing, worried. "Everything's gonna be all right. Nothing's gonna happen to me."

"Bless you, sweet boy." A mother's fret was all this was. Everything was good.

Or as good as could be expected.

Crickets sounded around the edges of Fishing Creek as Callie returned to her patrol car, heavy-hearted. What the hell was going to happen to that boy if something happened to his mother first?

CALLIE PULLED INTO her drive feeling a tad frayed around the edges. She looked forward to getting home, except that meant heading straight into hurricane Sophie. While the yoga mistress was her dearest lady friend, Callie'd lived alone at a much slower pace than the woman who woke most mornings at full throttle. Callie's own bed might not be an option tonight, though, with the onset of mold and mildew which thrived in this environment in normal circumstances.

Then a sense of guilt bubbled up at the reluctance of spending the night with a friend. Sophie was indeed dear and would do anything for anyone she loved, *but* . . . there was that disclaimer again . . . the energy that woman threw at the universe could be extreme, and a lot of times, the blowback could be fierce. Callie's home life was so much simpler.

Sophie's daughter Sprite and Callie's son Jeb continued as an item going on a year now, attending the same college, coming home to mothers who were next-door neighbors. Actually, they were so tight an item that they'd decided to travel for the summer, neither coming home to see a mother except for possibly a couple weeks come August for a short visit before school started back.

God, Callie missed that boy. With a deep passion, she understood Minnie's love and concern for a son.

However, with Jeb's mother a police chief full of security issues and Sprite's a free-wheeling yogi spirit wielding sage sticks, Callie could guess why the kids chose to travel. The past year had been the first of their lives they hadn't dealt with momma-drama.

She sighed an empty-nest sigh.

Hopefully, the rest of the night would prove uneventful. July was top season for any beach, but unlike the other Carolina beaches, Edisto slowed at dark. No blaring beach parties, no neon-flashing souvenir shops on every corner, and no chain restaurants. She hoped Edisto could remain that way. More and more people were discovering the secluded island, and with discovery came their recommendations on how to change it.

Where were the electric car chargers?
Where's the McDonald's?
Where was the Marriott?
What, no Uber?

Callie hoped it never got to the point she had to build a lockup. Taking the occasional lawbreaker to Walterboro suited her just fine.

The short mile to her and Sophie's residences on Jungle Road took no time, and the tasks awaiting her swept away the melancholy. Her house was a wreck and needed cleaning.

Lights were on, ordinarily a concern, but she'd left Sophie there to do whatever it was she was able to do with that fiasco. Anything would be a blessing. Callie didn't expect the tiny creature to have accomplished much alone in the couple of hours, but there was that unpredictable energy.

Callie parked and went inside.

Her mattress stood end up against her fireplace, her headboard against the kitchen bar. The dresser backed up to her living room sofa, but only after the dining room set had been shoved against the wall, almost blocking the walkway. Her Queen Anne chair had taken a somewhat regal place in the kitchen. The roar of box fans could be heard all the way outside, well before Callie stepped in and spotted one of them in her bedroom doorway, and through the open back door, a myriad of towels and quilts hung over the railings to dry.

After navigating the maze, Callie peered into her empty bedroom, windows wide open, then retracted and headed to the back door. Sophie stretched capri-clad legs on a chaise lounge on the porch, peering over drying linens toward the marsh, nursing a carrot juice. "Hey, girl," she said as Callie stepped out. "Water is sopped up. Your insurance agent is coming by at nine in the morning, by the way."

"You filed my claim? How does that even happen?" Callie said.

"Your agent is my agent, honey. Enough said."

Why should Callie be surprised?

"Oh," Sophie continued, sitting up, "I called Jeb and told him about things, by the way. He offered to cut their trip short to help, but I told him the mothers had this covered. Go fix yourself a ginger ale. I'm ordering takeout now that you're here. Figured you'd have a cow if we went to my place leaving yours opened up like this, so we'll manage back here for a while until it gets a little bit drier. What do you think?"

Callie was surprised but not exactly stunned. She already knew that if you channeled Sophie in the right direction she could move mountains. You just had to make sure it was the right mountain. "How did you move the furniture?"

"Those landscapers across the street."

Okay, now Callie *was* stunned. "I don't know what to say to that, Soph."

"Besides thank you?"

She hurried over to sit at the foot of Sophie's chaise. "Oh, no, Soph, I'm eternally grateful for all of this." She swept her arm toward the house. "I owe you, big time."

Sophie moved the celery stalk aside to take another sip. "Yes . . . you do."

"No, I mean . . . why the landscapers?" *How* Sophie convinced them was more the question.

"Thomas already told them you were the police chief." A coy hand went to her collarbone. "A move I would not have made, by the way, but since the cat was out of the bag, I seized the opportunity."

That damn sure gave Callie pause. Sophie's creative thought didn't travel on normal wavelengths. "What opportunity would that be?"

A sly grin crept up. "Told them you wouldn't arrest them for being Peeping Toms."

There it was. There was the Sophie one had to be leery of. "You threatened them. Soph, don't do that. That was all on me today. The entire lunacy of this afternoon was on me. Those poor guys—"

"Those poor guys were new out here. We don't know them. They might've come back with ulterior motives to check out you and your house. I wanted to be proactive . . . show we were tough."

"By making them move furniture?" What was Callie to do with this woman?

"By telling them how many people have died out here since you took over."

Well, okay then. Callie had nothing to say to that.

Chapter 4

CALLIE SHOVED pajamas she never wore into an overnight bag. Why wasn't she sleeping in Jeb's room, in her own place? But Sophie had offered, and it was hard to tell that woman no, especially after all she'd already done. She was so excited about having a houseguest that her chatter had proven relentless, drowning out the night song of frogs and crickets. She might even be keeping the neighbors up from her perch on the back porch.

"I started to pack your bag, you know. It's not like I can't read you." Sophie kept on, shouting from her outdoor spot back into the house. "You understand how I can read people. It's how we get along so well. It's how we got along from the start. Can you believe it's been over two years since you got here? Now you're practically a fixture."

Callie's stomach growled, which made her think of Mexican food, which made her wonder why she hadn't asked to sleep over at Mark's.

Sophie entered the house and spoke up from the living room. "Want me to put on some Neil Diamond? Something soothing after such a difficult day?"

"Um, sure."

Wasn't long before "Song Sung Blue" started up.

Sophie had taken to Callie from the git-go, before Callie assumed the police chief role. She'd helped and hindered, enraged and entertained through the ups and downs of family, work, and Edisto society. As a result, her pushy self believed that she grasped all Callie's traits, habits, history, and buttons, but Callie wasn't as open as her neighbor thought. Their relationship undeniably held a yin-and-yang flavor.

For instance, Sophie had nursed her back to health after Seabrook died, but in acquiring a house key, had assumed responsibility to keep her best friend sober by periodically rummaging around Callie's place for a gin stash. She'd found one . . . twice.

Sophie could pry—sometimes wide open without shame and other times discreetly hidden behind an air of silliness, but it worked. Sophie had a contact list ten times longer than anyone on Edisto, and Callie had capitalized on that meddling nature more than a few times.

A friendship not a soul on the planet would've forecasted. Whether Callie wanted the help or not, Sophie gave it, because that's what Sophie did.

Tomorrow was Wednesday. Thank the heavens and entire host of angels. Sophie had a yoga class in the morning or they'd be girlfriend-talking into the wee hours of dawn. The class took place in a bar on the back side of the Pavilion, overlooking the ocean. The pushed-back bistro tables and chairs made for an open floor with personality and a cheap venue, yet the simplicity of the ambience made Sophie look genius. During tourist season, she collected a mint under the table. The natives, however, benefited from a monthly discount.

Sophie knew her yoga stuff, claiming she could likewise access the pulse of a particular degree of the spirit world.

Wait a minute. . . .

Callie returned to the bedroom doorway, speaking up over a fan and holding up her weapon. "How are you feeling about this under your roof?"

Sophie shook her head, no thought whatsoever. "Can't do it."

Callie shifted her weight to the other side of the doorframe. She should've thought of this sooner. "This gun goes wherever I go. How about I stay here in Jeb's room and not put you out?"

Setting the phonograph needle back in its place, Sophie turned off the music. "Are you telling me you cannot, for even one night, do without that thing?"

"Yes, that's exactly what I'm saying. It, the badge, plus I was toying with bringing my uniform, which I'm fully aware you—"

Her pixie shag shaking in a fervent negative, Sophie crossed her arms. "Magnets for negative energy. Callie, there's something really wrong with a person who cannot part with a weapon of destruction."

Sophie stood fast against inviting the universe's bedlam into her home. Her stash of sage was renowned for cleansing evil from her place, your place, anyone's place. Even locking her doors was a sign of negativity, she claimed, another issue Callie'd ruefully forgotten. She'd never sleep a wink over at Sophie's with blinds up, doors and windows ready and willing for some wannabe burglar. Or worse.

No, ma'am. Open door . . . open carry.

The pout came out, also renowned. Sophie might be pushing fifty, but her childish pout had an adult power all its own.

Callie made a conscious eye sweep of her living room. "If your house flooded, would you want to stay here? With me and all my wicked, injurious, trouble magnets?" She went for humor, but from Sophie's expression, she'd missed the mark.

Sophie's hands moved from crossed to her hips. "I'd never sleep."

Callie raised her brows in a silent ditto.

"Delivery!" shouted a voice from the front porch.

"Come around back," yelled Sophie, since furniture blocked easy access to the front. She scurried around mattress and headboard to the rear porch. "About time," Callie heard, her friend's singsong voice alive and well again. "We were about to faint of starvation!"

And like that, Sophie was back to being Sophie. Her anger was of the flash-in-the-pan variety, which made her all the more endearing.

She'd ordered from El Marko's, bless her, knowing good and well that Mark would bring it himself. He and his infamous paper bag, Callie had grown quite fond of both.

As Mark climbed the stairs, the motion sensor flashed on, spotlighting his Hawaiian shirt of the day in aqua and green. Paired with his dark hair and eyes, the color accented an incredible tanned image. Three years Callie's senior, he had tinges of gray at his temple. Enough to add *striking* to the adjectives Callie would choose to describe him to others . . . if she were so inclined to brag.

He rose taller than both women by about eight inches, though he fell a couple short of six feet. Reaching the top of the stairs, Mark gave Sophie a loose one-armed hug before handing her the bag so he could wrap Callie up in both arms.

Locked in that hug, Callie opened her eyes to see Sophie slyly grin. Her wink said it all.

Yeah, friends didn't get any better than Sophie Bianchi.

SOPHIE ATE AND LEFT, having passed the torch of tending Callie to Mark, and the frogs went to sleep long before Callie and Mark wound down talking.

At first they talked about nothing and anything, the mundane and the fantastic. After hearing of each other's day, they went to their go-to supply of conversation . . . cases. His with the SC State Law Enforcement Division. Hers with Boston PD . . . then those incredibly weird ones on Edisto. The commonality of law enforcement bound them, and a man with that sort of history powerfully attracted her.

Her own son had pointed that out to her.

Her husband, Jeb's father, had been a US Marshal.

Callie's lover Seabrook had been the former Edisto police chief.

Her former Boston captain Stan lived out here on the beach now. He'd followed her when he retired both the career and ex-wife and left them up north. She and Stan had come embarrassingly close to blurring the line between friend and bedfellow when they both first arrived, each lonely and lost without that prior life they shared.

Mark carried on about a current case, one that a past buddy had called him about that day, asking for advice. Catching the thrill of involvement in his voice, she wiped up remnants of salsa and beans, nibbling on chips as she listened.

She loved his stories, and he was attentive to hers. Their cursory understanding of each other's worlds had made for an easy bridge to cross from stranger to friend after a few bumps of alpha behavior. Regardless of the gender, cops gravitated to other cops. Not unlike those who come back from war not wanting to talk about it, yet still needing to hang around those who'd been there, too.

Also like real warriors, they avoided the deepest corners of their personal history. No open dialogue about the life-altering, tectonic shifting parts of their lives that drove them both to Edisto.

Natives out here left baggage on the other side of the big bridge . . . the one tourists only saw as the gateway to their one-week vacation. Mark had immediately fallen in line with Edisto's don't-ask-don't-tell method of year-round living. One day she would ask about his obscure limp. One day she'd explain about the burn scar on her arm. Neither had yet seen the need.

"In spite of your day, you're looking rather good," he said, scrunching up wrappers and cramming them in the paper bag, shifting attention to her.

She laughed. "Been thrown up on, flooded out of my house, exposed nude to total strangers, and coped with a building knocked off its foundation. Normal, Super Woman day on Edisto."

He chuckled, which contagiously widened her smile. His laugh touched something positive in her each and every time, and he knew it. There was a strong sense of caregiver in the man, which wasn't lost on her.

In other words, they fit.

Her father would've liked him.

Jeb, however, still held doubts.

"Anything earth shattering at El Marko's today?" she asked.

"A family tried to skip out on their tab. The heat made people order alcohol. Had two drunks almost make trouble. One family dispute bordered on the rowdy."

Licensed and trained, Mark kept his own weapon behind the bar along with a set of cuffs, but his charisma diffused most situations. His personality clicked into place in the community like the last piece in a forty-dollar puzzle. He hadn't involved Callie or her guys in a call to his restaurant since Brice went nuts over Aberdeen last December, and while Callie had first worried about his self-policing, she'd since come to appreciate the one less worry on her plate.

What wasn't to love about this guy?

And Callie didn't love easily.

"It's late," he said, "for you anyway. I'm usually closing a restaurant about now."

"You leave Wesley in charge?"

He nodded. "The kid's pretty damned reliable. Kind of glad we fell out when we first met. I only hired him out of spite against you." His foot nudged her. She nudged him back.

"So, what's your plan tonight?" he said. "Surely you're not leaving your house open."

"No." She rose from her too-comfortable position in her fold-up chair. "I'll lock up and do my best to sleep through those fans still going in there. Might leave that bedroom's windows open since they are way off the ground and too far from the porch to be reached."

He stood and surveyed the mess. "I'd feel better if you had some-one with you."

She took his hand. "I bet you would, you know . . . feel better."

They locked up the back door, then the front, and decided they would make do with the guest room upstairs. They'd hear the fans less, plus, Callie wasn't quite comfortable with her boyfriend sleeping in her son's bed downstairs.

"CHIEF!"

Even asleep and deep in Callie's unconscious, pressure in her core prodded her to react to something unseen . . . yet catastrophic.

The man's voice held an urgency. Sincere danger. She wasn't sure about what or where he was.

"Damn it!"

She awoke to the harshly hissed curse. Mark rubbed the top of his head, forgetting about the sloped vaulted ceiling, as he leaped up to determine who relentlessly pounded at the front door below.

"Chief! Chief!"

Only then did she hear the distant ringing of her landline phone, a requirement of a first responder on the island. However, her wall phone was downstairs in her kitchen, muted enough not to be readily heard over the fans drying out the bedroom carpet.

Then Mark's phone rang from the floor, knocked off into the messy bedspread. He jerked the spread around, hunting.

"I'll get him," she said, kicking off the covers and rushing past Mark, grabbing his shirt on the way to cover up since his was bigger and easier to slip on. She reached the front dormer window, cranking it open with one hand, buttoning the button between her breasts with the other. "Thomas?" she yelled down. "That you?"

He ran down the front steps to ground level, searching up. "Chief! Another fire. This time it's serious. Myrtle Street, one of those two older houses owned by Booker McPhee. They've called in St. Paul's Station *and* Colleton County's."

Instinctively, she peered west and spotted the gray smoke.

"Meet you there," she yelled down. "Raysor on duty yet?"

Don Raysor was a deputy on loan from Colleton County who'd turned permanent about four chiefs ago.

"He's already there."

She was already closing the window. "Go on then."

She turned to see Mark almost dressed. "I'll get out of your way, but I sort of need my shirt," he said.

"Sorry," she said, breathlessly stripping it off before running to the bathroom for a quick shower . . . only for the shower not to work. No water. "Damn it!" she yelled. She ran back to the bedside, grabbed hers and Mark's bottled waters from the nightstand and returned to the bathroom, emptying them in a small towel and did a onceover dash of a cleanup. She left enough liquid to gargle with before running back out. "I can't meet the insurance guy. He's due at nine."

Mark handed her bra to her. "I can handle that. My day doesn't start until ten."

She snatched the bra, threw it on, and kissed him in passing. "You're pretty awesome—" and she stopped herself.

She'd almost called him Mike.

Where had that come from? Mike Seabrook had been dead for well over a year.

Suddenly, Mark and Mike were way too similar, which meant her subconscious had promoted him to that level. The realization caught her off guard.

"What is it?" Mark asked, curiously waiting for her to finish, not catching the slip.

"I was struggling with a nickname and fell short," she said and kissed him quickly again. "We'll work on that. I'll call you later."

"Call me on what?" he yelled down the stairs. "You don't have a phone."

"My backup work phone is at the office," she said, a bit disgusted she hadn't retrieved it last night. "I always used my personal cell." Then she whispered, "Damn." Friends *were* the citizens she served, work had become her social life. All had melded together, and she'd quit carrying the second device some time back. Guess she'd go back to toting two phones.

She threw on the uniform, her backup nylon belt with some of the basics, sans radio and phone, and ran down the steps, the outside filling her ears like cotton balls after a night of those droning fans.

A family SUV crept along Jungle Road, nervous about the patrol car on their tail, until they turned off on Marianne, letting her kick up her speed. She glanced at the clock. Was it really only five till seven? Why weren't these people still in bed? They were on vacation.

It was early. Too early. Early morning was an off time of day for a fire. She'd never heard of a house fire happening at dawn. Occupied houses were normally asleep and had been for hours, leaving little excuse for a fire to catch. Houses being worked on hadn't welcomed their contractors quite yet.

An uneasiness crept under her skin. Trouble was she wasn't sure how much was instinct and how much nerves from the past. She tried to will down the threatened repeat of yesterday's nerves. While her pulse had jumpstarted at the jolt out of her REM sleep, it hadn't settled once learning the crisis was another fire. She could pray this one turned out like Brice's, but Thomas sounded pretty distraught. The boy didn't panic.

The last time a house caught fire was Papa Beach's place a few weeks after she'd moved to Edisto. Again, up surged memories of his murder, her personal messiness, and how close that fire came to burning her own place down.

Some had blamed her presence for both the fire and the murder. Those same people wouldn't be far from wrong considering the murderer/arsonist had followed her to South Carolina.

She tried to deep breathe but couldn't. The past . . . the present. All suddenly muddied together, the past oozing out from behind that wall she perpetually tried to guard.

No. Quit forecasting doom and gloom. Hopefully, it was another rag fire.

But rag fires didn't merit three fire departments or shoot smoke that high.

A choking lump of fear wedged in the base of her throat. Damn it, it was dawn at Edisto, for God's sake, not dusk in Boston.

The house in question was under renovation. It had changed hands more frequently than most. The house was half-livable, the most recent owner having found the repair funds and hired a contractor, per the loose chatter on the street . . . losing all sorts of rent by not being available this time of year. In spite of funding difficulties, he'd bought the house next door not long after the first. People did that out here.

Or people didn't have their stories straight.

Callie reached the police station, darted in, snatched her work phone from its charger along with a handheld radio, and ran back out. Her lone admin person, Marie, hadn't arrived yet, but no doubt she'd arrive any time since the fire invariably came across her personal scanner. Marie was hard-core legit Edisto PD, even without a badge.

Callie tore up Myrtle Street heading toward smoke, unable to swallow the pressure building in her throat. She would be curious to see who showed up to watch the fire and stick around long enough to see the results.

She rounded the curve, and her breath caught. The number of vehicles didn't surprise her. The fact that both houses were on fire did.

Chapter 5

CALLIE PULLED IN A drive four houses up, throwing on her sunglasses. Early morning and the temperature had already reached eighty-seven degrees per her dashboard. Post Fourth of July heat started early and, atop a fire, would promise hell on Edisto today. The sun was already crushing.

So was the pressure in her chest.

Edisto's truck was front and present, meaning Leon Hightower, his assistant chief, and all the volunteers would be on hand. The St. Paul's fire truck parked next to Edisto's, a hose connected to a hydrant two houses down on the corner. The town had recently had twenty hydrants blasted for rust, ever the cost of storms and salt air. The firefighters re-painted them. At the time she'd honked at Leon, paintbrush in hand, as he put the finishing touches on this particular one.

She closed her eyes to center herself then opened them to take measure. Flames reached for the clouds, falling far short of the images in her head. Damaging, but the firefighters had easily contained them from spreading to neighbors. Still, both houses managed to be injured.

The smoke color ran between white and gray. Thank God not black, which Callie's limited education on firefighting told her could mean a more volatile situation, more possibly fuel related . . . more often a fire set with intention. Smell choked the air, seemingly more of wood than gas, or rubber.

The smell . . . nothing brought back memories faster than smell. Again, she closed her eyes. Flashbacks popped up of her standing on a curb, fire trucks and firefighters in front of her, behind her, beside her . . . that heat.

One hand on her hood, she fought to detour her focus from the curdling fear to the crime. The cause. The culprit. She reached for the muscle memory of working a case.

She dug in to maintain her gaze on the big picture from four houses back, her mind sifting the options. Had workers come early and, being half-asleep, accidentally set something afire? A lit cigarette? A match not put out before being tossed? A spark from the wrong tool falling on wood shavings?

Callie could only hope an accident at this point. They needed arson out here like they needed a three-ring circus.

She caught herself rubbing her forearm scar, a permanent reminder that actions had consequences. This incident was already stealing her breath.

While fires were insanely scary for her . . . they were extremely dangerous for Edisto. No ambulance, for one. The closest had to come from Walterboro, and critical situations merited a medivac chopper from Charleston. She'd already called dispatch to put them on notice, just in case. The fire department consisted of mostly volunteers, not to downplay their roles, and houses were built close enough to light each other off on so many streets.

Phobia or no phobia, a fire was a heart-stopping concern.

Right now she walked outside of her own skin, somewhat disconnected, her reactions questionable. Not good.

Callie had pulled past Deputy Don Raysor to park, a welcome sight and part of the island's fabric. He was handling the southern access at the corner of Townsend Street, and she could use his seasoned, reliable presence about now.

She swallowed to push down the uneasiness. It wasn't working. "Who's here?"

She had to speak up at the big, burly man over a decade her senior who made double of her. The most seasoned uniform on her force. He knew Edisto Island, Edisto Beach, Colleton County, and every soul, address, creek, and acre on them, his territory far and wide and known to every first responder in the region.

"All but Manson," he said. "Keeping him available for later . . . in case."

In case could mean any of a dozen things from an officer getting hurt to the others having to work the day and end it too exhausted to pull a double shift. This was an all-hands situation.

Right now, however, there wasn't much traffic. Not this time of day, especially on this road, but regardless, that traffic had to cease for now. "Thomas is handling the north end of the street, at the corner of Louise Street. Others are detouring access from Palmetto. As people wake up, it'll get worse, but hopefully the guys on the fire will contain it quick."

That meant five of six officers working, two on their day off. Bless 'em.

"Colleton County Fire isn't here, but they're on standby. One of those houses up there was cooking pretty good before any of them arrived, but it looks better."

A car approached, and Raysor shook his head at the driver, motioning for him to turn around.

"I'm renting—"

"Fire, sir. Can't let you through. Which house is it?"

The man pointed. "Four houses that way. I only went out to pick up breakfast." His whine bordered on complaint.

"Then we evacuated them," Raysor said. "Suggest you call your people, and y'all take it to the beach. Right now, nobody's getting in."

"But it's damn hot out here."

"Like a summer beach in July, sir."

His brow furrowed deeper. "Son of a—"

"Yep. I hear you. Help us out and turn it around, please."

Scowling, the man did a three-point turn and left fuming, phone to his ear.

One would think he'd thank the officer, glad his family had been channeled away from the danger, but some people didn't believe danger could enter their world . . . until it did. The town would deal with the complaints later.

Callie'd seen the behavior more times than she could count.

"Stan's over there somewhere," Raysor added, stepping out to address yet another car, this time a native who Callie knew would give Raysor hell, not that he couldn't handle it. You could almost say what you wanted, how you wanted, to the people who lived here. They knew the drill.

This was the height of the season, residents understood, and safety was paramount. Every rental was rented, with day-trippers increasing the population by thousands. Even if the fire was contained quickly, one of her guys, maybe alongside one of the volunteer fire guys, would have to watch the site for the rest of the day to keep the curious from tripping over damage, contaminating the scene, even getting hurt and feeling the need to sue.

"Radio if you need me." She turned, halted, inhaled, seeking a calm, and moved toward the fire . . . but took her path across the street. Reaching the address, even keeping a distance, the heat coated her.

Properties on all sides had been emptied of people. A Palmetto tree, with sloppy dangling fronds, flashed alive in flames, emulating a giant lit match. Shouts redirected attention of one hose, and in seconds, the threat was dowsed.

This was the first time she'd seen Leon and his crew in choreographed action. Intense, they functioned in a loose synchrony, even with a visiting firehouse in the mix. She was proud. She was tense. She was glad she didn't fight fires for a living.

She'd rather face a bullet.

Both houses continued toasting in spite of flames lessening, one with far more gusto than the other, flames having gutted the side nearest its sister. The two-for-one appeared more than a case of chance to Callie, but she wasn't the pro. Luck had smiled on the owner of the untouched, occupied house on the opposite side, though, but disaster had certainly visited Booker McPhee, the owner of the two on fire.

Unless insurance was involved. Or, rather, unless *enough* insurance was involved.

"Look out, look out," shouted a man in gear, right before a wide porch floor gave in.

Exclaims of *Watch out* came from every direction. "Back up," someone yelled.

New sparks danced up in spirals, the hoses adjusting with the change.

Callie's heart tried to escape through her throat.

Of course she'd jumped back like the rest, but it wasn't enough. She kept stepping, her need to move further away clashing with her training to go in and help. How was she supposed to do this? Why wasn't her body in better control than this?

Her pulse throbbed and throbbed in her throat, and no amount of swallowing helped.

She snatched her gaze away from the flames to behind her, trying to see instead the ocean three blocks over. Unable to, she studied someone's green lawn. Something cooler. Any colors other than orange and yellow. Anything to break this loop in her head.

But nothing drowned out the crackles, the cooking smells, the shouts, the almost-human voice of flames struggling with a will to live.

Instinctively, she counted to ten, slowing herself to count correctly, as she was taught. She hadn't had to count to ten in a very long time.

"Chief," the radio cackled, "Thomas here."

Tasting nasty heated air, she sucked in one last deep breath to regain control and cued the walkie. "I'm . . . on site, Thomas. Over."

"Everyone okay?"

"A deck floor came down. They're on it."

Thomas had no clue about her and fire. She wanted to keep it that way.

He keyed back. "I've got people from two restaurants over here with drinks and stuff for the firefighters."

They did this for hurricane relief all the time. "Not yet," she replied. "Tell them to be patient until Chief Hightower gives me the okay."

"Ten four, Chief," he replied.

Just like the Edisto folk to come through. For now, however, everyone waited while people did their jobs.

Leon directed the crew like the pro he was. This was as bad a situation as they'd ever handled out here short of a hurricane, and he addressed it like he managed such on a daily basis. At least from her vantage. She longed for this to be over and them to have a chat as to his deduction on how the fire started.

This wasn't Boston, but chances were that in her fifteen years there, she'd assisted in more fires than most of Leon's volunteers had put out. She'd had training, learned how to assist, to the point cops could assist.

She knew residential fires comprised the grand majority of fires in the United States, numbering in the hundreds of thousands. What made the acid in her stomach churn was that someone died in a residential fire every two and a half hours.

Houses under renovation, however, were a very small percentage of residential burns. One to two percent. A fact, given what else she knew, to be an eyebrow raiser to Callie.

Fires took place more in the winter, too, and if occupied, on Saturdays and Sundays. Unoccupied houses under repair weren't quite as predictable but still, they ran in the Thursday-through-Saturday range. More incidents took place in the afternoon and evening. Heating equipment, electrical mistakes, mishandled construction tools like soldering irons or torches.

This was summer, early in the morning, and these were unoccupied dwellings. Callie had a loose professional feel for the norm. She wasn't feeling this one anywhere near normal. This fire either defied the odds of accident, or was set.

Brice's words kept banging in her ears. *Someone else set this fire.*

"Get your ass back here!"

One arm waving, Stan's voice boomed over the melee long before Callie spotted him. Her retired Boston captain trotted after someone, calling them down. Following his line of sight, she caught a piece of Monty as he disappeared on the other side of the St. Paul fire truck.

Oh Monty, not today.

Instincts kicking in, she ran around the front of the truck to cut him off which wasn't hard with him weighted down with a cooler in his hands, a sleeve of cups in a plastic bag crushed under his armpit.

She snared one of the cooler handles. He tried to snatch loose, his frown angry until he registered who she was.

"Chief. They need to drink. It's too hot." He peered over his shoulder and, seeing Stan, tried to shake Callie loose again. "Let me go! I need to help."

"Stop it, Monty," she said, attempting to steer him to the other side of the truck. He wouldn't budge.

Stan arrived, reached out, and laid a heavy hand on the young man's shoulder. "I'll take him."

Tucking his head down in his shoulders, eyes clenched, Monty screeched and tugged. "No, no."

Callie gave Stan a slight shake of her head, and he let loose.

"Give this gentleman the cooler, Monty," she said, gently assisting him to release his grip. "Give me the cups."

Took her two attempts to coax his hands off. Aware of the delicacy of the moment, Stan took the cooler and used his softer, inside voice Callie'd heard him reserve for crime victims. "I'll set it on the end of the truck for them, my man. I'll tell them who sent them the refreshments. But only real law—"

With tiny head movements, Callie caught his attention. Telling Monty he wasn't legitimate help would irritate him, and they didn't need the man wound back up.

Passing the cups to Stan, Callie put her back to the fire and brushed her palm up and down Monty's sleeve. "Thanks for bringing it this far," she said. "Even I'm not allowed in the middle of firefighting, Monty. Frankly, I'm in the way standing here."

Stan hushed and disappeared, doing as he promised the eager wannabe.

Monty allowed her to keep her hand on him.

"That's why I'm standing right over there," she said, and led him to where she'd been across the street. "Here's where we stand guard, watching for people who break through or get in the way."

A small smile crept back on his face. "Like her? Can we go get her?" He pointed toward the Edisto fire truck.

Her? Who . . . *son of a biscuit.*

A striking girl in her twenties that everyone out here knew quite well picked her way around obstacles to get a closer look. Ponytail a la Edisto, Alex Hanson represented WLSC-TV. She'd probably been staying at her grandmother's place on Jungle. Not the first time she'd intruded on a scene at the beach.

"Yes, exactly like her," Callie said, anxiously patting at Monty to stay put. "But listen to me. While I'm taking care of her, you save my spot here and watch for others, okay? This spot, between here . . ." She pointed at the ground. ". . . and here. It's important you keep this place occupied, okay?"

He looked at her like she was nuts. "Of course I got that, Chief."

Callie fast walked to where the young woman had disappeared behind a vehicle. Monty might not know better, but Alexandra Hanson most assuredly did.

"Alex," Callie yelled, but the girl didn't hear or had learned to ignore mighty well. Callie swore the girl speeded up, her Canon camcorder on her shoulder.

Which made Callie have to venture closer to the heat.

Alex wasn't deaf. Her mouth was moving. She was recording.

The heat cooked Callie's skin, hurting her scar. She wasn't walking into fire for this stupid girl. "Alex. Stop where you are! Police!"

That would take her finger off the damn record button.

Pausing, then pretending she hadn't, the reporter almost kept walking, but in a second thought, she turned and innocently replied, "Ma'am?"

"Ma'am, my ass, Alex. Get back across the street. *Now.* Let these people work."

"Chief Morgan, this is a breaking story. Since when does Edisto have a disaster like this?"

"Water, here!" shouted a fighter.

Alex pivoted, and in a smooth reflexive swing, the camera swung back up.

Callie turned as someone in the melee shouted, "Man down!"

Callie bolted toward that shout. Stan reached her side out of nowhere. While firefighters continued to train water on the blaze, the two of them assisted the man who'd succumbed to the heat. A St. Paul firefighter moved burnt wood and kicked away smoldering construction trash to pave their way through the smoke and confusion, where a woman in a St. Paul shirt motioned for them to set him down.

"I'm a medic," she said. "I'll take it from here."

"Ambulance? Chopper?" Callie asked.

"Ambulance on its way," she said. "Ten minutes out."

Callie stared at the man, feeling she shouldn't leave, frozen in place. "Chief."

"Yeah." But she couldn't take her gaze off the man being tended. No blood. He was drenched with sweat, cheeks dangerously flushed, eyes red. . . .

"Chief, I got this."

"Sorry. Of course you do." Callie turned back toward the fire, angry . . . incensed. Fists clenched, she stared at the damage, the threat against life, unable to do a damn thing about any of it.

She hated it. She despised it. She wanted to kill it.

"Callie!"

She turned. Stan motioned for her to follow. He headed across the road, but she couldn't take two steps without looking back over her shoulder at the houses.

He didn't stop until he'd reached the cooler shade of oleander shrubs lining the carport of a rental on the other side of the street. He positioned himself so she had to face him, the incident at her back. "Look at me," he said, gentle at first.

She tried but kept snatching glances back.

"Look at me," he repeated, bold. Almost harsh.

Jerking at the tone, she did as told, noting he glanced over her head to make sure nobody heard.

"Wake the hell up, Callie."

His treatment of her struck a nerve. "I am awake, Stan. How can I not be awake? Look at this hell."

"Stop it," he ordered, putting a palm against her jaw when she tried to peer back again.

She lurched away from the touch. "What's your problem?"

He bent over and lowered his voice. "You're losing your shit, Chicklet."

Her nickname took her back to Boston, back to when she was on her game, her family intact, and she'd imprisoned enough criminals to make three detectives proud.

Stan had seen her after that old fire, fought to help put her back together . . . tried to keep her from trashing her career afterward, which he hadn't been able to manage. This man came down to Edisto to save her from herself when she was seriously headed over a cliff.

He was the only person beside Seabrook who understood how deep this wound went, and Seabrook was dead.

"You're past all this, you hear me?" he said. "That was over four years ago."

But all she could do was glare. Fuming, livid, infuriated at what something totally inhuman had done to infiltrate her resolve, what the hell was she supposed to say? There were no words. There was only a festering.

"Suck it up," he said. "I know you can." He unconsciously scratched at sweat rolling down his temple.

She blew out once, but it wasn't enough. She sucked in hard and exhaled with stronger purpose. "I know," was all she could muster. Words, his or hers, could not touch this feeling.

When he rested a hand on her shoulder, she noted the beaded moisture under his forearm hairs, and she stared at that instead of back in his eyes.

"I'm not letting you go back to being that Callie Morgan," he said. She shook her head. "I won't."

For the longest time he said nothing else. She patted his moist arm, assuring him he could let her go.

He removed his hand letting his finger wipe a trickle of sweat off her forehead. "And I better not see you touch a drink, either."

For some reason she had more trouble promising him that.

His pat on the shoulder came across half captain and half friend, maybe something a little conditional. She knew he meant well, but most of all she knew he would keep her secret.

She peered back to her original spot on the grass. Monty was gone. She looked across at the fire, now under control.

But she was far from it.

Chapter 6

ALEX HANSON HAD escaped. Callie wanted to ask how Edisto would be presented in her story, learn who was interviewed, give her a warning about pissing in her own sandbox when it came to putting any sort of bad light on where her grandmother still lived. With her television station being an hour away in Charleston, she was probably halfway to the big bridge by now, to get it into production.

Besides, no reporter wanted to be cornered by Chief Callie Morgan.

While she could call Alex, the girl would give her the runaround about press rights, not divulging sources, all the bull crap that journalism was noted for these days, assuming she answered her phone. In Callie's experience with press people, they espoused their rights, tread over everyone else's, capitalized on carnage, then went home bragging about the rules they'd broken to get the story. And Callie was noted for telling them so.

Not that she didn't like Alex as a person. She was cute, and she was Edisto. Across the street and two houses down from Callie, the elder Mrs. Hanson was a dear, a cookie-making machine, and grandmother to Alex. This was July, so Alex was vacationing, maybe seeking the annual human interest piece about beachcombers.

But Callie's gloves came off when Alex turned reporter, as the young lady was fully aware. Everyone knew why. And nobody contested it.

After the relentless news spotlight on her husband's murder in Boston, and Seabrook's on Edisto, Callie'd cemented a dislike, one could say, for the profession. No salvation for them whatsoever.

Most chiefs played the press. Callie didn't even pretend to make nice with the Holy City's television stations and papers. Case in point, Seabrook was killed by a reporter after which Callie blew said reporter to hell.

So the mayor and town council sort of let that part of her job description go unnoticed. Someone else could handle public relations for the town of Edisto Beach, and anything law-enforcement related was handled by the mayor. Therefore, Alex normally made herself invisible around Callie, adeptly avoiding the chief when Edisto made the news, but Callie knew where she lived if she needed to have a word with the young woman.

Now that the air was soup-thick with steam, and the fire was out, Callie couldn't suck in a breath without it clinging to the back of her throat. A sickening mixture of charcoal, burnt chemicals, and sweat hung in her nose, on her hair and clothes. Soaked under her uniform, she walked the scene. Crime tape was up. Studying the wet swamp of ruin, she waited until Chief Leon was free.

Every person, place, and thing carried a water-logged feel, and the pace had switched from frantic to slo-mo. She looked up the front staircase, wondering how much of a loss this first house was. Thank God it wasn't occupied. The second house not as bad, but still . . . *Shell Shack* and *Shark Shack* remained standing. She might not be able to talk construction, but she could guess the extra red tape involved if the stilts and main supports went down. Support pillars were a bear to install, and not cheap.

Her guys still handled traffic. They were letting only those through who resided on the street. It was almost noon, and if the temperature didn't hit a hundred today, it wouldn't miss by much. The humidity would make it feel ten degrees hotter.

St. Paul's truck had left. Once Edisto's truck left, she'd park an officer on the site and cut the others loose.

Leon finally walked over, water bottle in hand, wet to his bones, hair flat, saturated, and awry. With his suit and equipment gone, he appeared an exhausted, sodden echo of the man who'd just fought the devil out of some serious flames.

"Wow," Callie said, holding out a hand to shake. "Wish I had a beer to offer you. You look whipped."

"Been a couple years since. . . ."

"Papa Beach was the last time," she said.

He pointed the water bottle at her. "Yep, that was the last real fire. Regardless how long, the sight of something like this"—he motioned the bottle at the spoilage—"makes it come right back all 3D and Blu-ray."

She wished she could share how deeply she related to that. "Everyone okay?"

"Yes, they are, and thanks for helping our guy out," he said. "He got a bit too hot, is all."

She nodded. "Thought so." She gave enough pause to change the subject. "Time for the question of the hour."

"How did it start?" he finished. He rubbed a hand across his cheekbone and along his jaw, stopping to scratch the itch on his dirty chin. "CCFR doesn't do Edisto Beach, so we're asking SLED to take a look."

Colleton County Fire and Rescue didn't cover the beach in its distant location at the far end of the county, and the South Carolina Law Enforcement Division was the go-to investigatory arm to call when a case exceeded the expertise or manpower of the normal jurisdiction. They had to be asked before coming in.

"You think it's arson then?" she deduced.

"Not sure it isn't," he replied. "You okay with that? Wanted to ask before inviting someone else on our turf."

Callie did a little shrug thing with her mouth, a wave of her hand. "Fine. Whatever you feel needs doing, I'm on board with. Tell the mayor what he needs to know." Meaning what he'd have to know to handle the press. "What's your unofficial take?"

Leon's gaze went over Callie's head toward a pile of damage under the house, in the ground-level parking area. "They had building supplies stacked up over there," he said with a nod. "And patio chair cushions in and around them."

Callie waited for more, and when Leon didn't continue, she added her two cents. Maybe playing devil's advocate, if she could call it that. "These were two beach houses under repair, thus the building materials. Beach houses have beach chairs. Beach chairs are often stored in the storage room, especially in unoccupied addresses like this. Workers maybe used the chairs to take breaks."

More nods from the fire chief. "Yeah, but who sits on cushions without the chairs? The frames are still inside the storage room and on the porch. Polyurethane foam goes up like that." He jerked his chin, too tired to bother snapping his fingers.

Okay, interesting. "The owner isn't local," she said. "But the contractor is. Harbin Webb. Come to think of it, I'd have thought he'd be here on a Wednesday morning, or at least have shown up once this started. The whole beach has to be aware by now."

Leon downed the last of his water, sweat dribbling across his

Adam's apple as he emptied the bottle. He wiped his mouth with the back of his equally wet hand. "Maybe tied up on another job?"

"Too tied up to check out one of his projects burning?" She discreetly scanned the area. "Not even to come by afterwards to assess the damage? At least learn enough to call the guy who hired him and give him an update?"

Leon shrugged.

A gold Hummer rolled up, parking in the drive of the rental across the street.

"Like she's doing," Callie said as the engine shut off.

The driver had no qualms about parking in many of the drives in town since her real estate sign hung on about seventy percent of them. For Sale or For Rent, Janet Wainwright's red-and-gold logo told visitors she was the main mover and shaker when it came to Edisto property.

"Surprised she didn't show up sooner," Leon said under his breath, "to tell us to spray extra water on any houses that are hers."

Callie gave him an "um hum" as the retired Marine got out, her nephew Arthur exiting the other side.

"Remind me to show you something afterwards," Leon whispered out of the side of his mouth as the realtor approached.

Relatively tall, sinewy lean, tanned from her life living on the beach, her white hair cropped to a military tightness, Janet Wainwright made an impression. She had been a drill sergeant on Parris Island, the east coast Marine Corps Recruit Depot, and she moved with the ramrod posture they'd instilled in her eons ago. She made hard eye contact with everyone, friend or foe, and cut through bullshit like a hot knife through butter. "I would appreciate a report, please," Janet said, unable to hold any conversation without a demand involved.

Janet was closer to seventy than sixty, and if you didn't respect her for her age, you did for the fact she could probably kill you a dozen different ways.

Arthur Wainwright had graduated two months ago with a business degree and relocated to Edisto to work full time and complete his education at the knee of his aunt in hope of assuming the reins one day. He was the only potential heir she had, *potential* being a key adjective. Nobody doubted Janet would strike the kid out of her will in a skinny minute if he didn't measure up to her standards, and everyone also knew he'd almost lost his place in the will last December messing around with a friend involved in island thievery and an accidental death. It took a

Charleston lawyer and Janet's deep pockets to negotiate probation for Arthur, but the friend was serving serious time.

Oh yeah, nephew walked the straight and narrow, now, falling just short of salutes when his aunt gave directives.

Like with Brice, Callie had acquired more experience than Leon had when it came to taking verbal lashings from Janet. Leon updated Janet on the fire, but Callie strategically filled in holes to keep him out of the Marine's crosshairs. The real estate broker might be hard core and difficult, but she protected Edisto Beach's economics with the same devotion she pledged to the Corps, never falling short of a hundred-and-ten-percent effort. Callie had developed a Janet language after all their run-ins, so she did her best to keep the Marine's attention on her in lieu of the exhausted fire chief.

Callie noted no Wainwright signage on either of the burnt houses. "I take it neither of these is yours?"

"No, ma'am. Didn't sell them to the owner nor arrange the contractor. Used to rent these out three years ago, but once they changed hands, in a direct seller-to-seller deal, I quit being involved." While talking she inspected not only the houses on either sides of the burnt ones, and not just the two across the street that she managed, but also the two damaged ones. Callie knew good and well Janet was measuring opportunity with a powerful analysis.

She didn't get to be queen of Edisto's real estate business by waiting for it to fall into her lap. Janet mentally deduced loss versus probable insurance coverage versus the chance she could buy, sell, or take charge of refurbishing these two potential money makers. She owned four of her own, valued at three million or better, their rental income lucrative.

"Are you familiar with all the houses that Harbin Webb works on these days?" Callie asked. "I'm sure you manage the rentals on most of them, and you probably sold them to the current owners."

"Most of them."

"Is he working for you?"

Janet scoffed. "Some, but nothing major like this. You repair in the off-season, Chief Morgan. Nobody takes a house off the market this time of year." She caught herself. "At least nobody with any sort of real estate savvy. Why isn't Webb here? Is he arrested by chance?" Janet's mouth pursed in expectation.

"No, he's not arrested," Callie said. "Why would you think that?"

"It's a question. No reason."

"But like you, we wonder where he is," Leon replied.

Webb's absence was loud enough to put finding him at the top of Callie's agenda today. Anyone with half a brain would look at the contractor. He'd need to finish the job to get paid, though,. and insurance was a slow paymaster. "Tell me where he might be."

Janet prattled the house names off like she'd practiced for the question. "*Wave Runner, Bad Buoy, Riptide, Bikini Bottom* but not *Bikini Top*, and *Turtle Time*."

Nicknames were as much a part of a house's location as the street it was on. These houses were on five entirely different roads, from one end of the beach to the other. *Bikini Bottom* and *Bikini Top* were an A/B affair, like a duplex only two stories, each level a separate rental.

"Of course, that's only Aunt Janet's houses," Arthur added. "He might have others."

Janet looked at him like he'd spoken in tongues. One didn't mention what Janet did *not* have.

Dark hair and almost Italian looking thanks to his tan, Arthur could give Thomas a run for his money in terms of the island's eligible bachelor, if he weren't on such a short leash. Not extremely tall but pretty enough. He held up a finger, started to speak again, but a snap glance from Janet shut him up.

Poor guy. The kid had a mighty deep foxhole to climb out of. His December escapade had embarrassed his aunt, and she didn't suffer fools gladly.

"A job for you," Janet said, tipping her head toward the young man. "Find Webb."

He pivoted and almost stepped out to leave. "How will you get back to the office, Aunt Janet?"

She sighed and shook her head, pointing. "We'll talk in the Hummer." He wilted back into his place as sidekick.

Gracious. Callie found their dynamics painful to watch.

Janet peered back at Callie. "We'll let you know when we find him, Chief Morgan." She returned to her Hummer, the kid following.

"Poor guy," Leon said.

"That's become his middle name," Callie said. She'd heard a dozen different people say that to Arthur's back. "Seems that's one of the prices he pays to inherit the kingdom."

They watched Arthur open the driver's door for Janet, close it reverently, then trot around to his side. Not one to wave, Janet faced front and center down Myrtle Street on their way out, her nephew doing the same.

"I mean it, poor guy," Leon repeated.

"Radio me if you need me," Callie said, wanting to find Webb before Janet. "Or use the station number. My personal phone took a swim."

He chuckled at the remark. "Wait, before you take off, one of my guys found something of interest before Janet interrupted." Canvassing the immediate area for ears, he lowered his voice and motioned for her to come closer.

Intrigued, she shortened the distance.

He pulled an evidence bag out of his pants pocket. "Didn't want to show you in front of the Marine and her private but thought you'd find this of interest." He held it up. "Don't jump to conclusions, but it sure makes us have to talk to him, don't you think?"

"Crap," she said under her breath, reaching up and letting it lie lightly on the tips of her fingers. Not nearly as gold and shiny as she'd seen it last evening, but even grimy and smudged black, she recognized the Amazon badge that Monty liked to wear around his neck. And he hadn't been wearing it earlier when she pulled him away from the fire.

"Maybe he dropped it," Leon said. "He wanders a lot."

"Helps the contractors," Callie added. "It's how he earns a lot of his spending money."

Leon nodded. "True, true."

They both fell silent, not wanting to add too much to the conversation for fear of how it sounded.

"I'll look into him, too," she finally said, not telling Leon that she had now put Monty ahead of Webb. She especially wanted to be the first to talk to Monty. He trusted her. She'd probably been the last one to see him wearing that badge last night.

She turned to leave.

"Wait. I'd rather not talk over the radio about all this," he said, then thought a second.

"Use the station number," she said. "Again, good job today."

"You, too, Chief. Good team effort."

She walked the four-house distance to her car, armpits damp, back trickling perspiration. Deputy Raysor was one of those policing from his patrol car, blocking the road, air turned on high. She reached him and tapped on his window. "Once the fire truck is gone, everyone can go. Since they're calling in SLED, we might need to keep one guy on site. I'll let you decide who."

"Where will you be?" he asked.

"Hunting," she replied. "If you see either Monty Bartow or Harbin Webb, radio me."

Raysor took his standard growl to a lower one. "You don't think it's arson, do you? We don't need that."

"No, we don't." She realized they were murmuring quietly despite having nobody within eighty yards. Not even traffic.

Raysor still held a pained expression, waiting for more of the story.

"Monty's badge was found in the ashes," she said.

"Shit."

"And Webb hasn't shown up to weigh the damage. Wouldn't you—"

"Just when you think you know people," he grumbled.

She pat him on his hairy arm. "You *never* really know people, Don. Everybody has their secrets."

"Not in my family," he said. Don Raysor was kin to a third of Colleton County, and while that was a lot of folks to keep up with, admittedly, his family members were deeply in each other's business.

She pat him again and left for her vehicle, after reminding him to keep Monty and Webb to himself for now. She'd cruise the town roads for Monty, and failing that, she'd go out to see his mother. He always came home to Momma.

She started at the current end of the beach and drove past three of the five properties Janet had mentioned. Renters occupied two of them. Repairs were more difficult this time of year with owners scrambling to keep each sunny, summer day obligated to a paying customer.

She curved around to Dock Site, past Brice's place, and continued east toward *Bikini Bottom*. There was Webb, retrieving something from the toolbox in the back of his truck.

Chapter 7

PRIOR TO THE bathroom flood, living a mile from the station gave Callie the advantage of taking a mid-day shower and donning a fresh uniform in the steaming months of July and August, but with her house trashed with wet carpet and furniture in disarray and her other uniform not washed, thanks to everything upside down, she hadn't had the luxury of changing before beginning her hunt. Not today.

She'd prefer talking to Monty first, but Harbin Webb was more convenient with him right in front of her. From the sight of Monty's moped against the wall of the house, however, she'd lucked up with a two-for-one. Finally, a high point to her day.

"Webb," she said, pulling alongside the man's truck. The contractor had a rather giant-looking wrench in one hand, the other hand rummaging through the toolbox on the tail of his truck.

"Chief," he replied, wary.

She'd give him the wariness. They weren't fully acquainted, never having had to be, and for the police chief to take interest in him, in front of anyone who might happen by, wasn't a good look.

Harlin Webb fell in the mid-range in terms of price and familiarity in the beach area. A regular contractor, neither top shelf nor cheap, he made a common living repeatedly repairing homes that salt air, hurricane season, and disrespectful tenants brutalized. No doubt he'd repaired his own repairs a half dozen times at some addresses.

Like most of the outdoor employed, he had a leathery shell from a lifetime of sun, his blue eyes dull and squinty. No fat, but no muscle either. An example of a life of ladders, screwdrivers, saws, and paint, and his stained clothes and fingernails defined it. His left sneaker let his pinkie toe stick out.

She had a pair of shorts she loved like that.

She made for a rather melted presence, and if he stood closer, he'd note her odor. She didn't care for him to whiff the smoke quite yet and give away her purpose. "Can we talk?" she asked.

"Where?" came the reply.

Not *why*, not *how come*, not even *is something wrong?* Even traffic violators asked, *Something wrong, officer? Where* indicated he didn't want to be seen speaking to the cops.

"Is the house occupied?" she asked.

He shook his head.

"Then let's take it to the air-conditioning. Be there in a second." Before he could reply, she pulled into the duplex's drive, up under the house, trying to give the man a little respect by making the patrol car less obvious.

Inside, as tired as she was from standing all morning, she remained on her feet, not wanting to transfer her aroma to the rental's furniture. Seeing paper cups on the kitchen counter, she grabbed one, filled it from the faucet, and drank it dry. As wet as she might be under her clothes, her body screamed for water.

She tossed the cup in a grocery sack of trash. "Where's Monty?"

"Working out back," Webb replied. "He came by a little while ago and asked if he could earn a couple dollars. You know how we are with him around here. He's a good guy."

He sniffed, tried not to show he had. He'd picked up on the smoke.

She wandered to the back window. "There he is." Monty pulled nails from old boards, put them in a coffee can, and stacked the wood on a homemade trailer. "How long's he been here?"

"An hour maybe, why?"

She didn't answer, remaining in place to keep one eye on Monty, to make sure he didn't come in on them, or leave. "And how long have you been here?"

"Since seven."

"Aren't you going to ask about the fire?"

Thank goodness he didn't say *what fire*, because she'd gone off on him. Edisto was too tiny for him not to know. Especially since Monty had come from there.

But Webb didn't miss a beat. "Figured someone would get to me sooner or later." He motioned toward the hallway. "You mind if we talk while I work? I'm under a hard deadline on this place. Renters show up Saturday."

He left before she responded. People had to make a living out here, and a poor result on one house could mean losing two others, or more.

"Where were you this morning between five and six?" Callie had gotten Thomas's wake-up yells at a quarter to seven. A fire truck was already on its way by then. She didn't know where Webb lived or how far he had to travel to reach his work on the beach.

He'd squatted as though to work on the tub, but he stopped at the question, peered around himself, and laughed in a way that bordered mocking.

The bathroom they had entered was a wreck in terms of plumbing, and the tile that had to be taken out to get to the damage. Chipped grout, busted ceramic blocks. There were a couple of dinged-up spots on the bathroom counter and holes in the sheetrock. Webb would be hard pressed to get this project done in time for the weekend.

The contractor had his hands full, but the question merited an answer. "Better yet, start with waking up this morning, then bring me to now."

"Got up at five. Out the door by five thirty. On the job by six."

"Can you prove it?"

"No."

"Which job?"

"This job."

Still he hadn't asked why.

"Where do you live?" she asked.

He gave her a long second of attention then, head down, returned to his task. "Herbert Smalls Road," he said.

On the island. Not close, but under a thirty-minute drive.

"Can anyone vouch for you?"

He jerked his chin toward the rear of the house. "Ol' Monty back there."

Callie started to lean on the door frame, but sheetrock dust coated it. "You said yourself he only got here an hour ago, so 'no' might be the better answer, don't you think?"

Webb rose from his squat, tool still in hand. "Why are you crawling my ass, Chief? You've never needed to look into me, so back it up, little lady."

"Drop the wrench first," she ordered.

His eyes widened, then squinted, but he hadn't let loose of the tool.

"Now," she ordered again, hand moving toward her weapon.

His hesitation felt contrived. "What, you mean this?"

"Yes, that." She stared a hole through him and eased back as he set down the wrench with a clunk.

Not one to pass judgment quickly, Callie's jury had already come back in with this verdict. The man was an ass. Whether he hated authority, cops, women, or short people, she didn't care the reason. "Are you doing the repairs on *Shell Shack* and *Shark Shack*?"

"I am."

"They caught fire this morning."

"I know."

"So where have you been?"

"Lady. . . ." But he stopped himself reaching into a pocket for a vaping pipe, taking it slow for her sake.

She started to ask if he was allowed to smoke in this rental; most didn't allow smoking, but that was not her oversight. Plus, he wasn't exactly smoking. A blueberry scent drifted out of his mouth.

Like a shrimper wearing Dior. Not an exact fit.

"I'm aware," Webb finally said, perching himself on the edge of the old tub. He took a deep breath and took his time blowing it out. "Believe me, I'm totally aware. Been told no less than twenty times this morning. Visits, drive-bys, phone calls, and texts. *Your houses are on fire.*"

He took another puff. "Y'all ain't letting me on the property anyway." Then letting the pipe hang between his fingers, his forearms on his knees, he shook his head. "Too big a fire for me to put out, first. Nothing I could do. This house, on the other hand, needs my constant attention until it's done. I'll be working long hours up to the morning the tenants arrive. Figured someone like you would find me soon enough. What's the damage?" he asked.

"Substantial. Are you insured?"

"Depends. What's 'substantial'? House-coming-down substantial or redo-the-repairs substantial?"

"Not my call," she said.

Not the slightest blip in his heart rate about this. Not that people got overly bothered living on Edi-slow time, but this man was letting this setback roll off his back in an exorbitantly easy manner.

"Anyone hold a grudge against you?" Callie asked. "Anyone who might do this to spite you?"

That raised a brow. "They're calling it arson, are they?"

Callie kept quiet, still waiting for Webb to answer.

"Nope," he finally said. "Don't know nobody stupid enough to pull something like that against me. Don't owe nobody. Ain't pissed off nobody. Not that I know of."

"You don't appear too upset about the setback," she said.

He took one last drag on his pipe and put it away. "Ain't got time to get upset. Attitude is everything. Keeps my blood pressure low. You need me for questioning, or can I get back to work?"

"Would appreciate you looking at the site when you get a chance, but avoid crossing the crime scene tape. SLED is on their way to examine it."

"So it *is* arson." He shook his head, reached for his wrench, then in a second thought watched her as he slowly lifted it back up. "I'll head over there when I can," he said. "I'll be here when anyone has an accident report to give me so I can file my insurance. Imagine someone ought to tell Mr. McPhee. Would that be you or me?"

"Let me do it," she said.

"Good enough. Let him get angry at you, plus one less thing on my plate. We done?"

"I'll be in touch." She turned to leave but turned back. "I'll be talking to Monty for a little bit downstairs."

"Why? What's he got to do with this? He a suspect?"

Now he shows interest?

"Who says he had anything to do with the fire?"

His expression went back to its standard nonchalance. "Nobody. Connected the wrong dots, I guess."

"Thanks for your time, Mr. Webb."

"It's just Webb," he said, and gave her his back.

She exited the way she came in, out the front door so as not to touch or taint anything. She felt icky, and stepping outside in the heat only made it worse. Monty was singing to himself, and she walked past her patrol car through the breezeway to the backside. He had to have seen her car.

She'd debated earlier, driving away from the Myrtle Street fire, about whether to bring Monty into her cooled office for questioning, or to catch him like this, in an environment he'd be more natural in. She decided on this. He was on the clock, and no point robbing him of the little bit of money he was trying to earn.

"Hey, Monty." An oak and three palmettos shaded the backyard, but the man's red cheeks and flattened wet hair told her he was almost too hot. She looked around for water and found a six-pack cooler under the carport.

"Here, come sit down and drink something," she said, the mother in her coming out, wondering what his own mother would think at how hot he was. She probably packed his cooler, maybe gave him a few bucks for lunch. Regardless of the time of year, hot or cold, Monty lived his days out and about, so a mom like his would have a game plan to ensure her son was covered. Like Webb said, people around Edisto would tend to him, too. Maybe she ought to take him to El Marko's.

For the moment, however, they sat on the back steps under the shade. Unfortunately, the shade also made for the incessant swarms of no-see-ums and mosquitoes. Monty reached into the cooler and brought out a Gatorade and a bottle of bug spray, spritzing himself, then unexpectedly, he shared, spritzing Callie's arms and face. Spitting, she turned her head, palms up, the Skin So Soft about to ruin any thought of Mexican for lunch. "Stop, stop, I'm good, Monty. Thanks."

"Bugs are bad," he said, coating himself a few more times. The bottle went back in the cooler, and he offered Callie a sip from his Gatorade. The thought of the two flavors almost turned her stomach.

"Thanks, Monty. I'm good."

They sat staring at the lush greenery barrier between *Bikini Bottom* and the house on the other side, perspiration trickling down the side of his head, like it had started back on hers. But this was nice, really. This was calm. This would do.

Callie reached over and used the towel around his neck to wipe off some of his excess moisture. He let her with a smile. "There," she said. "Sorry we could not use you more this morning, Monty."

"I'm not a firefighter," he said.

"Nor am I," she replied.

He brightened. "Alex is fast, you know it? She's a professional newscaster now, you know."

Yeah, Alex went from the occasional *Edisto News* reporter to blogger to reporter for WLSC-TV, mostly due to coverage of Callie's cases. Alex was slick, and the fact she was young, agile, and adorable empowered her, making her all the more cunning. Part of how she'd avoided Callie. She was attractive and smart, with the island proud of her.

The little vixen.

"For sure she's good at her job. I'm trying to do mine now," Callie said. "They think someone may have set the fire this morning. It's my job to help find whoever it was."

His innocent look darkened. "People should not catch houses on fire. I helped build on that house. Webb paid me to help him on Friday, and now it's ruined. I almost feel I should give him back his money."

"No, no, that's not how it works, Monty. You gave him your time, and he paid you for it. The money is yours to keep." She let that subject settle and close. One had to speak to Monty linearly. He couldn't juggle many balls at once.

"Don't see you wearing your badge," she said, tapping her own. "Did you lose it?"

His puzzlement took her aback. "I don't wear it when I'm a construction worker, but you want to see it?"

"Yeah, as a matter of fact, I do," she said, sensing it normally not far from his grasp . . . doubting he would lay hands on it.

He leaped up, and she followed him to the moped. A basket on the front and a tall basket on the back, Monty went everywhere prepared. She'd seen him pull out a first aid kit once, and a couple of bungees another. He likened himself a bit of a MacGyver boy scout kind of guy.

She needed to read him. Then maybe confront him. She'd have to see. That badge, however, would not be in the basket.

Rummaging, he lifted a drawstring bag and dumped a small box out of it into his hand. He opened it then sucked in a breath. "It's gone!"

Callie approached closer. "Could you have left it somewhere?"

He brandished the box, top in one hand, bottom in the other, the fake-suede impression of the badge empty. "No. It goes right . . . here."

"Maybe it was lost at the fire, Monty. What time did you show up at *Shell Shack* this morning?"

His panic wasn't going away easily. "Don't keep up much with time." His pitch went up. "Where is my badge?"

He hunted under the seat, in a smaller compartment, then in the basket in the back. He ran to his cooler, Callie sticking close, then back to the moped.

Callie went for a calming approach. "Monty. Let me buy you lunch. We can talk about it in the air-conditioning, okay?"

"I got up," he mumbled. "I drove to the beach. I drove around asking for work. I heard about the fire. I went to the fire. I came here."

"Can you estimate the times for any of that?" she asked, trying her momma voice. Reaching, she aimed to rub his shoulder, reassure him like she'd done Jeb once upon a time, to make him believe he was smart enough to remember.

But he jerked away. "I don't do time, I said!"

He couldn't prove when he drove to the fire or when he was elsewhere where people could alibi him. This wasn't going well.

"Gotta go home," he muttered to himself, like Callie wasn't there.

"Let me escort you."

"No!" he yelled. "It's not dark. Momma will think I did something wrong. Leave me alone, Chief!"

He leaped on the moped, no thought to telling Webb.

"Monty, let me buy you some lunch. If we both cool down, we might be able to trace where it is."

But he was too focused on some unexplained plan in his head to hear. He tore off on the moped. Chances were he'd do the speed limit. He always had. He said he was headed home, and maybe that was the better place for him.

Callie needed to talk to Monty's mother anyway and start the timeline from that morning, then try to retrace Monty's activities from there. Minnie might not be such an easy nut to crack.

Maybe she'd wait until later, when the temp was cooler, when Monty had had time to settle, when Minnie might better understand that cooperation would serve all of them well.

"Did he set fire to my job?"

Callie jumped. Webb stood on the other side of her car.

"You eavesdropped," she said, none too pleased with being caught off guard.

"Simple question, Chief." Not threatening but none too pleasant. Far from protestations of calm he'd communicated in the torn-up bath.

"Pending investigation," she countered. *Not that your own alibi is in stone yet, either, Mr. Webb.*

Chapter 8

ARTHUR WAINWRIGHT rolled up at *Bikini Bottom* in the Hummer. "Don't tell Aunt Janet you beat me finding Webb, Chief. Please don't." Then he shouted over at the contractor, no notice of the stiffness between Callie and Webb. "Sorry about your houses, man."

"Appreciate it," Webb said, returning to his nonchalant role. Then as if he and Callie hadn't been talking, he returned upstairs.

"Does he seem upset to you?" Arthur said. "I never can read him. I'd be royally pissed if my job was torched."

Being unreadable was probably a trait Webb honed. Being benign made him less noticeable and kept him in the background. Contractors could do that, having learned to be invisible while repairing a family's home with them still in it. The behavior also allowed them to overhear conversations that weren't necessarily meant to be heard. They were quite clued into the island.

Callie backed herself under the shade. Arthur turned in, not inclined to leave the Hummer's cooler air. "Actually he's quite the opposite. Not very upset at all," she said, though not trusting the contractor's laissez-faire behavior. "How much have you worked with him?"

Arthur pondered a second. "I don't know . . . he's nothing bad, nothing stellar. Aunt Janet might have a longer history. He does all right for us."

"How are his finances? He ever stiff his subs? Ever walk off a job?" She almost asked if he drank on the job, but that sounded rather hypocritical, and she wasn't sure what the kid had heard of her own past, um, drinking on the job.

"Not that I know of," Arthur said. "Listen, Webb is found, and I've got other chores to do. My aunt keeps me patrolling these streets like I was on the police force. I kinda feel your pain sometimes. Please don't tell her. . . ."

"I don't rat, Arthur. All is good."

He slid on a silly grin. "Good to know. Thanks. And I really mean it.

Gotta have allies on this beach if I'm gonna live here full time, or she'll eat me alive."

"You gotta get out from under her roof," Callie said. "And whatever you do, don't make people choose between the two of you."

"Working on all of that," he said. "But moving? Um, real estate ain't exactly cheap around here." As a real estate agent under Janet's broker's license, he ought to know, and his aunt wasn't about to hand him one of her places rent free.

Cute kid though. Arthur wasn't much older than Jeb. She almost yearned to tussle his hair. "Be good," she said as he left, like she always told her son. He winked.

Arthur wasn't two houses down the road before Thomas drove up, his hand out the window holding something. "Thought you'd like this!"

Her phone!

"Bless you to heaven and back, Officer Gage." She took it like a long-lost talisman, her power back in her control. "You have made my day, kind sir. I thought it was done for."

He puffed out a little laugh. "After your last twenty-four hours, it wouldn't take much to make your day, but I'm happy to serve, m'lady."

This time she couldn't help herself. She ruffled his hair.

"Hey, I just combed that." He peered in his rearview mirror, finger-raking it back in place before smirking at her and leaving.

What was with these young guys being able to so easily tug on her heart? Or mess with her. Or make her momma-bear instinct rise up and take charge.

Like with Monty. Though he was thirty, he had the mentality of someone fifteen years younger, and right now she wanted to find him before anyone else did. He wouldn't find that badge, and she wanted to be there when he realized where he left it.

Then she needed him to admit the why. Why he was at *Shell Shack* and *Shark Shack*. When did he arrive there? Who else might have been there as well, because Monty acting alone felt improbable to her.

Look at her. She quasi-suspected him, and if she did, others would. Anyone, like Brice or the property owner, would jump at the chance to blame Monty. He was too easy a target.

Before she forgot, she sent a group text on her vitalized cell to Mark, Marie, Stan, Jeb, Sophie, and Leon, the familiarity of her personal phone so welcoming, and let them know she was back in business communication-wise. By the time she clicked her seat belt, started her car, and adjusted the air-conditioning, all but Jeb had replied, mostly thumbs-up, praying hands from Sophie for *namaste*, her signature reply, and a set of lips from Mark.

That went to everyone!

God, the man had no shame. And he was a nut with visuals in his texts.

Stan replied with a laughing emoji.

Back to normal, to a degree. Her house wasn't fixed, but the fire was history, *thank God*. Odds were they wouldn't see one for another two years, hopefully more, and she could lower her guard, put her fears to rest, and pray the day wouldn't dredge up the old nightmares when she finally put her head on a pillow tonight.

Wet had become the theme of the afternoon. As sweaty as she was, with beach waves in her ears and a wet, soggy carpet at home, the impact of those flames was rather quelled, and she felt sheepish about the earlier panic. Stan had recognized it right off the bat. Hopefully, he'd recognize it gone just as quickly.

The best news was nobody got hurt. Could've been a lot worse. Nothing tragic enough to send her to drink, as Stan tried to warn.

She headed toward Monty's house, having radioed Marie and texted Chief Leon her schedule with an extra note to keep quiet. She preferred to keep Monty under wraps for as long as she could.

The fire chief replied that SLED would try to arrive on-island within the next couple of hours, and Callie pushed the gas a little more. They would want to meet with her. They also might want to meet with Monty. Again, she had to reach him first.

An incoming front and its hot wind pushed against the car as she traveled down Oyster Factory Road, and she hoped it passed on through. The cattle gate wasn't latched when she arrived and, in fact, hung open. Not Monty's protocol, especially so protective of his mother. Apparently, he was still distraught.

Callie lumbered through. Summer heat had blanched the knee-high grasses yellow, and with the wind, they bowed in undulating waves. The brush under the trees, however, remained green, their roots deeper and able to easily reach the high-water table. She arrived at the house, Monty's moped parked in its spot under the carport.

She knocked, noting the windows and doors shut, the window unit sounding like a vacuum cleaner, occasionally rising in its heavy hum, as if clenching its teeth to spit out a little more air.

Minnie answered. "You want to tell me what the hell happened?" she demanded from behind the screen door.

Callie had imagined placating the woman, but Minnie's acerbic expression nixed that. "Ms. Bartow, there was a fire. Monty was there, which I'm sure he told you about, but—"

Minnie waved with impatience and held the door open for Callie to come in. "Don't stand there and let all the cold air out."

Callie scooted inside, not one for wasting someone else's money. Damp and standing in the living room, she shivered at the drastic change from outside to artificial cold. "I found him on one of Webb's repair jobs, Minnie, and he flared up about his badge going missing, so I followed him here. Was hoping to calm him down, maybe help him retrace his tracks. Also, I was hoping to talk to you."

"Stand right here."

A rather cool reception, but okay. "Sure, we can stand here and talk," Callie said.

"No." Minnie said, as if having a sour taste. "You stand. I'll go get my boy."

Callie better understood, and Minnie left. Taking note not to touch anything, she didn't want to leave any residual of her odious self on this poor woman's furniture, a contribution to the depreciation of the thrift-store décor. Maybe that was part of the cool welcome. Her aroma.

In spite of the tiny rooms, Callie couldn't hear more than muddled conversation. At least until Monty yelled, "No, Momma!"

"Monty!" A hard emphasis on the front end of the name blew out of the mother.

A door slammed. The one off the kitchen. Callie moved to the living room window to catch sight of Monty rushing to his bike, pushing it with a vengeance to get it revved, and giving it the gas to get gone quickly.

Callie hoped she didn't have to spend her entire evening chasing that little moped.

"Okay," Minnie said, striding back in, her voice huskier than last night, her demand for accountability evident in that one little word. "You sure got him upset."

Say what? That wasn't Callie yelling with Monty in the back room. "Where's he going?" Callie said, torn between coordinating with the mother, who could help, or chasing Monty.

"Gone off hunting his badge. He said it wasn't here." Minnie stared harder. "He also said you were accusing him of something, so you ain't chasing him quite yet. You ain't leaving until we get something straight. What exactly would you be accusing him of, Chief?"

Callie chose to soothe these feathers first. "I didn't accuse him of anything."

"He's not stupid, you know." Minnie still hadn't asked her guest to sit.

"May we talk?" Callie wasn't three feet from the sofa. The recliner, its end table with a set of reading glasses and a newspaper was Minnie's, an upholstered chair to the left of it obviously Monty's from the basket of assorted *Star Wars* paraphernalia beside it, the plaid cushion worn on the front from his sitting on its edge.

Taking her chair, Minnie's bottom lip and brows pinched. Then she nodded sharp for Callie to be seated on the sofa.

"There was a fire on Myrtle Street this morning," Callie said, easing just on the sofa's edge, elbows on her knees, leaning forward, giving the appearance of assistance. "They suspect arson, but the investigation just started. Nobody has been accused. Not Monty, not anyone."

Minnie's stare darkened. She wasn't buying it.

Callie cleared her throat. "They found a fake police badge in the ashes, like the one Monty wears. I don't think anyone else around here has such a badge, Minnie."

"Is it his?"

"Like I said. He's the only one we know of, and while we haven't finished checking forensics—"

"Can you prove it's his?" the mother repeated.

"No, not yet, but can Monty show us he still has his?"

Minnie crossed her arms, pushing ample bosoms almost up under her chin. "Burden of proof's on you. Who else are you looking at?"

"It's early in the investigation, Minnie." Callie was not about to name names. Bobby McPhee, Harlin Webb, the neighbors, enemies of any and all of the above, had to be located and interviewed.

"We need an attorney?" Small talk wasn't this woman's strong suit, but before Callie could say she couldn't really advise one way or the other, Minnie blurted. "We can't afford an attorney."

"When and if the time comes, the court can appoint one for you."

Callie hardly ended the sentence before Minnie tossed out, "How'm

I supposed to know when that time is exactly?"

Callie really hadn't wanted to go this far. Monty was an island fixture, and Callie was not charging him unless the evidence was pretty damn solid, and while they might be headed in that direction, they weren't there yet.

"When and *if* he is charged, Minnie."

The room lit up. The women hunkered, looking stunned at each other, then both snapped attention to the paned picture window. A clap of thunder trembled the floor, rattled something in the kitchen, forcing both to hide again beneath hunched shoulders.

"God Almighty, that struck close!" Minnie yelled.

A sizable drop, then two, hit the glass. Then a few more. With heat backed up under fat clouds, with this much moisture in the air, with them living on coastal South Carolina, such storms rolled in and out at least twice a week. Like this one, such weather loved to tease with wind, then hint with a few plump drops . . . then decide whether or not to explode in a frenzy, soaking everything down with enough noise to not hear one's self think.

As though someone had pulled out a tablecloth all at once, a wall of rain pummeled the yard.

Monty wouldn't have had time to make it to the beach. Callie sure hoped he pulled over someplace. "Maybe I need to go after him," she said, reaching for her keys.

"Rain isn't gonna kill him. He has a change of clothes in that bike basket, and someone'll tend to him. Always do."

Callie looked over at this woman with newfound . . . wonder? That wasn't a very motherly thing to say. Everyone was aware the Bartows didn't lead a smooth life and made do on many levels. Guess to Minnie there were worse bumps in their world than getting rained on. Callie worried more about the lightning.

Didn't take three minutes for the rain to reduce from a cacophony to a shower, the thunder muted rumblings in the distance. Minnie backed away from leaning on the windowsill. "Well?"

Callie stood back. "Well . . . what?"

"Do I get an attorney yet or not?"

"If you know one, yes. If you don't, better to wait."

Minnie spit out a sarcastic scoff. "Meaning we're poor."

There was no sugar-coating this discussion. There probably was no sugar-coating any discussion with Minnie Bartow. "Meaning he hasn't been charged, Minnie."

"Hmm."

Callie headed to the door. "If you find his badge, call me, okay?" She went to pull out her card.

"I got the number," she said. "Marie and I go way back."

Calling Edisto PD's office manager was close enough.

Hand on the doorknob, Callie said, "Thanks, ma'am. I really want to help."

No response from Minnie one way or the other, so Callie let herself out. She waited on the front porch, timing the shower. These things usually let up quick. When she deemed the time opportune, she leaped down the front steps.

The bottom fell out again.

Rain down her collar, in her shoes, saturating her hair, Callie could only keep going.

Throwing herself into the front seat, she reached around for something to wipe her face, snaring a thin roll of paper towels under the seat. She wondered what this deluge was doing to the crime scene. Or if SLED would delay coming out. If Leon was right, the fire started outside and was now indubitably flooded. That couldn't be good.

Peering back, Callie noted the living room window where Minnie now stood vigil. Though Callie'd tried hard to be empathetic, the Bartows would struggle seeing Callie as an ally now. Still, she'd do all she could to shield Monty from unnecessary distress. At least until she couldn't.

Sticky and unable to see through her fogged front window, Callie blasted the AC through the defroster. While she waited for better vision, she went for her phone . . . only to find an empty pocket.

Thomas had just given her this phone. Had she put it in the wrong pocket? She patted herself over, felt between and under the seats. She checked the glovebox though she'd never put the device there before.

The front window began to clear. She wondered if she dropped it in the house.

She glanced over again to see if Minnie still watched, but in bringing her attention back from the window to the car, Callie spotted the phone. On the ground, in a puddle.

Chapter 9

"NO!" THROWING herself out of the car, as Minnie watched from her window, Callie weathered the rain again, scooping up her cell, instinctively wiping it on a pants leg already soaked through.

"Son of a bitch," she uttered outside, but once in the vehicle, she screamed, "Son of a f'in *bitch*!"

Maybe it wasn't ruined, but she couldn't help but look at the phone as if it were a patient right out of the hospital, mostly healed but vulnerable to relapse. She gently touched it, to turn it on, like it had feelings.

Nothing.

Damn, damn, damn, damn.

She pulled out her work phone, something she wouldn't have been able to do before this phone situation. She hated carrying two phones. Out went a notice to the same people . . . Leon, Mark, Stan, Thomas, Jeb, and Marie. She'd lost the use of her personal cell again, and her work number was back in play.

What did you do? Stan typed, adding emojis with shrugs and eyes rolling, exercising his newfound pleasure of illustrating his comments.

Not even gonna ask, Jeb replied.

She didn't bother reading the others. Exasperated, she threw the phone on the seat next to the dead one and left. She reached the gate, wide open in Monty's explosive escape and decided another soaking wouldn't hurt. Callie jumped out into the rain and closed the gate behind her.

Driving slowly, she hunted for Monty. Under trees, on porches, even in the ditches. Most likely he'd taken shelter some place, drying off. Finally, she headed to the beach. No point hunting him in this mess. She knew perfectly well how dripping drenched he felt.

Taking a pointer from Monty, she made an executive decision to go home and change. She called Mark on the way. Forecasting dry clothes only made her sense her ickiness all the more.

"Got good news and bad news for you," he answered. "Which do you want first?"

"The bad. I prefer ending on a high note," she said, shifting in her seat, her underwear clingy and bunched under her right butt cheek.

"Insurance adjustor wasn't happy meeting me about your house in lieu of you. Seems he saw you as some sort of celebrity," he said.

She bitterly chuckled. "He wouldn't be so impressed seeing me right now." *Was that the rain letting up? Yes*, the sun was trying to peek through the clouds, but that also meant a steam bath when she left the car. "So, what's the loss estimate? I assume that's the bad part of the bad news."

"Thirty thousand, give or take."

"Give or take what? My first-born child?" Building supplies had gone up more than she thought. She'd heard the complaints since Edisto was forever in some state of construction flux between new houses on the last remaining lots and old houses needing facelifts every five to ten years due to the harsh salty, coastal living. "That's like adding on a room. How is that price even possible?"

"When's the last time you added on a room? He's emailing you an itemization tomorrow. He said you could probably get quoters to shave off a few thousand with you being the police chief . . . and famous. I got the sense the guy had a teeny crush on you."

Was he chuckling? She struggled with the humor here. That much money meant more damage than she expected, which meant longer to do the repairs, which meant a monstrous inconvenience. The deductible she could live with, but the time spent ripping out stuff, moving her things, spending the night elsewhere, and, God help her, selecting colors, paint, floor covering.

Negligible security would reign during this time. With so many people having access to her home she'd wonder about contractors bringing their friends over when she was at work. How many copies of her key would be cut in the name of access and convenience? She could retain the right to let them in and out, but she'd be unable to watch them as they did the work, meaning she'd be studying her cam footage half the night to ensure nobody did untoward things in her absence.

And she had zero decorating taste nor an inkling of desire to pick out new items. She'd probably go safe with beige, feeling she'd get tired of anything any bolder. Paint was not to be noticed, in her opinion. Just backdrop.

Wait, she had two mothers, and her adopted mother had designed the beach house to begin with. *Chelsea Morning* had belonged to her parents before they tossed the keys to Callie. However, Beverly Cantrell was mayor of Middleton now, which probably didn't give her much down time. Wait . . . if Callie told Beverly that Sarah, her biological mother, was to orchestrate the renovations, then Beverly would find the time. Question was, which woman's taste did Callie want. No, wait. Which woman did she prefer to see the most of?

Or should she keep her mouth shut and recreate exactly what was there before? Was it considered dated? Did she care?

Mark interrupted her interior decorating. "You haven't asked what the good news is."

"What time is it?" She crossed Scott Creek, putting her home a mile and a half away. "I've gotta go home and change. I stink."

"You have no water," he said. "And don't be mad at Sophie when you get there either. She's working in the restaurant right now and feeling mighty good about herself."

Callie's focus snapped back into place. *Crap.* She forgot about no water. How was this going to work? And what was that about Sophie? "What does Sophie have to do with anything?"

"Um, that was supposed to be part of the good news." His silence showed an effort to reform the message.

As she drove by El Marko's, she tried to spot him inside the restaurant, feeling silly at the effort. Passers-by could barely see through the tinted windows of the place, and Mark walked to work so no car in the parking lot. "Are you at work or at my house?" she asked.

"Work. Where are you?"

"Driving past, why?"

"Shoot," he whispered.

"Meet me out front of the restaurant," she said, already turning around in a driveway. By the time she reached El Marko's, Mark stood out front, thumb up like a hitchhiker, his usual paper bag in hand.

He got in, picking up the two phones in the seat to make room. He sniffed. "Holy cow, is that you?"

"No, it's Santa Claus."

He buckled up and laughed. "No, I know him. I donate to his sleigh. He smells like cinnamon and sugar cookies. Nothing like this."

She headed back up Jungle Road. "Why am I nervous about opening my own front door?"

"You'll see."

"So, I *should* be nervous, huh?"

He dangled the bag. "Hungry?" He could be savvy with that bag.

Fact was, she hadn't eaten a bite. A bottle of water at the fire and a paper cup of the same at Webb's job had been it. Right now, she couldn't stand the sight of water . . . in her, on her, around her.

She almost wanted to eat in the car and enjoy a moment of un-interrupted peace before getting hit with the good news that wasn't good news when she went inside, but she parked and got out. She brought in both phones, in case the one decided to work. On the porch, she let Mark unlock the door.

"We didn't do any of this until after the adjustor left," he said.

"Any of what?" Unable to help herself, she peered through the glass. She couldn't see past the furniture in her hall. Her sofa blocked the entryway. Her floor lamp lay across its cushions surrounded by . . . shoe boxes.

Her phone rang, and she held out both, deciphering which to answer. The work phone.

"Chief? Three robbery reports," Marie said, slow and distinct.

"Wham, no point in wasting conversation, eh, Marie?"

"It's been a long busy day, Callie. Not sure we've ever had three in one morning. That and Booker McPhee tried to call you if you want his number."

Callie had whispered *son of a bitch* more times today than in the last year, but Marie was her bellwether and deserved nothing but gratitude for keeping the station on its game. "Not three missing items, but three separate burglaries at three separate addresses . . . this morning?" Callie turned to Mark. He tucked his chin and scowled at how ridiculous that sounded for Edisto Beach. They'd had a Christmas rash of burglaries, an anomaly, the culprit being that jailed friend of Arthur's, but even those thefts stretched out over a few days.

"Every single one on Myrtle Street," Marie continued, naming the houses. "All during the fire."

The weight of that dropped Callie to her rattan rocker, forgetting she'd get the tufted cushion wet. With every officer but one on duty, with all the firefighters present, she'd had some concern about an opportunist scumbag breaking and entering in other parts of the town, but right there on Myrtle? After families had been evacuated and assured all would be fine? How did nobody see the culprit? Assuming the culprit was solo. Could be a team. Could be three different people who thought alike. Could be misplaced items, too, lost in the hurry of evacuation.

Could be that Brice LeGrand and town council would have a conniption fit when they heard this.

"Text me the names and phone numbers," Callie said. "Let me grab a bite and change clothes, and I'll head over there. Anything else?"

"The SLED fire people said they can't come until tomorrow. Something else came up closer to where they were. Might not even be until tomorrow afternoon."

Might not happen at all if they talked to Leon about what the scene looked like after the storm. Put an iPad out there, pan the scene, and there you go . . . an analysis of the fire scene without leaving the office.

No, she wasn't holding her breath about them showing.

"Thanks, Marie." Callie hung up and fell back against the chair. "What the hell else can happen?"

"Oh, you should not have said that," Mark answered.

Her phone rang again.

He shook his head and grunted, "Told you."

"Probably Thomas or something." She looked at caller ID.

No such luck. The caller was Brice.

There on her porch, for all the world to hear, Callie started to put the councilman's call on speaker for Mark's sake, but God only knew how loud his complaint would be, or how profane.

"Chief Morgan," she answered.

"What the hell happened to your other number?" he fussed. "How are we supposed to get in touch with you if you don't turn on your damn phone? Is this your way of avoiding me, us, the citizens who need your attention?"

Yes, Brice. I've hidden from you all damn day long.

She could recite his speech. The bastard couldn't fathom how to behave in any other manner but as a bastard. When was she going to quit letting him under her skin? "The old number is my personal phone. You called me on the work phone but calling the station still works, and so does 911, but more importantly, what can I do for you?"

"Your damn job," he said as if pushing through his teeth.

Mark heard him and came closer to hear more.

"I'm listening," was all Callie felt she could stand to say before understanding how deeply in trouble Brice thought she was.

"One, a fire at my house. Two, the fires on Myrtle Street. I've called

Bobby McPhee, by the way, and he's not happy in the least."

The first was on him. Not calling the owner, however, was definitely on her. She'd meant to call McPhee before now. Brice probably cancelled appointments to beat her to the punch. Still, she had to do so herself not just out of courtesy or professionalism, but because he could also be a party of interest. "And the third issue?" she asked, halfway expecting what that third was.

"Breaking and entering right under your nose on Myrtle Street," he said, his gloating long-time practiced. "Three times, no less. Are your people blind or what?"

He stopped there.

"Was that rhetorical or did you seriously want me to answer that question?" she asked.

"The point is it's inexcusable. I'm surprised you haven't been inundated with protests. All it takes is those three families posting on social media, or leaving bad reviews on websites, or talking to neighboring tables in restaurants, and we have a crisis on our hands. What will this beach do without tourism?"

She bit her tongue not to squawk, *The sky is falling! The sky is falling!*

Edisto lived off of tourism, but based on the waiting lists to rent houses, she didn't see the gross income of the community doing anything but rising. Public image did matter, though. It dictated how well the community ran. It also dictated how long her officers kept their jobs.

"What are you *doing* about it?" he demanded when she'd thought too long.

"I'm about to change out of these smoky, damp clothes from this morning's fire and head over to Myrtle and speak to people," she said.

"Why aren't you already over there?"

"Because they just called the station? And Marie just called me? And I've been investigating the fire?" Once again, she kept the attention on her and off of Leon. He had a young family and needed his job. She, however, had been roped into police chief, ultimately doing it because that was who she was. After her husband and her father's deaths, she was financially sound enough to sit on the beach reading books with a drink in her hand every day, which was partially why she worked . . . to keep from being bored, and to keep that drink out of her hand.

"This is going on the agenda at the next council meeting," he said. "The lack of police protection and fire control. The public is watching, Chief Morgan. Alex Hanson is already trying to chase me down for a story about it all."

Alex should only know about *Shell Shack* and *Shark Shack*, unless Brice had volunteered that someone had set his storage room on fire . . . and the burglaries.

"Brice?" she asked.

"What?"

"Would you please let me go so I can do my job?"

His snort came through. "I'm watching you."

She waited for his hang-up.

There it was.

She sat with a phone in each hand, marveling she hadn't lost her cool.

"When it rains it pours," Mark said.

"God, don't say that," she replied. "I can't get any wetter. If I don't get changed, I'll find rashes in places I don't need them." She stood to go inside, forgetting that Mark hadn't quite delivered his *good news* yet, Brice's scathing call and Marie's notification having hijacked their attention.

But her first priority was to call Booker McPhee, and she put this call on speaker. She had no idea what to expect from this man, and a witness couldn't hurt.

"McPhee," came the curt reply.

"Mr. McPhee, this is Edisto Beach Police Chief Callie Morgan, calling to inform you about an incident at your properties here."

"Been told four times already today," he said. "What more can you add other than giving me a report to use for insurance? Even better, tell me who did it. I assume you picked him up. I mean, how hard can it be to police that beach?"

His voice gave Callie an image of a billionaire allowing her ten minutes of his time because a hundred other people were lined up for their own ten minutes of time.

"The investigation is ongoing," she said. "But tell me about the repairs. Do you trust your contractor?"

"Thought I did before you asked that question. Why?"

"Routine question," she said. "I'll ask him the same about you."

"Brice said it was probably arson. You confirmed that."

She shouldn't be surprised, but she could be irritated at Brice spouting off about a crime without knowing a damn thing. She wiped at a drip down her temple.

"You're repairing houses during peak rental season instead of the off-season. Is there a financial reason? And you still haven't told me what you thought about your contractor."

"You sure get to the point, don't you, Chief?"

He didn't sound flustered. He didn't sound irritated at her not having called earlier, but he did sound like he wanted to be done with the call, without really having the call.

"Trying to," she said, adding, "like I'm sure you'd want me to. You sounded like time was money when you answered. Trying to be efficient with that time," she replied. He'd used his impertinence to dodge the questions, instead asking more questions than she had . . . deflecting, in her opinion.

"Well, thanks for calling, Chief. Now, if you don't mind—"

"To receive an accident report for your insurance, you need to answer my questions. First, do you trust your contractor? Second, are there any issues with him we should be aware of like an inability to pay his bills or fulfill his end of this contract? Third, do you have sufficient insurance to cover this loss and rebuild the houses? Fourth, why did you wait until the height of the rental season to pull your houses off the market?"

"Chief, I trust Harbin Webb. He's given me no problem at all."

"Nicely done," she said. "And the other questions?"

"I'm insured just fine."

She waited.

"Good enough?" he asked.

"The last question," she reminded, looking at Mark to see if he was catching this evasive behavior as well.

"Look," McPhee started then stopped.

Callie waited. She enjoyed filling the air with silence when talking to a person of interest, which McPhee was fast becoming.

"Chief?"

"I'm here. You were explaining about repairing the house in July?"

"Yes, yes. Well, I honestly can say I let it get away from me. I bought those houses eighteen months ago, rented them for all they were worth, amassing a fairly long laundry list of repairs, some of them serious enough to jeopardize my insurance coverage. I live in Roanoke, Chief Morgan. My focus is up here. Webb got in touch with me and offered his services at a discount, which I found quite enterprising. I checked his references, he seemed good, and I gave him the jobs. Sloppiness on my part is the best way to describe it, I guess. Nothing to do with Mr. Webb." He finished, with a distant *hmm* on the end, like he had to show he was done.

"We need proof of that insurance," she said. "And proof of that contract."

"I was over four hundred miles away from that fire," he replied.

"I wasn't accusing you, Mr. McPhee. Don't give me reason to change my mind." Callie gave him the office fax and email, and both her numbers. "I look forward to those documents. Thanks so much for assisting us in getting to the bottom of this."

"You are more than welcome." He sounded magnanimous, like he'd cooperated all along. "Please keep me apprised of the results of your investigation."

"Oh, absolutely, Mr. McPhee."

Looking at Mark, she disconnected the call, waiting for his feedback.

"Something's not right in Roanoke," he said.

"You think?" she replied, mocking.

McPhee might physically have been in Roanoke this morning during the fire, but who says the man got his own hands dirty?

She rose from the rattan chair, her pants sticking to her. "I want another go-round with Webb." She started to tell Mark about Monty, but she'd made a promise to herself to protect the guy until she couldn't. Mark was reliable, but it didn't seem right to violate that promise.

Chapter 10

"IT'S AFTER FOUR," Mark said. "You started at dawn, you're soaked, and you've weathered flame and flood. I see no point in you enduring famine as well. You missed lunch. . . ." He held up his paper bag. "It's practically time for dinner. You can't function like this."

She peered up at him. He'd been an agent, not a police chief. Different in so many ways. He was being incredibly sweet, but in a place like Edisto, the chief of police was tethered to each and every one of its occupants. While your normal person saw small-town policing as an easy eight-to-five schedule, it could prove quite the opposite. On two and a half square miles of people seeking paradise, her role was to aid their mission, whenever the need arose.

Burgled tourists now needed settling and assurances. She had property owners with arson forefront in their minds. She wouldn't sleep well without finding Monty and addressing him in a subtle way others would not bother doing. A gripping concern had taken hold of her, and not necessarily about his innocence.

"But I've seen enough of you to know you won't quit till you have to," Mark said, dismissing the need for an explanation. "Those calls," he continued, "means your day has miles to go, doesn't it?" His grin crept up on one side, like her husband used to do. It had never failed to make her smile back. "Shall we go in?" Mark said, showing her the way to her own front door.

She was touched. Bless him, this man proactively lessened her load, showed he cared, and saw her perspective. She hadn't thought they made guys like that anymore. She damn sure didn't think she'd merited one.

She laid a hand on his chest and swallowed a lump she hadn't seen coming. "Thank you."

He studied her hand a second then tilted his head down to hers. "You're welcome." He studied her longer. "Are you okay?"

God, what was she not seeing about this man that could make him less perfect. She had no idea why fate felt she deserved another chance at a relationship. Sometimes his walking into her life scared her to death.

Her friend Slade flashed to mind, and their discussion about Callie having lost two romances in her life while Slade had Wayne and was too afraid of commitment. Callie advised her to go for it. Life was too short.

Now, here she was, afraid to practice what she preached.

Not that Mark had mentioned anything permanent. Not that she wanted permanent just yet. Wasn't even on the horizon. Visiting each other's beach houses suited her perfectly fine.

"And there she goes," he said. "Your thoughts just shot off on a tangent and got lost in the universe. As I keep saying. . . ." He tapped her on the forehead. "You think too hard."

Warmly, she smiled back. "I'm good," she said. "Really good. Thanks for taking care of the house. That means a lot." She almost thanked him for tending to her. She wasn't sure why she stopped short of that.

"Don't thank me quite yet. You're still homeless."

Yeah, she was. That was fixable and not the real problem. Her fire phobia had slipped up on her, and that nagged her more. Chances were there weren't going to be more times for that phobia to grab hold of her, but she wasn't eager to share the flaw with Mark quite yet. Maybe they'd have a discussion once she learned to manage it . . . on her own, like her drinking.

As Stan ordered in his old-boss manner, she needed to get in front of it. The public had to see a totally put-together person in charge of public safety, and she didn't need a man thinking he had to protect her.

In the meantime, she needed to see the house. Callie unlocked and pushed the door, which abruptly hit the sofa sitting about a foot from it.

"Sophie must've shoved that sofa further to make more room," Mark said. "Can you squeeze your tiny little self through?"

"Nope. Geez, all I want to do is go in and get a shower," Callie uttered.

"Like I said, that's not gonna happen." Mark shouldered the sofa back a few more inches. "No water until tomorrow."

"There will actually be water tomorrow?"

"Yea," he said, with a grunt.

"You hired a plumber, too?"

"Thought that part you wouldn't mind," and with a final push, he wormed his way inside. "He's a local Sophie recommended. Said he'd bill the insurance agent. He and the agent fish together."

She hoped that wasn't why her estimate was as high as it was.

The two of them slid behind the sofa, and it was only as she squeezed out the other side did the weight of Sophie's generous nature become evident.

The living room was void of furniture, curtains, even pictures on the wall, the emptiness revealing the reason why. The hardwood floor had already started buckling from the bedroom out into the living area.

Thank goodness they left blinds on the windows.

Sighing, Callie peered left into the bedroom, equally empty only minus the carpet and most of the padding, the subfloor splattered in *Rorschach* designs of moisture and ruination. She moved through, thinking it could be worse, especially after having seen what fire could do.

In the bathroom, there was not so much as a toothbrush on the counter. No rug on the floor. Not even her mother's bronze fish sculpture from the wall over the tub. If she'd had a better day, she'd have asked why they emptied the walls, but she hadn't the steam in her, so she traipsed back into the living room to see the kitchen. Only she couldn't see in her kitchen. It held her bedroom furniture, crammed counter to counter. There was no reaching the sink unless you crawled over the bar, and no getting into the refrigerator at all.

She still couldn't account for a dresser, her recliner . . . her record player and all its Neil Diamond albums. "Still waiting for the good news, Mark."

"Sophie went to a lot of work," he said way calmer than she felt.

"Used the landscapers to move everything, I take it?"

"Not sure who those guys were."

"Did you help?" she asked.

"Some. Those guys had stronger and younger backs than me, but I moved most of the lighter stuff. I can tell you where everything is, though. I kept notes on my phone."

She bet his limp had something to do with his inability to lift furniture, but that thought was for another day. She hoped the task hadn't aggravated his injury. "My clothes," she remembered, and ran to the closet . . . which was as bare as the bedroom.

Mark tailed her throughout the rooms, from upstairs to the downstairs guest room where she found the furniture pieces she'd missed. The guest bath. At least it still had its guest toiletries . . . only no water to use them with.

Callie threw hands on her waist and slowly pivoted. "Where have y'all put me for the night? And for goodness' sake, how long?"

"Want to sit on the back porch and eat this?" he said, holding up the bag again.

"No, it's too hot." She sat right there, on the floor, scooching up against the wall, then held out her hand for the bag. "And you're getting awful handy with this bag thing you do to diffuse conversation."

He sat beside her, despite her dampness and odor. "I talked to the insurance guy, then Sophie took charge. Be thankful."

Now she felt bad. "I am grateful," she said, mouth full of a burrito. She had underestimated their generosity. "I'm thrilled."

"And you're staying with me," he said. "Is that a problem? Something about a gun and your karma not becoming Sophie's karma. Sounded a bit selfish to me, but she was ripping up carpet at the time she said it, so who was I to question the logic of a *spiritual goddess?*" He grinned. "Her words, not mine."

Thank God she wasn't staying with Sophie. "But where are my clothes, makeup, underwear? My dirty uniforms."

He unfolded another burrito for her. Callie accepted the second without hesitation. They were small, right?

Mark grinned. "I do love watching a woman eat."

"My underwear?" she said from behind a bite.

"Sophie packed up what she thought you needed. The suitcases are at my house where we can go as soon as you finish eating. I threw your dirty uniforms in my washer. They haven't made it to the dryer yet."

Was this guy always a step ahead?

Oh, wait. Who was running the restaurant during July's tourist mecca? With his hostess Sophie missing to boot.

She took a faster bite. "You've got to go," she said. Damn but she was hungry. Still she needed to quit exploiting his good nature. "Do you iron, too?" she garbled, inhaling the beans and chicken.

"Yes, Chief, I know how to put creases in police uniforms."

"Damn," she said, swallowing the last bite. "Guess you could call this good news in a weird way."

"You calling me weird?"

She wadded up the paper from the burrito, finished off some nacho chips, and swigged down the rest of a small bottle of juice. She wasn't sure when she could stand looking at water again. "Not if you can find me a shower."

Mark rented a house on a long-term basis only two blocks from the restaurant, a tiny place with one bedroom and barely a suggestion of another if you counted a twin bed, a nightstand, and a three-foot-wide, free-standing closet. Sixty years old and bare-bones basic, *Reel Lucky* had as much porch as living space. The house had been built back in the day when a fishing cabin was just that and was difficult to keep rented in modern times. The house became one of few that preferred the monthly rent of a normal tenant to the weekly of squandering tourists who demanded much more. Having thrown his savings into the restaurant, Mark had no plans to buy a place until he could measure the success of El Marko's.

Callie'd never spent the night there. She couldn't explain why at first, but when she debated on whether to drive her personal vehicle or the patrol car, because people might notice, she nailed the reason. The police chief would be shacked up with the Mexican restaurant owner, for all to see and the gossip circuit to pass around at the speed of light.

Something else for Brice to toss onto her pile of ill-deeds and professional impropriety.

"Here," Mark said, as they locked up the house and walked down the front steps. "Take my key."

She took it, feeling oddly errant and sneaky.

"Drop me off at the restaurant, go get cleaned up at the house, and I'll see you when I see you," he said. "I rarely get home before eleven."

At the strip of commercial businesses, El Marko's on the west end, Callie dropped him off but not before he kissed her goodbye. Like a couple sharing a car to work.

"It's okay," he whispered, giving her another quick peck in after-thought before leaving. "Lighten up, Chief." He got out and leaned in. "I need a better nickname for you." Then he left.

At *Reel Lucky*, she entered, tentatively, expecting a disaster in terms of her things but instead finding the correct toiletries in the bath, the right underthings in a bag, and hangers of at least four days' clothes . . . in Mark's closet.

They'd worked hard to give her no excuse to complain while not getting in the way of her duties. She owed them big time.

Minutes later, Callie smelled a hundred percent sweeter in cargo pants, an Edisto PD polo shirt, her belt, and weapon. And both phones, the personal one still dead.

With Brice in his aerie keeping watch on her, and three families nervous about a burglar, she had to compartmentalize Mark and make tracks. Was it past five already? No problem. Mark wouldn't be home until eleven.

Then she wondered why that should factor into anything as she headed to Myrtle Street.

She caught herself keeping a watch out for Monty, his soft-blue moped unique. Then as she turned onto Myrtle, she did a double check of *Shell Shack*, hoping one of her officers remained on site . . . hoping for the off chance Monty was there hunting his badge.

Passing the fire site, she raised a wave at Officer LaRoache baby-sitting the scene, slowed and backed up. She needed to speak to him.

Smart of Raysor to assign this officer. Cobb LaRoache wasn't one to think outside the box or put in longer than his normal duty, and he'd become even more of a routine-monger after last December when he'd shot and killed a guy shooting at Callie. The incident only served to anchor him even more to a schedule, for some reason. Unofficially, they all obliged him. No one but LaRoache and Callie had killed a human being, and the others didn't want to join the club. She kept the occasional extra eye on him. Those demons never went away.

She paralleled to his vehicle, the drivers' sides together. "Hey, Cobb. How's it going?"

He'd lightened up a tad since December, but there was still a sadness in the creases on his face. He was a year older than she, with a son and daughter at home and his wife a schoolteacher in Walterboro. For some reason, Callie felt way older, like he was another young man to mentor, only without the innocence.

"Good," he said. "Looky-lookies coming around, but they see me and don't stop. When's SLED coming?"

"They might not," she said. "You seen Monty Bartow by any chance?"

He shook his head. "Nope. I can name you a dozen other locals but not him. A few stopped and chatted. Am I doing this again tomorrow?" Then before she could reply, added, "Please say no."

She liked him, even more so since December. "I doubt it, but still waiting to hear from SLED. Can you stay here through ten? I'll put someone else on then, and you can have tomorrow off."

"Deal," he said. "You checking out the burglaries?"

She blew out, expressing her exasperation. "Yes. Did you by any chance see anything this morning in relation to those? Didn't you have that end of the street?"

He peered down.

"Not blaming you, Cobb. I'll be asking everyone."

"Sorry, Chief. Honestly I didn't, though I feel like I should have seen something."

"We all feel like that. Listen, let me get to those calls. Have fun," she said, driving away.

That morning had been maddening and far from the typical Edisto day. They'd been told traffic duty was the majority of their job, not house watching. Who'd have thought anyone would've been so bold?

The first burglary was *Ocean Potion*, five houses up from the fire site, with a Wainwright Realty nailed to the lower porch. A mediocre house in terms of a beach rental, with the standard three bedrooms and assorted wedged, bunked, and abutted sleeping arrangements that allowed an eight-person rental to house fifteen counting the sofa. A woman answered the door, eagerly inviting Callie inside, and, from the looks of things, fifteen guests might be a low estimate. Callie imagined Janet's disgruntlement about the number.

The woman still wore her bathing suit from the day's activities, a viscose shift over it. She covered her ears and motioned to the back door. "Let's take it outside," the woman said over the squeals of three middle-school girls and an argument of two teens with a mother-figure in the kitchen. Two men, husbands most likely, sat sunburned, open-shirted, and more interested in cable news, debating election fraud with beers in hand.

Not a lot of concern over the burglary here.

The woman hadn't even introduced herself. "And you are . . .?" Callie beckoned.

"Amelia Cash." She shut the door behind them, shutting off the hubbub. "Sorry for all that in there, and sorry for your trouble, but better safe than sorry, you know?"

"Are you the one who called in a burglary?" Callie asked

"Listen," the woman went on, sitting in a rubber-form chair. She slid another one up close and motioned for Callie to take a seat, as if she were about to divulge a secret. "This morning was chaos. We hadn't finished breakfast when we got evacuated, and each one of us thought the other was taking care of locking up, putting things away, grabbing essentials . . . a wild mess."

With some victims, Callie felt it better to remain silent and listen.

"We came back to find the door unlocked."

Big surprise. Callie hoped there was more. No, scratch that. She hoped that was all. She raised her brows to show she paid attention.

"Well, there's a bracelet missing. If it hadn't been an anniversary gift, I wouldn't have bothered you, and while I doubt it's jaw-dropping expensive . . . my husband never told me and I didn't ask . . . I'm sure it bumps a thousand in value. Not worth filing insurance over since that would be a thousand deductible in and of itself, but still, I have to show I tried or Bob would be hurt."

Low-key and unbothered. No pinching pennies here. Made Callie wonder why they hadn't rented a bigger house.

Amelia spoke in sentences that strung into long-winded monologues skating on the dramatic. If Callie didn't ask a question, Amelia felt the need to add more. When the conversation strayed to Bob's overly attentiveness to his law firm, his insensitivities, and her inability to read him after twenty-seven years, Callie took back control of the situation. "Describe the bracelet."

"White gold. Six half-carat diamond charms."

"When's the last time you had it appraised, and would you be able to send that to me? Along with any sort of picture?"

"Oh, oh, sure. Hold on a sec."

Amelia scrolled through her messages. "Here. We posed out here on the porch when we first arrived." She turned the phone around to Callie. "Zoom in on that."

The resolution wasn't impressive, but Callie got the gist of the item. She forwarded the picture to herself. "I see."

"No appraisal, though," Amelia said. "Who thinks of appraising anything that isn't worth five figures?"

"Are you sure nothing else is missing?"

"Positive."

"Are you sure the bracelet isn't lost inside somewhere?" Callie'd seen their disarray. Weekly visitors tended to explode their belongings everywhere in a house not their own. Vacations meant lax family rules, and clean-up services forever found belongings under, behind, and beside nooks and crannies.

"Absolutely sure," she said, not insulted at all by the question. "I kept it in a zipped compartment on the outside of my purse. It went with me everywhere, even if I didn't wear it."

"So, someone went through your purse?" Callie had started taking notes at the description.

"Oh yes," Amelia said. "Because I'm missing five hundred dollars, too."

Callie paused at the incredulity of the afterthought. "I assume you want to report that as well."

Amelia shook her head, as if telling someone to keep the change. "Nobody's going to turn that in, and you won't be able to identify it as mine. Besides, Bob would fuss at me about leaving my purse behind like that. For all he knows, my bracelet was taken from off the dresser. Let's leave it at that."

Some tourists would lose their minds over five hundred dollars. Others considered that a tip. "Want to show me where you had your purse?"

Amelia grimaced. "Do I have to? The less Bob hears the better. It was on my dresser in the front right bedroom as you come in the door. Just put that in your report."

The woman only wanted to tell her husband she did all she could. Didn't take long for Callie to leave. A white-gold bracelet with diamond charms was obvious enough ... if it showed. And she wasn't too worried about Amelia Cash making trouble with Brice, preferring secrecy about the loss.

Quickly, she put out the picture to her officers and Marie, telling them to be on the lookout, in case someone had the audacity to pretend it was theirs and enjoy wearing it before it got pawned or, as had been known to happen in the past, was regifted to someone local.

With the interview taking barely forty minutes, Callie felt rather efficient after a day of anything but, and while the next house was across the street, she still drove, in order to park the all-too-obvious patrol car in someone else's drive.

This person, however, was not a tourist. This was the home of Dudley Vaughn. Dud for short. However little Amelia cared about her burglary, this man would more than make up for it. He and Brice had butted heads for years over council business, and Dud would waste no time haranguing Brice and any arm of Edisto Beach for incompetence ... in hopes of running against him in the next election.

Callie'd only met him once, a year ago, when he'd rear-ended a golf cart while driving without his glasses.

Dud was eighty-seven years old.

Chapter 11

CALLIE RAPPED hard on Dudley Vaughn's door, no doorbell available. Paint peeled around the frame, a soft gray that had been a deeper color when *Salty Kiss* was last painted maybe fifteen years ago. Or even ten. One couldn't tell the way things weathered on the coast. Doorbells for instance. People quit installing them since salt air rusted the contact points. A reasonable expectation, like Callie expecting Dudley Vaughn's age to slow him answering her knock.

But Dudley answered rather quickly, enough to make Callie wonder if he'd seen her across the street and hung close, awaiting his turn. Maybe he eagerly anticipated something to break up his days, since his twenty-four hours were probably limited to sunrises, sunsets, particular shows on television, and a meds schedule.

"Hey, Mr. Vaughn. I'm Police Chief Callie Morgan. You spoke to the station about a burglary, and I thought—"

"About time," he said, walking away like Callie was supposed to read his mind, or be smart enough to put things together, at least be astute enough to come in and shut the door. "And my name is Dud," he shouted over his shoulder.

She closed the door, noting it no longer locked, wondering if he knew that. Should he be living alone in a three-bedroom house with no security? She pictured him using only one bedroom, a bath, and the kitchen, the rest of the residence and its antiques left to slowly succumb to dust.

There was ache in his step, yet he moved with a cane that appeared more habit than necessity, not always touching the ground, and he led them through the living room into his kitchen. Maybe the burglary took place in a back room. She dutifully followed.

He wore khakis with a leather belt, a short-sleeved, button-up shirt tucked in. His white hair neatly addressed, Callie could make out how wide the teeth were in his comb from the accented, even lines he'd sculpted and molded into place with hair tonic, which gifted him with a soapy, floral musk.

The loneliness of the house pricked at Callie's heart. To think he dressed himself to a standard like this and probably saw nary a soul.

"Sit," he said, pointing with a gnarly finger to a table for two at a window that overlooked the fourth hole on the Wyndham golf course, if you peered hard enough through the fencing and green growth. He returned to the counter, stilted in his movements. Callie thought she heard him talking to himself.

Dud was a former Merchant Marine, retired somewhat around the time Callie was born per the other older natives on the island. He and his wife had moved to the water, there on Edisto, and for twenty years more, he managed the marina. After Sally died, Dud retired from that as well, sold both his boats, and confined himself to *Salty Kiss*, named by his wife for reasons secret to them.

He rarely came out in the heat, reserving his public appearances for cooler seasons, elections, town council meetings, and the occasional parade, of which Edisto had four. He ventured out in his golf cart these days, though, especially after last year's ticket he received from Callie, and hadn't been seen behind the wheel of the old Buick since. Rumor was the couple had no children, and nobody had the nerve to ask the man who his relatives might be.

Callie held her breath when the man turned around because he'd draped the cane on his arm in order to carry a tray and was intensely focused on holding it level. She was afraid to take over for fear of causing an accident, and Dud would not appreciate the coddling.

A hint of relief passed over him when he reached the table and placed the tray. Carefully, he set two bottles of Coke at the two place settings, then the glasses of ice, then a plate of Lorna Doone shortbread cookies. Clearly, he emulated what Sally might've done with a guest, keeping some sense of decorum in his wife's home. The gesture made Callie wonder how long it had been since he'd had a guest.

While most houses on Edisto kept their air-conditioning overly cool, Dud apparently was of the old-school thought that you didn't waste power. Callie'd seen it in many a senior's home. Either economics or his aged, papery skin and thin blood preferred the almost-eighty temperature which was not uncomfortable enough to cause sweat but warm enough to make you avoiding moving fast enough to generate one.

His ups and downs not nearly as easy as his horizontal movement, Dud bent, then bent some more, then trying not to, caved to gravity and fell the rest of the way into the seat.

"There," he said, sighing like they'd emptied a moving van. He jerked a beckon at Callie. "Drink. I know how hot it is out there." He took a nibble of a cookie. Callie put two on her plate.

"Thank you," she said, noting at how much slowing down she had to do with him, finding herself grateful for it at the same time. She hadn't realized how much busy-ness filled her day until made not to. Between his manners and the dated appliances, furniture, and the living room wall art she passed on the way in, Callie felt like she traveled back in time, and with that journey came a slower clock. "Tell me what was stolen, Mr.—"

His eyes jerked up.

"Sorry, um, Dud. Tell me what you're missing and how you came to realize it." She hadn't had a real, unadulterated Coke over ice in ages, and as plain as the cookie was, it hit the spot, too.

"A necklace," he said.

Callie waited for the description, but Dud looked out the window and released a sigh that ended on the slightest hint of a moan.

"Dud? You okay?" Callie hadn't expected much emotional attachment to these burglaries. This was a beach town, with everyone's serious belongings locked up back at home. Dud was home, though, and all he owned was here. She had to remember that. "What kind of necklace was it?" she softly asked.

From how he struggled to talk, Callie bet a year's pay the necklace belonged to Sally and came with a story that could take a tough old bird like Dud and wring all the starch out of him. Callie's chest thickened having to hold this conversation.

"It was Amita Damascene," he said, reaching to his collarbone as he envisioned it in his mind's eye. "Spent fifty dollars for it in sixty-four when I was in Japan. It's a dark chain."

Callie could see him imagining.

"It held seven plaques inlaid with gold on black in these *tiny* vignettes of Japanese themes." His voice rose squeaky on the work *tiny*. His gaze took off well past Callie, out the window. "Dragons, bamboo, irises, Mt. Fuji . . . a heron, I think. She always looked for excuses to wear it, and I couldn't bear to bury her in it. It held too much of her."

Unique enough, for sure. "Where was it in the house, Dud? How did the thief get their hands on it?"

Dud shook his head. "I kept it out, around the neck of that vase up front on the credenza. So I could walk by once I awoke, stroke it, and tell Sally good morning on the way to the kitchen. Then again to bed in the evening. I kept it in plain sight."

Oh, goodness. "No chance you moved it, or it slid off? I can help you look."

He squinted, lasering in on her. "I'm ancient, but I'm not senile. I never moved it so it would *not* get lost." He sucked against his teeth, making Callie wonder if they were his originals. "Believe me or not," he added, as if blowing her off, "I'm used to such treatment."

She could do so much better than this. She was not going to leave this man hopeless. Not as lonely as he was. "Do you have a photograph of it?"

"Will I get it back?" he asked, challenging.

"I won't even have to take it," she promised. "Tell me where it is, and I'll go get it for you."

"No, you won't." He seemed to pull his strength together before shifting to stand. "Unless you're too busy to wait."

"No, sir. Take all the time you need."

He went without the cane this time and returned more quickly than she expected. He must've put his hand right on it. She took the yellowed photo from him, smiling at his reluctance to release it.

The picture had to be fifty or more years old. One of those posed Olan Mills-type styles with a brushed blue background, him seated on an invisible stool and his wife in a chair to give the tiered appearance . . . his hand on her shoulder, a couple inches from the necklace.

"This is perfect," Callie said, and snapped her own pic of it. "And the photo is beautiful of you two."

He hadn't taken his eyes off it.

She let him stare a few more moments before she spoke. "Did they take the vase?"

He shook his head. "No."

"Come," she said, handing back the photo and standing. "Show me where it was, then I've got to be leaving, Dud. I have one more stop to make, and they are missing something important, too."

She'd read him correctly. He would not want to infringe on anyone else's time. He took her back through the living room, pointing out the oriental celadon vase, its slender neck perfect for displaying the necklace. Almost like it belonged there.

The thief had it easy in this house. Even if Dud hadn't evacuated, which she had her doubts he had, the culprit would be in and out before Dud could rise from his kitchen table to see what the noise might be. "And you didn't see anyone?" she asked.

"No, little lady, or I would've told you. Now you go on and do your job."

He'd gotten a tad nicer during their visit, but because the topic had engaged memories of Sally, Callie felt intrusive. He'd aged around his eyes in the short time she had been there, so at the door, Callie couldn't help herself. She hugged the man.

Stiff fingered, he patted her lightly on the back, her shortness still giving him a few inches of stature on her. "I'll be in touch," she said.

She felt his nod before they parted. By the time she'd made it down the steps, steps she suddenly hoped he didn't try to make too often on his own, the door had closed. As she got in her cruiser, she turned back and waved, in case he still watched.

She sat in the car and studied the photo on her phone, not quite ready to jump to the next house. A melancholy wave had stolen her, and she wanted to ride it a few moments more.

Callie knew loss. A few of her husband's shirts were still in her closet . . . or had been before being moved. She wondered what Mark thought of finding those in his moving the place. Her baby daughter's blanket owned a dresser drawer all its own, wrapped up to keep that baby smell captured in the threads as long as possible. Seabrook's red swing on his beach house and a lone shirt of his she'd stolen unbeknownst to his family.

The Edisto house her father gave her the keys to, his bourbon glass in the kitchen.

The chicken salt-and-pepper shakers of Papa Beach. They took her back to simpler times as a child when the elderly neighbor would fix her hot chocolate at his kitchen table, letting her play make-believe with those shakers.

With the exception of her daughter, a crib death, all of them had died as a result of her law enforcement criminal pursuits. The murderers had scarred her each and every time. Even now, while remembering the good of her people, she forced herself to remember how they lost their lives, her way of penance and respect for the dead.

Being alive hurt after loved ones died. Despite her abstinence, she could not deny the medicinal value of two, sometimes three, stiff gins before bedtime, and there was no way she'd ever get to the point she didn't want them.

Dudley Vaughn had sprouted that sense of loss anew in her . . . along with that craving for a drink to make it go away.

Thank God she wasn't going home to an empty house tonight.

Connections to things of departed ones made those items powerful. Amelia Cash might not care about her diamond bracelet, but Sally Vaughn's Damascene necklace held enough magic to keep that old man breathing. The stiff old codger had oozed love for her.

Dud remembered Sally alive and made no mention of how she died. To Callie, however, memories of how her people died often wedged aside the memories of how they lived, the intense ones frequently filling her head at night.

Dusk approached, part of why she felt moody, but she had one more burglary on her list, two houses down on the same side of the road. Again she marveled at how the burglar had been so presumptuous as to rob on the same street occupied by the entire police force and fire department.

Vitamin Sea wasn't as old as *Salty Kiss* but was better maintained, and when she pulled into that drive, a man hollered at her to come around back. Peering through under the house, she caught sight of grill smoke, then the scent of seared meat, along with the laughter of drinkers.

Three couples greeted her, each person hovering around thirty. If they had kids, they'd left them elsewhere. Loud and boisterous, the man cooking waved her over with a spatula. "Officer, hey. Come on around."

One of the other two men sobered at her arrival, seriously studying her uniform, but the rest smiled amiably. One of the ladies asked, "Is something wrong or is this about the burglary?"

Which led one of the other women to exclaim, her punctuation accented by alcohol. "Can you believe that fire? How often does that happen?"

"It's been two years," Callie said to her. "The fire department did a great job this morning."

"Have to admit they got us out of here fast," replied a man.

"In time for someone to pull a snatch and grab," added the guy who had eyed her. He took a pull from his drink, afterward speaking into the glass. "Wonder how often that happens, Anna?"

Callie had one name, anyway. She was hoping they'd have the manners to introduce themselves, but they hadn't. "Yes, I'm here about the burglary," she said, introducing herself.

The chef bobbled his forehead. "Oh, we merit the *chief* of police. That's cool."

"Everyone else is probably a volunteer," said Mr. Negative.

Callie needed a name to this character. "And you are?"

He pointed at Anna. "Her husband."

Callie pulled out her notepad. "So, Anna's husband." She turned to the others. "Are your names just as strange?"

They laughed. "He's Phillip," Anna said, poo-pooing her spouse. "We're the Calders."

"Are you missing the item?" Per the report, a Mrs. Calder had called Marie.

"Yes, that would be me," Anna said, her bubbly nature a contrast to her husband's sullen one. Protective, maybe. A natural ass, maybe. Callie's concern, not at all.

"They took my college ring," she said, holding out her hand, wiggling fingers, finally holding up an empty ring finger on her right hand, like she'd had to hunt for it. She'd had a few. "University of South Carolina. Year 2014. College of Hospitality. I own my own bakery in Aiken."

If Callie hadn't gone to USC, she wouldn't have taken the hospitality thing seriously, but the university indeed had such degrees. Those details would make that ring easy to spot. "Inscription?"

"My name. Anna Jean Talmadge." She leaned forward, her expression scrunched. "I might've gained a few pounds since then. It tended to get tight, and the sun makes me swell, so I didn't want to wear it." She leaned back. "When that fire started, we were told to leave so we headed to the beach to chill."

"Glad you didn't leave your wedding ring." Phillip came forward in his seat this time. "I'm a deputy with Aiken County Sheriff's Office. I assume the chances of recovery are slim. Your crime rate must rise this time of year. I assume you'll canvass your *frequent flyers*."

Frequent flyers were local habitual criminals. Phillip was showing off skills in front of his friends.

"Were your doors locked?" Callie asked, not falling into the *mano y mano* speak between cops.

Phillip scowled at her, like he was better than this. "These are old beach houses. Are any of the locks any good?"

The third husband, the one silent up to now, spoke up. "Hell no, we didn't lock the house. That's why he's so bent out of shape. Mr. Five-O blinked and got robbed." He jabbed his beer-bottle hand at Phillip, his smile mocking. "Serves him right. Drives us ape-shit nuts with his public service announcements. It just happened, man. You're human like the rest of us."

The guy's wife sang a song about bad boys and what you could do with them under her breath, barely loud enough to be heard. The chef's wife joined in. Then the chef. All but Callie and Phillip broke into song, Phillip's face reddening.

But Callie could read his mind. He thought everything was safe with cops on the street. He let someone else take responsibility for locking up and regretted it, especially since the victim was his own wife.

"You should've left it at home," Phillip growled to Anna. "Who wears jewelry at the beach? It screams for the taking."

"You need another drink, man," said the chef. The other couple laughed between them, the gist of their conversation being Anna and Phillip, from the whispered asides.

She didn't tell them there were two other thefts, and if she had been Phillip, she'd have asked, but since he didn't, she wouldn't fuel his animosity.

"Steaks are ready. Shrimp, too," announced the chef. Phillip turned to his wife. "Want to go get the salad and bread?"

She hopped up. "On my way."

Chef made the gracious gesture of inviting Callie to dinner, to which she declined just as graciously. It was seven thirty, give or take, and she relished the idea of grabbing dinner at El Marko's knowing she could hang with Mark until they locked up, then go home together. Like a mock trial run without calling it such.

She pulled out of their drive and drove south to run by the fire sites. Lines of wet black and gray traveled in streams along the edges of both gravel drives. The property was a muddied mess. LaRoache waved again. Good man.

But as she reached the perpendicular access from Myrtle to St. Helena Sound, Mikell Street channeled the last of the sun, in all its brilliance, straight up the four-block distance off the water. Like it had never rained. Like the light had waited for Callie to reach that corner, in that moment, to splash her in the face.

She gasped. Then in a late split second she told herself not to react. But her heartbeat still doubled.

Her memory smelled smoke.

And the scar on her arm remembered vividly the rawness of a night that changed her life forever.

Chapter 12

CALLIE FELT OFF her game the whole way to El Marko's. Mr. Vaughn's meeting clung to her as did the opportune geometry of that sunset hitting her in the car. Anyone else would go in El Marko's, sit at one of the colorful, hand-painted tables, and ask for a drink to settle the day, maybe say hello to a few folks who walked by. But she wasn't anyone, and one drink would wind up being three.

She groped at how to lessen her unbalanced, unsettled-ness. She couldn't believe the high point of her day had been a shower at Mark's that afternoon—without him in it.

She waited at the restaurant's hostess station, which was nothing but a sign asking people to wait to be seated. Instrumental Latin music came across loud enough to muddle the conversations and fill the place with atmosphere. The dining room was packed, and Callie almost changed her mind about being there, but she had no desire to be anywhere else.

She hunted for Mark. He must be in the back.

She hunted for Stan. He wasn't at the bar, in his usual chair.

Sophie bee-bopped up. "Hey, girl."

Callie welcomed the friendly face.

Her neighbor looked fresh. One never would've thought Sophie had emptied a house before going to work. The spring in her walk had energy to spare. Guess that's what twenty-plus years of yoga did for you.

She wore her pale-blue contacts tonight and, instead of Mexican primary colors, a cream shell and pastel-blue gauze pants with blouson legs. Matching toenail polish accented those size-ten feet. "So? What did you think?" Sophie asked.

Callie reached over and pulled her friend close, needing a hug. A big hug. A squeezing, meaningful hug. "Thanks so very much, Sophie."

"Oh," Sophie said. "Wow. Glad to help, girl." And when Callie didn't let loose, Sophie returned a second hug. "You've had a bad day, huh?"

Callie nodded into the pixie shag.

"You have a place to stay, right?" Sophie asked. "Mark said all was worked out, but if you need me, there's Sprite's room."

Callie patted and pulled loose. "I'm only grateful."

Sophie stared at her, the empath in her at play. "You all right? I mean, there was a fire, and you used to have some sort of thing about fire, right?"

Sophie understood the source of Callie's forearm scar, but not a whole lot more. "It wasn't in my house," Callie said, like that meant anything. "So I'm good."

Sophie's curiosity seemed satisfied. "Good." She pointed to the corner. "Your old man is over there."

Peering over diners' heads, Callie searched for Mark, instead spotting Stan alone at a table. "Oh, you mean Stan." She laughed. Felt good to laugh. "He's not old."

Sophie leaned in. "He's a decade older than you, and you two have a weird closeness that makes me wonder how well you know him naked."

"Geez, Soph. He's only five years older than you."

"Which doesn't mean I haven't wondered about him naked." Sneering, the yoga lady flashed a skeptic brow over her false lashes. "And you didn't deny the accusation. Never mind," she quickly said. "Mark's busier than hell." She looked around Callie to the people behind her. "A family of six has backed up behind you that needs attention. Go find Stan." And with that she pushed past Callie to do her hostess job.

Callie wasn't sure how she'd missed Stan other than she'd sought his regular place, but she couldn't ask for a better dinner partner. She wouldn't have to pretend what she felt or thought. Stan had seen it all.

Through a herd of people, Callie made her way. She didn't wear a uniform, but the cargo pants, badge at her waist, and utility belt said enough. Natives shouted hellos. Silently, tourists tried to interpret who she was and what brought her there.

"Need company?" she asked, taking her seat at Stan's table, the sight of his plate, the smells of the kitchen, the whole gamut of her senses leaping to life as her stomach screamed neglect.

"Always," he said, smiling that paternal grin she never tired of. Stan was her almost-everything man. Almost a father figure. Almost a lover. Once a boss. Almost the person she could be abandoned with on a deserted island and cover the bases. He interpreted all sides of her. The before and after Edisto. Before and after the deaths and calamities, the losses and wins in her life.

The tension in her shoulders relaxed.

"Haven't seen you since this morning," he said, meaning she should report how she was doing, while he picked at the remnants of tamales Callie knew were on the bland side. Stan's level of heat had always been a far cry short of hers.

"Haven't seen you either," she said, speaking in his own code. She leaned back from the table as the waitress came, setting her regular ginger ale order on a napkin, not bothering with a menu. "Enchiladas," was all Callie had to say. Mark's staff had her three standard orders memorized. This one would come out with one bean, one cheese, and one chicken enchilada with a stuffed jalapeno on the side. The waitress left.

El Marko's was seven months old, but already there was something aged, reliable, and rather comforting about the familiarity of this place. Like McConkey's, the Waterfront, or Whaley's, only Mexican.

Callie took a deep, long sip of the ginger ale, eyes closed, trying hard to pretend it was gin. She sighed contentedly at how the cool drink took her temperature down a degree or two.

"Staying with Mark tonight, huh?" Stan asked, pushing his plate back.

Contentment interrupted, she lowered the glass and scoffed at him. "Please tell me the entire town isn't aware."

"Telephone, telegraph, tele-Sophie," he said. "She told me, by the way, not Mark."

Nope, Sophie didn't keep too many secrets, but Callie appreciated how Mark did, and how Stan did in spite of the two men being fast friends as retired law enforcement. As far as she knew, each didn't talk to the other about Callie except in general terms. Of course, if they were that discreet, they could be keeping their conversations secret from her as well.

She took another hard drink of ginger ale, almost draining the glass. "Yesterday, today . . . a little much to handle, but I'm making it," she said. "I spoke to the three burglary victims on Myrtle Street. Brice is going to use that to his advantage at the next meeting."

Stan rolled his eyes. He wasn't a Brice fan. "We'll rally the allies. You're the darling of Edisto, girl."

"This time's different," she said. "I'm staying a step behind. Someone was damn slick and downright bold invading homes while we were on the street. And that doesn't even count the arson before Brice starts ragging on our incompetence regarding the burglaries."

"Y'all were focused on the fire, as was every other body on that street. It was a crime of opportunity someone spotted and seized," he said. "True, it'll be difficult telling who did it, because I don't even think *they* were aware they were going to do it until they did. They made a snap decision."

"Unless they set the fire to create their own opportunity." There wasn't a single home on that street with more than a visual doorbell, and those didn't last long in this salt. No security on the rentals. Renters didn't want owners snooping on them, and owners didn't want cams installed for renters to tamper with.

Dud's home wasn't a rental, but he wasn't high tech enough to have a Ring doorbell, much less a system. In her opinion, he hadn't evacuated, and even if he could recognize who stole his wife's necklace, he might be too afraid and vulnerable to say who. He sure seemed fractured to her, as if he'd let down his deceased wife.

Sad. While she had a duty to pursue all three thefts, that one drew her in the most.

The enchiladas arrived. Callie glanced back toward the kitchen and wondered why Mark hadn't at least made an appearance. Maybe he was down a cook. She unrolled her silverware from the napkin. "Wanna hear about the burglaries?" Which, of course, Stan did, and she spoke in between bites, ending on Dudley Vaughn for effect.

"Pisses me off," she said, her ire causing her to finish off the second enchilada in three bites. The jalapeno she finished off in two, savoring the heat seeping into her sinuses. Still, Dud's image remained crystal in her mind's eye, his sensitivities keen on her heart.

"A piece that unique will be easy to spot," Stan said.

"Or quickly pawned," she finished, making a note to revisit Dud periodically, just because. With barely more than six hundred permanent residents in the beach town, she harbored guilt at never having paid attention to him before.

Stan watched her. He loved to analyze her, and he could do it well since he'd had to read her so many times in their long past. "While I'm not happy about Dud," he said, "and that's quite the name, by the way . . . at least I see it's readjusted your, um, focus."

He didn't have to say the word *fire*.

He'd last seen her that morning, disturbed, so it only made sense that was his expectation in seeing her tonight. She liked to think she was over it, but the sunset on Mikell Street had stunned her more than expected. Stan didn't need to hear about that.

"Have you told Mark about my *focus*?" she asked. Before the flash of sunset a few moments ago, she'd have labeled this morning's glitch in her mental well-being just that, an anomaly, but something had resurfaced in her, and she was uncertain how it would manifest itself from this point forward.

Truth was, deep down inside, when those conditions presented themselves in the most perfect order, she wondered if she might be susceptible to flashbacks.

What was she to do about that? Was there anything *to do* about it except carry on? She'd dodged those four little letters, PTSD, for going on four years and had decided in the last year that they'd disappeared. She'd adapted, grown, improved, and forgotten about the acronym until she heard them in that deep, growling, Boston accent.

"It's called PTSD, Chicklet."

"I'm not seeing a shrink," was her knee-jerk reply. "You didn't answer me. Have you told Mark?"

His lips mashed, accenting the folds along his jawline, and Callie watched the muscle ripple up to his temple. "No, ma'am, I haven't," he said. "But if you are getting serious about him, you should. He, of all people, would understand."

"Why would you say that?"

"Which part?" he asked.

"Well, first, I'm not sure how serious we are becoming, so why divulge my flaws if I don't have to?" she said, not comfortable with his sounding too parental and his borderline venture into none-of-your-business territory.

Stan listened. He was superb at listening. Trouble was he also could take it all in, digest it, and throw it back at you in a different shape that made you doubt yourself. Sometimes she appreciated it. Other times . . . not so much.

She rode the fence on that right now. "*He of all people*, you said. What does that mean? What makes him so especially understanding?"

"His story to tell," Stan said. "Like yours is yours to tell." He grunted and shook his head.

"What?" she asked.

"You two," he said. "I want to lock you in a room and leave you there until you let down your walls."

She ceased eating

She knew her flaws, but Stan had revealed Mark came with his own, though she hadn't read Mark as harboring anything so serious as a phobia or flashback-inducing past. Stan didn't lie, so there was something. Would knowing each other's issues bring them closer or make them leery of taking their relationship further because of the baggage? She wasn't too keen on being the first to open up.

She went back to her last enchilada, wishing she'd ordered extra peppers.

True Confessions was too complex to worry about atop of everything else on her plate. She had zero plans to broach the issues, shortfalls, or hang-ups in hers or Mark's life. They enjoyed each other's friendship. They could keep doing that. Edisto Beach was noted for simplifying lives and leaving problems on the other side of the big bridge. Why not embrace the culture?

"I really wish we hadn't discussed this," she said, stabbing at her food. "It's pinging around my head now."

"Well, I haven't divulged a thing to either of you," Stan said, rearing back, arms crossed.

"You mean other than the fact that there is something that needs divulging?"

He thought he was so smart, too, making her almost ask questions about Mark. If Stan had played this manipulation with her, he had done the same with Mark.

Callie suddenly wasn't fond of Stan's matchmaking tactics.

"How was dinner?"

She jumped. Mark had slipped up behind her.

He chuckled and laid hands on her shoulders. "Oh, babe, I'm sorry. Didn't mean to scare you." He studied the two of them at the table. "I didn't interrupt anything, did I?"

"No, not at all," she said. *Damn.* In her contemplation about Stan and his motives, she'd lost track of her surroundings. She wondered if Mark and his retired LEO senses had noticed.

She twisted around in her seat. The sight of him warmed her, and when he leaned over to give her a kiss, she craned up to meet him. This is what she loved. This right here. The effortlessness of a friendship, not the long-range what-ifs of what everyone else expected two single people to eventually be.

"Turn the damn music down!" boomed a voice at the restaurant entrance.

People quit conversing.

She spun around to see the entrance, recognizing a voice she could identify in her sleep. The business day was over. What was so damn messed up to warrant his coming out like this?

"Chief Callie Morgan!" he yelled, louder, but since Sophie had actually done what he'd asked with the music, his words rebounded off the walls. Everyone went quieter still. Someone coming in turned around and left.

Unable to read whether Brice was grandstanding or seeking help for a legitimate concern, Callie started to stand. The onus was on her to handle this.

His back to the door, Mark hadn't turned, and he put a hand on her shoulder, pressing her back in her seat. "Wait a second. Let him show his hand," he whispered.

She wasn't comfortable having someone else take the lead, but she didn't want to make matters worse by debating with Mark. Brice was the problem.

"Monty Bartow was run off the road this afternoon," he bellowed . . . at her. "After you upset him and sent him running from his very own home."

"What?" she said.

"You," he continued, taking two more steps into the room, his finger aimed appropriately. "You accused him of setting the fires on Myrtle. A poor defenseless disabled boy who looks up to you for reasons I cannot fathom, had his heart broken because you accused him of arson. He left during that storm so distraught that he drove that moped of his into gale force winds and rain." Brice let that visual set in. "He's at home, laid up and hurt, by the way. Car almost hit him"

Sophie covered her mouth in surprise and looked at Callie like she contemplated whether Brice's opinion of fault was correct. And if Sophie would do so, so would the rest of the room, especially anyone who knew Monty.

"Brice," Callie said, standing, attempting congeniality. "Come over here and have a drink and some dinner. Let's talk." He stayed put, appearing determined to be contrary. Callie could've asked him to scream and he would've whispered. She could've reached out to him, and he would've recoiled. He was owning his attitude a thousand percent, especially with an audience.

He jabbed his finger back at her again. "You did nothing about the fire at my home yesterday, either."

Now he headed down a laundry list. No, she wasn't having these discussions here.

He shook his finger again. "You let those burglaries happen on Myrtle Street, right under your nose! You and all your well-trained officers stood right there and didn't see three houses get broken into and robbed!"

Even Sophie scowled at that, but while she corrected herself, the rest of the room didn't. Most had not heard of the burglaries. Grumblings floated table to table, carefree tourists now infused with doubt as to the safety of their vacations.

"Did you catch the burglar?" someone spoke, two tables over from Callie.

"I'm renting on Myrtle," someone else said.

"Still under investigation," Callie said, from a history of habit.

However, the one comment empowered another. "So why are you sitting there socializing, like there isn't a threat?"

"Yeah," said another. "Shouldn't you be out there hunting for him? I didn't pay this kind of money to fear who might slip in while I'm sleeping."

Murmurs and peeved glances infected table after table, while Brice remained standing in the limelight relishing the fertilized disgruntlement. The woman who'd announced she rented on Myrtle got up and left, her gentleman partner in tow.

Mark strode up to Brice, whose shoulders drew back. The restaurant owner pointed to a sign over the bar. "Read that."

Management reserves the right to refuse service.

"Mr. LeGrand," he continued, a hard push on the *Mister* part. "May I see you to a table? Maybe the bar." He dramatically peered up the line of barstools. "Sorry, but there appears to be a bit of a wait. We ask waiting patrons to step outside since we're limited in our space." While not intimidating, Mark made himself heard, and he exuded manners.

"I'm not here for your damn food," Brice replied, his manners nonexistent.

Mark feigned disappointment. "Then I must ask you to leave, sir."

"Not until I tell her . . . and everyone here"—he made a broad sweeping motion across the room—"that Police Chief Callie Morgan is abysmal in her role as this island's head of safety, protection, and security. Hell, she got the last police chief murdered, then had the gall to step into his shoes." His complexion had reddened; his glower homed in on Callie.

"Sir, I kindly ask you to leave," Mark said.

"No, *sir*," Brice said, an uptick on the *sir*, using the attempt at etiquette as a slur. "And while I have everyone's attention, I'd also like to say—"

Mark anchored strong hands on Brice's shoulders, forcing him to pivot toward the exit, and then took his arm to chivvy him along. "Then you have no right to be in this establishment and are no longer welcome. My customers deserve peaceful meals and did not pay to be a captured audience for your platform."

"But I'm head of town council," Brice said, unable to brake against Mark's hands.

"Not here," Mark said, his head motioning for Sophie to open the door.

"Quit handling me," Brice yelled.

To which Mark countered, "Don't make me call the police, Mr. LeGrand. We already went down that road last December, and I have no desire to see you jailed again."

Blistering red in the face, Brice cooperated, and Mark released him outside, Sophie holding the door open for all to see.

"Wonderful," Stan sighed.

Once Mark returned inside, sans Brice, the room gave a meager round of applause.

"My apologies," he said, remaining on that side of the room. Without making eye contact with Callie, he walked by several tables, speaking to patrons while motioning to his main waitress. He had a pat method of appeasing the distressed. Callie'd seen it before. A free appetizer sampler, one per table.

Then after seeing everyone tended to, he disappeared into the kitchen, leaving Callie still catching her breath. He had never looked back at her.

"Well," Stan said. "Crisis averted, I guess."

Averted? Maybe for the restaurant, but Callie's crisis had risen to Defcon 1. Diners stole glances at her. Though Callie didn't expect reassurance, Sophie acted too busy to come over and badmouth Brice. The chair of town council might be gone from El Marko's, but he'd make the rounds to the other council members, as well as the mayor. Tomorrow he'd hit the ground running to business owners, chamber members, and whoever else would listen.

Stan nibbled on nacho chips.

Mark remained in the kitchen

Callie had done all within her power handling those fires, as had her people. As had Leon and his people. So why did she feel vulnerable?

She put her napkin on the table. "I've got to go, Stan."

"Don't make him send you packing, Chicklet. For all you know he's outside waiting."

But she shook her head. "I can handle him. What I cannot handle is not knowing if Monty really did have an accident because I visited him. Sorry, but I have to pay him a visit."

He put his wadded napkin in his plate. "Let me go with you."

Laying a hand on his arm, she declined. "No. If Monty and Minnie are upset, they'll see you as me bringing reinforcements to gang up on them. I'm good alone. Tell Mark I'll see him after he closes up."

Without looking back or side to side, she crossed the restaurant and left, seriously bothered that Minnie had been so upset as to call Brice in an emergency instead of her.

Chapter 13

CALLIE MADE HER way back to Oyster Factory Road. The rain-drenched jungle green glistened in places under the occasional streetlights of scattered island homes. Unsure what she'd find at the Bartow home, her only plan was to see if Monty was all right.

Stan's concern that Brice might be outside waiting for her proved unfounded. When she left El Marko's, he was nowhere to be seen. Brice could be all mouth and hot air, his *motus operandi*, but he'd said enough to weigh Monty heavily on her mind. Was he hurt, or had Brice embellished the truth?

For sure, Monty left earlier in a huff, in the rain. She'd seen him. She felt partially responsible.

It crossed her mind that Brice might have laid a political trap of some kind. That possibility didn't quite gel, but the random notion did make her wish maybe Stan had come along. Brice wasn't dangerous, but he was devious in his own asinine way, and even someone as ridiculous as that man could hit pay dirt on occasion.

No telling what kind of state Minnie would be in.

The air was still thick with moisture. Rain had washed everything anew, but the wind had blown limbs and debris into the road. Most she drove over, some slowly like a speed bump. She got out once, digging in with her thighs to lift an eight-inch-thick piece of rotted tree trunk that had given in to the wind and water and come down. She was glad she'd gotten at least two of those enchiladas down before leaving. They served as the only fuel she'd had all day.

Upon arrival, she unhitched the gate and pulled in, scanning for wind damage, of which there appeared to be none. As she pulled up to the house, she noted the moped, covered in streaks of mud and leaves, parked under the carport, dented deep in two places that she could see.

Nobody came to the door at first, and no inside lights appeared on, but with the windows open for the cooler night air off the river, she heard someone turn down the television volume.

She rapped on the screen door. "Minnie? This is Callie Morgan."

Even with the badge and belt, she hoped she came across less threatening without her uniform.

She rapped harder, then peered through the screen. Nobody sat before the television. Were they dodging her? Monty, maybe, but Minnie? The mother had tattled to Brice, so maybe she hid in another room.

Monty wouldn't slip out the back and drive off this time, unless that bike ran better than it looked. "I'm sitting on the door stoop until someone speaks to me," Callie said loudly, then squatted to take said place and wait.

Didn't take two minutes for Minnie to show up. "I ain't asking you in."

"That's okay." Callie stood, dusting herself off, feeling a little damp from the rough concrete which had shared some of its moisture. "I only want to know if Monty is all right. I heard he was injured. May I see him? To make sure?"

"My word isn't good enough?" the mother spouted.

"My report has to say I saw the damage, Minnie." A small lie, but worthy.

Minnie pondered whether that was so, then turned her head, hollering, "Monty! Come to the door, son. Somebody needs to see what you did to yourself."

He showed up right away. He presented with a limp, his arm hugged against his belly, but the guy who adored playing police, who had relished Callie's praises, didn't even say hello. He didn't smile, didn't even make eye contact. She thought they had a better connection than this.

"Monty? You okay?" she asked.

He nodded into his chest, holding his arm closer, wiping a trickle of sweat from the side of his face.

"Did you run off the road?"

He nodded again.

"Did someone force you off the road?"

Another yes.

"Can you describe the vehicle?"

He shook his head.

"Can you describe the driver?"

No, again.

Then she tried a question that might penetrate that wall. "I'm so sorry. Is your moped broken?"

He glanced at her this time, the low-wattage yellow bug light in the coach lamp making the whites of his eyes appear jaundiced. She read sadness in his demeanor. Without the bike, he was back to walking to town, carrying his items in a backpack. Losing the bike had demoralized him.

But if Monty did one, two, or all of the crimes, he might need to be homebound for a while anyway. She hated having to think like that.

Wiping at sweat starting around the edges of her own hair, Callie waved off a mosquito whining around her head. "Can you show me your injuries?"

The lack of indoor lighting, the outside darkness, and the minimal light on the porch should've reduced insect attraction, but the high-pitched hums still hovered, eager for their dinner. The marginal illumination also created distorting shadows that prevented her from determining Monty's well-being. At least he was mobile. She went for her small flashlight. "Can I use this to see?"

Monty's gaze darted to his mother for direction.

Minnie dipped her chin once. "Show her."

Mother and son were little more than silhouettes coated in a film of yellow from the bug light, but when Callie popped on the flashlight, they took on a less ominous mien.

Monty's ankle had a bandage on it, thus the limp, but he was walking. Not terribly inconvenienced either. Callie moved the flashlight up to the arm. A thick bandage enveloped his wrist from the middle of his forearm to his hand, wrapped around his thumb tight to lessen movement. The bandage made it look worse than the ankle, and he favored it more. "Did you go to the doctor?" she asked, lightly reaching to touch it, then changing her mind when he watched, leery.

"No need for a doctor. Nothing's broken," Minnie said.

Which meant they couldn't afford medical treatment. "Who did such a neat job of patching you up?"

Minnie answered instead of him. "Mr. Hutchins's girl."

That made sense. Tia Hutchins had been an LPN for twenty years. "If you had to wreck, good thing it was there," Callie said, bringing the talk around on a good note. Or so she hoped.

She checked herself, deciding not to ask if he'd found his badge. She knew he hadn't. Leon had it, evidence from the fires. The chance of anyone else sporting an Amazon badge made in China was miniscule.

Plus, Monty didn't have it when Callie was last there, and he hadn't gotten any further than the Hutchins place on Highway 174 when he left.

"Can we talk about the fire?" she asked, avoiding looking at Minnie, not wanting to inadvertently give her permission to speak on his behalf again. Nobody declined, so she kept going. "Monty, did you see anyone set the fire?"

She hadn't blamed him, and he seemed surprised he was asked about someone else. He shook his head no.

"People have accidents, Monty. Like when you ran off the road by accident. Any chance you maybe, possibly . . . set the fire by accident?"

"No," he spouted, then talked into the ground. "I did not start that fire."

She caught his choice of words. "Have you ever set *any* fire?"

Again, he looked to his mother for guidance.

"He sets the fires in the pit around back," Minnie said. "He burns the trash and roasts weenies. You did say *any* fire."

Callie wondered if there was any play on words taking place here. Monty clammed up.

"Okay, okay," Callie said, wanting to rub his arm or soothe him or something. Minnie sure wasn't. Instead she glowered at Monty, then at Callie, maybe mad at the world for bringing calamity upon her household.

More mosquitoes. Sweat trickled, itching as much as the insects.

"Monty," Callie began again, "did you get curious and enter any of the houses on Myrtle Street while we were fighting the fires?" One theory was whoever set the fires had created a diversion to burgle the homes. Another was that one party started the fire and another took advantage. She didn't see Monty sharp enough to do the former, but the latter held fair potential.

Minnie reared back. "Like he went from house to house asking people if he could come in and snoop around? What the hell kind of question is that?"

"No, that's not what I'm saying, Minnie."

She stood at a crossroad here. Whatever she told Minnie could easily return to Brice. No point in his hearing half-assed details from Minnie. "Never mind," Callie said.

Well, that hadn't gone well. So Callie returned to a question that might shortcut all of this. "May I see how badly your moped is broken? I might be able to help."

That bike was Monty's baby, and even torn up and bent, it was worth showing off. "Sure," he said, leaving the stoop and heading to the carport.

Aiming to stay a friend, Callie followed.

"Lost my front basket, but look here," he said, motioning at the twisted front wheel. "And here." He noted the broken mirror and fractured headlight. Of course he noticed the superficial. Callie couldn't repair a vehicle to save her soul, but when he tried to start it up, the bike obviously incapacitated, she understood his sadness. He didn't care about his injuries . . . just those of his precious moped.

Monty rose each morning, dressed, did chores his mother told him to do, then struck out to town. He rarely went home until supper. His routine had been dashed to hell now, but Callie expected him to keep to his regimen best he could, even limping the five miles to the beach like he used to.

She smothered the bike with attention, making appropriate noises of interest, peering at scratches he showed her, even mud that didn't matter. She opened the back basket, as though seeking damages, and he let her. Water had flushed inside, and she moved things around as if hunting for leaks. No badge. No jewelry. No matches or lighter. There was a grocery bag, but it held sunscreen, a hand towel, thoroughly soaked, a diaper-bag-sized container of wet wipes, and dime-store sunglasses.

"That's enough," Minnie said.

Callie had heard her approaching, the woman too cumbersome in her movements to be missed. "Monty, mind if I speak to your mother a moment? Go back inside and prop that ankle up on a pillow before it goes back to swelling."

Minnie didn't correct otherwise, and therefore, Monty returned inside.

Callie watched him gingerly take his steps toward the house. "Good-bye, Monty," she hollered after him. "Call me if you need anything." At the threshold, he held back his good hand, not to wave but to not let the screen door slam behind him.

Before she could address Minnie, the mother whirled on her. "What are you up to? First the fire, then this walking into people's homes thing? My boy did nothing wrong."

Minnie wasn't Monty. She didn't merit Callie's sympathetic voice. "We believe the fire was arson, Minnie. Monty's badge was found at the scene." She thought a second, pondering whether this direct approach was best, but with this woman, there didn't seem to be any other way, "My officers evacuated the houses on Myrtle Street for safety's sake. Someone took advantage and stole jewelry items from three different families."

"Could've been one of your uniforms taking advantage," Minnie countered, standing with chunky hands on where her hips would be on that pear-shaped body. "Ever think about that?"

Callie couldn't read much more about her in the dark, but frankly, she was surprised Minnie hadn't exploded already. The population might be surprised at how often people thought a good offense made for a good defense. Cops saw it coming a mile away.

"This is why I called Brice LeGrand," Monty's mother said, low, jaw clenched. "He's known us a lot longer than you, and my family has known his for at least four generations."

Okay, this was different. Lineage mattered out here. How long your people had been here mattered. Whether they lived and died as part of Edisto Island mattered. While Callie's grandparents had bought *Chelsea Morning* before she was born, they'd vacationed, not resided in the Jungle Road beach house. Callie was the first to do that.

Forget that Callie's family went back as far as Brice's, only at a town up the road where her ancestors had been mayors, senators, and more. While his people helped found Edisto Beach, hers established Middleton, but the forty-five-mile distance gave her no more credence than a Yankee from New Jersey. Edisto lineage was tightly knit, and her stock was nowhere near the level of Brice's. Never would be.

"Brice is not law enforcement. He can't decide how an investigation is carried out," she tried to explain. "I want to make sure Monty hasn't done something, and if he has done anything, I want him to be taken care of in the best way possible. Work with me, Minnie."

"I filed a complaint," came the answer instead. "A real one. Brice said he'd see to it. My boy is hurt because he was scared of you. He's being blamed for things he didn't do, and you discount who he is."

Her boy got hurt because he went hunting for his badge in the rain, not out of fear of Callie. He hadn't been accused yet, but Callie had to rule him out. He was a person of interest. Overall, she thought she'd done well respecting the man.

"I want you off my property," Minnie said. "And I want you never to come back."

Callie exhaled hard enough for Minnie to hear. "I will leave, but if we need to speak to Monty, I'm afraid I'll be back." With a warrant, probably. "As I said, I'm with the police. Brice is—"

"In charge of your job," Minnie finished. "He hired you, and he can fire you, sweetheart. If he gets rid of you, my boy will be just fine."

Jesus, Brice. How cruel of you to make such a promise.

Besides, that made Monty sound guiltier.

If Callie had any doubts of Brice taking advantage of a poor family to cripple her, they were long gone now. He'd done it, and he would continue doing it.

There was no concealing the fire news, but her department and the fire department had hoped to avoid spreading the fear of arson. She'd hoped to keep the burglaries rather quiet for everyone's peace of mind, but Brice would paint her attempts at avoiding public panic as hiding her inability to protect Edisto Beach.

She loved this beach, this island, and these people. Most of them, anyway. Damned if Brice didn't sometimes make her wonder why bother with this job, though. She didn't need the money.

But she needed a home.

"Momma!" Monty shouted, slinging open the door. "Alex put me on the news. Told you she would. The commercial said, *Fire on Edisto Beach. Story at eleven.* And I saw myself! Can we stay up and watch, Momma? Please?"

"Sure you can, son. You've had a hard day," Minnie said, speaking to him but watching Callie.

He returned inside, probably planning to sit on the worn-out edge of his recliner's cushion, toy with his Star Wars figures, and wait for Alexander Hanson to do her magic on the eleven o'clock WLSC news.

"Might use this to prove he couldn't have robbed those houses," Minnie said, controlled and firm.

Might also prove he was in the vicinity of pulling them off, too, once Callie partnered the footage timeline with the estimated times of the thefts, but until then, no judge would call that reason enough to grant a warrant to search the Bartow home for the stolen items.

But what arsonist didn't hang around to watch? That discovered badge sure made him a person of interest in that crime.

Callie reserved those thoughts to herself. She wished Minnie a good night and left.

Ten o'clock. She almost headed home to her routine, then remembered the status of her house. Mark would still be at the restaurant. Stan would either be home watching television or perched on his barstool reclaimed after a tourist left. She really wasn't up to conversation anyway.

Driving back down Oyster Factory Road, the night ink-dark due to a moonless sky, a melancholy set in, most likely from the day's stress and Brice. She reached the end of the road, stopped to check for traffic, mostly nonexistent this time of night, and sat.

Right would take her home, to the beach. Left, however, took her north. Sitting in the dark, with no push to move in any direction, she exhaled, owning the fact she was feeling a bit hurt. No, a lot hurt. She remained idling at the stop sign.

She cringed to think that Edisto thought of her as anyone but a devoted servant to its well-being. Policing wasn't the respected professsion it once was, but she did it with her heart and soul as well as her head. She wanted people to feel safe, and she loved being a major part of the effort. Everyone needed to feel safe.

But safety meant more than physical protection. It meant protection from mental torment as well. That was harder to provide with the likes of Brice. Her badge would always have enemies; that she could accept. But to have one of Edisto's own attempt to undermine her at every turn, even after she'd come to his defense barely six months ago when he could've gone to jail, drained a degree of conviction out of her, each time a little more than the time before.

Turning off the air-conditioning, she let down her window. The air's heaviness pushed inside the vehicle, the moisture wrapping around her. Not what a normal person would do, but she loved humidity. She took in the scent of this jungle, the rainwater in the ditches, darkened by the unique mixture of tannins the incredibly rich flora of this island provided.

She ran the route through her mind, past the six churches to the seventh that stood proud on the right side of the highway. The one she couldn't drive past without history tapping on her heart. The cemetery's history, not the church. Not quite two years ago, Seabrook had been buried while she'd lapsed in and out of consciousness with pneumonia. After his service, reserved for once she'd recuperated, the minister had invited her to attend Sundays as a regular. She'd made excuses about Sundays being workdays for officers, the ten miles not always convenient, but the truth was she couldn't make herself sit in that sanctuary knowing Seabrook lay at rest thirty feet behind it.

He'd died for being stupid. He'd never been a natural cop.

However, he'd also died because she'd been too stupid to rein him in.

He'd died avenging his dead wife.

But he'd also died saving Callie.

However, the bottom line was that he was gone and sorely missed by many. She'd help cost Edisto one of its favorite sons.

She shouldn't have let him into her life, but she had. By the time she realized how much she loved him, he'd gotten himself killed.

Callie's conclusion after losing her husband and subsequently Mike Seabrook was that she didn't have a damn clue how to manage a serious relationship. And now she had Mark dancing around her, making all the proper gestures, being a gentleman. Bringing her meals all the time to ensure she stayed healthy, like someone normally invested in a significant other.

No, Stan was wrong. Mark didn't need to know her flaws. Who said he wouldn't be gone soon, too?

Her car still idled at the end of Oyster Factory Road. Any passer-by would suspect a cop waited to catch a speeder, but there were no speeders. She just didn't want to move.

She took in a deep breath, breaking her out of this . . . trance. What the hell had dredged all this up? She'd grown comfortable in this in-between sensation of feeling loyal to Seabrook while giving him up. Being noncommittal had suited her. Being friends with benefits with Mark was okay.

She called that moving on.

She put the car into drive and did that, moved on. It was ten thirty. She'd lost a half hour seated at that stop sign, with no better answers than when she'd stopped.

Chapter 14

CALLIE HADN'T GONE to Mark's place, where she was probably expected, sooner or later. She hadn't gone to Stan's, and no way was she going to Sophie's. It was after eleven, and she lay on her back in the red porch swing . . . at Seabrook's beach house on Palmetto.

Windswept was her thinking place. What started off as her promise to the Seabrook family to keep watch on the what was now their seldom-used vacation house, had really been a way for her to visit and pine for their son. However, as she healed, the porch morphed into a mental retreat. This was the beach. Who couldn't watch the waves and rethink one's messy life? People were afraid to interrupt her there.

The house sat on the north side of Palmetto, facing the beach front across the street. Ordinarily, nobody sitting on the north side could see the water, but *Windswept* faced an empty lot. The long-gone original home on that lot had washed off its foundation during Hurricane Gracie in 1959, much of it taken out to sea. The Seabrooks owned that lot, too, to preserve the view. She'd be foolish thinking they would continue paying that level of property taxes for long. Something would sell one day.

Callie had set the swing rocking, eyes closed, not that they needed to be with the darkness, and arm hung down she pushed with fingertips to keep the sway. Her thoughts pin-balled from one topic to another, and at the moment she needed to list all the issues then prioritize. She needed some kind of game plan for tomorrow, and the day after and the day after.

She had an arsonist to pursue, the most glaring issue, because that crime was the biggest, the baddest, and the boldest. It reflected most harshly on the town. The owner, Booker McPhee, had deflected, irritated he'd heard the news from Brice first. Webb had been in the middle of repairs on the house but shown little interest in the fire. Like the owner, he had outstanding bills to pay, and insurance companies never paid quickly. An arson investigation would drag out insurance payment, so unless Webb or McPhee was in dire financial straits, that would not be the route to take. Unless the two collaborated. That was an option meriting attention.

A full investigation would have to run its course, though. She hadn't spoken to neighbors on either side of and across from *Shell Shack* and *Shark Shack*. She'd have already addressed them if not for the burglaries stepping in her way . . . and Monty.

The burglary cases still entailed her talking to those present at the fire, to include her own officers. Thomas had been on traffic at that end of Myrtle, and Gerard Valentine did most of the evacuations for a dozen houses, to include the three that were burgled. Gerard came on after Seabrook died, along with LaRoache. LaRoache had five years' service, while Gerard had three. Edisto Beach PD wasn't exactly a springboard for police employment, attracting more of the entry and retirement levels— the first or last assignment in one's career. Some escaped to the beach from whatever hadn't worked for them before but left in a year or two after learning what beach policing was all about.

Experience or no experience, Thomas and Gerard should've had eyes on that block. Brice was right about that.

She had to touch base with the Edisto powers that be to offer assurance . . . and to counter whatever bullshit Brice was spreading. The lady at the Chamber of Commerce, the key restaurant owners, the real estate brokers, most importantly, Janet as the queen bee of the three brokers.

So, tomorrow . . . Thomas, Gerard, and Janet. Oh, and Janet's nephew, Arthur. Though he wasn't the most observant individual, he'd been there. Webb again . . . Booker McPhee again. She'd have Leon speak to his people. She'd have Marie put out descriptions of the three missing items: a diamond bracelet, a Damascene necklace, and a USC college ring, with double emphasis on the necklace.

She'd try to check on Dudley again. *Um, Dud.*

On a personal note, her Edisto home was a mess, and she was mad at herself about that for some reason. Mark said a plumber would be coming by but hadn't said what time or who was expected to let him in. She suspected he intended to take care of that. Not that he minded tending to her business, but should she let him? It was giving him a nod, wasn't it? At a minimum, it was taking advantage . . . wasn't it?

Yes, Mark. The fact she was spending the night, and an unknown number after, with him, kept pushing concern about him to the top of her personal heap. The favors were nice. The brown-bag dinners were appreciated. Her biggest worry was that Mark, and also Stan and Sophie, maybe everyone but her, would view this slumber party arrangement as the next step.

She didn't want a next step.

Especially now ancient baggage leaped back into her path. Fires, sunsets . . . not the drink, not yet, but the yellow fire and orange sunsets once had been intricately connected to the blue of a good Bombay Sapphire on ice. She ran her tongue over her teeth, missing gin more today than the first day she'd quit.

None of this was fair to Mark.

None of this was fair to her either, but *this*, in its tangled ball of knots, was *her* problem, not his.

Stop.

Start over. Back to the fires. She'd start her day with those interviews. Then Janet to get her take on McPhee and Webb and get her politically on board against whatever Brice was scheming. Then the other real estate brokers. . . .

She heard cars passing by, judging who sped and who didn't. Not many violators tonight . . . not with her patrol car parked out front of *Windswept*.

The footfall on the bottom step caused her to snatch her eyes open, taking her hand to her hip.

No car had pulled in. She hadn't heard voices. Not that night owls didn't stroll, but few dared climb stairs to a house they weren't renting, particularly with a cop car on site.

"Stan?" she called, though the steps didn't remind her of him. He was the only soul who dared sit with her at *Windswept*. Few spoke to her of Seabrook nor questioned her visits to the red swing on his house except for Stan, and in his defense, his goal was usually to pull her out of her doldrums and make her get on with life.

"No," came the male voice. "It's me."

Callie sat up and touched her hair, like it mattered.

"Am I trespassing in any way?" he asked, finally mastering the two dozen stairs to reach the porch. He paused for an answer, his hand on the railing.

No, this wasn't awkward at all. She slid to an end of the swing, feeling as if he'd caught her cheating. She thanked the heavens for the jet-black night that kept him from reading her cheeks.

Truth be told, his arrival did feel a little like trespassing. "Stan told you where I was," she said.

"He did." Mark took a place at the other end of the swing, and once the chair had adjusted, he used his heel to start a slow rock. A waft of the restaurant reached her nose. He came without showering, unlike his normal visits. "This is nice," he said while she kicked off her shoes and sat cross-legged. Upright, her feet didn't touch the floor. She liked having him push.

Mark didn't ask why she didn't show at his place, and he didn't ask what was wrong. He relaxed, like he'd had a long day, gazing out at the waves one could only see the whitecaps of with everything so dark, and only then because it was almost high tide.

"It's after midnight," he said.

"Guess it is," she said. "I don't keep up with that when I come out here."

She sensed that he sensed this place was sacred, and she couldn't help but feel touched by the respect. "What, no bag? No tamales or burritos?" she asked, smoothing things over.

"I thought you ate. Plus, I felt it was getting rather cliché. That and Mexican sits rather heavy this time of night." He waited. "Hope that's all right."

She lightly laughed. "Of course it is." Her head leaning back on the swing, she watched the water. She could've used that last enchilada.

"Hey, I'm not Stan," he said, filling in the silence, "but feel free to run through anything with me. I mean . . . police related?"

He was tip-toeing. Stan must've told him how important this porch was and how it was where she went to think. Sometimes where she and Stan met, him helping her think. They'd had a natural give-and-take to solving problems in Boston, and on occasion, he still served her well here, watching the waves.

"Thanks. That means a lot." Mark's offer was sweet, and she was touched, chagrinned at the wall she'd thought about throwing up earlier for no precise reason she could nail down now. She did tend to lighten up around him, think less deeply, and accept feedback, but she stopped short of a bare-bones exposure of her life.

She wondered how in depth that chat with Stan was. Not too terribly in depth, she hoped, recalling Stan's sage retort to her of, *Not my story to tell.*

"You and Leon were on the news tonight," he said. "As were

several others."

"Did you see Monty Bartow?" she asked.

He chuckled "Yeah, he was on there in all his silly self. He'll probably remember that three seconds of fame for the rest of his life."

The remark made her smile. Mark made her smile.

"Did you record it?" she asked. If he hadn't, surely someone had. She'd hate to have to ask Alex for a copy.

"No, afraid not. Bet Brice did."

Brice held a collection of ammunition at his disposal now: his storage-room fire, the Myrtle Street fires, the burglaries, Minnie's complaint, and now Alex's television coverage that, whether she realized it or not, debased the island.

Brice's animosity was not a new experience, and each issue, on its own merit, wasn't a threat, but pull them together into a theme, and in twenty-four hours he'd gathered enough grenades to make noise.

Mark shifted on the swing to better see her, the wood creaking. "Speaking of Brice, you're welcome."

"Not sure that's the words I had in mind," she replied, her comfort zone disappearing at the replay of Brice's tirade in El Marko's.

When Brice had called out Callie, Mark had told Callie to stay seated. His wait-and-see suggestion was to make Brice show his hand. His decision . . . not hers.

And that let Brice broadcast to the restaurant how inept Callie was, how Monty had been injured as a result, and how crime had taken hold on Edisto that she couldn't get in front of. Then on top of that, she couldn't even take care of Brice himself in his disturbing the peace, a violation meant for Callie to handle.

Instead, Mark had read the man, taken charge, and told everyone else what to do.

She hadn't enjoyed the experience then, and she especially didn't enjoy it in replay as she'd been made the fool . . . mostly by Brice, inadvertently by Mark. In hindsight, if she'd cuffed Brice and removed him from the restaurant, all those people would've assumed she was trying to silence him from bad-mouthing her. There was that. Still, Mark's solution stung.

"Unfortunately, despite good intentions you made matters worse," she said.

He lit the light on his phone. "Sorry, but I can't do this in the dark.

Explain to me what I did wrong."

Damn it.

She tried to explain, not sure she could be more clear without being a heel. "Brice chewed up my reputation spreading how weak I am at protecting these people . . . then you did the white-knight thing and stood up for the little damsel, underlining Brice's point . . . then you never turned things back over to me, instead tending to diners, maintaining the alpha role, then disappearing as if I didn't even exist, leaving me dangling in the wind." She had to catch her breath. "If Stan didn't see that, he's senile. What did he say?"

Mark's reaction was that of puzzlement. "He didn't comment on what happened but said if you weren't at my place to try here." He peered around. "He sort of sent me here, I think."

"What else did Stan say?" she asked, absolutely sure there was more. There had better have been more.

"He said if I chose to come looking for you, to tread carefully," Mark said. "The man speaks in encryptions. I asked him to explain, because I damn sure didn't want to walk into something blind, but he said it *wasn't his story to tell.*"

Like Stan said to her. And like him to play each of them against the other to force an aeration of each other's past.

"I did hear what Brice said about Seabrook, though," he said. "Nobody believes that you caused Seabrook's murder and stole his job. From what I hear, Seabrook didn't want the job and had to twist your arm to take it. He was your biggest supporter."

"He was," she said softly. A lump formed in her throat. "This is Seabrook's house," she said. "We ate on this swing. We dined at that table inside." She stopped short of saying they slept in the bed in the first room on the right as you entered the house. Once. Only once. The bed she'd saturated with her sweat from pneumonia, acquired after having aspirated water attempting a rescue in Scott's Creek.

Brice had put her in his crosshairs then, too, calling one of his emergency meetings that evening to fillet her in public. The mayor had come over to warn her, standing at that very screen door not five feet away, warning her of what might happen. She'd exchanged short sentences with him, calling to him as she remained in the bedroom, weak as a sick kitten. Sophie'd been tending her as Seabrook filled in for her at the station . . . the same evening she'd wilted, unable to be of any value to him as he went out that evening, alone, following the beckoning call of a killer.

Mark waited, recognizing she was lost in thought. She couldn't decide exactly what to tell him, what would help him understand . . . versus what was too painful, too personal to explain. Even Sophie knew more about Seabrook than Stan did, and he'd held her crying quite a few of those earlier evenings.

Who said Mark was ready for that sort of spillage?

That didn't even count the phobia about fire and dusk.

He knew about the gin from the fact she refused to drink.

He turned off the flashlight. She breathed relief, as if the click meant she didn't have to say more.

"Have I gone too far somehow?" he said, the question coming across caring and willing to accept her in whatever shape or behavior she chose to present.

Goddamn it, he reminded her of Seabrook in that way . . . especially that last day when he'd finally opened up to her.

This mishmash of the two men wasn't going to work. She wanted them separate. She needed each relationship in and of itself private and defining.

"If we're going to take this further," he said, again so smooth and loving, "I need direction, Callie." He inhaled, the silence of the late night amplifying his sincerity.

Here it was. What she hadn't wanted to hear. Without the ability to reveal her innermost feelings, how was she supposed to give this man her all? She wasn't sure she had that much to give him, frankly. There was a lot more wrong to Callie Jean Morgan than there was right.

"Not the place and time to do this," she said. "Way too much history. Not enough night."

"Callie," he started, then acted as if he caught himself. "You aren't the only one with history, but you won't even take a step to open up to me. I haven't dumped my problems on you for fear that wasn't what you wanted, because then you'd feel the need to reciprocate. Appears I was right in thinking any sort of pressure would only push you away."

She stared at the whitecaps, wishing she could see more in the dark. A moon, reflections, a boat . . . Charleston's lights off in the distance. Instead there was little more than black. He was trying, and it appeared she was not willing to when that wasn't quite it at all.

But these were her memories, her trauma, her past to choose

whether to hide away or tell. Trust sold at a premium in her world, hard earned at a high price. She'd lost so much giving way too much of herself to too many others.

Mark was a friend, and she shied away from thinking of him as much more while keenly aware of the magnetism. She enjoyed him, but the idea of letting another soul have access to her own scared her shitless.

"Don't mess this up, Mark."

She hadn't even thought out the words first. They just happened.

He stopped pushing the swing. "I got the impression from Stan, that this might be . . . a door we could walk through," he said, hesitating.

"Yeah," she said. "He's been pushing me to slice myself open and show you all my secrets, wounds, and favorite flavors of ice cream."

A zing of regret shot through her at that last one.

Seabrook used to bring her mint chocolate chip. She hadn't had a single spoon of it since he died.

What the hell was wrong with her? She wouldn't want to be on the receiving end of these words.

Too much on her plate was what was wrong. Now was not the time to discuss how to step up a relationship.

"Let's go home," Mark said, standing.

Her first instinct was to decline the offer and find her own bed, until she realized she couldn't. She unfurled herself, put her shoes back on, and rose from the swing. "Yeah, it's late. We've been at it since dawn." Suddenly, she was bone tired. The swing had served its purpose slowing her down, and the almost-conflict with Mark had finished wearing her out.

There'd be no luck for Mark in *Reel Lucky* tonight.

Her work phone went off, the personal one still defunct. The call was from 911 dispatch in Walterboro. What she heard stunned her.

"Gotta go," she said, taking the stairs two at a time down to the sand. "Fire at *Bikini Bottom*."

The name of the house meant nothing to Mark. She had no time to update him on the case. There was a bit of sadness to that reality, she thought, leaping into her car. And when she turned to tell him *goodbye, don't wait up*, he still stood on the porch.

She'd forgotten about his old war wound. The one he hadn't found the time to tell her about . . . for fear of pushing her away, he'd said. Maybe that slight limp of his meant he couldn't take those stairs as readily anymore. Maybe he decided to let her go do her thing. He'd already worked a long day.

But then, Callie pretty much implied she wasn't his to keep.

She pulled off, throwing him a wave. His was slower in return.

She ought to be mad at Stan and his poorly orchestrated attempt at a lovers' encounter. He really needed to stay out of their business.

Her light off, to avoid waking tourists, she'd almost reached Lybrand Street. *Bikini Bottom* was right ahead.

She wasn't as mad at Stan as she thought, though. She was angry with herself for being unprepared for such an obvious conversation. She'd known this was coming. If not today, soon.

Mark was trying. She didn't want to, which made her the bad guy.

And because of her moronic inability to articulate her parameters and past, she was fairly sure she didn't want to do much more than apologize for any rudeness and return to single-hood, unless he could accept reverting back to friends with benefits. Chances were she'd screw up much more of a relationship.

Damn, she wished Stan had stayed out of things. Things had been fine before he got involved.

The fire truck's red lights lit up the sky, bouncing off a dozen houses, throwing her pulse into triple time with expectation. She parked and leaped out. Nothing like the houses on Myrtle Street, this fire was more contained, but it was fire, nonetheless. One firefighter already had water going, but surely Leon had rolled out of bed for this. Quickly deducing the residence wasn't what burned, she scanned for the fire chief, finding him peering over what appeared to be a body.

Chapter 15

FLASHING LIGHTS from the fire truck coated them all. Leon's full garb for firefighting atop the muggy summer night already had sweat dripping down his cheek, his hair wet around his face. He placed an oxygen mask on Monty. "He's inhaled a lot of smoke, Callie. Chopper's on its way. Can you take him to meet them?"

Monty lay half naked, the charred shirt in the grass to the side, removed by Leon. Instinctively, Callie studied Monty's bare chest for movement, relieved to see the breathing, shallow though it was. Taken aback by the small pieces of shirt melted to his shoulders, she caught the mild scent of burned flesh amidst that of the wood, paper, and trash in the dumpster.

"No problem. I'll get him there," she said, kneeling, reaching out to touch Monty, then drawing back, uncertain in the dark what part of him was painful. "The driving range or the big bridge?"

"The bridge," he said, his trained eye scouring Monty for any immediate need before they put him in Callie's car.

Monty hadn't opened his eyes, his brow tightly knit. He released slight moans, showing he hurt. "It's okay, Monty." Again, she so wanted to touch him. "We're going to take care of you. I'll notify your mother. How did this happen?"

Leon caught her attention with a tap on the back. "Don't make him talk, Chief. No telling what kind of throat damage he has."

She nodded. She should've known.

Monty wouldn't open his eyes, afraid to move, his consciousness in question. Burns on his face, arms, and chest, second and third degree from what she could guess, but it was one thirty in the morning with no moon, and a flashlight didn't allow for accurate interpretation of his injuries. She guessed his arms, upper body, and face only, since his lower extremities didn't appear damaged, the pants not scorched.

"Okay, let's do this," Leon said. "It'll take you fifteen minutes to get to the bridge."

"No it won't." The fifteen miles was on twisty, two-lane highway 174, but in the middle of the night, lights and siren going, she'd make it in ten. Or less.

The other firefighter, a volunteer, showed up to aid them, and only then did Callie realize the fire had been confined to a dumpster and the fire was out.

They gently slid Monty in her back seat, and without further discussion, she turned the car east, made it to Scott's Creek at the town's entrance, then mashed the gas. They barely dropped below ninety, her hands white knuckled on the steering wheel, her focus purely on the road, watching for deer, raccoon, or other nocturnal nightlife so often out this time of night, prepared to plow through or around—whatever it took.

"Monty, I know it hurts, but they'll take care of you, I promise. I'm so sorry this happened to you, buddy. Can't have one of my favorite officers get hurt like this, you know? We take care of our own."

He wasn't responding. She talked, nonstop.

She made it in nine minutes. She exited and ran around, opening the door, cooing assurances to him. His moans were louder and more frequent as he more and more felt his pain. "We'll figure this out," she said, gently. "You let the doctors take care of you. Let me handle things here."

She heard the chopper before she saw it, and it soon settled on a span of the mile-long McKinley Washington, Jr. Bridge, the overpass that symbolized separation of pre- and post-Edisto life to the natives. Right now it served as Monty's bridge to the mainland's emergency help that Edisto Island could not begin to provide with its one-doctor office and three-times-a-week clinic in one of the church's fellowship halls.

In well-synchronized fashion, a woman and a man unloaded Monty onto a gurney affair and loaded him up before Callie could think twice. She handed them his wallet, confirmed his identity, and off they went.

Seemed like seconds. Probably was.

The chopper's *wump-wump-wump* diminished to a drone, then disappeared altogether. Callie remained behind, standing in the middle of the fifty-foot-wide bridge, catching her breath, somewhat stunned at what had happened.

There was no way anyone saw that coming.

They had no clue why Monty was on the site, nor how a dumpster could catch fire in the middle of the night. Another arson most likely.

Question was, did Monty set it or someone else? The first would be bad enough, but a challenged young man lighting up trash was nothing compared to someone else targeting him. Monty might've stumbled upon activity he wasn't supposed to. Or worse, been lured.

None of this made sense, but it was her job to make sense of it.

That evening she'd left Monty at home with his mother, eager to stay up late to watch himself on the eleven o'clock news. Somehow, he'd slipped out. She had no idea what would make him do so. Before the moped, he had a history of walking from home to the beach, but he was injured. Something had to be of dire importance for him to make that trek after midnight with a limp. Maybe he still had that old bent bike.

A shift in breeze caught her face on. The night was a beauty. The tide had eased out, and the damp, acrid pluff mud aroma filled the air. She ordinarily loved the smell, the night sounds, and brush of the salt air atop that bridge. No traffic.

While she'd love nothing more than to lean over the side of that bridge, watch the water and think, she had two tasks before her. First, tell Minnie about her son. Second, roll to the site and get a big picture gander at what the crime scene could tell her. Of course the morning light would shed more on the details, but impatience prompted a craving to look sooner than later.

She got in her vehicle, turned it around, and radioed Gerard, the officer on duty for the night, telling him to tape off the scene. Turned out he was already there. Good man.

Moments later, she turned onto Oyster Factory Road, entered the gate, properly fastened this time, and slowly approached the Bartow residence. Callie left her headlights on, hopefully to awaken Minnie with flickers off her bedroom wall rather than a sudden knock on her door at two in the morning. Never a good thing.

The yellow porch light came on. By the time Callie reached the stoop, Minnie stood in the doorway, a thin cheap robe held around her with one hand, the other resting on the screen door handle, like she needed the obstacle between them.

"Minnie," Callie said, not expecting to be asked in. "Monty has been taken to the Medical University's Burn Unit in Charleston. If you want me to take you to him, I'd be happy to."

Minnie's guard went up, a flicker of fear, then concern, as if seeking an excuse to go all the way to angry. "What happened?"

"We found him burned on the *Bikini Bottom* property. He'd been—"

"I don't keep up with them damn names," Minnie said. "Get to the damn point."

"For some reason a dumpster caught fire, and he got burned in relation to that."

"Why was he there?"

"No idea, Minnie. I was hoping you could tell me."

"How bad?" the mother asked, and Callie could literally see the woman choosing her strength over fret. Pragmatic to the core, which deserved respect.

"He was breathing on his own," Callie replied. "Burned on his chest, arms, and face."

The small gasp was quickly contained. "Is he talking any?"

"No, but we didn't want him trying to until they analyzed smoke-inhalation damage."

Minnie nodded. "Anything else?"

"That's all we know at the moment," Callie said. "Wanted to tell you first thing. I'm glad to wait for you and carry you to Charleston—"

"I got a car," Minnie said, and left, shutting the door.

She quickly reappeared in one of her formless dresses, sneakers, and sweater over her arm. A brush had been run once or twice through her hair before held back with a stretchy headband. Purse in the crook of her arm, Minnie locked up the house without the first acknowledgement of Callie waiting beside the patrol car.

Minnie held up the sweater in walking past. "Hospitals get cold." Then she repositioned the banged-up moped so it leaned on a post rather than on her car. "Told you I didn't need a ride," she said over the hood.

"Only trying to be of assistance," Callie said.

"What damn sense does it make to take me then leave me stranded in Charleston?"

Callie walked over as Minnie got behind the wheel. Callie stopped the door closing. "We'd get you home, too. I need to make sure you're okay to drive."

"I'm okay to do whatever it takes to see to my son," she said, and tugged the door from Callie's grip, cranked the engine, and backed out, the angle causing the front bumper to nudge the moped, sliding it to the ground.

The Bartows had always been self-sustaining and hardcore practical, but Callie also heard Minnie cry over her son's tardy return home the other night. She'd witnessed the mama-bear protectiveness and likewise saw the love.

Callie went over to right the moped and move it further out of the way. The kickstand wouldn't support it any longer, so she grabbed a broken concrete block from behind the carport and wedged up the bike. He must have wrecked hard to tear off the front basket like that.

Monty had kept a smaller one on the front and a larger one on the back. All that was left of the former were rubs and scratches on the front fender and along the handlebars from the anchor ties.

With nobody looking over her shoulder, she rummaged through the other basket, muddied up, crooked, a hole in one side. She wasn't hunting anything in particular, but if anything connected Monty to Myrtle Street or to *Bikini Bottom*, she'd be grateful. She found nothing but personal items that looked to have been there a while, now mud-coated.

She headed back to the fire site. Weariness dragged on her like a wet wool blanket, but before she put her head on a pillow, she had to walk that scene.

Hardly remembering the five miles back, she parked on the street. The crime scene tape was up, everybody gone.

An investigator worked a crime scene from the point of the crime and moved out, but she couldn't help but study the macro-version of things first. Nary a scorch on the house from what she could see under her flashlight's scrutiny. A tarp was bungeed over the dumpster now. Best to wait for daylight to bother looking in there. Monty's old bike rested against the house's steps, her guess as to his mode of transportation confirmed.

She decided she was doing little more than blindly trampling the scene and walked back to the car, texting Leon to see if he'd meet her first thing in the morning and review the incident. Then she texted Mark that she was on her way and didn't expect him to be up. Her phone said almost three.

Before their talk tonight, Callie would've relished parking herself at Mark's for a night or two, versus slipping home after a night's tryst. Very convenient booty call. However, tonight she'd kill to be going home, alone, not talking to anyone, not caring where she left her smelly clothes on the floor nor when she had to wash them.

She immediately felt guilty about the thoughts. She sighed. Weariness screwed with her head.

When she reached Mark's driveway, she took in the house, wondering if he'd tried to wait up or if his experience told him she could be all night and he'd hit the sack. She appreciated his not coming with her . . . was a little surprised he hadn't. Maybe a hint disappointed, which she had no right to be.

He often offered his services for little tasks like traffic control during craft fairs and parades. Most retired LEOs stepped up whenever possible, for a little taste of the good life.

But she didn't want him to see her around a fire. This one was minimal, thank God, but she hadn't known that when the call came in. She had no clue on how she'd react to flames raging in the heat of the night. The dumpster fire spiked her emotions . . . but not as badly as it could have thanks to the race to transport Monty. She would love to claim that as a plus in her PTSD column, as Stan now called it. However, she likewise didn't want to let any of that fire business lay claim to her mental acuity.

Test by fire. Literally. The only way she'd ever know how she ranked on the scale between panic and no effect would be to face the experience. Edisto didn't need the fires.

Being unable to forecast her reaction to a fire did exasperate her. Nothing drove her more nuts than not being in control.

Control. Maybe that was the issue digging at her about Mark. His not having access to her secrets helped her maintain control, the way she wanted it. She'd been quite comfortable before the fires, before Stan talked about fires, Stan's prodding leading Mark to feel he needed to know her on a deeper level. Stan meant well, but no. This was her decision.

She couldn't help but wonder if her and Mark's former comfort level was damaged. She stared up at the window, trying to decipher if Mark stared down. Then after what felt like too long, she gave up stalling and climbed the stairs, pulling out the key he gave her, feeling like a wife coming home to a marriage in trouble.

He'd left the kitchen light on for her, and no, he hadn't waited up. From the look of him sprawled across the bed, he was miles deep in REM. The bed was a queen, but he'd obviously grown accustomed to owning all the real estate. To slide into bed and move him over would wake him. He wouldn't mind. Mark never really minded much when it came time to accommodate others. Part of why folks flocked to El Marko's.

Part of why she liked him.

The insides of her eyelids could pass for sandpaper. The clock read half past three. She wanted to meet Leon at the fire scene around seven, her logic also being to catch Webb when he arrived, the contractor more of a person of interest than before. Mark, however, ran on a different time schedule due to El Marko's and didn't need to rise that early.

Gingerly leaving the room, she opted for the mini-bedroom, a twin bed plenty big for a five-foot-two girl who'd go comatose as soon as she went horizontal. She'd be back up and out before Mark even knew she'd been there.

Logically made sense. Romantically, not so much.

Regret clung to her about Mark, like she wasn't doing something right by him. It clung to her like the humidity, but the night was too old and she was too tired to weigh personal issues. She set her phone to six thirty, shut the door, stripped to her underwear, and fell onto the bed, falling asleep reaching for the coverlet.

Chapter 16

A HARP STRUMMED in the recesses of Callie's mind, and she couldn't register from where at first. Wait. Her alarm tone. *God, already?*

She crawled out of a dark hole of sleep, groping for the phone lost under the sheet. She'd kept it on the bed near her so she wouldn't wake Mark, going for the mildest, gentlest sound to go off at six thirty. The second chorus began as she fought to dig out of a sleep that wouldn't let go. She'd had three hours of shut-eye. She could function another day on that, but damn, her eyes were gritty.

Sluggishly, she dressed. Opening her bedroom door, she faced his, open. Mark slept with his bedroom door unlocked, as opposed to Callie who locked any lock available, and she took advantage and peered in on him. Still passed out, a few jet-black curls had fallen forward over his eyes making him appear younger, his salt-and-pepper sides hidden in the confusion of pillow and sheet. His left leg had escaped from the covers, the one he could be seen limping on if you watched him closely enough. The scarred one they'd never discussed, like the ropey scar on her forearm.

The room held his scent, and she took in a fuller breath. Not sweet, not musky, not overt anything in particular. Just him. She loved that residual of him on her pillowcase and bathroom towels when he stayed the night at *Chelsea Morning*.

He sprawled across a bed, as she was already aware, and he could sleep like the dead, but she'd never seen him quite this reposed. She wanted to remain there in the doorway watching him, like a parent watching their child dream, marveling at the blessing.

She hadn't expected this. Mark in his own environment gave her a different feel, drawing on her. Peaceful, homey, cozy, and . . . innocently suggestive. There was also a quiet strength there she couldn't help but admire, and admire she did.

Callie imagined his muscular back against her palms and wished she could slip in next to him and sleep the day away wrapped up in those arms. The man loved to be up against her. There was no rolling over after sex and assuming his own private place in the bed. The whole night the whole bed was his, to include her.

Shifting her weight, she toyed with bumping the door, accidental-like, to make him want to rise and send her off with a hug, a kiss, and a wish for a good day.

But she didn't. Because she couldn't grab sleep didn't mean he shouldn't.

Instead, he'd awaken in a couple hours, see she'd slept in the other room, come and gone without him being aware, and be disappointed. It couldn't be helped.

At least that's what she told herself while at the same time telling herself Stan was full of crap.

Damn it, but her old boss had gotten into her head. Either that or she was overthinking the consequences of this relationship. She hadn't started doing that until Stan's recent suggestions, but still, she could overthink like a pro, an age-old trait of hers that she despised.

The friends-with-benefits thing had suited her fine. A few years ago she'd have never thought she'd say that. She thought Mark liked the deal, too. Why not leave it at that? Because that's not how relationships evolved, Stan said. He thought they could be something better.

Stan should know Callie was afraid of making things worse by allowing so much intimacy that the loss of it later would rend her to pieces . . . again.

But if Callie became too much trouble to get close to, Mark might quit trying. Stan didn't have to lay that out there for her to see it.

She took in another long look of Mark, surprised at the prick of emotion behind her tired eyes, then tucked away her guilt and left. If she could do anything well, it was compartmentalize.

Gently, she pulled the front door closed and left, ensuring it was locked.

Callie arrived at *Bikini Bottom* after seven, her study of Mark making her five minutes late. Leon already walked the scene. Webb hadn't shown up. Of course, she was assuming this was the job he'd show up to that morning. Yesterday he'd made the job sound urgent and time sensitive.

Leon waited for her at the dumpster. He'd dropped a concrete block for her to stand on, which she silently appreciated. Being height challenged could be a bitch sometimes.

"Before we soaked things down last night, something had to have been dry enough to light this off," he said. "Had to have been tossed in after that storm we had, too, which means someone put dry material in between the rain after dark and Monty's arrival around midnight."

Excellent deduction, but that time frame could not do them a damn bit of good without cameras or witnesses, and who watched a dumpster in the dark between suppertime and midnight, unless they were dumping off the trash, which nobody would admit to. Anyone could read the writing on *that* wall. Admission would make them a person of interest.

But someone could've brought kindling for the purpose of setting off the fire, too.

"We can't jump to conclusions, Leon. People see a dumpster and toss all sorts of trash out of convenience. Some of this could've been furniture, from what I'm seeing. Who out here hasn't cleaned out their storeroom and used some contractor's dumpster?"

He stood flat-footed on the ground, watching her, waiting for her to finish. "But this burned with an accelerant."

Sarcastically, she stood back flat-footed and sneered over at him. "You really could've led with that. Did you find its container?"

"Nah. Think they took it with them."

She hopped down. "I would have. Haven't had a chance to check on Monty yet this morning, but I spoke to his mother before she left for the hospital last night. I'll give them a little more time before I call." The painful moans of that poor boy would revisit her every time she got in the car for a while. The way his sobs amplified in the small confinement . . . the way he uttered calls for his momma.

"I'm hoping none of his burns are more than second degree," Leon said.

"Me, too." Callie hopped down and began slowly walking the scene, hunting for anything that might help her make sense. "Leon, this is three fires in two days. What the hell is going on?"

He strolled at her side, speaking low, scrutinizing the grounds as well. "No idea," he said. "But they are three entirely different fire types. An accident, a probable arson, and this. Not sure what to call this one."

"Besides attempted murder?"

He stopped walking. "Didn't want to say that too loud. What are you thinking?"

Her hypothesis was barely more than smoke right now, pardon the pun, and, nothing against Leon, but she wasn't ready to talk what-ifs with him. What-ifs that might spread to the public. "I'll keep picking at the threads," she said. "Let me take a raincheck on that conclusion, but I'll fill you in when I can."

"Fair enough," he said. "SLED isn't coming, by the way."

"Not surprised." A dumpster fire wouldn't exactly motivate them, even atop the Myrtle Street fire they'd sidestepped for more pressing issues. SLED was always in high demand, and you didn't use them lightly. If they couldn't come, they had something more important.

Besides, Callie wasn't quite ready to broadcast the attempted murder concept to them yet either.

They'd rounded the house and passed Monty's old bicycle, then back around to the dumpster. She picked up a stick and headed to the side with the concrete block and looked in again, pushing debris around.

"What?" Leon asked, trying to follow her gaze.

"Nothing. Only trying to figure this out. You sure no gas can or bottle or other accelerant container could be in there?"

He peered in. "I'm pretty sure. I can have a guy look again."

Leon's department functioned heavily on volunteer hours, and she had her radio in her hand before she answered him. "No, I'll have one of mine sift through." One call to Marie would put Gerard on this. She preferred leaving Thomas cruising the roads and the beach. His people skills could diffuse a lot of small-time issues before they turned into more.

Webb's truck tires crunched the gravel drive turning in. His door hadn't shut before he spouted, "What the hell's going on, Chief?"

Why wasn't he this distraught over the Myrtle house fires?

"Fire late last night in your dumpster," she said, meeting him halfway. Leon hung a little back. "I need to ask where you were around midnight, Mr. Webb."

His weathered complexion darkened at the insinuation. "You can drop the *Mister* shit. I didn't do this."

"A man is in the hospital from it. Burned."

Webb crossed his arms, cocking a stance. "Maybe he shouldn't have been lighting fires. Who is it?"

"Monty Bartow," she said, watching for the reaction.

His arms uncrossed, and he squinted as if concluding something. "He cause the other fire, too?"

His quickness in casting aspersions on the convenient man with limited mental skills, showed Webb didn't care one iota about Monty. Or at least that was Callie's gut sense, but the average person might think the same as Webb. "You didn't answer my question," she said. "Where were you last night around midnight?"

"At home," he said. "In bed," he said harder.

"Witnesses? Wife? Girlfriend? Neighbor?"

"No. Live alone on ten acres. Go to bed early to get up for work. Haven't had a girlfriend in three years."

Callie checked the time. Seven forty-five. His lack of alibi was the same as for Myrtle Street, and she wasn't comfortable with that. Yet there was little more she could do other than keep him on the list as a person of interest. No sign of motive. The fires hurt him more than helped.

He waited. For more questions, for clues, for explanation on where to go from here, whatever, Webb watched her, and when she didn't query him more, he felt the need to fill in. "Somebody's messing with my livelihood." Then he got accusatory. "I'm about to start taking this personal. What do you intend to do about it?"

Callie gave a slow nod, showing she heard him. "And why would that be, Mr. Webb? Have you been threatened? Do you know of anyone with a grudge?"

He swept his arm through the air, toward the dumpster. "You don't call this threatening?"

"Not exactly," she said, noting how he dodged the question. "This isn't your property, though I'm not tossing the idea someone hates you. Can you name names? Are you in trouble with anyone?"

"No, and get out of my business," he said, an octave lower.

"I'm solving a crime, sir. Your business is my business, so we can determine you aren't the criminal."

"Damn beach cops, good for nothing but chasing speeders and drunks." Turning back to his truck, he snatched up his toolbox, the weight heavy and limiting, and he headed for the stairs. He stopped. "Anyone damage the inside?"

"Tell you what," Callie said. "I'll wait here while you give it a once-over yourself, but am I right in assuming that Booker McPhee doesn't own this house?"

Pausing on the third step, he snapped back. "I take my orders from that Marine bitch on this one. Ask her who owns it."

He didn't get halfway up before the gold Hummer arrived, coming to a halt sudden enough to skid a foot or two. Janet Wainwright peeled out of one side, Arthur the other.

"Report, please," Janet ordered. Callie wasn't sure she meant her or Webb.

"Appears only the dumpster caught fire," Callie said when Webb didn't say anything, "but Webb is giving the inside a once-over. Monty Bartow is in the hospital though, with burns."

"He set the fire?" Janet asked.

Here we go again. No doubt that rumor would take on life and travel the beach like a bad virus. Callie wasn't happy Monty was injured, but she was relieved he wouldn't be wandering Edisto Beach too soon, with half the natives and any of the tourists who listened hard enough suspecting him.

"We have no idea who set the fire, Janet. This one or the other one."

Webb stomped up the rest of the way and disappeared inside.

Callie waited until he was gone. "Janet, who owns this place?"

"The Randolphs. A couple out of Rhode Island," she said. "They haven't been down here in several years, and I manage it for them as a pure rental."

"Are they hurting financially? Any issues you're aware of?"

Cynicism creased Janet's expression. "Absolutely none. And if you're insinuating this was insurance related, you're on Mars with your investigation. They're comfortable, more than comfortable, and I've not had a second's problem with them financially or otherwise. Check that box off your list, Chief."

Callie would gladly check any box off her list. Nothing gelled. There were two, maybe three fires with no apparent connection. She had a lot of boxes to check.

Webb wasn't at risk for payment on this job, per Janet. And he seemed to pay more attention to it. Scheduling clashes? Maybe. Or could he be butting heads with McPhee over payment? Or could an arrangement have been made between the two men, using fire to collect insurance? No hint of the latter, but she wasn't ruling it out just yet. Not until she knew more about what made Webb tick. Up to now she'd thought him too respectable to pull anything like this. Up to now, she hadn't the need to wonder who Webb might've pissed off.

Janet went to the dumpster, inspecting, the nephew already nosing around. Janet tossed some sort of question at Leon, and he joined her and the nephew, pointing into the mess, probably explaining whatever limited conclusions he'd gleaned.

Why Webb? Why Monty?

They were the only commonality between the last two fires. Webb's work was being ruined, or threats being made. He acted disturbed and irritated, playing the victim card quite handily, but still, both cases involved him. The dumpster fire, however, did no real harm, only serving to point to the fact Webb might be involved. A setup? A threat? A warning to him for some sorted past?

And Monty. What an easy pawn to move into law enforcement's scrutiny, and without serious thought, he could appear quite guilty between the badge found at *Shell Shack* and himself injured at *Bikini Bottom*. Unfortunately, the only person who could answer questions about those irregularities was Monty himself, and he wasn't in the best shape to query yet. She'd call and check on his status when done here, and from there determine how to approach him. Him, not his mother. Minnie would lie to hell and back to protect her son.

Webb showed up on the porch, peering down, hunting for Janet.

"Janet? Webb has a report for you," Callie called, using the Marine's own verbiage to get her attention as Webb lumbered down.

"No damage," he said as Janet fast-walked to him, Arthur scurrying behind. Webb was flustered, and Janet's drill-sergeant behavior didn't help.

Janet struck a stiff static pose. "No missing materials? I don't want surprises here, Webb. I got insurance to cover incidentals, but I won't be conned."

"I'm not conning you," he said, a tad too loud, enough for Janet to raise a brow in warning.

"We still got tenants due in on Sunday?" he asked, self-correcting.

"Yes," Janet replied.

"Can I continue using the dumpster? Goddamn, if it isn't one thing after another," he finished under his breath.

Janet looked to Callie who gave him a nod. "Give us till after lunch. One of my guys is going to go through it once more."

Palms up, he turned to leave. "All I need to know. If y'all don't mind, I got work to do."

Still holding questions for Janet, Callie studied the landscape, giving the contractor time to go back inside. Yellow caught her eye under the dumpster, against one of the supports. She headed over.

Leon spotted her. "What do you see?" he asked, meeting her at the dumpster.

She lowered to her knees, elbows in the dirt, and reached under the edge of the dumpster, using a stick to slide out the nozzle of a two-gallon gas can.

"How the hell did you see that?" Leon asked. She reached up for Leon to assist her to her feet. Then she retrieved a large evidence bag from the cruiser and dropped it in.

"Webb!" she hollered, hoping he could hear.

"Arthur," Janet ordered, "go tell Webb to get his sorry self out here. The chief has a question."

Guess Janet did have her uses.

Webb appeared on the back porch, looking down the fifteen feet. He threw an empty caulk container over the side toward the side of the dumpster, making a point he needed access to a place for his trash. Arthur scooted around him to rejoin his tribe.

"What?" Webb called.

"Did you have gas cans out here, and are any of them missing?"

He peered around, thinking, his sight stopping to his left, on the opposite side of the backyard from the dumpster. "That side, closer to the house, near the garbage cans. Should be a gas can or two. My guy cuts the grass once a week." He pointed down, arcing his arm to indicate under the porch. "I can't see from here, but that's where we kept it."

"Yellow, black, or red spout?" Callie called up.

He had to think about that. "Yellow, I think. Yeah, yellow."

"Thanks," she said. He stared at her like *that's all?* then returned back inside. She went to Janet. "How stable is he financially?"

Arthur stood behind his aunt, watching the conversation, not having been invited to participate.

Janet gave her answer some thought before deciding to cooperate. "He built his own home on acreage he bought some time back," she said. "I believe he owns it all debt free since he built most of it himself."

Behind his aunt looking off in the grass, Arthur grimaced. Callie took note.

"Personal issues?" she asked, speaking to Janet, halfway watching Arthur.

Her sigh loud and irritated, Janet did her eye-roll thing.

Callie continued. "Gambling, drugs, bad investments, alimony, child support?"

"He doesn't bore me with his personal life," Janet replied. "We don't *share*. Even better is he doesn't talk *back*."

Yeah, Callie could see the Marine having little patience with people any further than what they could do for Wainwright Realty's bottom line.

"So this rigid schedule of yours doesn't ever jam him up? He ever put other house owners ahead of your requests? He doesn't ask for advances, does he? Has he ever gouged you on his prices?"

Janet cackled a laugh. "I'm not in the habit of paying asking price for a house, for rent, or for hired help, and disbursements are on *my* schedule." She paused, like she felt that needed to sink in for Callie to understand. "These people know better than to put another job before mine, too."

Arthur's whole head rolled with his eyes.

"We're not buddies. I have no time for contractor drama," Janet added. "Am I understood?"

Callie almost brought up Tate from last December. Tate, Sr. and Tate, Jr. The former had died, having worked with Janet for over a decade, loyal as hell. The latter had gotten in trouble, almost taking Arthur down with him, and Janet had paid all legal fees for both, almost getting shot in the process of going the extra mile for the kid. Janet had time for the right drama of the right people, but apparently Webb hadn't made that list.

A long route to a short answer. No, Janet wasn't aware of anything on Webb outside of repairs she hired him for.

Arthur, however, might be worth another chat . . . later.

She thanked Leon, then Janet and Arthur, and headed toward her patrol car, locking the evidence bag in the trunk first. Before she opened her door, another vehicle arrived. An old Buick.

Brice LeGrand.

Had he bugged her vehicle or what?

"Ain't got your boyfriend to take up for you this time, eh, Chief?" he said, strutting toward her.

Leon slipped in his car and left. Brice acted like he didn't notice or didn't care.

Janet ordered Arthur into the Hummer while she marched toward the council chairman, determination in her jaw. "Get the hell out of here, Brice, or I'll kick your ass off this place myself, you SOB. Can't have you interfering with this righteous public servant trying to do her job. Not everything is your business."

Brice pointed at Callie. "As town council chair, my business is her job and her job my business. This is the third fire out here in twenty-four hours, and I'm fed up with her irresponsibility in allowing these arsons to happen."

Janet yelled, "Blow it out your ass, councilman. She's working on it. You're in her way."

He braced himself, hands on nonexistent hips, feet spread. "You don't run this beach, Wainwright."

Janet leaned in. "Test me," she said. "If you don't keep out of my business, I'll start a recall for your position." She smiled, almost evil. No, full-on evil.

He forced out a *hunh* filled with sarcasm. "You think you want my job, do you?"

But the elder woman's mouth took a downturn, her sinewy neck taut. "A drunk baboon could do your job, Brice. That pissant job is well below my talents."

Then she looked toward the Hummer where Arthur made no pretense of not eavesdropping, but when everyone followed his aunt's gaze, he snatched his attention elsewhere.

"But now that my nephew is a full-time agent with me, on his way to being a broker, he has expressed an interest."

Brice overexaggerated a *Ha!* then followed it up with disbelieving laughter. "Riding your coattails, huh? No talent of his own, but might as well use his old aunt's reputation, huh?"

Callie sucked in a breath at his perilous audacity, and in her mind she took a step out of the verbal line of fire. Not at the *coattails* mention, mind you. No. Janet would own that top to bottom, inside and out. Even approaching seventy, Janet considered herself still spry enough to practice what she'd just preached in kicking Brice off the *Bikini Bottom* property. It might have been twenty years since she'd handled Marine recruits, but nobody doubted she remembered the skills.

"Brice, I'll find you later," Callie said. "Janet, I think I'm done here, and I'll let you know what I find." She peered back and forth between them. "And I'll tell both of you how Monty's doing." She took a breath. "I assume you care what happens to him?"

Neither could say anything but *of course*, and they practically said it in unison.

"Then thanks," she said, putting a period on the end of this situation.

They hesitated leaving, Callie guessing neither wanting to leave first, but, surprisingly, Brice took the high road and took off, Janet standing firm.

"We all are aware the hard time that bastard gives you, Chief," she said, watching Brice's taillights head north. "Glad I could be of assistance taking care of him for you." She did an about-face, joined her nephew, and left.

Yet again, someone else had stepped in to do her job, protecting the little cop lady.

That's when she heard chuckling overhead. Webb had watched it all. He returned inside the house, laughing harder.

Chapter 17

CALLIE LEFT THE dumpster scene disliking Webb even more. Sweat already glued her hair to her face and dampened her back. She debated whether to go to the station next or to Mark's. She felt sheepish slipping out on him at dawn. She needed to thank him for the roof over her head, his dealings with the plumber, the insurance adjustor . . . gracious, the meals out of nowhere when she forgot to eat. She owed him big time.

She'd allowed an awkwardness to slip in between them.

However, she didn't want to fall back into last night's conversation about how his taking charge at El Marko's had or had not undermined her presence. Unfortunately, that stood foremost on her mind because of the way Janet had handled the situation at *Bikini Bottom* and Webb's reaction as a spectator.

Both times involved Brice. Both times fueled Brice against her. She imagined neither Janet nor Mark seeing things that way, and the more Callie protested about Brice, or about being protected from him by her friends, the weaker and more spoiled she would sound. After all, these folks were in her court.

Too many times she found herself on the defensive around Brice. Gun-shy, she could even call it. He made his personal goal quite evident to commercial business owners and the handful of town employees . . . get rid of Police Chief Callie Morgan. She couldn't stop his efforts nor his opinions and would appear childish if she attempted to. Her strength came in proving her worth via actions, not words, and in her two-plus years there had been plenty action to show people that Callie understood law enforcement. This Garden of Eden had no clue the crime under its nose until she arrived, and she'd been able to control it, keep it at bay, even hide it behind the scenes in the ultimate effort to maintain the peace, reputation, and economics of Edisto Beach.

Brice's reasons for his nastiness . . . the why—or rather, the whys—were many and the history too irritating, painful, and private to go into with people. Brice knew her mother once upon a time, intimately, and it hadn't ended well, the decades in between not having done much to ease his bitterness. Also, Brice had been a rabid fan of Officer Michael Seabrook, and Brice blamed the death on Callie. Everyone knew it, and for a few months afterward the town folk tended to split, siding with one viewpoint or the other. All of them, however, were acutely aware that she blamed herself for not keeping the man she loved alive though a criminal wielded the knife.

That didn't even count the little things. How she handled cases. The tickets written, or the tickets not written. She presented the department's activities, budget, and progress at each council meeting. One month he'd accuse her of being heavy-handed, the next she wasn't doing enough. The rest of the council saw Brice for what he was, a nuisance riding on his grandfather's legacy, but Brice nagged like a no-see-um in summer. Ever there, ever buzzing, ever nipping at your ears. Sooner or later some of them surely believed some of what he said. Had to.

Callie going on the defensive would only air dirty laundry and leave her looking equally as pitiful as he did, though.

Brice's remark at *Bikini Bottom* still rang in her ears. *Ain't got your boyfriend to take up for you this time.* And he'd said it in front of Leon, Arthur, Janet, and Webb. An entire restaurant heard Brice at El Marko's where diners saw her take the back seat to Mark's alpha presence. Sure, it was his restaurant. People sort of saw her as his girl. But wasn't this her beach?

Then Janet barged in, taking up for Callie against Brice.

Callie tried not to pout, and made a decision. Mark's it was. He was owed a thanks, plus, selfishly, she craved some appreciation right about now.

She reached *Reel Lucky* at a quarter to ten. Mark's car was under the house, but when she let herself in, she found him gone. He'd walked to work. Admittedly, she was let down and disliked Brice even more for robbing her of the time she could've spent with Mark at the house.

So on to El Marko's. The venue didn't open until eleven, but lights were on inside.

Best to check on Monty first, though, and offer her assistance to his mother. She called Minnie.

She picked up on the first ring. "He's asleep," she said, not even asking who the caller was.

"Hey, Minnie, it's Callie Morgan." She left off the Chief part, hoping to smooth any ripples between them before they had a chance to start. "How's Monty?"

"Wasn't no accident, was it?" the mother said.

"Doesn't appear to be, no ma'am." But that didn't negate the fact Monty could've set the fire, screwed it up, and paid a horrid price.

"You catch the person?" Minnie asked.

"No, we haven't, but we've been there all morning trying to piece things together."

Callie received a sigh in return, and she was grateful for it over criticism. "How is he?" she asked again.

"Second-degree burns on his arms, hands, neck, and face. A few worse spots on his forearms. He inhaled smoke, and his esophagus is swollen. He won't be able to talk for another day or two."

This time Callie sighed with empathy for Minnie to hear. "That's good news, Minnie. It could've been so much worse. He must've climbed out of that dumpster pretty fast."

"That's what the doctor said. He'll have some scars, but nothing he can't live with."

Callie caught herself running a hand along her own forearm scar where the burning piece of debris had gouged her over four years ago in her husband's fire. A lasting memory. Seemed like ages ago some nights, and only yesterday on others.

Guess she and Monty would have something in common to bond over. She'd try to make him comfortable with the scars.

"Who would set my boy on fire?" Minnie suddenly asked, tears behind the question.

The choked words tugged at Callie. "I can't think of a soul, Minnie. Can he tell us anything at all?"

Callie imagined the woman shaking her head. "No. Maybe tomorrow."

"Any idea when he can come home?"

"Couple days, they say." Minnie left the conversation hanging, maybe collecting herself.

"Need me to bring you anything?" Callie asked.

"No." More silence.

"Well, call me if you need me. I'm here for both of you."

"Uh huh." The call disconnected.

Poor Monty. She couldn't think about him without thinking how riled he'd been ever since he lost his badge. He hadn't been thinking straight, and worse, he thought he'd let Callie down, which was anything but the case. The accusations flying around the island would make him so much worse.

He wasn't materialistic in the least, so he wasn't seeking treasures of any kind, so why else hunt but for his badge? The question, however, would have to wait until he could speak.

Her ongoing concern was that if someone overtly did this to him, did they consider themselves successful in the attempt . . . or a failure? Was the damage done that was intended, or had they intended more?

Most of all, she was struggling not to pin both fires on Monty. Webb and Janet had made that leap all too easily. How long before others did as well? Or already did . . . and were they right?

Pushing hair back, the sweat holding it there, she found El Marko's entrance unlocked. Leave it to Mark to welcome walk-ins before opening time.

The air-conditioning hit her like a wall, a very welcomed wall, shooting a shiver under her damp clothes, a vent overhead making the red, green, and yellow fringed streamers dance. The scents of cumin, cilantro, garlic, and onion weren't strong this early but were recognizable enough to trigger hunger. The background music had been set to low. She made her way back to Mark's private table against the kitchen wall and used a napkin to wipe her temples. Two customers already nursed iced drinks at a table

A waitress scooted out of the kitchen, aware of the couple already seated per the appetizer on her tray, but she jolted at the site of Callie. "Oh, I am so sorry. Didn't hear you come in." Callie had been there enough times as Mark's date and friend for his staff to define her differently from the other customers, an extra attention she didn't relish. She'd been a mayor's daughter her entire life, her mother Beverly the current mayor of Middleton, and privilege went against her grain.

Callie shook her head. "No rush. Tell Mark I'm here, please, and when you get a chance, an ice-cold glass of water would be phenomenal. It's already like an oven out there."

"Yes, ma'am."

Ma'am. The word flowed off the young woman's tongue. Callie grew up Southern, but her fifteen years in Boston caused her to forget about the genteel quality of the Carolinas, making her appreciate its customs all the more. She liked how Mark ran his restaurant, too. His staff didn't turn over as often as the other eateries, and people lined up for the rare job opening. He vowed to keep people employed year round, but after only seven months open, only time would determine his ability to manage that; however, Callie could tell they loved working for him.

She closed her eyes a moment, listening to the kitchen noises, wondering which one belonged to Mark.

"Hey, you aren't falling asleep on me, are you?" Two ice waters had arrived, carried by Mark.

She smiled, suddenly aware of how sluggish she was . . . and unsure what to say to him. "Don't let me take you away from prepping for lunch."

He shook his head. "We got it covered. Dinner is busier." He set out the glasses and took his seat. "How'd it go last night? I started to come see if I could help." He crossed arms on the table. "But after our discussion on the swing, I didn't want to interfere."

First, she drank her water, genuinely parched, legitimately hot, and, once quenched, royally embarrassed. "I might've overreacted about that. This is your property, and you feel the need to protect it. Sorry about laying all that on you."

"But the threat was directed at you, and I should've noted that," he said.

Now she really felt bad. Even if he was right, he was doing all he could to put her at ease.

He brushed a finger over her hand, the lightest touch. The man was a master at subtleties. "I hate to think that some incident like that could turn things clumsy between us," he said.

"It didn't," she said, when it definitely had. *Why did she say that?*

Because he was being magnanimous, the bigger person, without even having to *try* to be the better one. Then just like that, she wasn't bothered by it anymore. There was no point.

However, that didn't mean they'd taken their couple-hood to a higher level, which planted little ice shards in her blood. She wished they could live in the moment.

"I got in awful late last night, too tired to do much more than fall into bed, barely taking time to shed my clothes," she said.

"Should've woken me," he said. "I'd have helped."

She chuckled. "You looked so deep in sleep I hadn't the heart to disturb you. Being dark we couldn't see everything at the scene last night, so I had to meet Leon there this morning before the contractor showed." Recanting her late-night and early-morning activities only served to make her want a nap. The heat had sucked more life out of her, and not having breakfast had ebbed her energy even more.

"You look tired," he said. "You need more than water." He waved over the waitress. "Put in a breakfast order for the chief, please. Minus the peppers and onions."

The girl nodded and entered the kitchen door not four feet away. This might be Mark's private table, but he'd strategically chosen the one the public wouldn't particularly like. No point in occupying valuable real estate. He didn't mind the kitchen door opening and closing behind his chair, the closeness giving him a better ear as to how his establishment was running.

"What's the breakfast order?" Callie asked, surprised she hadn't heard of this before. The SeaCow restaurant was the epi-center for breakfast on Edisto Beach, across the road and within view of El Marko's.

"You'll see. It's my go-to if someone asks." He rubbed her forearm lightly with a finger. "How is Monty?"

At first she was a little stunned about his awareness of Monty. "You've heard already?" She hadn't had a chance to say who was hurt in the dumpster, but apparently enough people were already aware of the incident.

Thank you, Brice.

"Yeah," Mark said. "The staff wanted to start a collection to help him out with medical bills. My cook already decorated a big gallon pickle jar we're going to place on the bar. Everyone's aware of his financial limitations and are eager to help."

That was Edisto's nature. They pitched in in a skinny minute. George and Pink's was a fourth-generational farmer's market on the island, and a couple years ago their home burned to the ground. The community fundraising effort rebuilt them a new home, the ribbon cutting not a month ago.

"But I preferred talking to you first before we put out the jar," he said.

She lightly laughed. "That's up to y'all, Mark."

One brow raised, and he ensured nobody walked within hearing range. "I also heard he was the only person out there. Tell me about this fire. The one last night, not yesterday." He gave a short huff. "Hmm, that's rather unsettling to say, isn't it?"

"Yeah, three fires in two days is hard to fathom for Edisto Beach."

His eyes widened. "Three?"

Her sarcastic smirk tried to make light of the mention, but she still felt the need to whisper in reply. "The first was a reckless bucket incident in Brice's storage room. Linseed oil and rags. Fires two and three are the serious concern."

He looked wary. "Expect Brice to blame whoever did the others."

Palms up, she nodded. "Not his call. Leon and I deemed it an accident, sending Brice off the deep end."

"Any chance it wasn't an accident?"

Her reflex answer was to say no, but his asking told her there might be room for doubt. Someone had been watching from the neighboring house, but since when were nosy neighbors suspects?

Brice swore he did everything right, but he couldn't deny leaving oily rags wadded in a bucket, prime for combustion on a hot day. There was no other conclusion since he couldn't think of who might harbor malicious intent. Prank value? Maybe.

"Still, he'll be back," Mark said. "Is SLED coming to help on the others?" He had retired from SLED with some sort of disability retirement and a story Callie hadn't heard yet.

"Nope," she said. "SLED's not coming."

Mark's sneakered foot nudged hers. "Want me to make some calls? I might be able to change their minds."

"No, not sure I even want them here."

"Might I ask why? Only curious, mind you."

"Their sluggishness in deciding to come yesterday shows that if they come today it will be reluctantly, and the dumpster would sound like a prank to them," she said. "This is my territory. Edistonians rely on me. I have them more at heart."

He waited to see if she intended to add anything to that, then asked, "But you don't see the dumpster as an out-of-hand practical joke?"

"No, I don't. Monty diving into a dumpster that catches fire, at midnight, isn't making the first lick of sense. Especially with him already hurt from his earlier moped accident. Something enticed him hard to make a special trip into town in the middle of the night."

"Any persons of interest beside him?"

"Not for the dumpster fire. The badge found on the Myrtle Street scene doesn't look particularly good either."

"Hey, I'm all ears if you want to run over the details," he said, smiling up at the waitress when she set chips and salsa on the table. "And I'm keen to your opinion, Chief. I've seen you work before, remember. I'll be your CI, traffic coordinator, forensics, or investigator. Name what you need. I've about done it all."

Mark's investigative experience wasn't lost on her, and Callie relied on his input quite often when she needed validation . . . or sometimes redirection. Between him and Stan, they succinctly told her when she overlooked something, spun off wrong, took someone's remark too seriously, or not seriously enough. It was nice having friends with the same skill set so handy on a beach with a limited department and no budget to hire much more than beat cops.

Breakfast arrived.

"Hold the *all ears* a moment," he said, scanning the meal for shortcomings. He deemed it worthy, thanked the waitress, and motioned for Callie to eat.

The plate held four quesadillas, beautifully toasted.

"You've told me you didn't like Huevos Rancheros because of the peppers. Nor do you like salsa in the morning. So here you go. Chorizo, cheese, and egg quesadillas." He reached over and snared one. "They made enough for me to sample, of course." He took a huge bite, sucking in at the bit of heat remaining from the skillet. "Better blow on it first."

Being hot, the first quesadilla went down slowly, but nothing went cold before she finished the others, with a cup of coffee mysteriously appearing halfway through.

"I think we were supposed to split the meal in half," Mark said, laughing as she chewed the last bite.

"You work in the kitchen everyday around this stuff. I'm not apologizing for taking advantage. Ummm, that was incredible," she said. "I could almost marry you for the food alone."

She froze.

He froze . . . then tried not to be obvious by diverting his attention to moving the empty plate aside.

That was the last thing she ever expected to say to him. Particularly after thinking for the last twenty-four hours about how to put on the brakes. She was too tired to trust her words now.

"I'm not holding you to that," he said, but his words didn't quite have their usual jovial nature. "I keep telling you there's no proposal on the table. I want you comfortable around me, Callie, not obligated. Absolutely not tentative."

He could read her like a book, sometimes interpreting her faster than she could form the thought. The book metaphor was a common joke between them, having originated the first morning she'd awoken with him sharing her bed, her second-guessing what the hell she'd done. He'd teased what an easy read she was and kidded how he was a fast reader, which he was. He read people quite capably, from his years on the job. He probably felt he had her issues pegged.

He still didn't know about her fire phobia, though.

He knew some about Seabrook but little about her husband John and the incredibly dark couple of years after. She hadn't wanted to chase him off sounding PTSD damaged. This beach was too small to avoid people.

Stan had pushed them toward each other from day one. Her reluctance to forge a concrete relationship dove a lot deeper than losing Seabrook.

"Let's start from the top, with the first *real* fire," she said, feeling more comfortable talking about subjects like arson, breaking and entering, even attempted murder.

After discussing the jewelry heists, she brought activities back around to the dumpster meeting that morning, delivering nothing more than facts. The who, what, when, and where of everything, but not the why and much of the how. She hushed and waited for his interpretation.

"Everything points to Monty," he said.

"Right," she replied, "but I'm not going there yet. I don't see that kid doing this. He has no priors. He sees himself as law enforcement. He's proud of working on these houses, even offered to return his pay to Webb after the Myrtle fires. Trust me, it's not him."

"Well, I'm pretty sure I'm not putting that collection jar on the bar quite yet," he said. "You'll want to talk to your officers who were guarding Myrtle about who they saw coming and going. The contractor, Webb you say? Yeah, he's suspect number two. But Callie, I'm sure you realize. . . ." He left the rest unsaid, ending on a *hmm* knowing she could finish the sentence.

"Monty," she said. "But you don't know him like I do."

"Those are the hardest ones to deal with," he replied, adding, "the ones we know, I mean."

She slowly sipped down the last of her coffee. "I know. Listen, I gotta go."

She'd already stood, like always, feeling guilty not paying the tab, but Mark had nixed the issue enough times for it not to be a matter for discussion any longer.

"Chief," came a call from the front.

Thomas hustled across the room, his expression serious. Her heart fell at what else could've happened while she ate quesadillas. She hoped to God Brice wasn't involved or he'd label her negligent on the job again. How dare she eat, sleep, or do anything but police his island! Peeing practically warranted disciplinary action.

Shameful how that man had to pop into her mind before she wondered what the heck was wrong.

Thomas got up close and leaned in. "Mr. Hutchins called me. The old man who lives on 174 about two miles out? He's on his way to the station to see you."

Odd. "What's the problem?" It wasn't unusual for a civilian to call their cop of choice, and Thomas was often that cop out here, but to then ask for the chief?

"He's bringing Monty's basket. Apparently, it fell off his moped when he wrecked yesterday evening. Said you needed to see it."

She headed toward the door. Then, in afterthought, she went back and gave Mark a quick kiss.

"Meet me here for dinner," he said. "I'll be thinking on this for you."

"Thanks, kind sir," and the endearment made him smile.

She accompanied Thomas out the door. He'd parked his patrol car next to hers. "Hey," Callie said, before he reached his vehicle. "I sort of dropped my phone in a puddle."

He raised a sceptic brow. "The same one?"

Her sheepish grin gave the answer.

He came around his car to hers. "Give it here, and I'll see what I can do. When did it happen?"

She retrieved it from her glove box, and even to her it looked rather lifeless. "Um, during the storm yesterday."

"It's been sitting there wet all this time?" he exclaimed.

Another sheepish grin.

He snorted in jest. "Don't hold out much hope this time, Chief. This phone has probably breathed its last."

Nothing would surprise her anymore, and a dead phone fell low on her list of issues. Right now she headed to the station, wondering what Mr. Hutchins had that was so urgent . . . worrying how badly it would make Monty look.

Chapter 18

WHEN CALLIE WALKED into the police station, Marie had the elder Mr. Hutchins in a chair next to her desk, a cold bottle of Coke in his hand, a shopping bag on the floor stretched from its contents and standing up on its own between his feet. "Hey, Chief," they both said, in a staggered unison.

"Hey," Callie said. "Mr. Hutchins, come on into my office. Sorry I wasn't here, but I've been out most the night and had to jump back at it about dawn. Thomas told me you requested my presence, so here I am."

"Ma'am, I'm an old man, retired longer than most people been working. I already figured you'd be busy. I had my son drop me off, and then I sent him home, telling him how much safer could I be than waiting in a police station, in the air-conditioning. Said I'd call him when I finished my business. Your helper here has been keeping me entertained and"—he held up the soft drink—"refreshed."

Marie gave a quirky look at her boss. "He's the one keeping me entertained. He tells the best stories about this island, Chief, and I thought I'd heard them all. Get him to tell you about the haint on Raccoon Island."

The gentleman must have a sharp mind and sharper memory to beat Marie on Edisto stories unless she only courted his favor. Callie led the way, and Mr. Hutchins rose, took his bag, and lumbered in. Callie left the door ajar for better circulation. The outside temp was already low nineties, the humidity making everybody and everything that dared outside sticky and spent. Even inside, one could feel the dominance of summer.

Sitting in one of the two chairs across from her desk, in a room barely able to hold the three people the chairs were for, Mr. Hutchins held the bag in his lap, setting his Coke bottle on the edge of Callie's desk once she gave him a smiling nod of permission. "So, what can I do for you, sir?"

"Well. . . ." and he thought a moment. "That young man who lived with his mother on Oyster Factory Road wrecked during that God-awful storm and wound up in the weeds on the front of my property yesterday."

"I heard."

He grinned, admirably. "My Tia fixed him up pretty good. How's he doing?"

"Well, he got himself in another accident, Mr. Hutchins. He's at MUSC."

With an exaggerated tuck of his chin, he reared back. "Say what? Is he hurt bad?"

"Burned," she said. "He might come home in a couple days, or so I heard."

"Um, um, um. That boy can't catch a break, can he? His ankle and arm, losing his scooter, and now this." He leaned forward. "How's his momma? Those two are about joined at the hip and all each other's got. We know how that family is."

"She's with him," Callie said, wishing Mr. Hutchins would let her get to the purpose of the meeting, but she'd been raised to talk the personal niceties first before jumping into the meat of a discussion. The first made a lot of difference on how successful the latter would be. "She's hugging close to his bed. I've talked to her."

His smile pushed wrinkles around his mouth, moving his worry aside. "Chief, you're a good-un. We're lucky you finally moved here. I met your daddy a few times before he passed, and he seemed to be a good-un, too."

The mention of Lawton Cantrell softened her. She'd give anything for him to walk in the station and admire his daughter in her role. They'd been close. He was her Captain. She was his Scallywag.

Niceties like this took place for serious reason . . . to remove the edges of communication and build a bridge between the communicators. Besides, island time was nicknamed Edi-slow for a reason. Those in a hurry were reminded of the bridge across which they came to get here, and how easy it was to go back. Finally, Callie had decided they'd made sufficient small talk to cover all bases. "About your bag there, Mr. Hutchins?"

"Oh, oh, I'm so sorry." His words were soft spoken and melted into each other. Such a kind man. He opened the bag, reached in, and lifted out a basket, holding it over for her.

Callie held off taking it, moved his Coke out of the way, along with some folders and a pen cup, and motioned for him to set it on her desk. She said nothing. He needed to connect the item to the incident without her direction.

When he didn't talk, he did a slow wave of a hand. "Belongs to the boy. Belongs to Monty," he said, clarifying. "Came off his scooter when he wrecked."

Spots of mud clung to it here and there, but Mr. Hutchins had cleaned up the exterior. One zip tie was missing, the lid hanging askew, a hole having ripped through the weave while the second worn black tie held on.

"Did you look inside?" she asked.

His thin, almost bald head moved side to side, but also all which-aways in his emphasis to speak. "My son wanted to, but I told him no. Whatever's in there belongs to that boy and 'tain't our business."

"Find anything that spilled out?" she asked, in an afterthought reaching in her desk drawer for a pair of evidence gloves.

Mr. Hutchins's eyes widened at the gloves. "No, ma'am." Then he hushed, choosing to only watch.

Callie could read his thoughts. She'd read people like him a long time. What could start innocently as a good Samaritan returning a lost object could slide into something criminal by simple possession of it. Throw in the authority figure slipping on blue latex gloves, and tensions raised. Folks either got super curious at times like this or incredibly leery, wondering how any of this would rub off on them. Mr. Hutchins fell into the latter.

Callie stood and lifted the lid, laying it back, releasing a whiff of stale dampness.

They had no lab or CSI affair on the tiny island. Not even a one-man jail. Improvising, she opened a cabinet behind her and pulled a clean trash bag off a roll and spread it over her desk blotter. She reached into the basket to lay out each item, one by one to take inventory . . . and to read Mr. Hutchins.

First came sunglasses in an old-fashioned case with rusted hinges. Then a key chain on a long lanyard, protecting one single key which Callie guessed was to a house. A dirty, mostly used tube of sunscreen, a ruined travel-sized tissue pack, and a miniature first aid kit missing most of its Band-Aids. She sensed a lot of Minnie in these items.

Discretely, Callie stole looks at Mr. Hutchins. He hung on each second of the discovery, staring at the items as if he expected gold bars or a brick of cash to appear. Or worse, anything that might point to him in a poor light.

Callie hesitated, finding something she hadn't expected. She lifted a dainty chain, clasped closed.

Her heart fell at the insinuation of finding it.

Mr. Hutchins's hands went palms high. "I had no idea that was in there."

"It's okay, sir. Not saying you did."

Without much effort, she identified the piece as Amelia Cash's missing diamond bracelet . . . especially when it appeared looped through Anna Calder's college ring. And with a little more teasing, the bracelet broke free from a cloth in the bottom, and it came up circled inside the clasped Damascene necklace. Each piece of jewelry protected the other from getting lost. She left them connected as she laid them on the desk.

She kept searching, strategically lifting a small leather change purse and a wet t-shirt wadded in the bottom, fast mildewing from the stink. Holding it up, she let it drop loose and fall open to make sure nothing was hung up in it. That was it.

Jesus, Monty.

The necklace's antiquity was unmistakable in the small scenes in the seven plaques, but even dirty, it displayed more beauty than she'd imagined from Dud's description. A gold-and-black enamel snow-capped mountain hung front and center, and up the sides were scenes of birds, cherry blossom trees, and pagodas.

Mr. Hutchins waited for more, looking from basket to Callie, then back again. "Is that it?"

"Yes, sir, appears to be. And you never looked inside? Never took anything out or put something in?"

With lots of animation in his denial, he almost scooted his chair back with his antics. "No, no, no. Never seen any of this stuff. We picked the basket up, wiped off the outside, and put it in this bag. Went by the Bartow house first, but after finding nobody home, I suggested we bring it here."

Thank goodness for that, at least. Still, no telling if the basket contents had been pilfered, jostled from the fall, or even recreated to hint at guilt.

"Who's *we?*" she asked.

"Me and my son," he said. "And he didn't do nothing either."

Something told her they'd seen the jewelry and opted to pass the basket on to the authorities, which was fine, but if she were Monty's attorney, and was cutthroat enough, she'd insert enough doubt in that chain of custody to remove as much blame from Monty as possible.

Look at her, already thinking about Monty's defense . . . after she had to arrest him.

"Thanks for bringing this in, Mr. Hutchins. Do you need Marie to call your ride or do you have a cell phone?"

The man stood, eager to leave. "I have my phone," he said, reaching into his pants pocket. He opened the little flip mobile, fat and tiny compared to the current sleek smartphones.

She'd meant for him to go outside and call for his ride so she could make calls of her own. She silently waved and mouthed *thank you*. He only waved back while talking, his son wanting to hear the details right then and there, and he sat back down to relay his tale.

Okay. On to Plan B. Callie put the basket in its own separate trash bag, then after snapping pictures of everything, she dropped the connected jewelry into an evidence bag, the remaining items in others as Mr. Hutchins watched from his phone. Then she left the room with the empty basket and gave Marie the items inside to log into evidence.

She wasn't calling Minnie to announce her arrival. Monty might not be able to speak much, and his hands might be too bandaged to write, but if his face wasn't too covered, Callie could read him when he saw the basket. All evidence pointed to Monty as criminal, and even with him in the hospital, she needed to ask the hanging questions and officially note the reactions of both mother and son.

To think she'd hoped to catch a two-hour nap.

"I'll be at the Medical University Hospital talking to Monty and Minnie Bartow," she told Marie.

"You look awful tired," Marie replied. "Go over there on the sofa, or better yet, go home and grab a few winks."

But Callie wouldn't be caught dead napping on the sofa in plain sight of Edistonians during working hours. God, how that rumor would spread. And at present she had no home. Mark wasn't at *Reel Lucky* so that was an option, but the truth was she needed to address Minnie and Monty in the early stages of this double-fire, triple-heist series of crimes. Waiting around had bad optics. Waiting around also let people think harder about covering their tracks.

"I'll try to be back before you take off," Callie said, "but don't count on me." Meaning no appointments or promises to others.

Marie gave a small salute, hardly missing a beat from her keyboard.

Callie headed toward the door only for Brice to walk in before she reached it.

"How about the robberies?" he said.

Son of a bitch. Little did he know she held the stolen items right in front of him. "Brice, I have to be somewhere."

"Anywhere I'm not, right? Two fires now, yet you can't believe me when I say mine was set. These two fires are arson, right? Before you answer, I've already spoken to Leon."

She gave him her best concessionary bow. "Then you have your answer. He's the expert on fires."

Callie tried to pass him. He sidestepped into her way, and she stiffened. He leaned in. "Arrest that boy before the whole beach catches wind of his activities. And you better find that thief. We can't have this kind of crime spree, Chief Morgan. If you can't control this town, we can hire someone who can."

Nothing would please Callie more than pulling Brice aside and engaging in a verbal one-on-one, but it would serve no purpose. And they *could* replace her, but never in a hundred years would they find someone with her experience. Or so she kept telling herself.

However, she was fully aware that one of these days they might cut off their noses to spite their faces and hunt for someone else.

Enough of this. She'd had little sleep, robbing her of patience, diluting her resolve to be bigger and better than people like Brice.

"You're going nowhere until I hear about the burglaries," he said up close in her ear.

"I'll go where the hell I want . . . when I want . . . and when it comes to talking about crime on this beach, I decide who, when, why, and how I tell it," she uttered.

He tilted back, as if he had to get a better view of who this stranger was before him.

"Do you need a memo?" she repeated, her voice a hint louder.

Brice looked over at Marie, to make sure she heard. The officer manager held a phone to her ear.

But Callie didn't give a damn who heard. "Get out of my way, Brice. I have no time for your shit today." Not waiting for another round of barbs, she exited the station, heart pounding, a dull, sleep-deprived headache taking root.

But Brice wasn't about to let her leave. "Who the hell do you think you are?" he yelled from the entrance. She'd only made it halfway to her patrol car.

"I think I'm chief of Edisto Beach police," she yelled back. "Until I'm not. Take your best shot at making that happen."

The words weren't out before she noted the other people who heard. Leon and one of his volunteers stood outside the firehouse entrance. No chance Marie hadn't heard. Two walkers on Murray Street, right in front, strolled slower, listening for more. And as luck would have it, the clerk from Town Hall was returning to work, walking from her parking place.

"Be happy to," Brice hollered back. He continued saying something else, but Callie didn't hear. She'd gotten in her cruiser and shut the door, cranking the engine to make sure she didn't hear. She'd literally heard enough to understood that she'd said too much, but for some reason, this time she was coming awful close to not giving a damn.

Chapter 19

"HELLO, MINNIE." Callie entered the hospital room smiling. She set a box of chocolates, no nuts, on the bed table with one hand but said nothing about the big bag in her other. "These are for you, Monty. How do you feel?" She took a breath in afterthought and spoke back to his mother. "Is he supposed to talk?"

"Doc said not much, and only what he feels like. It's more like a hard whisper," Minnie said. More sedate in her appearance than usual, the woman was leery but open to visitors. Staring at four walls watching someone sleep could make one crave any kind of distraction.

"That's great," Callie said, meaning it. "May I sit a minute? I wanted to see how he's doing, update y'all on everything, and ask a few questions."

Minnie nodded, and Callie dragged a chair to the side of Monty's bed.

"You feeling up to me sitting with you a bit?"

He gave her a nod, and the smiling hurt his face from the starts and stops he made with his mouth, but he didn't complain.

"Well, we haven't found anything in the dumpster, and we haven't found anyone who might've caused the fire. Everyone on Edisto is thinking about you, though. I've had a lot of people ask how you're doing."

Everyone loved to be missed.

"Monty," she said, easy and slow, "did you go to the dumpster alone last night?"

He could answer that with a move of his head so he didn't have to talk. He gave a yes.

"Excellent. Thank you. Did you see anyone else while you were out there?"

Negative this time.

"Think hard, Monty. It was real dark last night. I might've driven past if not for the fire. I do not know how in the world you drove your bike in the dark that far. Are you sure you didn't see anybody? Nod if you are sure."

He obliged.

"Did you use a flashlight or maybe light a fire so you could see better?"

Lifting a heavily bandaged hand, he did a slow side-to-side movement.

"Flashlight?"

A nod.

"Did you light a fire in the dumpster? Maybe on wood scraps?"

"No," he said, catching Callie by surprise. The words came out stronger than she anticipated. "Did not set the fire."

"Okay, okay," she said, almost patting him to soothe the moment, then patting the mattress instead. "What were you hunting for in the dumpster?"

Licking his lips, he answered, "My badge."

"Your badge? Why would you go in the middle of the night, without telling anyone, to hunt your badge?"

He sighed at her complex question, leaving him so much to answer to.

"You're making him talk too much. Reword the question," Minnie said.

Callie shrugged and apologized. "What made you go there?" she said.

"Phone call," he said in a raspy whisper. "Said my badge was in the dumpster." He swallowed, and the chief grabbed the water glass with a straw in it, giving him a sip. "I cannot help you without my badge."

Minnie glowered. Callie expected some pushback from Mama Bear but had hoped not this soon. Minnie wasn't fond of Monty playacting police and was shrewd enough to see that nobody took him seriously doing it. On top of it all, the badge now had served as a magnet to his potential demise.

The misunderstanding, the bait of the badge—the whole mess hurt Callie's heart, and she couldn't blame Minnie for resenting her and the department. Minnie might not be able to take out her anger on the unknown culprit who set her son on fire, but she could condemn the police for implanting his desire to serve them.

Callie could attempt to mitigate, and Monty needed to hear a positive message. "Oh, Monty. It's not the badge that makes a police officer. It's his head, his heart, and his desire to serve and protect. I'm sorry this happened. We can always get you another badge."

Monty's reaction, minimal as it was, conveyed a happiness . . . while Minnie's mood only darkened.

Callie tried to continue their conversation. "Do you know who called you about the badge?"

He shrugged.

"But they said they saw your badge in the dumpster?"

A nod.

"You rode your bike all the way there in the dark. That's incredible, Monty, but also scary. Once you got there and climbed in the dumpster, did someone throw gasoline on you?"

"Yes," he said, gazing down into the sheets, realizing he'd been duped. "Smelled it."

"Somebody set him up and went after him, you mean," Minnie said. "I done told the boy enough times not to dumpster dive for stuff. Someone took advantage of knowing he looked in dumpsters. What the hell are you gonna do about this, Miss Almighty Police Chief? How am I to take this boy home with someone wanting him dead?"

Callie cringed at that last part, a concern Monty did not need to hear. Not now and not here.

Monty loved dumpsters, having found one of his moped baskets in one. Even Sophie had found a small table for her porch at one down the street. A lot of Edistonians took a gander in a dumpster, often on site of any of a dozen repair jobs on the beach.

Anger built a fury in Callie at what had almost happened to Monty. She would fight to solve this, but she didn't need to express herself openly in front of him, nor in front of Minnie, incensed enough on her own accord.

Simply put, the man was set on fire. Someone had called him, baited him with finding the badge, and lured him into the dumpster.

Only Monty was quicker than they calculated and smarter than they perceived. He might have a fifteen-year-old's thought processes, but his adult reflexes had worked in his favor escaping the fire.

Minnie looked about ready to boot Callie out, but this conversation wasn't over. Callie lifted the sack and set it on the edge of the bed, Monty watching it closely, Minnie as attentive. Methodically, Callie lowered the bag from the top, exposing half the basket without letting the dirty item soil his hospital sheets.

Monty's face lit up. "My basket!" Coarse sounding, but he identified the broken basket as his.

"Where'd you find it?" Minnie asked, hesitant about where the conversation headed.

But Callie remained fixed on Monty, only talking to him. This next part of their chat was important. "Mr. Hutchins found it on his land, and when you weren't home, he brought it to me. Wasn't that nice?"

Monty tried to touch it, forgetting about his bandages. "Yes."

"Do you remember what was in it?" she asked.

Pointing toward the broken lid, he acted like he hadn't heard.

"Yes," she said, "it appears one of your plastic ties came off, but that's easily mended." She let him picture that a moment. "Monty, listen to me. Look at me."

He did.

"Do you remember what you had in this basket before the accident?"

"Sunglasses. . . ." He thought hard.

"Yes, those were still in there. Go on."

"A t-shirt, in case I messed up what I was wearing. My house key." He looked at her, panicked.

"The key is in there, Monty. Keep thinking."

He relaxed, mentioned the tissues, then shrugged.

"First aid kit," Minnie added.

"Yeah," he said, looking over at her.

Callie opened her phone to photos and showed him the pictures she'd taken. He watched her scroll, agreeing with bobs of his head, pleased at his meager belongings being found.

Callie had to be careful here. While some cops liked to take advantage of people in the hospital, so easily cornered and questioned, their guard often down due to medication, Callie wasn't so inclined. She was judging behavior more than anything else here, and thus far she was seeing an innocent man. She debated on whether to show him the jewelry, whether to wait for his pain meds to dissipate, maybe even until he found an attorney. Too many people on Edisto were beginning to hear his name associated with the fires and thefts.

Minnie got a call, her gaze darting from phone to her son in the bed.

"Take it, Minnie," Callie said. "I'll stop asking questions, sit here, and keep him company."

Moving to the corner of the room, Minnie answered.

Keeping an eye and ear on the mother, Callie turned Monty's

attention to the broken lid, telling him how it could be fixed.

"Wait a minute, Nell." Turning back toward Callie and Monty, stone-faced, Minnie put the phone on speaker. "You bleeped out there a moment. Say that again?" She held out the phone.

"Everyone's saying he got careless setting fires and burned himself to a crisp," said the caller whose distinctive voice Callie quickly recognized as belonging to a woman who worked in a souvenir shop. "They say he's set a half dozen fires so far, and it was a good thing he messed up or there might've been more."

Minnie returned toward the wall, but not before Nell added, ". . . and he stole jewelry worth thousands of dollars. Where would he sell something like that, Minnie? Wanted to give you a heads up before the police come chasing you. That Morgan woman has a reputation for catching whoever she's after. Make sure—"

The call was taken off speaker. "I've got to go," Minnie said low. "Let me know if you hear anything else."

Coming back to the foot of the bed, Minnie's previously plain complexion held ample color, her eyes steely. "How dare you." Kathy Bates couldn't have said the line any chillier . . . or harder.

Callie's first concern was Monty, but when she twisted to see him, he focused on his bandaged hands drawn up in his lap. "Monty, I'm not here to blame you—"

"Quit talking to my son," Minnie yelled. "I'm his guardian, and you have no right. I may not have a PhD, but I have enough sense to tell you to back off and be well within my right, and his, to do so."

Holding still, Callie selectively chose her words. "No need to get upset, Minnie. Sit. Let's talk about what's fact and what isn't. That caller didn't exactly have her facts straight."

"Shut up!"

The yell took Callie aback and sent Monty burrowing into his sheets. Minnie swept her hand across the tray table, slinging the plate's half-eaten macaroni and cheese and Jell-O toward Callie.

Callie dodged the most of it, the noodles, cheese, and red slime finding home on the wall. "Stop it, Minnie."

"You phony! You're trying to frame my boy!"

On her feet and on her way toward the mother, Callie attempted to talk first. "Quite the opposite. I'm seeking the truth, and the only way to find it is to ask you and Monty questions."

A nurse poked her head in the door, saw the food splatters, the angry mother, and the cringing patient and disappeared.

Puffed up like a toad, the mother seethed, her breathing forced and fuming. "You can't do your job so you blame a poor, handicapped boy. My boy. He's gotten hurt twice trying to please you. Trying to be like you. And you turn all that against him when you can't find who really broke the law."

Minnie's fist reared back, projecting enough for Callie to easily move out of the way. "Stop it, Minnie," she said in a firmness warning of repercussions. The woman had pounds on her but no knowledge on how to use them, but they didn't need violence of any manner on a hospital floor. Nor in front of Monty.

Her heart ached seeing him balled up, tears on his cheeks.

Two security officers rushed in, the culpable party unmistakable. They grabbed Minnie's arms and looked to Callie for information.

"Edisto Beach Police Chief Callie Morgan," she said. "Came to pay my respects, but this boy's mother here is pretty distressed over what happened to him. Understandable. It's still an open case."

The shorter of the two security guards, being half as wide as he was tall, spoke like he called the shots. "These things can be stressful, ma'am," he said to Minnie, but to Callie, "More than happy to call Charleston PD," he said, as if he held Public Enemy Number One in his grasp. The second officer cinched in his grip on the other side of Minnie, in an echo of the offer.

Callie shook her head, but while they held Minnie, Callie went to Monty, leaned over, and told him to get better, and returned the basket to its bag. Turning to the guards, she said, "No need. Release her. Might be better all around that I leave." She stood there to ensure her request was honored.

The short guard lightened his hold. "Can you assure us you'll behave?" he asked Minnie. "We cannot have such outbursts in a hospital. A lot of sick people are in these rooms, and they don't need this." He dipped his head toward Monty. "He especially doesn't need this. Hear me? Can I get a promise from you to be civil while you're on these grounds?"

Her cheeks' capillaries spidery in fluster, Minnie gave them a flat, "Yes. I promise."

"Are you sure?" the guard continued.

Callie read the flare in Minnie's fixation on her. "Yes, she's sure," Callie said.

They let Minnie loose. "Remember, I'll escort you off this property in a heartbeat," the short guard added.

Shifting her dress and sweater back into place, Minnie seemed to have taken her emotion down a few notches. She sniffled and took another breath for good measure. "I'm upset about my boy, is all. You'll have no more trouble from me."

Smiling at the officers, Callie indicated she'd take it from here, and they left. She didn't have a chance to make her own exit before Minnie spoke, teeth clenched. "You do not talk to my boy again. Anywhere. Not without me."

With a final glance at Monty, who'd loosened up but remained wary, Callie told them goodbye.

Waiting at the elevator, Callie noted the reflection of the taller guard in the polished doors. "That could've been worse," he said, making conversation.

"Yeah, thanks for your help," she said, thinking it could have gone a hell of sight better, too. Would take her a long time to mend that bridge, but the bigger concern was Monty. Poor guy.

In her car, Callie made Marie aware she was leaving the hospital, a routine call, but Marie wouldn't let her go. "Callie," she said. "Rumors are flying about Monty. Brice is shooting off his mouth to anyone who'll listen."

Damn that idiot, a man who could think of nobody but himself. No wonder his wife got tired of him.

She needed to talk to a lot of people today and put some of these pieces together. She didn't wish another fire on anyone, but dang if that wouldn't prove Monty innocent with him pent up in the hospital. There was a niggling in her saying these crimes weren't his, and like any crime on Edisto Beach, they were time sensitive. All too often, though mostly misdemeanors, crime was performed by visitors, and since visitors stayed on a Sunday-to-Saturday routine on a beach with only private rentals and no motels, criminals came and went on a schedule. Anything Callie investigated could fall apart come Saturday.

This was Thursday.

"Marie, get Raysor to take those evidence bags I gave you to Colleton County's forensics with as much rush on it as he can for the prints. They can schedule DNA, but I don't expect quick results."

"Got it."

"And call Gerard and Thomas. I need to speak to both today about their handling of the Myrtle Street fire. Gerard first. Have him there by the time I arrive. I'll call in Thomas later."

Marie didn't salute back so quickly this time. "Are they in trouble?" Only Marie could get away with asking.

"No, but what they saw could be important so tell them to have their thinking caps on."

She chuckled. "They'll be scared to death."

Callie only wanted them sharp, and their memories sharper.

Two down and three to go.

The car headed southeast toward home. She left a message for Stan to meet her at El Marko's for dinner at seven. She'd call Raysor in a minute, allowing Marie to do her thing first. That left Alex and her reporting expertise . . . meaning everything she'd seen and recorded on Myrtle.

The call to Alex went straight to voice mail. Callie left a simple message. "This is Chief Morgan. Something's come up. Need your help." Too little and it wouldn't sound important. Too much and Alex might talk herself out of returning the call.

Callie might like the girl thanks to her history on Edisto Beach, with her grandmother somewhat of a homespun saint, but she hated journalists. Alex knew it. Time to see which Alex replied . . . the Edisto girl or the reporter.

Didn't take Alex two minutes to call back. Callie put it on speaker, needing both hands on the wheel as she ate up highway to get home.

"What's up, Chief? Find your arsonist?"

"Not yet," Callie replied. "To do so I need a favor from you. Can I see your raw footage from that day of the fire?"

"Which part?"

"Any and all of it," she said.

"Why should I?"

Alex's trademark personality was sass, and Callie gave it a pass. "To help us find an arsonist before he hits anyone else . . . to include your grandmother's place. This is your home turf."

Alex didn't immediately respond. Callie had touched a spot. "I heard about the robberies and the second fire," Alex said. "Heard Monty Bartow is responsible, is that true?"

"Is that the only rumor you heard?" Callie replied, choosing not to correct the girl that these were burglaries, not robberies. Robberies were person on person. "Somebody's channeling only what they want you to hear, Alex." Meaning Brice, most likely. "I'd think you'd want facts to avoid embarrassment. Send me the footage, let me solve this thing, and you'll be the first correspondent to know. I'll even try to call you for the perp walk when they're cuffed. No promises, mind you."

She could almost hear Alex thinking. "You believe the arsonist was watching the fire that day."

Actually, Callie didn't see this person as some crazed opportunist or deranged mental case. The burglaries made this appear more measured. There was the off chance Alex caught the perp, but this footage could also give Monty an alibi during the jewelry heists. The footage could show a lot of things or absolutely nothing, but Callie had to try.

"Give me your email," Alex said. "It's probably more than you expected."

"The more the merrier. Thanks, Alex. I'll—"

". . . owe me one?"

"Yes."

Okay, twenty more minutes of driving.

She called Deputy Raysor. Sometimes she wondered if Colleton County had forgotten about him being on loan to Edisto Beach until she reminded herself he was related to a third of the county. He picked up on the second ring. He was always good to pick up. He liked to sound inconvenienced. "Yeah."

"Marie get you?" Callie asked without salutation.

"Yeah. Headed there now."

"Can you talk to me at the same time?"

He growled. "What, you calling me a moron or something? What's up?"

"Take me to the day of the fire."

"Listening."

"You were manning the southern end of those two blocks on Myrtle, diverting traffic."

"Right."

"How long were you there?"

"Until the fire trucks left."

It was times like these when she adored a man of few words. Raysor was a master of abbreviated conversation.

"Did you ever see Monty Bartow? I mean at any time. I'm working on a timeline for him."

"Negative. Never came to my end of the street."

Meaning Monty came from the other end, the north end, the end closer to the burgled homes.

"Did you see Harbin Webb that day?" she asked.

She must've caught him off guard with that one, because he had to think.

"Nope. Didn't see him at all. He a person of interest?"

Callie had reached the big bridge and wished she had the time to enjoy the view of the Intercoastal Waterway. "Why?"

"My gut. He's a bit too self-absorbed for my taste."

"Not that I'm discounting your gut, as big and beautiful as it may be, you have anything more concrete than that?"

"He's a loner, doesn't share his business, and doesn't play well with others. Works alone."

Having watched Webb's distaste for Janet firsthand, she could see that. "Could you see him starting a fire?" she asked.

"Depends on the motive," he said.

"Can you see him burgling houses for jewelry?" she asked.

"Hmmm. My gut's telling me no on that one. Can't see him fencing jewelry for money. Too many easier avenues for him, I'd say. Plus, people are always wary about contractors robbing them. He's smarter than that."

That's what she was worried about. Webb might be smarter than people gave him credit for, but for the life of her, she couldn't find a motive either.

Signs still pointed to Monty.

"I'm at the station," he said. "About to carry this evidence to Walterboro. Need anything else?"

"No," she said. "Thanks. If you think of anything else, call me. Drive careful."

"Out," he said, hanging up. Again, a man of few words.

No doubt she'd pass Raysor in her return. She was past the Serpentarium on Highway 174.

Mulling over the loose ends, prodding her thoughts for motive, she kept pushing aside the pyromania theory that most people gravitated to. Those types of fires were maybe ten percent of fires set. The balance were set for insurance fraud, vandalism, and concealing other crimes. She wasn't casting aside the theory that someone set the fire and capitalized on it to steal the jewelry. The concept made the most sense. Why such a big fire, though, which would draw a horde and risk attention? And why not steal more than they did?

During the Christmas Secret Santa caper last December the thief stole one present from under the tree in each house he violated. Only one instead of raiding the whole cache of tempting, brightly colored gifts. The answer was a motive that took forever to define, having little to do with wanting to burgle a home. The mission was bigger and more personal.

Callie kept coming around to the burglaries being a distraction, or some sort of statement, not for monetary gain. People suspected Monty rummaged the dumpster to pilfer treasures, at which point a match or lighter had been mismanaged setting something volatile in the dumpster afire. However she'd learned someone baited him to go out there.

Whoever did this was still out there. They weren't a pro, but they weren't too damn stupid, either. With no clue as to their endgame, Callie was concerned about a repeat fire. Maybe even another attempted murder. On one hand, someone might be in over their head since Monty survived. On the other hand, they might feel smug and dare to do more. In either case, from her experience, things got worse at this stage before they got better.

Chapter 20

OFFICER GERARD VALENTINE was waiting for Callie when she entered the station. "My office," she said, leading the way. He tossed a questionable glance at Marie only to get a motherly look of pity in return.

Callie shut the door for privacy.

Gerard had worked Edisto for a year. After Seabrook and another officer, Francis Dickens, died within a week of each other, town council, in its earnest need to woo Callie to stay and fill the void in the police department, had hired three new uniforms. Two from Charleston and one from Wilmington. With limited upward mobility and even more limited pay-raise potential, the two in their forties left within six months. Council let her hire Gerard Valentine. She selected younger this time in hopes he'd stick around.

He sat before her desk, worry evident. He'd never been called in before.

"Gerard, I need your accounting for the day of the Myrtle Street fire. This is nothing disciplinary, by the way, so stop frowning. You make me want to mash out all those creases in your forehead. Did Marie stir you up like that? She loves messing with you guys."

He eased up somewhat. "Um, word has it that Brice is going to can you for the fires."

No way her surprise escaped him. Brice was accelerating his retribution, his embellished storytelling, whatever you called it. This was about as bad as he'd ever been. "Where'd you hear that?"

"From Brice, um, Mr. LeGrand. He contacted all of us."

Jesus. The others would blow him off. Raysor would've done more than that, and she bet Brice had skipped him, under the pretense he was on loan and not a real town employee.

What an ass. A pot stirrer of the highest order.

"Forget all that," she said. "This isn't the first time he's played this game. You're newer to it than the others."

He eased up more.

"Back to my asking you here, and I don't have a lot of time to waste on the likes of Brice LeGrand, okay?"

"Yes, ma'am."

"That day, your job was to go door to door and tell people to evacuate the houses on Myrtle, right?"

"Yes, ma'am. Or at least those on that block."

She accepted the correction. "Explain what you did and how you did it."

She could read him. He expected a complaint of some sort, and being in the dark, he wasn't sure how to respond. "Replay your actions for me," she said. "That's all."

"Well, I'd go to the door, knock, and tell them about the fire. I'd ask how many were in the house. Then I'd stand there until they exited, rushing them, of course, since some wanted to totally repack the house and bring it with them. I didn't go inside any of the houses."

She nodded, pleased with his response. He finished describing the logistics of his actions. Then she listed the three houses missing jewelry. *Ocean Potion, Vitamin Sea,* and *Salty Kiss.* Last names Cash, Calder, and Vaughn. Again, she limited the details, wanting him to fill in the blanks. "Do any of those stand out for you?"

"The houses or the people, ma'am?"

"Either. All. Any."

"I recall the houses. Do not recall the last names," he said.

"Did you watch them lock their doors?"

He hesitated. "No, ma'am. Once they were outside, my job was done. I rushed to the next house. I was the only one, ma'am."

"That's okay, Gerard. That's okay." He sure was nervous. How hard had Brice come down on him? Made her wonder if Brice had warned Gerard to choose sides.

He commenced to discussing each house's reaction. "Lots of people in *Ocean Potion.* That one took a bit. Just couples in *Vitamin Sea,* and they cooperated better than most. Nobody answered at *Salty Kiss.*"

"You didn't escort anyone out of *Salty Kiss*? That would've been Dudley Vaughn, a man in his eighties."

"I'd have remembered him, Chief. Maybe family or friends had already collected him."

But he had no friends or family to see to his safety. He hadn't left at all, probably hiding in the kitchen, in the furthest reaches from the front door and out of view of windows across the porch.

"Did you ever see Monty Bartow in your coverage of that end of the block?" she asked.

"The guy you're liking for all this?" he replied.

Her scowl pulled him in check. "I'm not ready to *like* anyone quite yet, officer. Answer the question, please."

Accepting his error, he shook his head, eager to appease. "Never saw him."

"What about Harbin Webb?"

He hesitated. "Sorry, Chief, but who is he?" With barely a year under his belt, he hadn't nailed the names of all the residents and business owners, much less the myriad of contractors and subs.

"A contractor," she said. "And don't go spreading that name around."

"No, ma'am. And I'm sorry, but he could've walked right past me, and I'd have never known," he said. She held out a driver's license photo of Webb, and Gerard still denied any recollection.

Gerard appeared to have done his job, and Callie thanked him, assuring him all was good before releasing him. She liked the guy, and how well he kept his mouth shut would determine if she should like him even more.

Thanks to him, she had to go back and see Dudley Vaughn, who hadn't been exactly forthcoming.

At almost four thirty on a Thursday night, the day had zipped by. There was a bit of a clock on this one if the culprit was a visitor. However, her gut, a lot smaller than Raysor's, now told her this person was local, at least regional, more savvy than someone who came to the island for a week to hit a job or two and leave.

She put in a call to Thomas.

She hadn't finished her notes about Gerard before her youngest officer waltzed in. Not nearly as sweaty as one would expect an officer at the beach in ninety-plus-degree heat, Thomas might not be crisp, but he wasn't wilted. "What can I do for you, Chief?"

He wasn't as concerned about being disciplined either. Instead, he was rather keen on hearing the dirt.

In a repeat of Gerard's interview, Callie asked him where he was during the Myrtle Street fire, for what period of time, and who he saw.

"I handled traffic on the north end of Myrtle," he said. "No more and no less. I do as I'm told." He grinned, impishly. Yeah, way more color in his personality than Gerard.

"This isn't a performance review, Thomas. I'm in need of facts."

"Yes, ma'am." But he still grinned. Took a lot to wipe that infamous grin off Officer Gage. Ask the tourists.

He hadn't assisted in the evacuation and instead deterred traffic with his usual prowess of keeping people happy despite the problem. Thomas had an eye for people and names, and besides Raysor, he'd been on duty the longest, despite his young age. He could spot who should and should not be there.

"Did you see Harbin Webb at any time?"

"What, trying to drive through?" he asked.

"Driving, walking, flying, somersaulting, did you see him?"

"I know his truck, so no in terms of driving," and he coyly tilted his head. "On foot?" He got serious, reaching back into his memory banks. "Once those houses started emptying, I might've lost track of who was who since they were mostly tourists. He isn't coming to mind, but that doesn't mean he wasn't there. My eyes were on street traffic."

Thomas plainly registered that Webb was a person of interest. "But if he was there, and if he didn't want to be seen, he could've easily slipped his way in and around those houses. I was on the corner. Those houses were three and four down from me. Again, sorry."

"No problem," Callie said. "What about Monty?"

"Nope. Him I'd have noticed, because I'd have been worried he was inserting himself into policing, redirecting traffic or something." He let out a breath. "Is he really your main suspect? I've listened to the rumors, and I've blown off Mr. Brice twice today. Truthfully, do you think our Monty . . . ?"

She liked how he referred to Monty as theirs.

"Do you seriously think our Monty would set fires and steal? Why? Where would he fence the pieces? He can barely get to the beach, much less a town or two over where there's a pawn shop." Leaning forward, he showed genuine concern for the boy. "I hear people throwing him under the bus right and left, but he's missing motive. He has friends, a family, a home, a way of life. I don't see him as a firebug. Sorry, I'm not buying it."

Bless Thomas.

"We have his fake badge," she said, having kept that bit of intel close. That would clinch Monty's lynching if that got out. "Leon found it in the fire debris. It's in evidence. And I know Monty's missing it, because he was hunting for it in the dumpster that caught fire last night."

Thomas sat back. "That's not good."

She did the same, rubbing the nape of her neck, wondering what she was missing, because otherwise, this case fast pinpointed Monty.

"You know I'm the one who got him that badge, don't you?" Thomas said, a sadness coming through.

"No, didn't realize that." She thought Monty bought it himself.

"In hindsight, I maybe shouldn't have done it. Sort of emboldened him, I think."

Releasing a soft laugh, she pictured Monty directing traffic, holding up his badge to show people he was legitimately Edisto Beach police. "Yeah, you turned a groupie into a monster." Thomas meant well, and she loved him for it.

"I even gave him a badge number," he said. "Started to use his birthday, but he wanted his mother's birthday instead. Number 1212."

Callie's birthday was in December, too.

"Trust me," he said. "He loved that badge as much as his mother, and he would turn over this island to find it. I'm not surprised he was in that dumpster in the middle of the night if he thought it was in there. How is he, by the way? Sorry I didn't ask sooner."

"He's got assorted burns that'll take time." But she was thinking of what Thomas said. "Would you look at the badge for me?"

"Sure. I'll get it." He started to rise.

Callie got up. "No. Let me. Be right back." She wanted to see him when he first looked it over.

She soon returned, and, holding up the badge still in the evidence bag, she showed him its front.

"Looks like it," he said. "Turn it over and you'll see 1212. Dorothea at the arts and crafts market at Bay Creek Park engraved it on there for me. Didn't charge a thing."

Callie turned the badge over and adjusted the transparent bag, pulling the plastic tight across the back.

Frowning, he reached out. "Can I hold it?"

"Of course," she said, handing it over.

He turned the badge over and around, studying close then not so close. Then, bewildered, he passed it back. "That's not his badge."

The back was plain. No number.

Pulling out his phone, he punched buttons and scrolled, doing it way faster than Callie was capable. "I can show you where I placed the order."

"I believe you."

He'd found it already and held up the phone, showing her his Amazon account and the date the badge was ordered.

She nodded that he could put it away. "What does this say to you, Officer Gage?" Callie asked, taking her seat again. She wanted him to see it, say it, and most of all, learn not to always take discovery at face value.

"This was found in the ashes of the fire, right?"

"Yes, sir."

"Who handed it to you?"

"The fire chief, Leon. Said one of his men found it."

Reaching out for the badge again, he drew it near, mashing on it, and Callie imagined him craving to touch it for real, maybe even putting a fingernail to it to test the smudges, because she felt the same. "I hate to say this, but how well do you trust Leon Hightower?"

To which Callie had not a thing to say.

She hadn't thought about Leon. He'd beat her to the dumpster, too.

And she thought Webb and Monty were the only commonalities in both fires.

THOMAS LEFT, HIS duty tour over, leaving Callie perplexed, fingering the evidence bag. If this was a plant, where was Monty's real badge? Someone went through a lot of trouble to pin the fires on Monty, but the underlying motive escaped them all.

Marie had left. The silence suddenly caught her attention, and she checked her watch. *Crap!* She'd told Stan to meet her at El Marko's at seven, and it was already ten past.

In five minutes, however, she'd left the office and reached the restaurant, grateful for the town's small footprint. She found Stan at Mark's VIP table, appetizer half eaten.

"I normally eat at six," he said. "This Mexican food sets heavy, and I'll be up half the night if I eat it too late."

"Quit fussing," she scolded. "Dang, it's busy tonight." Then she got it. "People doing their last hurrahs eating out on a Thursday before leaving Saturday morning. These restaurants will be slammed tonight and tomorrow night."

As if to prove her point, Mark whooshed out of the kitchen, delivering a tray of food to a large table. He finished up and stopped at Stan and Callie's table. "Picked a busy time to come in."

"We're the least of your concern." Callie snagged one of Stan's nachos. "I mainly came to pump Stan for ideas. Take your time with us, please."

"Ha!" Stan huffed. "To hell with that. I'm starved."

Mark pointed at each of them. "Your regulars?"

"Yes," Callie responded without giving Stan a chance to say differently. Mark vanished, the kitchen door swinging only inches from hitting the back of Stan's chair. A waitress delivered a water for Callie and replaced Stan's empty beer.

"Go ahead," Stan said. "You're consumed with a case. It's all over you. Need my validation or are you stumped?"

"Stumped."

He squinted his eyes, tilting his head. "Nothing on you, but I love it when you're stumped and come running to me."

Sneering, she purposefully snared another nacho, scooping a double dose of the cheese and meat on it, stealing his snack. "No shit, Stan. You old retired farts have to find meaning somewhere. It's my duty to provide you purpose."

He puckered. "Touché. What's the deal? This about the fires?"

"And the jewelry heists," she said, resting crossed arms on the small square table. This man had helped her solve hundreds of cases, and despite the retirement joke, he loved puzzles. He loved making *her* solve them even more.

She updated him about the moped basket, about seeing Monty at the hospital with an aside about Minnie losing her temper.

"So you've recovered the loot. Always a good thing," he said. "Give yourself at least that much pat on the back. Notified the owners yet?"

"No," she said. "That's tomorrow. Need to see Dudley anyway."

"And Dudley is who?" He half glowered though he didn't mean to, more quizzical than anything else. Stan's big face was a comedy in expressions, especially with the buzz cut over them that he couldn't seem to let go of, even in retirement.

"He's the eighty-something gentleman robbed of his deceased wife's Damascene necklace." The mention of him dredged up pity.

"You talk like you know what that is," he said, finishing the appetizer as the meal showed up.

"I do now," she said.

"So, is it Monty Bartow or not?" He talked into his dinner plate, admiring his food. "The public has pretty much solved this case for you, or so goes the word on the street. How is the boy, by the way?"

She gave a soft-fisted knock on the table, not enough for neighboring tables to notice but enough to take Stan's attention from the food. "I'm sick of this. He did not do it, Stan, but the court of public opinion is going to crucify him regardless because of who and what he is. He can't help he'll never be more mature than fifteen. He can't help his financial limitations. He only wants to be liked, to be of assistance, to be a part of the community. Who the hell else would walk or bike five-plus miles to town to see how he can help the police department, a contractor, some of the restaurants?"

Stan listened.

"A badge similar to his was planted at the Myrtle Street fire," she said, then described the difference. "He's missing his. Someone coaxed him to that dumpster and lit him up once he climbed inside. I can't determine who, what, or why people are damning him. Brice spreads these rumors so he can undermine my job, the bastard, and all this hurts Monty and his momma even more. Undermines justice, frankly."

She snatched her rolled napkin up and shook loose the utensils, slamming them onto the table when they tried to slide into her lap.

"You're exhausted, Chicklet. You do this every time there's a case where the pieces don't fit."

She ignored him, thoughts flying. She couldn't get Thomas's comment out of her head, and she criticized herself for not thinking of his analysis sooner. Leon Hightower was involved with not only the two fires, but Brice's third. Yeah, but so was she.

Everyone's a suspect until they're not.

With all three fires, she could retrieve the 911 calls, note who called, then cross-reference where Leon was when they were made . . . or when the fires were probably started. She could do the same for herself.

Easy to confirm. Now she felt stupid letting Thomas's innocent remark knock her off-kilter. Maybe she was too tired to think straight, and maybe she couldn't deny what Stan was saying. Sleep escaped her when there was a case as did meals and anything to do with staying healthy. She didn't develop those habits until John was murdered and she went on a one-year binge of hunting his killers. Some of those bad habits from way back when had stuck.

A tapping brought her back to the moment.

"Where the hell did you go?" Stan asked, no longer humorous. He set down his fork. "Are you all right?"

"If you're talking about the Myrtle Street fire, that was an anomaly for me," she said. "The dumpster didn't bother me a bit." Mainly because that fire was out before she got there.

"Fires aren't your only demons," he said. "You're obsessing, Chicklet. I know you better than anyone."

"I'm trying to keep Monty from losing what little quality of life he has. And I'm royally pissed that someone is waltzing around my beach getting away with arson. The son of a bitch put that jewelry in Monty's moped basket, probably wiped the pieces clean for prints hoping Monty would handle them out of curiosity. God, I'm praying he didn't. I sent the pieces to Walterboro for forensics." She kicked herself for not finding the chance to show Monty pictures of the jewelry before Minnie lost her temper.

The longer this case dragged on, and she did consider the arson and thefts conjoined, the more she favored Webb. While he had no alibi, he couldn't be placed at either of the crime scenes either. Even if she didn't arrest Monty, unless she solved this case, he'd be labeled. Minnie would hate the police. And a lot of people who helped Monty before would turn their backs on him from here on out if she didn't find the real criminal. No more little jobs for him to give him purpose

Then there was Dudley and maybe hope in interviewing him again. The house hadn't been empty as Gerard thought. Just nobody came to the door. Callie knew that the old man liked to watch out his window, and having no place to evacuate to, too feeble to handle the heat, he most likely hid and pretended he wasn't home. He may have seen the thief. That excited her.

"Eat," Stan ordered, apparently recognizing the facial expression that telegraphed her intent to scurry off in pursuit of a lead. "You can't afford to lose weight. I need a margarita." He waved for a waitress. "Ginger ale?" he asked Callie.

"Make sure it's the Blenheim's," she said. Mark kept the spicy good stuff under the bar for her. A South Carolina brand, the high-level kick of ginger delivered a bite and served as the closest Callie could come to alcohol. Thank God for her investigator friend in Columbia, Carolina Slade, for recommending it to her.

The waitress took the drink order.

"How's y'all's cohabitating going?" Stan asked, once the girl left. "You two have no excuses now."

Callie looked stunned.

"You and Mark," Stan said. "Under the same roof?"

"I get that. Excuses for what?" Callie asked.

"To air your feelings, your differences, your sordid and assorted pasts. You have all the opportunity you need to get closer. I like you two together, Chicklet."

She laid down her fork. "Stop it, Stan!"

"What's to lose? You two seem—"

"I said stop it."

This time the neighboring diners heard.

Realizing she'd spoken too loud, she leaned in, though no less chilled. "You want me to order a gin and tonic? Keep this crap up. And I'll make it a damn double." She shoved a forkful of chicken enchilada in her mouth. Her stare remained lasered on him. "I'm fed up with the matchmaking. You hear? I'm not tied to anyone. I see who I want, when I want."

"My goodness," Mark said, droll, a water in one hand, his other hand on the back of a chair. He'd slipped up to join them a minute, and in the hubbub of the restaurant, Callie hadn't heard him. "Had no idea I was that much of a dilemma for you."

Her stomach sank. "Mark, you only caught part of that. I didn't mean—"

But he was already shaking his head, pushing the chair back in. "You're welcome to sleep in my place for as long as you need. You've already chosen the spare room anyway, so we can both come and go without disturbing the other."

Stan lowered his attention to his plate.

"Mark," Callie said, trying again. "Sit down . . . please."

"Dinner's on me," he said. "Y'all have a good night."

He returned to the kitchen.

Chapter 21

CALLIE DIDN'T DARE follow Mark to the kitchen, not with this crowd. Not in the state he was in. Not when she really hadn't anything to say to justify what he'd heard. Instead, she peered down, rubbing her temples. She'd been talking to Stan, but while her remark wasn't directed at Mark, the mindset was clear enough, and it swept him up in the generalization of it.

I'm fed up with the matchmaking.

She loved being around Mark, but she wasn't ready to commit long term to him or anyone else. Why was that so hard for everyone to understand? And why did it feel so mean of her to think that way?

Why was it so terribly difficult for her to offer this man more than companionship and "benefits" if he wanted more?

A throbbing started behind her eyes.

She heard Stan scoot his chair, then his hand ran across the top of her head. "I am so sorry, Chicklet. I overstepped."

"You meant well." She slowly opened her eyes, shoulders feeling like they weighed a hundred pounds each. "Let's just eat." She put a piece of enchilada in her mouth. What started off as her favorite entrée on the menu tasted like wet cardboard now.

They finished their meals in silence. Mark remained in the kitchen.

Callie emptied her ginger ale, put a generous tip on the table, and stood. "Going to grab a few things from my house then head over to Mark's and hit the sack early." She toyed with staying at home, but she still had no water. She would have to pee and shower at Sophie's, and she wasn't ready to be interrogated by the island's gossip queen. To be honest, Callie simply wasn't in the mood for anyone.

Stan reached over and wrapped big fingers around her wrist. "Girl, I only want what's best for you."

"I know," she said, watching his hand instead of meeting his gaze. While she was bone tired, she was also emotionally spent. She loved this man like a mentor, like a brother, borderline paternal except she'd almost slept with him once. "I have no energy left to discuss this, Stan. Let me go."

He did, then with one last glance at the kitchen door, Callie left the restaurant.

She ran into Arthur outside. Literally, she bounced off him, with her as eager to get out as he was to get in.

"Hey, Arthur. I'm so sorry," she said, sidestepping to give him room.

"Hey, Chief, no problem. They got any seats left?"

She couldn't remember if there were seats or not. Her attention had been elsewhere. "Not many," she said, making it up. "Got a minute before you go inside?" She motioned to rockers sprinkled across the concrete porch that traveled the full length of the short strip mall, the chairs Mark had recommended to the landlord when he opened in December. Store names were etched into the backs of them to both advertise and deter theft.

Arthur sneaked a quick look across and down the street to his aunt's office.

"She expecting you back?" Callie asked, following his attention.

"No, but she's in there," he said, meaning Janet would get suspicious seeing her nephew in a tête-à-tête with the police chief.

Callie got it, but she also got this. "Ever seen her take the time to stand on her porch and study the people and traffic outside?"

"Um, no." Of course not. The woman came and went almost in a run, a snappy march, one could say, with purpose to be someplace. "Okay, then," he surmised. "Guess I've got a minute."

He took the white rocker. Callie maneuvered into the yellow, an item or two on her utility belt clanking against the wood as she positioned herself so she could watch both El Marko's and Wainwright Realty without turning her head.

"I caught your expression at *Bikini Bottom*, by the way," she began. "Figured your aunt didn't need to hear our conversation, and out here in the open appears innocent. You're waiting for an open table, and I'm ending my day."

Arthur watched the road, the bicycles, walkers, and cars wafting the hot air in passing, and he waited for a question, still uncomfortable.

"Tell me about Webb," she said. "Janet said he was all right. You, on the other hand, made clown faces behind her back, negating her words almost as soon as she said them. What gives?"

Ensuring no ears could hear, he leaned on his knees, motioning for Callie to do the same.

"If you don't want anyone to take notice, rock like a normal person, Arthur," she said, back against the chair, practicing what she preached. "Now, about Webb?"

"Last summer he begged me and four others to buy in on some marsh acreage. He promised we'd make a mint."

Callie remained relaxed, lightly rocking. Someone came out of El Marko's, and she peered over, halfway expecting Mark to come looking for her. "And you declined his generous offer?"

"Wasn't anything generous about it," he said. "The guy assumed I'd talk my aunt into investing because he didn't have the balls to. I didn't have that kind of money."

"Did she buy in?"

"No, but I also advised her against it."

"Did he find a way to get his money?"

"Oh yeah, he and some guys I never heard of, but I think he got his butt handed to him. He's about to lose his shirt if he doesn't sell his share. He doesn't have the sort of experience to get a project like that off the ground."

Arthur might be freshly graduated, but he'd been mightily groomed by his aunt, and she was an impressive real estate broker.

"What else?" Callie asked.

"The Myrtle Street job isn't right."

To that she almost stopped rocking. "Go on."

"This is the wrong time of year to be repairing a house."

"Not a secret, Arthur. You're just repeating your aunt and, frankly, common knowledge. How is that Webb's fault?"

"It's not his fault, per se, but he suffers for the poor timing of the owner, who's losing income by doing the repairs now. Booker McPhee isn't doing well in terms of those houses, and he might be letting go of them as soon as they're repaired. Webb told me one of his checks bounced. McPhee asked him if he could be patient enough to wait until the houses are sold."

Which would force Webb to continue doing repairs on his nickel. He could file a mechanic's lien on the house, encumbering the title until he was paid, but nothing made up for the lost days.

Would he have set the fire to ensure payment via insurance? Still not wise because the insurance company paid the owner. A fire would've set all this back further, and still, Webb had no choice but to complete the job to get a dime.

Unless he was in cahoots with McPhee. A big risk for a respected contractor, though. Callie worried she was still reaching . . . worried she was looking too hard at other people to keep the spotlight off Monty.

"How long ago did that check bounce?" she asked.

"Three weeks."

"Why didn't your aunt tell me? You can't tell me you knew and she didn't. She'd castrate you for holding this kind of information from her."

Callie was asking him to talk out of school, putting the nephew in the precarious position of outing his aunt versus defying the police. He grinned weakly.

"I'll try not to tell her anything," she continued, hoping to assure him. "And if I have to ask her about Webb, I'll try to act like I heard from another source. So talk."

He couldn't help himself. He leaned forward again. "My aunt made McPhee an offer," he said under his breath. "She's a shark smelling blood. Can't help herself when a piece of property becomes vulnerable."

Which almost made Janet a person of interest except she had the patience and bank account to wait out a man inept about beach real estate. Janet Wainwright had better sense than this, surely she did. Hiding what she knew about Webb, and now McPhee, still hinted at motive which kept her in Callie's sights.

"Would she . . .?" Callie asked, not finishing the sentence.

"Never," Arthur replied, not needing to hear *set the fire*.

"Might make McPhee sell sooner."

"She'd get the houses sooner if they didn't catch on fire. Nobody wants to deal with a fire sale. She would prefer not to deal with rebuilding after a fire. She's a career Marine. She's successful. Potential harm outweighs potential gain."

The boy sounded smart. Callie couldn't see Janet behaving in this manner, either, but nobody bested her in a real estate deal. "Had McPhee agreed to sell yet?"

The nephew ran a hand over the arm of his rocker, like he was feeling for something, which told Callie her answer. "Not yet, huh?" she said.

"Not to my knowledge," he answered. Mouth flatlining, Arthur rocked forward and stood. "Don't you dare tell her I told you any of this. I'll deny it. Christ, she'd gut me and feed me to gators."

Meaning she'd disown him, which was way worse.

"We're good," Callie said, and waved toward the restaurant. "Thanks for taking the time."

He didn't even say goodbye and disappeared into El Marko's.

Blowing out a long breath, she decided she was done for the day. Lifting out of the chair proved onerous. Her days and nights and lack of sleep in either were catching up. Her brain numb, her legs like lead, she couldn't take two steps without imagining going horizontal and closing her lids. Slowing down in the rocking chair had been her undoing.

The evening was going on nine thirty. Tomorrow she might bug Janet, definitely speak with Dudley. Revisiting Webb and McPhee went on her list, too, to ferret out their relationship, delve deeper into their financial standings. And, of course, Minnie and Monty, which she hoped might happen on Edisto if he was released. Revisiting Monty at the hospital had already proven to be less than productive.

She stepped off the strip mall porch and walked to the parking lot via the edge of the street, a downhill vantage so she wasn't noticed through the restaurant's plate-glass window. No point letting Stan and Mark see her, as if she were waiting for them, or moping for attention.

She was too exhausted to talk about emotional stuff.

Changing her mind about going by her place, she drove the two blocks to Mark's *Reel Lucky*. Dragging up the stairs, she let herself in, threw off her clothes, and stood under a lukewarm shower in a prefab stall in need of a caulk job until she thought she'd fall asleep leaning in the corner. Not bothering to blow-dry her hair, she toweled it best she could.

The shower had upgraded her from comatose to semi-conscious so she looked for a uniform for tomorrow. She had two full sets, both having been worn and exposed to smoke, sweat, and summer heat, and Mark had mentioned having thrown them in the wash. *Wait*, he said they might be in the dryer. He'd also mentioned how familiar he was at how to iron the appropriate creases, and embarrassingly, selfishly, she wondered if he'd bothered completing the task, but she found both sets in the dryer, a full day's wrinkles set in.

The man did have a restaurant to run, and after their misunderstanding, she shouldn't rely on him to tend to her. He'd done too much already.

What a damn day.

She couldn't find the iron, and there wasn't an ironing board. After slamming the dryer door too hard and backing into a vacuum cleaner whose handle slid to the floor, her exhaustion frayed her coping skills to the point of throwing something to release the pent-up emotion.

Chelsea Morning might not have water, but her place had power, and in a snap she could put her hands on an iron. Otherwise, she was down to jeans for work in the morning, and that was not the image she needed to present to at least four people she planned to interview. Even if she wore the badge on her belt, she would come across too unassuming, particularly with her size and height.

Crap. She threw on running shorts and a tee with no bra and left the house. She pulled up short, finding a bag on her car under the windshield wiper.

No weapon. No badge. She'd been at Mark's for a half hour, tops. She scanned the lot best she could in the night, stepping up the drive to study the ones on either side. Not even a car, though around there, anyone was smarter to prank on foot. It was easier to hide beneath a house, skirting from place to place easily hidden by lush greenery and storage rooms.

Taking the butt of a dried, dead palmetto frond, she swatted gnats away before reaching over and bopping the bag. Nothing. This was stupid. She tossed the frond and lifted the bag, light with only one item inside. Shining the light on her phone, she noted words on the outside.

I'm sorry. Don't skip breakfast. Stan

Suddenly feeling the fool, she peered inside at a protein bar. Chocolate mint, like she liked her ice cream

Good Lord. She threw the bar back in, rolled down the top, and tossed the bag on the passenger seat. Must be ten thirty now.

Stan was trying to apologize. She kicked herself for leaning on him so hard, because of all the people on this island, he cared the most as to what came of her. He retired to Edisto because of her, for God's sake, telling people he had nowhere else to go.

Cops didn't retire easy.

She got in the car and headed to *Chelsea Morning*. Freshly showered, she didn't want to walk the two-thirds of a mile, but she needed that iron and, as backup, find something else worth wearing in a box or dresser drawer somewhere. The clothes Sophie had packed for her were too casual.

She turned onto Jungle Road, the traffic next to nil this time of night. Edisto wasn't a late-night place.

The bag toppled over, and Stan returned forefront in her mind. Nope. Cops didn't slide into retirement. Sure, they bragged about doing so, like they were anxious to put the crime behind them and bask in the luxury of unscheduled days ahead. Truth was, if they didn't keep a toe in the water of law enforcement, they faded away.

She was Stan's toe in the water.

She needed to remember that.

Then she wondered if she was becoming Mark's as well.

Like Seabrook had been hers, back when he was police chief, and she thought she had taken an early retirement.

Law enforcement people might be hearty, but they had their weaknesses.

She wasn't sure how long she could do this social juggling, and Mark's presence had brought her emotional ineptness to the forefront of her world of late. She was horrible at this. A loner since birth, and someone who abstained from crowds—hell, a coffee klatch drew her up short— and she saw friends as beautiful one moment and painful the next. Yes, she realized that made her a nasty, selfish, antisocial bitch. However, the pain and loss of those she loved would aways prey on her mind, her heart, her willingness to let go one more time.

She reached home, and the motion sensors did their job, accenting her arrival and staying lit until she could trudge up the stairs to her front door. Peeking inside, she noted someone had left the bar light on next to her kitchen, which was good, she guessed.

Sophie and Mark had done a remarkable job taking care of her business while she tended Edisto. Word to self . . . wake up tomorrow and take ten minutes to think of thank-yous for these people, and Stan.

Inside, unable to touch the light switch in her traversing of the maze of furniture tucked Tetris fashion in the kitchen, she made her way to the laundry area and laid hands on her iron. She reached another light, flicked it on, and entered the living room scanning the hardwood's water damage. The floor appeared dry. The floor also appeared warped, and the closer to the bedroom, the smellier the carpet.

She found a suitcase, then rummaged through drawers to find a few necessities. She decided to peek in the fridge to make sure something didn't need to be eaten or at least stored at Mark's. After she shoved obstacles aside, she managed to open the door to find no more than condiments. Between SeaCow, Whaley's, McConkey's, Waterfront,

Pressley's, and El Marko's, she'd developed a habit of thinking about a meal last minute.

Maneuvering back out of the kitchen, around obstacles, she tunneled back toward the front door, lifting the suitcase here and there over things, the iron in the other hand. She stopped at Jeb's open bedroom door. At least his stuff wasn't damaged.

She kept the bedroom door closed when he absconded to college, admittedly to preserve his scent inside. She missed him each and every day, and this late, this tired, and this moody, she missed him more.

Setting the suitcase down and the iron on the floor, she took a moment to wander in, noting the random items on his dresser, on the spread, a wall around the bed. Per habit, she closed the door. Callie moved lamps and knickknacks off the nautical spread, as if they smothered Jeb's memory.

Then she sat down and rubbed her hand on the quilt. Seahorses. This had once been her room when her family did summers here, and in adulthood, after a particularly difficult day, she retreated here.

Lying down, she took in a navel-deep breath, taking in the familiar of her son . . . and her home. If she thought too hard, she'd feel lost.

On the outside looking in, people would consider her a success story. Healthy, financially comfortable if not affluent, a house at the beach, chief of police, a beautiful son in college, and a decorated steward and protector of the community.

On the inside looking out, with the onslaught of the firebug, with Brice's capitalizing on her weaknesses, with Mark disappointed in her, all she could see were wounds that would not heal.

Her body melted into the bed. Before she could worry about Mark worrying over where she was, she lost consciousness. If Mark missed her, he'd look here first.

Dreams came quickly, her mind unable to settle. Thoughts of fire and smoke traipsed in and out of one scene after another until she felt the heat, smelled the burning, choked on the smoke.

In her dream she coughed, swallowed, finding clean air harder to find.

She coughed herself awake. She was confused as to where she was until she found herself in Jeb's room, surrounded by furniture and decorations that weren't supposed to be there. Glass exploded somewhere near the living area. She bolted upright.

She pushed through the dullness of a too-weary brain to orient herself. Late at night. Check. She was home. Check. Her home remained a wreck. Okay.

Her cough tickled up again, then again, not going away.

Damn! Smoke seeped into the room under Jeb's bedroom door.

That was no dream.

Chapter 22

CALLIE FAST-ROLLED off the bed and ran into the adjoining bath to wet a small hand towel only to remember no water. Still she coughed into the rag until she could cough no more. Then she plastered the white terry cloth across her face and took deep breaths before returning to the door. "Hello?" she shouted, touching the handle. She jerked her hand back. Hot. "Anyone out there?"

She'd been trained about opening doors in a fire and how doing so could create a funnel for flames. Better to break a window and escape outside than risk the fire coming into the bedroom. One of Jeb's two windows faced the front porch, the other the ground, two floors down.

Even without seeing flames, the heat rose. A smoke-only incident didn't make you sweat. This was legit.

Unlocking a window leading to the porch, she pushed up. No budge. She hit the frame, frantic, again pushing up, digging into her back muscles for strength. *Son of a bitch* . . . nothing. She never painted windows. Had to be the swell of humidity and heat.

The towel loosened and fell. She retrieved it off the floor and did her best to tie the thick cloth around her nose, her t-shirt neckline already wet with sweat. She grabbed a seashell-coated candlestick off the dresser, her mother's, normally on a bookcase in the living room, and she wielded it like a bat and smashed the base against the glass. Shards shattered inside and out, some nicking her bare legs. After running the stick around the window's frame, she threw it aside and snatched up the seahorse bedspread to cover the opening.

Her heart pumped wildly. This was panic. This was fight or flight with flight winning by six lengths.

Get to the street. Run!

Her toe touched a plank. With a stretch, finally her foot flattened on the porch.

You're safe. You're outside.

But it's fire! Run!

Her pulse threw itself against the walls of her neck. Double-time.

Triple-time. Too many times. Darkness crept into her periphery. Her fire anxiety raced to take over her consciousness.

Count, damn it!

One, two, three, swallow . . . four, five . . . um, six, seven. . . .

The black subsided, her heartbeats slower but still racing.

Backing off the fear allowed other senses to leap into action. Heated odors gripped her, caustic, pungent. . . . Hands shaking, she pushed hair from her mouth. She tasted smoke, heard hundreds of crackles, each overstepping the other. She froze in place.

No, no. Don't stop here.

She needed a deep breath, but not here . . . not here.

She gripped the porch railing, willing herself to stabilize. *Okay, okay, you're good, you're good.* Her heart continued to beat itself wildly against her ribs, but she was getting away.

Two stairs down, a scream erased all rational thought. She froze in her tracks.

John, Jeb, Seabrook, Sophie . . . she listed names of loved ones, dead and alive because her mind couldn't sort right now.

Collect yourself!

Did the scream come from the back half of the house? Inside? Outside?

Man? Woman? God forbid . . . child?

Her breaths came irregular and chopped.

God, she had no phone!

This was only supposed to be an in-and-out trip. Five minutes.

Only then did she realize she was all the help someone inside had.

Quickly, Callie worked logistics. Option one . . . go back in through the window and violate the seal on Jeb's bedroom, possibly sucking fire into the room. Or run around to the back and find an open door, a broken window, or create any sort of access.

God, let them be outside.

She pivoted and took off, the motion sensors capturing her as she took stairs two and three at a time, leaping the last four to the ground, hitting the gravel in a skid, and turning in a run. She sped under her house, past her personal car, then out through the other side and up those back stairs.

She lock-kneed on the middle landing. Up and to the right was her bedroom, and she couldn't see anything but flames through the window.

Fire ate up her home. Like it had destroyed her home before.

She couldn't move.

The scream. What about the scream? Where was it from? Nobody was back there. Fear zipped through her at not hearing more screams . . . until she heard one. Weaker.

Her instincts overrode her fear. Coughing, she reached for the towel. *Shit, where's my towel?*

Whumph!

She spun at the muffled clap of air. Without remembering how, she'd reached the back porch, and through the door she saw where the fire had channeled up the stairway outside her bedroom door, forging its way into the upstairs guestroom where she'd taken Mark the day everything flooded. Backing up . . . peering up to the second level, she couldn't see the blaze but recognized flickering shadows through the dormer window that revealed how quickly the room was being consumed.

Move!

The screen-porch door hung on her left leading to a sitting area. With a yank, she ripped the small hook out of the wood and snared a beach towel from a plastic storage bin where she kept seat cushions. In a fell swoop, she dowsed the towel with water pooled in potted impatiens.

Turbaned, her upper body and head wrapped in the big terry cloth, she reached the back door, incredibly grateful to find it ajar.

The heat raised her scarred forearm before her eyes. "Hello?" she shouted. "It's Callie. Where are you?"

No answer. She moved closer. Which direction should she hunt, because choosing one way could mean losing other routes as the demon spread. The heat cut into her skin, the environment crackling like popcorn. She prayed even all these years later that the bullet had killed her husband before the fire reduced his body to ashes.

The flames crawled like a sci-fi creature, climbing the walls to her right, sticking to the ceiling on the west side of the house. Her sofa leaped to life in the entry hall, outside of Jeb's room. Like an animal, orange and yellow pounced from piece to piece, consuming fabric and wooden legs as if flesh. The pieces being crammed tightly in preparation for contractors only fueled the blaze.

She backed up, the heat cooking her bare arms and legs, her cheeks hot almost to the point of blistering. "Where are you? Please. Shout! Talk to me!"

She almost shouted *John*, then coughed, choking on the smoke.

She winced, scolding herself to keep her mind on the present.

Taking the path of least resistance to her left, she followed the wall, not yet too hot to touch, and prayed for a different angle that might show her someone. Smoke billowed, filling her surroundings, giving her a visual of no more than four or five feet, deteriorating by the second.

No way they were standing amidst all this.

Maybe they climbed into the laundry area off the kitchen and shut the door. Under the cabinets, maybe. She reached the small fireplace and looked in, not hopeful. She could no longer see her bedroom, and she almost couldn't make out the kitchen.

Callie shouted "Hello! Hello! Anybody there!" over and over, still slipping to call her husband's name. If she didn't force back those memories, she'd succumb. Being inside already demanded all her attempt for control.

Nobody called back. Nobody cried. The screamer hadn't made a sound, and Callie feared the worst . . . then wondered if she'd imagined the screams. She could have. She couldn't tell. For a brief moment she forgot why she was even inside the house. That lapse was enough to make her lose her way.

"Hello—" abruptly turned into a hack.

Where was she? The living room. She thought she had a wall within reach, but she'd wandered from the fireplace, and none of her belongings remained to orient her. Smoke enveloped her. Sweat soaked her clothes.

She coughed into the towel, the moisture in it gone. The cough kept going and going. Air out, none in.

Raw, her throat threated to close, shutting out the threat.

No, she couldn't just drop and give up hope.

Drop, yes, drop.

She went to her knees, then deeper, putting her face as close to the floor as possible. There. She found less polluted breaths but nothing clean enough to give her much strength. She may have bought herself a little time. Little, meaning seconds.

Oxygen-depleted muscles fought her when she decided to retreat. Why the hell had she tried this rescue? Who said this person hadn't tried to kill her?

Splitting creaks and snaps jerked her attention overhead. The biting smells stung her sinuses. She could only open her eyes in guarded snatches of time. If it were day she'd be able to find the door. . . .

God, she couldn't find the door!

Where the hell was Leon?

Her old suspicion crept back. What if he caused this?

Lights flashed . . . or was that the fire . . . or was it her mind playing tricks?

That's when she saw shoes. Her shoes that Sophie removed from the closet? The hazy darkness made detail difficult, distractions everywhere.

The fire's voice whispered in her ears.

Surrounded by quivering heat, nothing tangible told her where she was.

Blinking, forcing herself to focus on the shoes, she glanced, closed her eyes, and slid. She bellied forward, the effort made easier by the empty room.

Yes, those were feet. They lay top down. The person had screwed up calculating the wrath of the fire.

Like she had.

But determination flooded her, forcing her on. Nobody had reached John. She hadn't been there for John. The fire department hadn't gotten there in time for John, but she could be here for this soul, and the failure of five years ago gave her momentum to see this through.

Stretching her left arm, she missed touching the person, having miscalculated the distance. She inched closer.

Until she didn't.

A grip of one ankle, then both ankles, pulled her backward. "No, no," she cried, but she couldn't be heard over the snapping, popping roar.

Snatched her up by the waist, someone carried her out the side door onto her screen porch and down the stairs.

"Stop squirming, Callie. It's me," Leon yelled, putting her down and dragging her stumbling to put distance between them and the burning, tripping over oak roots in the way.

"Somebody's in there." But her rasping still defied understanding.

Not too gently, he pushed her to the ground across the street, hastily threw oxygen over her face, then did a quick look-see for burns.

"Stop!" she screeched, two octaves below her norm, reducing her to a deep hacking spell. After two whiffs of oxygen, she yanked off the mask. "There's someone else in there!"

He stood. "Jesus." He trotted to his two guys on hoses, yelling in their ears, then came back.

Callie leaped to her feet. "Go! I saw them!" An unsteadiness washed over her and forced her to reach for a tree.

Leon helped her back down and shook his head, angst in his eyes. "I'm sorry, but we barely got you out. I'm not risking the lives of my people to recover a body, because that's what we'd find." He hunched, face to face, resting a hand on her shoulder, ready to tend to a distraught soul. "Who was it?"

Coughing, choking, the words came out in pieces, some repeated to make sense. "Don't . . . know. Arson," she finally managed to say, unable to tack on the qualifier, "I think."

He wasn't surprised.

She teared up, or her eyes ran from smoke irritation, she couldn't tell which, but they wouldn't stop. A person was dying in her house, and she didn't know who.

A woman's cheap, common sneakers.

"St. Paul's is on the way, along with an all-hands callout to the volunteers," he said, reading her query. "Best we can do is keep it from spreading, Callie. We can't save it."

Thomas appeared out of nowhere, did a quick triage analysis of how his chief was, then bolted toward the fire.

"Thomas!" she yelled into the mask.

The officer ran beneath and through the parking area, hunkered down, and disappeared.

Déjà vu filled her head, Callie pinned underwater in Scott's Creek along with a former officer, his eyes wide in the swirling, murky brine. Thomas dove in and saved her. Francis drowned.

That same panic about choked her now.

Callie worried about and loved Thomas in equal measure. His tendency to be a hero scared her. She waited. Everyone waited. For too long they waited.

The police cruiser surprised them appearing from their right. Thomas had driven around the block to return her vehicle. He parked it a few houses down and trotted to his chief. "Had to save the squad car," he said, attempting jest. "I'm the youngest guy in the department, and I don't want to have to walk these blocks this time of year."

Nobody laughed.

"Are you okay?" he said, his gentleness touching as he crouched before her.

"You crazy fool," she said, embarrassed at his seeing the tears.

Her propane grill exploded on the east side. Callie jerked, scooting back. A timber collapsed, sending sizzling, electric sparks into the night sky. With a squeal, she crab-walked backward, scrambling, escaping. . . .

She dug her heels in, stopping only once she hit against a tree.

Her head pounded; her chest hammered. Her bearings were gone. Time and reality made no sense.

Thomas stayed down on her level. Only as he reached close did she realize she whined noises of desperation. "Chief . . . Callie. Shhh," he said, soothing.

More people had arrived, most watching the destruction, not seeing Callie tucked under a wax myrtle, wrapped in a knot, wedged against a young oak. Every native on the beach knew her address, and once their thirst for disaster had been sated, they'd hunt for her. Everyone would want to see how the lady chief handled catastrophe in her own backyard.

He stared from her to the field of people. "Chief."

She forced a breath at his warning, not deep without feeling the smoke, but she sought. . . release, maybe? With a staunch effort, she released the muscles in her thighs that shoved her against the bark. Then she leaned forward. Thomas backed up and stood, his attention still hard on her. She recalled where she was, and the gravity of it all.

She hadn't decided if she could stand.

"Thomas!" The low voice came from her left, Thomas's right, but it rang more frantic than Callie'd ever heard him.

Thomas searched for the familiar caller, and upon recognition, waved for him to come over, and come over fast.

Mark appeared.

"Callie, sweetheart, are you okay?" He started to kneel, but she remembered his bum leg and held out for his hand, so he'd stand her upright. He did so. "Come here," he said, taking her in after she acknowledged she was fine.

He rubbed her back until she thought her skin would peel off. "You're shaking," he whispered, and she thanked the heavens he hadn't announced it to the horde.

"I'm okay. Leon pulled me out," she said. The simple admission enabled her a bit.

"Callie!" The booming voice was as good as a favorite blanket.

"Stan!" she called, catching sight of his height over the masses.

Taller, Mark raised both arms, sweeping them to pinpoint their location on the side of the silt road. Stan trotted up, and even in the night, with firelight on one side of his face and a streetlight accenting the other, he appeared pale . . . and scared.

Without even noting Mark, Stan rushed over and swept Callie away from him, taking her up in a hug, her arms accepting him in kind though unable to reach around his waist.

"Chicklet, Chicklet . . . let me look at you." He eased her back so he could see.

Crazy needy for him, she peered back into those all-knowing eyes. Their emotional connection, their past, their having stood on the side of a street like this once upon a time as a person burned inside, sweeping them both back to Boston. In a rush of emotion, she crammed herself against him before she lost it.

Like a father with a sixth-grade daughter, Stan gathered her back up. "She doesn't need this. I'm taking her to my place. You don't mind, do you, Mark?"

But what could he say? He nodded, watching to see how Thomas interpreted this. "I'll tell Leon," her officer said.

"I go nowhere," she said. "They'll have questions for me. This is a crime scene."

"Callie . . .," Stan started, peering down to her, empathetic. "You don't have to—"

"Is she okay?" A woman spoke from a few yards over.

"Not sure," replied another. "Is she, Stan?"

Dozens gathered, to observe and make assumptions.

Callie pushed back, this time telling herself to stand on her own, regardless of the terror stabbing in and out of her core. The entire Edisto world held her on display.

"My house," Stan repeated low. "A shower, then we tend any burns. Maybe a sleeping pill, because no point in you enduring a bad night after all this. I suspect—" He left off the ending.

He meant her nightmares, and if this night didn't spike fresh dreams of an epic nature, nothing would. As a minimum, the shock of the evening would revive any other of her assorted bad dreams. She might as well remain on site.

"I wait right here," she repeated. "Thomas, tell Leon where I'll be when he needs me."

Thomas trotted to Leon. Stan shadowed Callie and took up protective residence at her side.

But when she turned toward Mark, she spotted only his back a half block down Jungle Shores, heading toward home.

"Oh, Mark," she whispered. Then she wasn't sure what else to say. They'd excluded him, without a grasp of why Stan was important to her on this night of all nights. All because she hadn't wanted to expose her past to the man.

Now seated beside her on a timber on the edge of the lot across the street, Stan extended another hug around her. "Mark is tomorrow's problem, Chicklet."

But to her he'd become a heavier one atop of all others.

Callie'd lost her home, her personal vehicle . . . a t-shirt of Seabrook's, the dress shirt of John's . . . a blanket, the last remnant of Bonnie, her baby lost to SIDS the year John died . . . the turntable . . . her Neil Diamond collection.

Stan was a thousand-percent right. This day was a lot to absorb. Without him, she'd be drunk as a skunk by midnight.

If she'd taught Mark about her past, he might've better understood her reaction to the present. In regard to some things Sophie knew more than Mark.

No.

She stiffened with the jolt of fear. Sophie lived right next door, her house reflecting the pyro . . . her home at risk of sharing the blaze.

Where the hell was she?

Chapter 23

CALLIE ROSE, FEAR a slow crawl into her reality. She trotted toward *Hatha Heaven* next door, then ran. How could she not have noticed Sophie missing? *No, no.* She ran harder.

The restaurant was closed. Sophie should be home. She followed happenings on the beach like a dog on scent. She should've beaten Stan and Mark to the fire.

She cut short screaming Sophie's name. Calling for her would send a frenzy through the crowd since the yoga mistress made a point of connecting to every resident and half the tourists. She was the only Sophie on the island.

Stan hadn't caught up, but Thomas had and read her concern. "What's wrong, Chief?"

"Find Sophie," was all she had to say. He obliged and bolted into the crowd, hunting, avoiding spreading fear by looking and not inquiring. Callie strode the road, staying in the middle of the fray, attempting in her challenged height to see her friend amidst neighbors giving their condolences.

"Have you seen Sophie?" she asked those who knew her, but nobody had. For once she prayed to find Sophie in the middle of everyone's business, like Callie ordinarily scolded her not to do.

Callie could *not* lose someone else. To fire, to anything. She couldn't. She'd lose her fucking mind.

A grip on her elbow hitched her breath. Leon pulled up close. "Come with me."

Callie knew those words and a thousand others she'd heard like them. A soft warning of worse to come. "It's not like Sophie to not be here," she said, preemptive, wanting to cut him off from his news, much like the victims she'd counseled in her past who avoided hearing about tragedy by speaking instead.

"Thomas and Gerard evacuated the surrounding houses," he said, in a kind way reminding her that everyone else could still follow procedure. Which was crap since Gerard had supposedly evacuated the houses on Myrtle, too.

"Callie," he said, a little more forceful. "Come with me."

She jerked loose of him. "Leon, don't frickin' patronize me."

He drew close, speaking subdued. "We found your body. Coroner's on his way."

Callie locked her knees to keep from collapsing. No, not again. This was not fair. This was not right.

Stan caught up and took a hold of an arm before she lost strength. "What is it?"

Leon let her tell him, his gaze with Stan communicating Callie might be distraught. She spotted the unspoken exchange. Recollecting her senses, she stiffened, her shoulders popping in response.

For God's sake, she'd done this business longer than Leon had. She could count the bodies he'd seen on one hand. She'd quit counting after fifty eons ago. All these things she told herself more so than standing in defiance of those around her. "They located a person in there," she said to Stan, steeling herself. "Any idea who?" she asked back to Leon, a bit harsh, her heart mad and insane with needing to know while incensed they treated her like a child . . . while understanding why they were.

"Was hoping you could help with the identification," he replied. "Female."

Female? Oh my God, Sophie.

He continued, "We found keys in her pocket." He held up an evidence bag containing a set of keys with a couple of charms. "Think they're for a Saturn. An older model. And we located a gas can near the body. We may have our arsonist."

The gender took her aback, but like whiplash, the Saturn key abruptly detoured her from her initial fear. "Jesus, Leon."

"You know her?" he said.

Holding out her hand, she took the bag gently, in case the contents were fragile from the heat. With tenderness, she shifted the keys until she could study the charms on the chain. One was nothing more than a shell design, half melted, likely from one of Edisto's own souvenir shops, like a child would buy for a mother for her birthday. The other charm, however, confirmed Callie's suspicion. Though damaged, she made out a Y on the end, and with minimal rub, she revealed the capital M.

On one hand she was relieved. The body wasn't Sophie.

On the other hand, she was stunned.

Stan tried to regain hold of her arm, as if she'd crumble from the news.

She pulled loose.

God love him, this overprotective side of his wore thin, especially in public where it would spread to others like a cold, giving others permission to feel sorry for her and question her abilities on the job. The case had taken a shift, its urgency replacing her personal shortcomings. Work called. Thank God work called. She'd already lost her mind too many times, and work would aid to her take hold. She needed to keep her shit together to weather this night and how many other nights it took to deal with this blight on her island, and there was no time for weakness

She turned her back to the fire and reined her emotions in. Line things up, she told herself. What was she faced with now?

Her own home gone, a crime suspect in the hospital, an attempted murder, a jewelry heist, witnesses still needing attention . . . and now a body.

But why this body, why this person . . . mostly, why in Callie's house? Why Minnie Bartow?

She reached inside and gripped hold of rationality. Everyone would expect her to cave losing her home, which admittedly hovered around the edges of her judgment, but that had to remain secondary . . . for the moment . . . for longer . . . for as long as it would take to solve whatever this was that was way bigger than *Chelsea Morning*.

This was difficult, but truth was the drive to work kept her personal issues at bay. She liked things better that way. This couldn't be about her.

She motioned Thomas over. "Hunt the road for a twenty-year-old Saturn." Her mind's eye recalled the faded worn vehicle under the lean-to carport. "Tan color."

Stan beckoned toward the flames, which had lessened, though nowhere near subdued. "You're already tired and will be no good if you don't get some sleep. Come catch some rest at my place."

Leon waited for her reaction, not echoing Stan's suggestion she leave the scene, because clearly he recognized there was work to do. They'd become a crime-solving duo of late, and Callie suspected he wanted her to remain. If this were someone else's house, she'd stick tight and see this through, leaving only once the firefighters left. Tired or not, she'd rather be proactive than wallow in her karma. She had enough adrenaline in her to hang for a while.

"Stan." She motioned back to the ground under the streetlight as a place for him to retreat, then had a different thought. "Why don't *you* go home? You don't have to be here." She wished Mark had hung around instead of Stan now. Mark wouldn't be a bird dog on point for every emotion, because he wasn't familiar with her triggers. In hindsight probably another reason she'd kept them to herself.

But Mark had left feeling he was of no use to her at all. Another layer of guilt on her. She had so many layers of guilt that she'd become a pro at shuffling them like a deck of cards, playing the one most timely first and letting the others languish until drawn. Mark wasn't her biggest call-to-action at present, but still . . . she missed his being here.

Enough about herself. She had to ponder Monty . . . and Minnie. What were the signs she'd missed? If Minnie started this fire, did she start the others, and what was Callie to do about Monty?

Stan took up residence on the bit of sand she'd motioned to, patting the ground beside him. "At least catch a nap here."

"Wait, wait. Here I am. Callie!"

The voice halted Callie from dropping down to her patch of ground, and she leaped up. Sophie scurried from her house next door, two chaise chairs folded, one in each hand, dropping one once, scrambling to gather the cumbersome items too awkward for her size.

Callie rushed over, taking one chair to give her room to hug her friend. "Where the hell were you, Soph? I was so scared I'd find you fried to a crisp in there." She doffed her chin toward the fire, blinking back the moisture in her eyes she hoped nobody saw.

Sophie wore her pale-blue contacts, giving her an eerie appearance reflecting the flames. "Wait, someone died in there?"

"Yes, you moron, and I thought it was you."

Sophie watched the firefighter hosing her own home. "How the hell am I supposed to sage all this out of our lives?"

Almost comical.

Callie nudged her, hard. "Where the hell were you?"

Sophie dropped her chair and stood in the middle of Jungle Shores Road, listing off the reasons on long, manicured fingers. "Worked late at the restaurant. They wouldn't let me inside my own house, but Hattie motioned me over to her place, and we sat in her yard watching." The list went on, the conversation heavily detailed in the goings-on of the neighbors up and down Jungle and Jungle Shores Roads and none of

Callie's immediate concern unless they'd seen the arsonist, but Callie gathered nobody took notice until they saw the inferno.

Thomas trotted up. "You found her."

"Now talk to everyone standing around and ask if they saw anyone go into my house tonight other than me."

He scooted off, beginning with a couple not ten feet away.

Moving to Stan, Sophie and Callie assumed their chairs. Someone appeared with another chair for Stan, and he adjusted himself next to Callie. Someone else gave them waters. The air was thick enough to drink, everyone sweating, nobody caring with the scene before them . . . knowing a person died in there.

"So," Sophie started, "what are we thinking here? Body dumped in your house to make you look guilty about something? Sounds like something Brice would do. Or have you pissed off somebody different?" She counted on her fingers again. "Or. . . ." She half spun in her seat. "Ooh, is this one of those Russians or somebody from your Boston days, seeking vengeance, and they tripped and hit their head and burned up. You were quite the badass up there in Yankee-land I hear." Her animations had quickened, expressions almost cartoonish. "Oh, what if they come after me because I'm your friend!"

Callie almost asked Sophie where she gathered her Callie Morgan history. "Nobody's after you, Soph. Let me think."

"Might help keep you together to, like, talk about it."

"Appreciate the offer, but please?"

Sophie's expressions ran through indignant and pouty to understanding and a nod, like everything else in her life, flighty.

Callie reached for her pocket, aiming for her phone. Not there. Still at Mark's. This was only supposed to be a trip to grab an iron. Even without the phone, hope sprang from the remembrance of her personal security system . . . then wavered.

"Soph? When you moved my furniture after the flood, did you find my cams?"

Sophie took on a deer-in-the-headlights expression. "What did they look like?"

"There were five of them," Callie began, which only made Sophie look puzzled.

"Three were round, two rectangular, about yay big," she added, measuring with her fingers. The furniture may have been moved around, but if they found the cams, and left them out . . . even one of them. She couldn't recall seeing them as she navigated the house seeking the iron.

"I protected them very nicely, thank you," Sophie said.

Callie's hope rose. "What do mean protected?"

"I tucked them in your underwear drawer. Wrapped each one individually. I wasn't quite sure that was them, but I didn't want them getting lost or broken." She winced. "I need to buy you better underwear. Especially if you're expecting to further anything with Mark." She hesitated. "Was that okay? I mean, about protecting your cams?"

Callie tried not to sigh too hard. "That was thoughtful of you. Thanks."

Well, no recording of anyone coming in, or setting the fire. When she retrieved her phone, she'd check the outside cam footage. She'd strategically set them to cover all sides, all corners, all accesses.

Her heart rate no longer galloping, it still maintained a steady trot with the occasional flip. The flames were dying thanks to Leon, his men, and the assistance of St. Paul's Fire Department, and Callie tried to sort her thoughts, the remaining embers still making the effort a challenge.

Were Minnie and Monty working together, or rather Monty working for Minnie because Callie couldn't see Monty developing any of these concepts on his own. Their involvement downgraded Webb to a lesser degree of suspect. Did Monty set the Myrtle fire as a screen for Minnie to steal? The theory that the fire had spontaneously prompted some opportunistic bastard lost its credence when the jewelry appeared in Monty's bike basket.

But the dumpster part made zero sense.

What would happen to Monty now?

Three fires, not quite connected except for the fact they were on Edisto Beach which hadn't had a fire like these in years. Burglaries weren't foreign to a beach town, but the manner of the burglaries suggested staging. And damn, the badge. Minnie would not set up her son . . . unless she was diabolical enough to think Monty's handicap would buy him a pass. Theories too disconnected.

A flash went off. "Gotcha," Brice gloated. "Proof of you not doing your job, again. Why aren't you in there with those *men*—"

Stan flew out of his seat faster than Callie thought the big man capable. Like the old days, he reared at Brice like an old-fashioned adversary, not touching him, but within inches, all but doing so. Enough pressure to send Brice stuttering and threatening a half block down the road, Stan all over him every step of the way.

"He'll have that picture turned into a poster-sized visual aid by the next town council meeting," Sophie whispered. The crowd had died to a quarter of what it had been, yet she honored the need for discretion. Sometimes Sophie got things right.

"Out of context. Besides, I have witnesses," Callie said, though she wasn't exactly feeling the assurance she tried to give her friend. That picture, atop of a burned body which she hoped Brice hadn't snapped a photo of, and a person in the hospital whom she hoped Brice hadn't visited, would fuel his own personal fire. Arson and theft, multiple cases of each, might give Brice sufficient heat needed to convince the council to approve what he'd been trying to do ever since Callie set foot on the beach. The man's recent divorce should've tempered him, at least depressed him such that he didn't have the energy to be so caustic, but apparently not.

Thank you, Beverly. Your past is definitely affecting my present. Whatever caused her mother to butt heads with Brice, before Callie's mother married her father, must've taken up permanent residence in that toxic persona of his.

Again, something for the back burner. She was fast running out of burners.

Thomas rotated throughout the scene. As suspected, nobody saw anyone enter *Chelsea Morning*, including her, and he'd located the Saturn only two blocks down in the drive of an empty house. He'd swapped shifts with someone to stick around for continuity, and Deputy Raysor would relieve him in the morning. Thomas greeted the coroner's vehicle and directed him to a safe place to park.

Stan returned, satisfied Brice had received his message to stay gone, and resumed his guard. Callie wondered how long it would take for Brice to use Stan's behavior against her, too. Mark would be next.

At three a.m., the all clear was given to allow Sophie back in her home. She begged forgiveness for leaving, blaming a yoga class she had to teach at nine. Callie borrowed her bathroom quickly, coming back to Stan whose arms were crossed and stationed strategically propped in his chair, asleep.

The island would explode in gossip, Minnie's name leading the circuit. Callie had to reach Monty. Not that she could tell him his mother was dead. That fact wasn't official. Keys didn't nail identity.

Callie might as well call the hospital. Damn, again, no phone, hers still at Mark's. She nudged Stan and borrowed his out of his Hawaiian shirt breast pocket, him having no problem mumbling his access code.

With nursing understaffed due the recent viral outbreak, Callie placed three calls before reaching the right party. The nurse had no record of release yet, stating they'd have a better idea once the doctor made his rounds in the a.m.

"He's a person of interest in a serious crime," Callie explained without actually explaining. Then in case, she asked, "Is his mother there? She'd be one to spend the night. You know how she loves that son of hers."

The nurse softened at the sound of humanity. "She is definitely a Mama Tiger, but no, she isn't here. Left after he ate and fell asleep. Said she'd be back, come to think of it."

"Probably tired and catching up on sleep," Callie said. "If she isn't back by the time he's ready for release, call me. Monty works with my department on some things, and he has no other family." The nurse promised to note his chart.

Callie hung up but held onto the phone, thinking.

Mark wouldn't rise until nine or ten, but she couldn't wait that long. Her day had multiple missions, and each step could dictate the next.

She'd at least wait until dawn to go to Mark's house, but she could be proactive on one item on her to-do list. The key chain and the Saturn might be Minnie's, and the body a female, but Callie needed to check Minnie and Monty's home for the record. Thanks to Thomas, at least Callie had a patrol car to do that, and she could do that now.

She pocketed the phone, caught Thomas, and told him she was headed to Minnie's house instead of sitting around. With a look hinting of pity, he said he'd cover things at her house. She hugged him in thanks for that and for saving her cruiser.

With huge relief, she sat in her car and took in its familiarity. She'd just lost a lot of familiar, and somewhere over the next day or two, she'd realize she'd lost everything she owned. Everything but Jeb, thank God. He merited her call, but not this time of morning. Risking the chance Sophie might talk to him first, or Stan, she accepted that Jeb might get pissed not hearing from her first, but he'd understand, too. He'd lived with a cop his entire life. She turned over the engine and headed the five miles to the Bartow place.

With no cars on Highway 174, she reached Oyster Factory Road in brief minutes.

After four in the morning, the streetlight at the Bartow house barely cut the pitch of night, and the yellow bug light on the porch hung dark, as if telling Callie the obvious . . . nobody was home.

But somebody had been there . . . and left evidence.

She stood cautious and wary against her patrol car at the sight, wishing she'd gone by Mark's first after all. Standing in the middle of nowhere, nobody in sight, in ash-smudged shorts, t-shirt, no bra, and ruined sneakers, she likewise yearned for her weapon left at Mark's atop a second-hand nightstand.

Reaching back into the car for Stan's phone, she wanted pictures before calling for backup. *ARSONIST* was painted big and bold across the siding in two-foot-high, spray-painted lettering.

Chapter 24

SHE CALLED MARK.

"Huh? Callie?" He shook himself awake. "What's wrong?"

"I'm standing outside Minnie and Monty Bartow's residence. It's been vandalized. We believe the body found in my house was hers." She gave him the Bartow address. "Can you bring my phone, a change of clothes—any kind—my work shoes, and my belt?" Then she added. "My weapon.

She could've returned and done this herself, but she didn't want to leave the scene. Thomas managed the fire. Any other of her officers would have to drive further than she would going back to the beach. She could go in the house, but she'd rather not alone. Best to kill two birds with one stone, get her things and gain a second set of eyes, trained eyes. Maybe also assuage some guilt.

"Be right there." He hung up without waiting for her goodbye.

He'd clicked into cop mode, just like that. Like she did. He'd never begrudged her for doing so, either.

Frankly, this man did just about everything right, and standing there in the dark, she felt awfully flawed compared to him.

But there had to be a wrong to him. God knew she had a long-enough list of them on her side of the tally board. A tally that neither one of them had fully seen.

For instance, she'd always been her own worst enemy. Her mother always said so. Callie worked long hours to avoid these private moments and the inclination to think too hard. Outside in the dark, without even cricket songs to distract her, she thought in circles, which now made her wonder if the avoidance of herself was part of her attraction to Mark.

A warm wind blew across her, bringing the whiff of brine from the brackish river.

She inhaled deeply, appreciating a distraction that didn't last long. She wondered how people put up with her sometimes. She was the police chief. Everyone could accept that since the title came with a professional standard which she upheld, but the non-cop Callie was riddled with issues, with miles to go before she deposited them into the *history overcome* category, folded and stored in a box somewhere.

Like she thought she'd done these ridiculous fires.

Rubbing her bare arms, feeling something gritty on one, she brushed herself. She pushed off the car to study the giant lettering closer. Phone in her left hand, flashlight app on, with one tentative finger she touched where the paint, red in the light, had run at the base of the N.

The paint was dry, the culprit long gone.

Still, her radar had kicked in, senses heightened, and she tried to feel any eyes on her. Listening hard, she eased over to the A, and touched with another finger. Dry. *See? Long gone.*

A limb snapped to her right, behind the carport. Her hand went to a naked waist.

Silly. Any sound came across exaggerated when the whole world slept, distant from urban existence where traffic meant someone you recognized.

She was about to write off an errant raccoon in its nocturnal hunt when another pop sounded twenty feet farther. Or so she hoped.

She slipped to the cruiser's trunk and almost unlocked it to retrieve a shotgun for those rare opportune instances where her handgun would not do or, in this case, wasn't available.

No, how ridiculous. She hadn't heard anything new. Scouring the edge of the woods, she could see no further than six feet in, so she listened hard. Another noise crunched maybe twenty yards into the trees.

"Police," she shouted, going with her down-and-dirty voice. "Make yourself known."

Nothing, nothing, then a lone snap. Then gone.

And there she stood feeling asinine. She returned to the car, albeit sideways, an eye on the trees.

Her ears perked at a car's engine. For a moment she couldn't read whether it was coming or going until it got louder.

Mark's Bronco slowed as it arrived, the man taking in what he might be walking into, his headlights bouncing off the word *ARSON*. He parked, lights left on, spotlighting the criminal act front and center.

"Sorry to wake you," she said, moving to the driver's door. "Thanks for coming." If he handed over the clothes and weapon and backed out, she wouldn't hold it against him.

He shut the car off, and when he exited, he wore his own firearm on his belt. He handed her a paper bag in one hand, her Glock in the other.

She motioned for him to set down the Glock. "Stand over here," and she positioned him to where his door blocked one line of sight and he blocked the other. She laid out the clothes on the car roof's edge, peeled off her sooty ones, and changed, hopping up on the hood to don the shoes.

"I don't understand what's going on," she said, tying the last shoe. "The hospital hasn't seen Minnie since eight p.m. Her car was parked near my house, a body with her keys found in the fire. We're pretty sure it's her." She stood and secured the weapon on her belt. "And sadly, I believe she was after me." She pointed to the word on the house. "She'd already blown her temper at me, meriting hospital security intervention, then came home to this."

"And. . . ."

"Optics," she said. "Even if I didn't paint the letters, she blamed me for allowing her son to be shamed and hurt. I may not have held the paintbrush, but she felt I was the catalyst. This was her last straw."

He had no remark.

He had no opinion.

It was as if he took whatever she said as a given. This time she could read him. He wasn't sure he was in her life for more than this, backup and validation. Another gun, another pair of eyes, traffic control when the officers had their hands full.

Uncomfortable, Callie fingered Minnie's keys in the evidence bag. "I'm gonna check out the house." She paused in case he had advice. He didn't.

Mark following, Callie gingerly used the proper key to enter the residence. The keys and vehicle lent themselves strongly to the assumption Minnie was dead, and Monty was still hospitalized. If that body turned out to be someone else's, that was another situation altogether, but she'd play those odds all day long.

Inside, Callie flipped on lights in every room. Simple living. Few electronics other than the cable box and the Nintendo. No landline or wireless. A sewing machine set up in what appeared to be Minnie's bedroom, and a file cabinet in the dining area that housed Minnie's limited income tax business.

Outside, they found no paint can, no footprints thanks to there being no flower beds, only grass up to the brick on ground too hard to make tracks in even after the previous rains. Daylight might show tire tracks, but what were the odds of those mattering? They did a cursory glance around the property, to no avail.

They returned to his vehicle to shut off the headlights, and they assumed their seats inside. "Could use your two cents," she said after some graceless silence.

She noticed he only stared ahead, so she asked a question. "What would SLED do?" She might as well call upon his former profession and attempt to cross more than a professional bridge.

"A crap load of forensics," he said.

No doubt forensics mattered and had been known to break a lot of cases, but she leaned more heavily on people as windows into a case. What they said, how they said it, why they decided one thing or another, their habits and their tells. Forensics only backed up what she read in people. Too many cops these days let forensics lead them by the nose, missing a lot of obvious along the way.

"But forensics are only good so far," he said, as if he had read her thoughts. "Call the boy. Is he well enough to talk?"

She scanned to the east, a straight shot down the drive and across the road. Faint tinges of pinks and lavenders diluted the navy of night at the hint of dawn. "It's still early."

"Who gives a damn how early it is?" he said, with a mild edge. Even if his temperament was due to lack of sleep, he was right. Things were more important than sleep. His, hers . . . Monty's.

She tossed Stan's phone in the glove box in exchange for her own, and after the same dead-end attempts of before, she reached the same nurse, making her grateful she'd called before shift change. "Has Minnie Bartow returned to her son's room?"

"No, ma'am."

"Then could you please transfer me to Monty's room and make sure he's awake to take the call?"

"Um, patients need their sleep."

"Are you going to make me drive from Edisto to the hospital to wake him up myself?" Callie said.

"No, ma'am. Hold on a moment."

Mark watched, no sign of approval or disapproval.

"Hullo?"

"Monty, this is Chief Morgan. How're you feeling?"

"I hurt, Chief Morgan."

Poor thing. "Sorry to hear that. I hope that changes soon. We need you back."

That seemed to wake him up. "I was afraid you were mad at me," he said.

"Goodness, no, Monty. I need your help. And I especially need your ideas on some issues. Are you awake enough to answer?"

"Yes, *ma'am*."

Callie envisioned him sitting straighter in bed. "Let's go over the dumpster fire," she said. "Do you recall anything new?"

"Didn't see anything, I said."

Mark leaned, listening to the phone on speaker.

The woods noises gave her an idea. Clues could be more than sight. "Maybe you saw nothing, but what about smell? Did anything capture your attention? Someone had to be nearby to dowse you like they did."

He waited a few moments. "I smelled old food," he started, probably recalling lunch remnants and neighbors emptying their household refuse when nobody looked. "Also smelled cut wood, maybe caulk from that bathroom job. Then gasoline smelled more than anything. You mean like that?"

Callie dared a slight smile, like she sat beside him. "Yes, like that." He would smile back at the stroke.

"Now, what about sounds?" she said, saving the best for last, her own experience about the noises in the woods still keen. "Close your eyes and think about sounds. Real late at night noises stand out, so relive that evening and tell me what you heard."

Again, he quieted, like a child thinking hard to answer right. She bet he had his eyes shut.

"A diesel Ram," he said.

Callie stared in disbelief at Mark, who looked equally amazed. "How would you know that?" she said.

"I play games," he said. "I listen, I watch. I count white cars under carports, and I guess types of trucks with my eyes closed. I see which storage rooms are open, and peek inside. . . ." He stopped, like he'd said too much. "I just know stuff," he added, wrapping up.

Disappointment stirred in Callie. Storerooms. Brice. Gracious, surely Monty hadn't lit that bucket. Brice would take both of them down if that got out, but as threatening as Brice was these days, this issue was the least of their concerns.

Burning down whole houses mattered more.

Burning bodies inside of them mattered most.

She made a writing motion to Mark, silently telling him to take notes. He turned on his recorder, instead. "Show me how good you are at the trucks, Monty. Name me some on Edisto. When I'm parked, bored, and watching traffic, I might try this. I might even start teaching my officers this trick."

"Oh, okay," he said. "The man at *Big Chill* has a GMC Chevy Silverado. The people at *Turtle Time* own an F-250 Super Crew. Sometimes SUVs can trip me up if they're big enough, but a lot of them are on truck bodies making them sound similar, but I remember sounds, Chief."

Mr. Lancaster from Charlotte, and the Kirbys from Columbia. Monty knew his trucks. "Who drives the Ram?" she asked, hoping he'd slide into the answer without hesitation.

"Um, don't remember," he mumbled.

She didn't believe him. He knew. Of course he knew, and he was afraid of what he knew.

Time to put out an unofficial notice to her guys to be on the lookout for the Ram. She wished she had model and color, but Edisto wasn't that big to make this search too terribly complicated. After all, it was a contractor's type truck.

Webb drove one.

"Listen, Monty," she said, shifting subjects before he turned too uncomfortable to cooperate. She wished she were with him. "We're hoping the doctor releases you today." Truthfully, she wished they'd keep him for the week, until she could get a handle on who'd attacked him, but someone would get to him sooner or later with Edisto news, and he'd be alone and frantic wondering where Minnie was . . . or hear she was dead. "Your momma can't get there to pick you up. I saw her earlier." No lie. Just not the whole truth.

"Why?" he asked.

"She trusts me. Do you trust me?"

There was some hesitancy, but he answered, "Yes, Chief."

"Good. The doctor is supposed to call me when to come get you. Let's cross our fingers it's today, okay?"

"Okay."

"And if anyone else comes to see you, call me."

"Yes, ma'am."

His tired tone spoke of disappointment and lack of sleep, but he took her direction.

"Get well. Call me if you need anything, and I'll make sure you get it," she added, hating the mild deception, wishing he felt better, praying nobody else bothered to call him today. "Take care, buddy."

"Yes, ma'am."

"Is the nurse still there?" she asked.

"No, ma'am. She left. They stay busy."

"Okay, go back to sleep. Tell everyone I said to take extra special care of you."

Hopefully, he would and be a nuisance doing so, as a reminder that he was a special case, in more ways than one. They'd remember him more in their daily duties the squeakier a wheel he became. The more eyes on him the better.

Minnie wasn't coming back. Responsibility for Monty wasn't officially on Callie's shoulders, but the weight most assuredly rested heavy.

Speaking of Minnie, Callie realized she had her own phone now. She flipped into her security app. The last file was last night. The interior cams showed black, the inside of her underwear drawer per Sophie. The exterior cams, however, held footage. The front, east, and west cams showed nothing abnormal until the fire got underway and took them out. The rear cam overlooking the back stairs and porch, where Callie had broken back into her own home once the fire had caught, confirmed her strongest suspicion.

The resolution so-so, the color in shades of black and white both due to the cam quality and the night, Minnie appeared from the top right, her hair clasped in a barrette which made her easily recognizable. She approached the base of the stairs burdened with something of weight from her off-balance walk, and she looked straight up the stairs into the cam tucked into a corner eave, like she pondered how to navigate so high a climb. She transferred the weight to her left hand, the item a filled gas can, and leaned the other direction to allow her right hand to grasp the railing for support up the two flights. At the top, bosom heaving, she dropped the can, peered straight at the porch cam, and flipped her middle finger. Taking a thin cushion off a folding chair, she held it against the door's glass, shifted herself to handle the awkwardness, lifted the gas can, and swung the container hard enough to smash the glass.

Callie's soul sank at the blatant hate.

Minnie's hospital temper tantrum was more than a flash-in-the-pan reaction to her son's injuries. As tight as mother and son were, in hindsight and shortsighted, Callie understood that Minnie blamed her for all of Monty's recent ills. Callie had introduced Monty to danger as evidenced by his yearning to be a cop, the public's accusations against him, and his near-death experience.

Minnie's last purpose on this earth was to settle a score. The mother saw Callie as the stimulus for all of Monty's woes. She'd tried to destroy her and *Chelsea Morning*, and had proven to the beach that someone else could set fires other than Monty. He had an alibi.

Callie dropped the phone in her cup holder, a hand over the bridge of her nose. The small beginnings of bird song announced the dawn. The world had turned from ebony and gray to purples and blues, the sky allowing a little more of the pastels to shine through . . . and she found no beauty in any of it.

Monty's plight weighed so heavy.

She scrunched her eyes, blinking the dryness out of them. God, she was tired. Edisto was supposed to be an easier lifestyle where she could *get over herself*, using the phrase of her beloved father.

Callie lightly snorted. *Supposed to be.* The beach had been anything but easy since she accepted the job, but whining about easy didn't get the job done.

She had to fix this. *This* being Monty, Brice, the arsonist, the thefts, the any and all of . . . *this*.

A grackle announced itself off to her left in an irritating caw, ready to tackle his day. She, however, hadn't slept a wink and wouldn't see a bed today. She wondered what time Dudley woke. Early, she bet. And she best catch a hold of Brice and feed him the proper narrative before he came up with one of his own. Then, say, by nine, she'd call the hospital again. Doctors should've made their rounds by then. Those results would dictate the rest of her day.

Then she remembered Mark, who sat two feet from her elbow.

He watched, waited, his patience practiced. She wasn't getting much of anything right, was she? "I owe you a big apology," she said.

"I haven't decided about that yet," he replied, a slight squint in his eyes that she couldn't read was humor-based or not.

She tried again when he didn't elaborate. "I owe you a ton of thanks for being there, for picking up the pieces of my random life."

"But not for scaring you," he said. "Right?" he added. "My presence scares you?"

She lost her train of thought attempting to pick up on his. Is that what he believed? "What you heard me say to Stan last night in El Marko's was more for his ears than yours," she said. "He was being pushy."

"Stan means well," he said.

Nothing she didn't know.

Mark tipped his chin. "He doesn't want to be your go-to guy for the rest of your life, though."

That gave her pause. "Did he tell you that?"

"In a roundabout way. He doesn't like telling me too much of your business."

Stan had told her the exact same thing about not tattling Mark's personal life.

"He wants you to land someplace and be happy . . . *Chicklet*."

Her smile deepened. Her memories of Stan were warm, rich, sometimes sharp around the edges . . . and irreplaceable. He could challenge her, praise her, and kick her backside around the block better than anyone, and ever be waiting for her with arms wide when it was over.

"See, look at that reaction," Mark said. "When do I get to nickname you and earn feedback like that?" His innocent question came out in a subtle plea.

When does he rate her approval, was more what she heard.

She rubbed eyes, attempting circulation into the numbness she felt, stopping with both palms on her chin. "Let me think on it."

"You think too damn hard, you know it?" he said, proving he was probably the better analyst of the two anyway. "Sometimes it's cute. Sometimes it's a pain in the butt."

The car's shadowed interior disabled reading nuances. Disappointment? Pity? Sympathy?

"And there you go again," he said, and reached over, lowering her hands off her chin. "Here's my psychological take on. . . ."

You, she finished in her head. Maybe *us*.

"This," he said, with a sluggish back and forth from her to him and her again.

She stiffened, not sure she was up for the assessment. Not this tired. Not this early in the day. Not ever, if she were being truthful. "I'm sorry," she said again, hoping to nip this in the bud.

He shook his head. "I'm not asking for your apology. We're both gifted with fucked-up pasts, which might serve as an attraction."

Her surprise drew a snicker out of him. With a sweep of his hand from head to toe of himself, he said, "You saw this as perfect, huh?"

"Except for the limp . . . and now the four-letter word," she replied, trying to match his wit and falling pathetically short.

"Callie," and he sighed.

Again, she wished she could read him better. What did she expect dating an investigator?

He leaned back, hands off her. "Our only history of each other dates to December. You didn't accept my advances until a couple months ago." He shrugged. "Maybe I came on too fast."

"No," she said, softly. "You did everything just about right."

He studied her, the morning softening his expression. "You are so much sweeter than you let people see."

She couldn't remember anyone ever calling her sweet. "It's Friday," she said.

The sharp turn in the conversation raised his brow, the unsaid being she either wasn't willing to discuss their relationship or didn't know how to take the compliment, but he let her change direction. The series of unsolved catastrophes beckoned more.

"It *is* Friday," he said.

"A busy day for you and El Marko's."

"Are you asking me to accompany you someplace?"

"Maybe," she said after a brief pause.

"I'll give you until eleven."

"I'll take it," she said. "Let's park your car at your house. My car is enough. I need to hit these stops . . . and hit them fast."

Chapter 25

ON THE DRIVE BACK to the beach, Callie left a voice mail for Arthur in lieu of Janet. These days his cooperation outweighed his aunt's.

She took Jungle Road toward *Chelsea Morning*, each passing house raising reluctance in her gut like a fast-growing mold. She needed to see the damage but dreaded experiencing the ruin in the daylight. Neon crime scene tape caught her attention first, then the blackened remains, and as she slowed, her throat did a vise-like move, and she had to remind herself to breathe.

As Monty had been blamed, now the community would blame Minnie for setting her fire, underlining Monty's guilt. The court of public opinion could be a fickle yet powerful force. The public needed quick solutions. The public preferred its peace. Callie wished them to know the truth.

She'd think about where to live later. She tried very hard not to think about how much easier it was to think about the job and not her life.

Exiting the patrol car, she took soft steps through blackened silt peppered with curled and brittle ash. An acrid stench greeted her long before she reached the tape, and she knew from experience the odor would hang in her sinuses for days. She took in the dark, burnt wood and melted siding of what had been snow-white panels with black shutters with ferns accenting rattan settees on the front porch—the pots now broken and plantless, the outdoor furniture twisted wreckage of frames. The cushions had provided tinder making her recall Leon explaining how well patio cushions provided great flash fires.

She'd stood outside like this more than four years ago in Boston, at dawn. Why fate felt she needed to relive another such moment was beyond her. Back then . . . like now . . . what remained was a shell of a structure, not unlike the charred body that had burned with it, the body then, like the body now, relocated to a cold table in a heavily air-conditioned morgue. What remained held little resemblance to what had been alive.

She couldn't stop trying to remember how this place, and her life, had looked less than twelve hours ago.

Pockets of people walked or biked by already, the early exercisers and the neighbors daring enough to snoop with the authorities gone. Some took phone pics with one hand while holding morning coffee in another.

"You ought to have a fire inspector check it over before going inside," Mark said under his breath, suddenly at her side.

She thought, *I know*, but nodded instead. "I've got to call Jeb. He'll be awake by now."

He waited for her to do so, and when she made no effort, he asked, "Want me to do it?"

Callie almost gave him the go-ahead, but her son would interpret Mark calling as a weakness in his mother, then extrapolate that into depression which would drag drinking into the conversation. The kid was too young to understand life wasn't that linear. Trouble was, he had life experience to fall back on to validate his concerns. "No," she said. "I'll do it."

She lifted her phone. She'd moved Jeb here from Boston with so many assurances they'd be safe. She'd been wrong so many times.

Her phone rang before she dialed, the Edisto Beach mayor. She refused the call. No, she could not do this right now . . . accept the condolences, answer a question about where she'll live, then respond how she'll solve the case. Like anyone had such a contingency plan. She'd done this before, and the answers weren't any easier the second time around.

She texted Jeb. A coward's way out, but she didn't care.

BEFORE YOU HEAR FROM ANYONE ELSE, THE HOUSE CAUGHT FIRE. IT'S PRETTY BAD. I AM FINE IN ALL WAYS, SON, SO PLEASE DO NOT WORRY. I HAVE FRIENDS. WILL BE SWAMPED ALL DAY, SO PLEASE, LET ME CALL YOU LATER WHEN I CAN. LOVE YOU. MOM

"Callie? Did you hear me?" Mark touched her shoulder, giving it a rub. "Come to my place, take a shower, and rest. Stan or I can field your calls about the fire, and your guys can handle the station. You look too spent to go knocking on doors."

But Mark misunderstood. He saw her depressed and stricken with grief when she couldn't be further from either. The loss was real, for sure. The violation was more than real. However, anger festered as much as any other emotion, and not far behind that anger was a vengeance at what she labeled an attempted murder of her she absolutely did not understand. She didn't roll over in Boston, and she wouldn't roll over here.

They'd managed to flip her switch.

"Your demons came home to roost, huh?" taunted a voice she really didn't want to hear right now.

In two long strides, Mark positioned himself between Callie and Brice LeGrand. "This is tasteless even for you, Brice. Get your ass out of here."

"I'm checking on what she's done about all this," Brice said, demanding and playing to the meager crowd. "I have an obligation to the people."

But Callie chose not to channel her infuriation on him. While his job gave him reasonable rights of oversight, she couldn't afford to let him rattle her or use her as an issue with "the people." Not with two house fires in as many days, two small fires atop those, one death, and one hospitalization. No one was going to stand between her and the truth . . . like once upon a time in Boston, she could not afford Stan in her way, either.

She stared at her home, incensed, though her home's scorched vestige was not what filled her thoughts.

Brice sidestepped Mark, as if Callie couldn't hear around him. "Why are you letting this maniac continue his spree, Chief? Look at the price we've paid . . . you've paid . . . for not doing your job. Do you have any inkling of an idea who is torching Edisto Beach? Do I need to call in SLED?"

Mark inserted himself into the man's personal space again, backing him up two steps. "Shut up, Brice. She lost her home, for God's sake. I was SLED. *She* calls them, assuming she needs them, not you."

"Not if she falls apart and can't do her job."

"You are such a son of a bitch." At least Mark had the awareness to control his tone and who heard him.

Cameras clicked. People whispered to each other. Some called their friends.

In a big inhale, Callie made a choice.

She turned and eased around Mark, laying a hand on his chest in a gesture to stop this alpha confrontation in front of the world.

Minnie may have burned *Chelsea Morning*, but the first fire had led to the jewelry heists leading to the dumpster fire, ending with Callie's home destroyed. The original arsonist had jump-started a domino effect, making his egregious actions her issue, her case, her job, not anyone else's, and yes, she'd decided to take the whole ball of wax personal.

"No," Callie said, first to Mark, then to Brice. She approached the latter, stopping before him toe to toe. She welcomed the fact he refused to step back, saving her the trouble of how to say this.

"I have a good idea who's behind the arsons," she said low and steady. "And an even better idea how to nail him."

Brice's stare widened at her gruffness, his body stiffening at her gall to defy him in public, but her message snared him, and he couldn't help but ask, "Who is it?"

She held his gaze, and in those split seconds ran through her options.

She had insufficient evidence. She had no witnesses. She would call Colleton County about prints on the jewelry though she expected nobody's but the old man who discovered the pieces in his rain-soaked yard. She'd already done a fruitless search for prints on the uninscribed badge.

But a person driving a Ram, on an explicitly defined property, *Bikini Bottom*, had tried to kill Monty for reasons she was beginning to piece together in a loose logic. They would not have attempted such without a reason, because she'd ruled out the arsonist being a mentally-driven firebug. Like she said, all was loose logic.

Naming a suspect at this stage ran the risk of painting her with a wide, vindictive brush, and for once she did not care.

She wasn't at the end of her rope. She was tired of shit happening on her beach and her being blamed for it. Call the problem Brice. Call the problem public opinion. Call the problem simple fatigue of law enforcement being blamed for society's demented cache of ills.

Brice studied her with an assortment of slideshow expressions. "I asked who you think did all this. My money's on the Bartows," he said.

Which meant by noon the island would proclaim the Bartows guilty. Monty would have learned to set fires at the knee of his mother, and with her not being there and Monty's defenses being limited, the rumor would spread and anchor. Minnie would have died trying to kill Callie for her son getting hurt, who, in turn and according to rumor, probably got burned trying to set fire to a dumpster and tripped up doing so. Brice had already written the script.

Forget the fact they'd never done anything like this in their entire lives living on Edisto Island.

Callie made a decision.

She bent to whisper in Brice's ear. "Harbin Webb."

Brice squinted. "What are you saying?"

"He is my suspect. He is my target. He is my mission."

Leaving Brice stunned at the blunt iciness of her answer, she left and walked the perimeter of the disaster, the seed planted. People would expect her to pine over her loss, so she put herself out there on her property, giving them their expectation and as many photos as they desired to take. However, she barely saw the place, because in her mind she was elsewhere . . . several elsewheres, with alternate plans depending on how this played out.

She barely heard Mark's steps come up behind her. He needed to care for her, and she might as well let him. Brice needed a story to tell his constituency, as if he were on top of solving Edisto Beach's problem, and she gave that to him.

Stan was who she had to avoid.

Stan could read Callie. Stan had previously watched Callie go off the rails once the situation turned personal. Stan had come to Edisto to pick up the pieces of that. This time, however, she was more skilled and more aware of how discreet she should be.

In essence, she was doing what law enforcement wasn't supposed to do . . . picking out the guilty party before she had the evidence.

"What did you tell Brice?" Mark asked about the time they finished one lap around *Chelsea Morning*.

"I said I was working as hard as I could," she said.

Mark let her answer sink in. "What did you really tell him?"

She hesitated, still disputing with herself on how and where she was taking this plan, and she hadn't realized how hard she clenched her teeth until she had to speak around them. "Do you really want to know?"

This time he hesitated. Roles were reversed this time with him attempting to read her, taking long enough to register he hadn't succeeded.

"No," he finally said. "Don't think I do want to know."

She exhaled. "Thank you for that."

"Do you want me to go with you or not?"

The powers that be might crucify her either way, but they would crucify more any officer she took with her. However, they couldn't touch a civilian. "I wouldn't decline your offer," she said, to which he dipped his chin and motioned toward the patrol car.

She'd conveniently forget about Stan's phone in her glove box. For now.

CALLIE CALLED MARIE, reporting in that she was on the job, addressing the arson cases. Deputy Raysor and Officers LaRoache and Valentine, or rather Gerard, could tackle the beach. Thomas needed the day off after the night before.

"Jesus, Callie, you sound robotic. How is your house? How can I help?" Then after a few seconds, Marie added, "How are you?"

"I'm good. I'll be in touch." In afterthought, she added, "Thanks for being there . . . for being so reliable."

"What else would I be?" came the reply. "Callie? Are you really okay?"

"I'll check in later," and hung up.

She approached Myrtle Street from the southern end on purpose. Webb's white Ram parked at *Shell Shack*, the contractor nowhere in sight, but she didn't stop. Mark quizzically peered over at her disregard for the address but kept quiet.

"We're headed to Dudley Vaughn's," she explained, motioning to the old man's house ahead on the right.

Once she pulled into the drive, she left the vehicle running, the temp already ninety. "You stay here. Two of us might intimidate Dud. Besides," and she nodded back from where they'd come, "I need to know if and when that truck moves."

He nodded.

"Thanks," she replied, and closed the door.

By the time she reached the top landing, Dud stood leaning on his cane from behind the screen door, his button-up shirt fastened to his collar. "Saw you coming," he said, half-stern and half-proud, and he held the door open for her, like the old-fashioned gentleman he was. "How are you?" he asked, the routine etiquette of his question indicating he'd heard nothing of her own fire.

"Fine, Dud. How are you?"

"Fine, fine. . . ." His response faded in his wake as he automatically made his way toward the kitchen, probably wanting to set out Coke and shortbread cookies again.

"Wait, Dud." Callie stopped at the credenza and the celadon vase naked of its jewelry. "I found your necklace, sir."

He halted, and in short sideways steps, turned to see her. "You did?" His stare moved over Callie in little jerky movements, in wonder of where she'd hidden the prized possession.

"It's being tested for fingerprints," she said. "I'll bring it to you soon."

He deflated a little but seemed to accept her explanation. His rheumy eyes fixated on hers, waiting for another reason as to why she'd visit other than to return the treasure.

"Who took it, Dud?"

He kept staring.

"Sir, the other day when the fire happened down the street, my officer knocked on doors and vacated houses for safety's sake. To include yours." She let him recall that. "Both times I've visited, you've spotted me before I reached your porch. You people watch, Dud." She gently motioned toward a Queen Anne chair in front of the plate-glass window. Sheers protected the person on the outside from clearly seeing the resident behind them.

"You sit here a lot per the wear on the cushion, and that day there was a lot of activity to see. When my officer came to ask you to leave, you didn't answer. In fact, you hid. He assumed nobody at home."

Dud cut eye contact.

She'd guessed correctly. Dud had not left, having no place to go and nobody to take him.

"Which meant you were here when the thief came in."

His sheepishness accented his frailty, and she escorted him to his favorite chair. He sat, her hand at his elbow. Once he settled, she peered outside. Mark still sat in the patrol car. From that vantage, she could see who might come up the stairs to within a couple feet of the door.

"If Officer Valentine hadn't come by and made you hide, the thief would've entered and seen you," she said.

Dud diverted his attention to the street, on the patrol car, on anything or anyone other than the police chief who'd figured him out. "Guess I ought to thank the officer," he said.

Callie's phone rang. She reached into her pocket, noted Mark's ID, and diverted the call to a canned message, a motion she could do blindfolded. She had Dud where she needed him, pliable and compliant, and she didn't have an identification yet.

She squatted in front of Dud, congenial and caring and showing she listened.

"I remained in the kitchen, hiding," he said, sounding disappointed at himself . . . or disappointed at his age, his lot in life, his unplanned seclusion, any or all of the situations representing how sad his life had become. "If the thief had searched further than the living room, he'd have found me."

He didn't have to fill in what might've happened.

"But you saw *him*," she said, trying to soothe for what had been beyond his control.

Moisture oozed from pink-rimmed eyes to lodge in the crevices of his cheeks. "He'd break me in two with one hand. Don't ask me to identify him, Chief Morgan. Please don't." He swallowed, his folds of loose skin wobbling.

"Dud . . . Mr. Vaughn. If you tell me who stole the necklace, we solve more than a theft. We believe this individual is involved in setting fires, more thefts, even attempted murder. You're the best witness we have."

He was the only witness they had.

She hoped she was making headway. "Other families lost valuables. Owners lost their rental houses. A young man is in the hospital. A lady is dead."

"Dead!"

He paled, and Callie rerouted back to the beginning. "Who was it, Dud? We'll protect you."

Her phone rang again. Without looking, she diverted the call, maintaining eye contact with Dud. "Please."

Dud sank deeper into the back of the chair, a man appearing to give up. "Harbin Webb," he said. "I only recognized him because of work he did across the street earlier this year . . . next door last month. Both times he'd asked me if I needed work done since he was already on the street." His sigh carried a wheeze with it. "I thought him a good man till he stole my Sally's necklace."

A knock sounded at the door.

"I'll get it," Callie offered. She opened to find Mark.

"I kept calling you. Webb left," he said. "Saw us, packed his tools, and left."

She radioed her guys. "Who's near Myrtle?"

"Gerard here. I am."

"Get to *Salty Kiss*, ASAP. That's the home of Dudley Vaughn. He needs protection until I tell you otherwise."

"Don't leave me." Dud's thin words raised a deep well of pity in Callie, while at the same time stoking her fury.

She hung up and eased back down to his level. "I'll stay right here until Officer Gerard Valentine arrives," she said, but she counted the seconds. Webb left for a reason. She prayed it was no more than putting distance between her and him, but he'd left too many loose ends. Dudley Vaughn was one. Monty might be another.

Chapter 26

CALLIE PUT A BOLO out for Webb. Deputy Raysor, through his connection at Colleton County SO, would post a county guy at the big bridge's entrance to the island, and the only route off by land, a move they automatically did when a suspect was unaccounted for. Then she called Arthur about the time they reached Jungle Road.

"Has Webb called you?" she asked, the demand all but an ultimatum as she exceeded the speed limit.

"Hold on a second." The hand over the phone obvious, he came back a few seconds later. "I was in her office," he said, traffic noises in the background. "Not a good look talking to you without her permission."

She slowed as she reached the realty, pointing at Arthur on the Wainwright porch as she drove past. "I don't give a damn about your aunt right now, Arthur." While he had been somewhat forthcoming talking to Callie, he'd also been clandestine about offering said service. "Has Webb called you?"

"No, ma'am."

Callie pressed the gas and moved on. "Seen him?"

"No, ma'am."

"Call me if you do."

"Yes, ma'am."

"Now, give me directions to this development he's involved in."

Like a bootcamp recruit, Arthur rattled off the road and acreage and approximate proper lines of the water frontage. He remained on probation from his last legal mishap only a naïve kid of privilege would've found himself in the middle of. He couldn't afford to screw up.

"Poor guy," Mark said when she hung up.

"Book sense," she said, "but his common sense falls short sometimes." They reached Highway 174, and Callie took her speed up a notch.

Mark settled into his seat. "Where we headed?"

"Webb's home first. Then his real estate development."

One eye on the road, she hit redial to a recent number.

"Not while you're driving. Put it on speaker and hand it here," Mark said, taking the phone.

This time it took only two attempts to reach the nurse's desk. Callie identified herself and asked if Monty's doctor would release him today.

This nurse took her job more seriously than the other who'd left at the seven a.m. shift change. "We only speak to family."

"I'm Edisto Beach Police Chief Callie Morgan, and Monty Bartow is a person of interest in one of our cases. He also works part time for me. His mother has been in an accident, and I'm contacting him on her behalf. Is he being released today or not?"

"Sorry, ma'am, but I cannot release that information. There's nothing listed here with your name on it—"

"Ma'am, who do you intend to call to come get him then?" Callie's voice reverberated inside the confines of the cruiser.

"His father," spat back the young nurse. "Malachi Bartow. We spoke to him moments ago about picking him up."

"He *has* no father!"

Son of a bitch. Webb. Had to be.

"Ma'am?"

"Do not release him to anyone, do you hear?"

"How was I supposed to know?" spouted the nurse.

Infuriated at a nurse who'd block the police yet let a stranger waltz in and take a patient, Callie cut the call and called the hospital operator herself, asking for security. Surely they had record of Minnie's temper event yesterday. In abbreviated conversation, she explained Monty was mentally limited, his mother incapacitated, and he had no father. She requested a uniform watch his room, calling her when Webb arrived. Under no circumstances was he to be released to anyone but an Edisto Beach uniform.

She hoped they took her seriously.

They reached the turn to Herbert Smalls Road, and the nurse's revelation gave Callie a dilemma of taking the time to scout for Webb at his home five miles in or continuing to the hospital. The father pretense weighted her decision to head to the hospital. She called Deputy Raysor and asked if he'd run out to Webb's house and look it over.

Mashing the gas harder, she clenched both hands to the wheel and headed toward West Ashley, outside Charleston, praying the nurse didn't honor Webb's pretense as a father and that security took her request to heart. Monty looked like an adult but couldn't function as one, and letting him loose, especially as damaged as he was, only made him prey for Webb.

Webb had his sights set on Monty. She was sure of it.

"Get us there in one piece," Mark warned as Callie almost caught air crossing the McKinley Washington Bridge off the island.

"I still don't have the motive," she grumbled. "Whatever he was up to fell apart. He'll be groping for an out," she said. "Nothing can pin a thing on him without Monty and Dud. Gerard is with Dud. We must get to Monty. After that, we chase down Webb. He put all these events into motion and lost control. The result is one person dead, one injured, and me homeless. That doesn't even count the heists."

"How are you so sure it's Webb?"

"Oh, I know," she said, gripping the wheel tighter.

"But can you prove it? You have a mentally challenged man who thinks he heard Webb's truck, and an octogenarian who thought he saw him while hiding in the kitchen, both afraid, neither incredibly, um, credible."

Her jaw clenched, Callie couldn't argue with Mark's synopsis. "Then we push Webb until he caves."

"You sound like an episode of 'Hawaii 5-0'," he said, not in jest. "In today's environment, cops are guilty until proven innocent. Webb has popular opinion in his court, Callie."

"Brice, maybe, but not Webb," she said.

"One may support the other," he said.

"I can't help that, Mark."

"I'm helping you keep your head," he countered. "Follow the evidence, not the culprit. Otherwise, you'll wind up down a rabbit hole with the bad guy in the wind."

She wished she could stop her eighty-mile-per-hour car and have this conversation on the side of the road. She wished she had the luxury of sitting in a diner over coffee for a philosophical discussion of why people hated cops these days, but she played the odds right now, with time on Webb's side. He hadn't been spotted again on the island or the beach, and she could only assume Monty was his goal, and he had a jump start on them.

Webb wasn't a hardcore criminal, but his nickel-dime plan hadn't worked, and his effort to stitch up the holes and repurpose his plan only worsened his situation. All because he wasn't a hardcore criminal. He didn't know how to be bad quite the right way.

Whether McPhee was involved had yet to be determined, but Webb was in financial trouble. He set the Myrtle fires, she was pretty certain, planting Monty's badge to sway suspicion. Then, maybe in afterthought, he'd decided Monty was too potentially damaging to keep around. While the court of public opinion ran high about Monty being the arsonist, Webb had tried to rid the beach of him, in hope of closing the arson cases. The faster the cases closed, the sooner insurance paid . . . the sooner he got out of financial trouble.

Whether he painted *ARSONIST* on the Bartow house was questionable, but no doubt someone did it because of the story Webb had spun.

Callie had a long history of being pretty damn good at proving her assumptions true.

She reached Adams Run, choosing to pass the two-lane highway 162 for the two miles further to US Highway 17, a four-lane where she could pop on the lights and maximize her speed. The stop sign at Highway 17 appeared a quarter mile ahead when she got the call from Marie at the station.

"Incident at *Salty Kiss*," Marie said. The intonation triggered something in Callie, and she lightened pressure off the gas. That was Dudley's house. That was Marie not sounding so together.

"What is it, Marie?" Callie looked over at Mark, wondering if his puzzled expression mirrored hers.

"Gerard's patrol car caught fire outside *Salty Kiss*. Lit rag in the gas-tank neck. He's fine." She held back, and Callie pulled to the side of the road, sensing more to be said.

"How's Dudley Vaughn?" Callie asked. Her gaze hung on Mark as if their combined powers could mitigate the news.

"He died, Callie."

Callie's breath caught. A flood of anger, frustration, and sadness rose up inside her, and it squeezed her hard. "How did he die?"

Marie wept on the other end. Not loud, no sobs, but her broken words said enough. "Coroner's on his way," she said. "And Colleton County forensics."

Callie scowled. "Start at the beginning, Marie. No, wait. I'll call Gerard. I want to hear it firsthand."

Callie must've sounded peeved, which wasn't unusual when the mission was literally blowing up in her face. Marie replied, "Don't blame him, Callie. He's beside himself."

"I'm sure he is," she said, easier. "Thanks, Marie. I promise to get the facts before anybody gets upset with anyone." Marie was solid, but for her to cry showed how sensitive she was about Edisto's people. "Honey, we'll figure this out."

"I know you will. Thanks." The sniffle came across sloppy and wet, making the heartbreak all the more real as she hung up.

Callie dropped her head in her hands, fingers pressing her temples, pushing up and down her hairline. Mark reached over to stroke her back, but he'd barely touched her before she straightened. She was rabid. This whole mess remained just out of her reach, and out of her control. She sucked in with intense effort, needing to collect herself. "I've got to call Gerard."

"I'm sorry, Callie. This is wearing you down. Remember that when you speak to him."

She almost snapped at him and asked what kind of person he thought she was, but that would only underline his point. She wasn't so exhausted not to see that. Her feelings weren't as compartmentalized as she preferred right now, but they weren't yet flapping in the wind, either.

She phoned instead of radioed, for no other reason than to keep this off the air. "Gerard? Are you okay?" Gerard was her least experienced, and he took errors too much to heart. He'd have been eaten alive in a big city, and she wondered if that was why he'd transferred to Edisto.

"Chief, I'm so sorry." He sounded a hint wobbly, inhaling once, then twice.

"Start at the beginning." She took a deep breath of her own.

Gerard cleared his throat. "Mr. Vaughn sat in his chair, watching out front. I gather he does that. I asked him if he wanted a Coke. I went to fix it for him when he shouted for me then shouted something about my car. I ran back. There was a rag hanging out the filler neck to my gas tank." He cleared his throat again. "I told Mr. Vaughn to sit tight. I turned the front door lock and pulled it closed. I managed to yank the rag out before too much happened."

Mark jerked at that. "This is Mark, Gerard. You were foolish trying to beat that fire to the gas."

"Yes, sir."

"But I'm glad you're here to tell about it."

"Yes, sir."

Callie spoke. "Go on, Gerard. Get to Mr. Vaughn."

"The front door was still locked when I tried to get back in, and he wasn't answering, so I ran around to the back. The door was closed, but not locked, and its glass had been broken. I'd checked every door and window on that house when I arrived, Chief. I promise. Someone broke in."

Callie turned the car around. "Don't touch the kitchen," she said, ready to nail down facts. "Now, tell me what happened to Dudley." Still on a two-lane road, houses scattered but driveways still too close to the road to go much faster than the limit, she stared ahead, counting down the miles to when she could drive more freely.

"That's the thing, Chief," Gerard said. "Mr. Vaughn collapsed on the floor, not a mark on him. Crumpled—like he stood and his body decided otherwise. No sign of anyone else in the room."

"Take care of the scene. We're on our way," she said, hanging up to immediately call one of her old reliables.

"Raysor," answered the deputy with his tell-tale growl. A blue-collar Stan.

"Your guy on the bridge still there?" she asked.

"Till I tell him otherwise," he replied.

"This bastard is still on the island. Let's keep him that way. Someone tried to blow up Gerard's patrol car, and Dudley Vaughn is dead."

"What? They sure it's Webb?"

Of course Raysor would ask as any law enforcement member would. "No, they aren't. I think the only person who saw him was Dudley, and the sight of Webb scared him literally to death." Fury spiked in her yet again at the old man's life, or ending of it. She couldn't prove Webb sabotaged the patrol car, but she'd bet her career on it. "Webb is staying one step ahead of us, Don. I can't seem to catch up to him."

"You sure we're after the right man?"

"As sure as I can be without forensics," she said.

"Doll," he started, using the nickname she used to hate that had become this redneck's form of appreciation. "Be careful with this."

"We catch him and rule him out, if nothing else, Don. Got it? He's the focal point right now." She turned onto the road. "I'm on my way. Hang around there at his house, if you don't mind," she said. "Webb has no place to go unless he has a boat. Is he a boater? Does he fish?"

"All I see out here is a small johnboat—maybe eighteen feet, twenty horsepower, so not too serious. Nothing to escape in unless he has a huge head start."

The help at her disposal was limited, and Raysor was seasoned. Where could she use him most?

"Tell you what," she said. "You stick to that neck of the woods. Scour that area for him but stay in touch. I want more than one person in his way if he decides to bolt off the island. I'm on my way to Dud's home."

"Will do, doll. Hey," he added, "unless he royally screwed up, cut Gerard some slack. He's good at beach jobs, but he's never been really tested."

Not the time to worry about that, but also nothing she didn't already know . . . don't jump on Gerard with both feet when she got there. "I hear you."

"Good. Raysor out."

Stan, Raysor . . . and Mark beside her. Overseers, mentors, advisors . . . sometimes overcompensating males thinking they had to keep her on some proper path. Lack of faith in herself began to show through one too many cracks.

She and Mark reached the big bridge, and as they sped past the deputy guarding the island side, they raised a hand. A few miles further to the right would be the turnoff to where Raysor held his ground. She took note of it as they passed.

"Lots of disjointed pieces to this," Mark said after a two-mile silence.

"Some of them are clicking into place," she replied, her stare steely on 174.

"They don't click right without proof."

Mark was doing his best, his subtle best, to keep her from crossing a line. He sensed her hunger to take this guy out and create the narrative afterward. He was right. That was the direction her thoughts had taken since her house burned down. Webb had started a sequence of bad events that needed to stop. However, if she couldn't stop him by the book, she'd freelance. Not that she wouldn't listen to Mark . . . to Raysor . . . to Stan. She'd listen until their advice didn't work anymore . . . or didn't mesh with her own.

"Cover this from the beginning for me," he said.

He was making her retrace steps and evidence, working to keep her honest and alert. To pacify him, she recanted everything from Myrtle Street to present. The dialog took them to the beach, and they soon reached *Salty Kiss*.

After the formalities of greeting a forensics tech at the patrol car, Callie took the front stairs at a trot not to address the living inside but for Dud. Mark hung back in the entryway as Callie softly stepped to the old man's side on the floor, the assistant coroner taking notes.

"Heart attack most likely," he said, without being asked. Richard Smith had met her three other times and, personally, could take or leave Callie, but for some reason, addressing this feeble, delicate gentleman on the floor tempered him. "We'll confirm with the postmortem. You're welcome to take a shot at proving whether fright induced it, but nothing I can do will help. The old guy was just . . . old."

Just . . . old. What a lonely place to reach in one's life. Callie kneeled, her heart full and beating harder to compensate. She'd planned to visit him, maybe take him out to eat on occasion. He'd just entered her life and had been there but a flash. "I'm so sorry, Dud. Enjoy your Sally."

She rose, gazing a long moment at him. Then she shifted gears and moved toward the kitchen. A tech was starting to mark the site. "Any joy for me here?" Callie asked, expecting nothing miraculous. Not on this case. Nothing worked right on this case.

The tech pointed to the floor. "Whoever it was ran out, slipped on the glass pieces, and while he caught himself, he managed to lay a hand on the tile."

Callie's heart dared beat a little faster.

The tech squatted, her pen acting as a pointer. "Blood there. Not much, but doesn't take more than—"

"Blood?" Callie shot a look at Mark, daring to think positive. "Anywhere else?"

"We're still hunting outside," she said.

"We'll take it," Mark said, gripping Callie's wrist. "This is where forensics reigns supreme," he said, smiling at their new upper hand. "Use it, Chief."

Oh, he didn't have to remind her that DNA trumped all the what-ifs in the world, but she didn't have to have the results back to have the power. All they had to do was find the son of a bitch and pretend they were indeed Hawaii 5-0.

Chapter 27

THE MARINA WAS barely a mile north of *Salty Kiss*. Callie called the folks there, then the manager at Pressley's, a popular restaurant that resided above the marina's office and store. Both sites, top and bottom, held a broad vantage of the entire marina's access, slips, and dock, and the more eyes on Big Bay Creek, the better. Today was bright. Today was sunny. Everyone knew who Webb was, some already having heard Brice's rumors about the contractor. He should be easy to spot in any attempt to take a boat and disappear.

"Don't attempt to confront him," Callie warned one, then the other.

"He's not a problem," said one lady. "Our guys will stop him."

"Please. Everyone becomes a different animal when the police are after them. We have no idea if he's armed."

"Most contractors are," she said. "A couple of us might have carry permits, too."

Not what Callie wanted to hear. "Please, do nothing more than shout at him to stay away from your businesses, but call me ASAP."

"Sure thing, Chief." Callie heard her shouting to someone in the background as she hung up. The natives, in particular the long-term ones, didn't take much to troublemakers on this beach. They weren't fond of arsonists or thieves, either.

Plainly, Brice had performed well, disseminating the news that Webb was wanted. May be bending the rules on her end, but it put the beach on notice, made them aware.

A deputy still covered the big bridge, Raysor several miles closer watching Webb's home vicinity. Gerard would remain at Dud's. LaRoache maintained watch on the north side of the Scott's Creek causeway that divided the town from the island. Her two other officers rolled, eyes peeled for the Ram, which everyone now assumed a 2014 model and white. Thomas remained the token off-duty officer, so somebody would be fresh tomorrow.

Webb remained loose. He wasn't off the island, and chances were he hadn't left town, but as a contractor, he was familiar with every hiding place around every building. She wasn't worried he'd escape. She worried what he'd do trying to.

"Mark, you want me to carry you to work?" she asked, noting the eleven o'clock deadline drawing nigh that he'd given her earlier.

"Already called Sophie to open for me," he said. "You're short staffed."

"It's Friday."

"Yes, it is."

She wasn't up to arguing. She was up to ordering who went where, when, and how, and if he could tolerate that, guess he was along for the ride.

"Tell me what to do," he said as if prompted.

She held up her phone. "Let me do this, then we'll join in the search."

She'd been meaning to meet with Arthur again, but there wasn't time, so she called. She wanted every ounce of intel on Webb, and like most people, if they heard someone was in trouble, they suddenly remembered all the wrong that person had ever done.

No answer. She left a voice mail.

Then she called Janet. No answer. Janet could be with a client, though. Clients always came first . . . above police, above the mayor, above God. Janet got where she was being who she was and being unabashedly honest about it.

Callie dialed the main Wainwright number, the office. Janet had discharged many a staff member for not catching the phone. She hadn't made her millions by being unreachable, and voice mail didn't cut it. Receptionists manned the front desk like an old-fashioned switchboard operator, answering within three rings or they were terminated.

No answer.

Three calls. Three voice mailboxes.

"Let's go," Callie said, walking to the front door. "We're running by Wainwright Realty. If you want to bail there and walk across the street to the restaurant, you won't hurt my feelings." She already moved down the stairs.

Remembering his old limp she turned to see if he kept up, but he was right behind her. "It doesn't slow me down as much as you might think," he said. "Let's go." When they reached the bottom, he added, "Don't bother dropping me off. Webb is escalating, and you don't have enough on your team. You need someone with you." He didn't have to include he was armed and well-trained with two decades of experience.

She sped up, radioing Officer LaRoache. "Any sign of that Ram?" she asked.

He stood guard right outside town across Scott's Creek, on the island side, checking each vehicle leaving the beach town. From that side it was a lot easier to corner them on the small two-lane road channeled by a salt-water marsh on both sides.

"No, Chief. And I'm checking everybody."

Webb was still within the confines of Edisto Beach. Wainwright was on Callie's way off the beach, and Callie's quickest route was to catch Palmetto and stretch out until she reached Mary Street, the hard left taking them almost head-on to Wainwright's parking lot. With island exits manned, she could afford the brief detour. Nobody answering their phones worried her.

She came in from the side, studying the parking lot, and stiffened. A white Ram pickup was wedged between a van and an SUV around back.

Callie's phone rang as she threw the transmission into park. She answered the phone with her right, pointing at the truck with her left, noting Janet's number on caller ID. "Chief Morgan—"

"The son of a bitch took Arthur," Janet barked. "He locked my receptionist and me in the front closet. One of my agents just let us out."

The receptionist cried in the background, a third party, probably the agent who'd released them, soothing her. Janet, however, sounded ready to empty a magazine and drop bodies.

"Any chance he's on the premises?" Callie asked, Mark having already withdrawn his firearm.

"No, he left. Took Arthur's Ranger." The two-door, extended cab was well known and nowhere in sight.

"I'm going after him," Janet said. "I'm not waiting for you."

"Stop it, Janet, I'm right outside. I'm coming up."

Damn it, Callie said under her breath, leaping out of her car. She took the two flights of stairs into the real estate office two steps at a time, only to find the agent and receptionist but no Janet.

The agent nodded toward Janet's office, a warning in her tone. "Bet she's gone in her gun safe."

"Her what?" But Callie didn't wait for the answer and bolted into Janet's inner sanctum. "Janet?"

A door hung open to what Callie had always assumed was a file closet, meaning banker's boxes, extra copy paper, and years of real estate contracts. She should've known from the lock on the door and the Marine's history that Janet Wainwright kept firearms at the ready.

"You're not going after them," Callie said. "We've had this conversation before, and last time I let you get involved you hid a weapon on you against my orders. You almost got killed, and you did get somebody shot."

"You can't stop me." Janet's guttural response from the closet surprised Callie. The old woman was afraid, and this was the only way she knew how to respond.

Callie went to the open closet to find Janet's head immersed in a twelve-gun Liberty vault. "What are you doing?" At quick count, Callie recognized eight firearms in Janet's arsenal. What the hell kind of fire power did she have at home? Maybe even in the Hummer.

"Oh, no," Callie said, moving into Janet's way when the real estate broker emerged, each hand filled, one with a .45 handgun and the other a twelve-gauge shotgun.

Callie reached out for the shotgun, but Janet turned to protect it beside her. "No, Chief. This is my fight. Nobody comes on my turf and harms my people."

Callie raised her voice, drawing Mark into the room. "You are wasting time and giving Webb time to escape, Janet. Shut up and tell me what happened!"

The Marine's glower would melt the sunglasses off most people, but she and Callie had confronted, fought, and collaborated too many times to catch either too far off-balance. "Janet! Talk."

Thin lips mashed almost white, her angular jawbone clenched tight, the aunt weighed her options and spoke. "Webb barged in here, in this very office . . . nobody barges in here . . . and asked Arthur if he could borrow his truck. Stunned, as he had every right to be, Arthur said no. I chewed on the imbecile for the manner in which he entered, trying to bully his ass out of here . . . not wanting to let on that I heard you were on his tail. Before I could get from behind my desk, he fisted Arthur in the chest and sprawled him across the floor." She gestured to the hardwood in front of her built-in bookcase, grumbling curse words. "And he yanked me by the arm, almost over the top of my desk!"

Callie expected a more damaging reaction from the Marine against Webb, maybe putting him on his back, yanking a shoulder out of socket, or breaking a nose, but Callie made herself remember Janet was in her late sixties.

Janet huffed once, her wrinkled cheeks rounded by the hard and angry effort.

With care, Callie took the shotgun from her and propped it against a bookcase. "He held a gun on Arthur and ordered you outside to the receptionist, then locked you both inside a closet." Regardless of Janet's strong-armed tactics with her nephew, Janet would not have risked a hair on Arthur's head. "Did he say where he was going?"

"No, only that he needed the truck, but then he snatched Arthur by the arm and took him. I'm telling you, the idiot was flying by the seat of his pants, Chief."

Janet was highly embarrassed, mad, and fearful rolled into a ball of rare insecurity. She was accustomed to being on top and in charge of everything in her universe.

But Callie couldn't have Janet in the midst of this. She was trained but had proven to be a loose cannon in times past, and her age slowed her skills.

Callie called Officer LaRoache.

"Chief?" he answered.

"We're now hunting for Arthur Wainwright's blue Ranger," she said, hearing him talking over the road noise coming toward and going away from him as he scanned each vehicle. "He kidnapped Arthur and stole his pickup."

"Wait . . . what?" he replied, and Callie's gut sank at those two words.

"You saw him," she stated.

"I saw Arthur," he corrected. "He was driving. Had a load of real estate signs behind the seat, and a canvas over what he said was more of them in the back. Said he was headed out to post new listings." He hesitated before adding, "No sign of Webb."

She knew the answer before she asked the question. "But you didn't look under the signs or the canvas?"

"No, ma'am."

"Callie out."

She hurried out of Janet's office, calling in to amend the BOLO, tapping Mark en route to the exit. "He's left the beach. You coming or staying?"

"Coming," he said, hustling behind her.

She reached her patrol car to hear Stan's phone ringing in the glove box. Stan was hunting his phone, her, and now probably Mark, but she hadn't time to explain. Mark offered to take the call.

She radioed Raysor, backing out hard enough to skid before taking Jungle Road. "Hold on," she said to him, and she barely slowed reaching LaRoache, shouting, "Stay here. The big bridge is blocked, and Raysor's in between. Be ready to haul if I call you."

He shouted "Yes, Chief," but she'd rolled on, only seeing him mouth the words in her mirror.

She returned attention to Raysor. It was mid-day, and the traffic leaving Edisto wasn't enough yet to slow her. "He's headed your way, Don, only he kidnapped Arthur Wainwright and swapped to Arthur's truck. A blue, late-model two-door Ranger, license tag EBEACH2. Last I heard, Arthur was driving . . . Webb hidden behind the seat or in the bed, uncertain which."

"Gotcha. What's the plan?"

She had LaRoache blocking the beach, the Colleton County deputy blocking the big bridge, and now Callie coming at him from the south and Raysor from the north. "We pinch him between us," she said. "You come no further than Jane Edwards Elementary School. I'll stop at Trinity Episcopal. That'll leave four turnoffs between us, all on the north side. Nothing on the south. If he takes a side road, they all dead-end, and we still have him blocked unless he takes a boat. We'll deal with that if and when it happens."

"Armed?"

"Yes."

Raysor growled in his mode of displeasure.

"I know," she said. "Slowly head down the highway. I'm already coming toward you. Call your guy and update him at the bridge."

She hung up. "I don't understand this man," she said, under her breath. "Money is all the motive I can think of, but damn at this guy's methods. He could get himself killed." Then to Mark, "Keep an eye out down the side roads."

"He's not a natural crook," he said.

"Which makes him volatile," she replied.

She'd already slowed. No point in racing. Webb wouldn't hurt Arthur while in transit, and he was blocked from both ends. Even if she missed him, or Raysor missed him, the others stood in his way.

Sun flickered through the two-hundred-year-old oaks that rose from either side of the road, stretching their canopies to meet each other overhead. Callie left her sunglasses in the console's holder, her gaze drilling as far ahead as she could see, hunting for that Ranger bumper and its unique tag.

Mark tossed Stan's phone back in the glove box. "He's pissed."

"He can stay pissed."

"Then he said be careful."

"Only way to be," she said, the discussion of Stan over.

They traveled in silence, perusing the side roads, knowing each one dead-ended into water or circled back to 174. She reached Trinity and eased onto the property and stopped beneath a massive oak, its ferns and wafting tendrils of ten-foot Spanish moss helping to disguise the patrol car as nothing other than a resident visiting the library on the grounds, or a member of the congregation parked to volunteer.

They waited.

"He's gone to ground," Mark said, "Or one of us would have seen him by now."

"Yes," she said, hoping that's all Webb did . . . hoping Arthur did no more than sit petrified behind the wheel. She almost called Arthur's phone, to get a read on the situation . . . *wait a minute.*

The last time she'd involved Janet in hunting someone who worked for her, Janet admitted she mandated People Finder on her staff's phones, in particular Arthur, her repair people, and her agents. She phoned Janet.

"Found him?" Janet answered without any sort of salutation.

Callie assumed she meant Arthur, not Webb. "No. Listen to me. Look up People Finder for Arthur's phone and tell me where he is."

"Damn it all, why haven't I done that already? Hold on."

Janet was flustered and scared and not thinking as crystal as her norm. "There he is," she said. "Webb didn't turn off his phone, thank God."

Callie didn't tell her that the app worked whether the phone was on or off. "Where is he, Janet?"

"That can't be right," she said, vinegar back in her tone.

"What?"

"Says he's in Scott's Creek, right outside town limits."

Damn. "Thanks, Janet. I'll be in touch." Callie hung up before she had to explain.

Webb had tossed the phone in the water as they left Edisto Beach, or made Arthur do it.

Callie waited at Trinity, and Raysor waited at Jane Edwards School.

Webb was someplace up and down these short roads. The wait was excruciating.

How many times had she chased someone on these roads? She could count her blessings for living on an island versus a place like Boston. On this side of the big bridge, you had only dead-ends into water and remained on the island. Almost like the magical characteristics of a Brigadoon. One way out.

In Callie's experience, people were more inclined to make brash, life-altering moves once trapped. Hopefully, Webb didn't harm Arthur out of sheer frustration of the corner he'd painted himself into.

Janet would never forgive Callie if he did.

Callie might never forgive herself. This case had been so stupid from the very beginning.

Chapter 28

CALLIE STARED AT the highway as if not doing so would let it vanish into vapor. Other roads ran through her mind where Webb could hold up. Point of Pines Road, Peters Point, Legare, Red House, even Botany Bay. She'd called upon volunteers to keep a watch on each and every road, one of many advantages of being a small community and the plus of everyone knowing Arthur. However, all saw nothing . . . but they'd watch.

"Here he comes," Raysor shouted over the radio, like his favorite horse rounded the bend to the finish line. "I've blocked the highway, and he's spinning around to head back your way."

Callie flipped on lights and siren, threw her car into gear, and kicked up buckets of oyster shell and crusher run exiting the church property onto the highway. Though buckled in, Mark held on to the door and the dash.

"He's almost at you!" Raysor yelled. "Hah!" he yelled. "Try it, you bastard. We're nailing your sorry ass. We're gonna. . . ." Raysor slung slurs and promises, his enjoyment of the chase ringing loud.

"There he is," Mark shouted, pointing ahead.

Instead of playing chicken with the blue Ranger, not willing to challenge Arthur who had no idea how to safely drive a truck at high speed on narrow roads, Callie braked and twisted her vehicle around until it obstructed both lanes.

She could imagine Webb's cursing orders to Arthur. "Turn around! Turn around!" Unsure what else to do.

And turn they did. Callie roared into gear and pursued, expecting to chase the truck back into Raysor's roadblock now only a mile ahead. She hoped Raysor knew to—

Wait. She took a chance.

Callie took Oak Island Road almost on two tires.

Mark's laughter bounced off the car ceiling, his own adrenaline up. "I remember this road! It circles around."

But Callie only drove. Yes, they'd been out here chasing Janet's hired hand back in December . . . the month El Marko's opened and the first time she dared to partner with Mark. Thank God she had, because she understood this road better now and hoped she had a plan.

They flew down the asphalt two-lane, past the New First Baptist Church's sprawling cemetery. With no traffic, the patrol car sailed down the straightaway at eighty, even ninety at one point, forty over what the speed limit should be if it were posted.

A couple miles in they passed the private road to Oak Island Plantation on the right, reminding Callie to watch for residences and drives farther ahead as they took the back bend of the circular route. She held her breath hoping nobody felt the need to run out on errands in the middle of the day.

The asphalt ran out quicker then she expected. The silt held traction for a short spell, but before she could lower her speed, the rippling of the unscraped road jarred their teeth and stole her tires' grip.

They slid left, the built-up dirt of the road bed and reduced speed giving Callie enough grip to regain control. The road held an assortment of secluded housing—a two-story plantation home, a trailer, a boxed-brick home, each of which had almost acquired a patrol car for their front yards. To avoid hitting a mailbox, Callie veered right into the edge of an open field that miraculously appeared out of nowhere.

Without conversation, she turned, threw an arm over the seat, and backed into the road again—thrusting the transmission into drive and taking off, daring the laws of physics to do that to her again. The delay might have been enough to alter her plan.

She mashed the gas, taking them back up to the range of another skid, but she had to risk it. There was little time. The silty dirt ran deeper, but at least they'd passed the residences. All they had was empty road, assuming they could stay away from the pines and oaks growing three feet off the sides, and the further they went, the wider the tree trunks grew, the broader the canopies, the deeper the brush, all creating a vegetation tunnel.

They exploded into light and tilled farmland, and Callie floored it again, knuckles white against the black steering wheel.

Mark had remained quiet to now. "You sure you—"

"He took Steamboat Landing, Mark. Behind him is Raysor. We're to his left. There's no outlet on his right."

"You think that he thinks we stayed on 174, and he'll take the road we're on to circle around behind us?" he asked.

"Yes. Then he's between Raysor and LaRoache at each end of this loop we're on. All we have to do is outmaneuver him road by road, dead-end by dead-end, until we run him into the hands of an officer."

"Unless we catch him first."

Callie grinned with a wry humor behind it. "My preference."

"I've got to say it . . . this is a damn turn-on, Chief Morgan."

To which she could not disagree.

Her preference was to stop Webb out here, away from most civilization. Whether she sideswiped him into a ditch or he slid sideways on silt into trees, she hoped to bring this to a close outside of civilian sight. Arthur mattered to her most, but nailing Webb out here ran a close second. The fewer involved the better. The fewer witnesses, the best.

Oak Island Road had turned into Jenkins Hill where the silt got deepest, and no way the Ranger had passed them. The T into Steamboat Landing was a quarter mile ahead.

Suddenly the Ranger flashed into view, skating sideways like skis attempting to slow on a black diamond slope, missing the turn. In their view and out of it, just like that.

Callie rushed to meet what she hoped was a finale to the chase, a fishtail skid reminding her to hold control. "See him?" she asked Mark, because she didn't.

"Not yet, but he's there," he shouted, every bit as eager as she.

Let him leap out of that truck bed and run. Let him have flown from the truck bed only to wrap around an oak. Give this crap an ending.

Just keep Arthur safe.

She braked, gliding into a stop at the T.

The Ranger had spun almost a hundred and eighty. Arthur stared out the driver's window. Wincing, he mouthed *sorry*, then ducked as his passenger smacked him upside his head. Webb had relocated to the front.

He shoved Arthur back, glared across his prisoner, and flashed a handgun at Callie as a warning. Then, as if his own foot were on the gas, the truck spun. It didn't head back toward Raysor. It didn't try to pass Callie on Jenkins Hill Road either. Instead, it tore up the silted one-lane of Steamboat Landing, the goading a *come and get me* message.

So she took him up on the challenge and followed, radioing Raysor to assist.

"Where does this lead?" Mark hadn't been to the end of Steamboat Landing.

Arthur had, though. And surely Webb had.

"Nowhere," she said, unable to see for the billowing dust. She backed off at the neon-orange *Road Narrows 5 MPH* sign. She kept pushing but wouldn't risk running up on a truck bumper in case they stopped.

Pulse throbbing, she gritted her teeth, admittedly hating this man, more so than most she'd pursued in her life. He wasn't incredibly vile, or as hardcore evil as half the people she'd chased in her detective days, but his casual destruction and disregard of people and lives had hurt, upset, and indirectly killed Edistonians. He'd ruined lives with his aspersions. He'd cost her *Chelsea Morning*, but for some reason that didn't rile her as much as what he'd done to Monty, who would never be right again after losing his mother. Callie could rebuild her home. He had nobody to come home to.

People like her were supposed to stop people like Webb. She was supposed to notice them before they did damage, if you believed her resume and long list of awards and recognized talents. Webb wasn't genetically deviant nor related to some mob. He wasn't a villain with grandiose plans that caused him to step on all the people in his path. He wasn't anything special, yet he'd gotten the best of her simply by muddling through his crimes. This case would leave scars.

Her wheels slid, and she lifted her foot, Mark bracing himself on the dash. "Whoa," he said. "If there's no outlet, we don't need to do this."

She regained traction and sped in robotic fashion as if on a track, her mission certain . . . stop this son of a bitch.

At this stage of the road, the sides not only narrowed but also grew three feet high where years of scraping the dirt road had piled sand, dirt, and dead leaves with small rambling roots anchoring the wall. Oaks grew thicker, moss heavier, the sun seeping through filtered, spotty in epileptic flashes across their vision.

Railed fencing cropped up on the right, then almost like a spotlight, the vista opened on the left, overlooking marsh grass, and in seconds, Callie could see sunlight literally at the end of the tunnel. They weren't far.

"Can he take any turnoffs?" Mark asked, looking uncomfortable with the surroundings.

"All gated," she said. "Big money and security out here. He's not getting through any of them."

As if to confirm her words, Mark's head swiveled fast right at the passing aluminum livestock gate, chained and locked.

Then the scenery stretched open, wide and low across a low-tide marsh. Even at low tide, a pickup wasn't turning in that muck, and before they blinked, a creek paralleled them, warning any driver they best not try.

Movement in her rearview mirror caught her attention. Raysor roared to meet them, lights flashing. He loved rolling those lights and kicking up dust, and he'd be as pissed as she was at what Webb had done to these people. Their trust, their safety, their whimsical Garden of Eden sentiments about being free and secure on this island had been damaged

Webb had been part of that Edisto fabric, which made the deception even more appalling. The contractor had dug his hole deeper with his every move, and Callie could not fathom why. He wasn't smart, but he wasn't dumb. Whatever he was, he'd lost his friggin' mind. Callie just didn't want him to take Arthur with him . . . wherever this took them, which right now meant the public boat ramp at the end of Steamboat Landing.

Surely, Webb wasn't planning a showdown.

But Webb wasn't the one driving.

Her blood pummeled each and every artery, but she held her breath steady . . . then she held it, period.

"Callie?" Mark warned, staring as hard ahead as she did.

The Ranger's brake lights came on, then off. On, then off again.

"Oh hell," she whispered, bringing her cruiser to an abrupt stop after sliding a good six yards into one of a dozen buried pillars blocking parking from the water. She bailed out of the car.

Water plumed far and wide as the Ranger plowed into the saltwater of Steamboat Creek.

Callie pointed for Mark to take the small fishing pier, his feet echoing on weathered wood. She rushed to the other side, where the sandy dirt ran straight into the water, scanning for Arthur, but the cab was too far ahead of her to see inside. The truck's rear end bobbed, then dipped forty degrees as the heavy front took on water and sank.

She kept waiting for the screams, at least voices of excitement. Some kind of noises calling for help. They didn't come.

The brackish water gave the rear end a buoyancy, but the soft, quicksand-ish mud in the bottom would suck in those front tires, helped by the weight of the engine. She kicked off shoes and waded in. . . .

Jesus, the cab was going under. Between the dark water, the angle, whatever position the occupants were in, she could not see either of them.

She threw aside her belt. Damn it to hell . . . she wished she had the opportunity to choose which side to tend to first. Arthur was younger, more able to tend to himself . . . Webb's side was closest.

She knew who she preferred to live.

Goddamn it. She leaped, further praying Mark and Raysor were retrieving Arthur on the other side.

Still too far away. She swam out, scanning. Not being tall, she instantly went in over her head, positioning herself far enough from the truck not to get carried under. She went under, searching for Arthur.

In a shock of déjà vu, her feet hit bottom, the mush swallowing her up to her ankles. Underwater memories of Scott's Creek roared back.

She'd almost drowned getting hung up under a car, feet mired. She'd lost an officer. Thomas had saved her. The creek had enveloped her. Her heart thumped, amplified under the water.

She kicked loose of the memory, then the muck, returning to the surface. Five feet out from the passenger's door, she spit out the salty taste and tread water. The passenger door was ajar. Wait . . . it hadn't been when she went under. Maybe she'd misread the situation.

From behind, hands took her back under, yanked her clothes, then her shoulders, until she felt him over her, weighing her down. Eyes open, she hunted for leverage, options, but the water swirled with stirred mud from the truck's splashing entrance, and now her frantic movements to kick free.

Drowning victims were saved out here by swimming up from behind, to avoid the panicky person taking down the rescuer. Webb had used the lesson to gain control and take down Callie.

Her lungs on fire, she hadn't had a chance to grab air before going under, and she hadn't but a precious few seconds to decide how to escape.

She went limp. She went to the bottom. He had to come with her or find his own air. And if she couldn't hold her breath long enough, she prayed Mark or Raysor were up to speed on their CPR skills.

His boots kicked her once in the back. Then one kicked her in the head. Then as if happy he'd made contact, he kicked her in the head again.

She lost her bearing. Was she up, was she down?

The bottom . . . she couldn't tell where it was. So she gave up and let gravity tell her when and how to sink.

She settled in the creek's sludge. Her ears rang, yet muffled silence surrounded her at the same time. She settled belly down, acting unconscious, yet she could feel water swirling above her from his legs kicking and treading.

A solid metal object, stark and opposite to the softness of water and mud, brushed her palm. Like a baby's hand instinctively gripping its mother's finger, she took hold of it. The object somehow oriented her. It was heavy, it was down . . . it was a weapon.

After a failed attempt to get her feet under her due to the mud, she reached around her for some other anchor . . . and gripped Webb's pants leg. He hadn't left, waiting for her to come up for air. Feeling the tug, he kicked her again.

She only gripped his pants tighter, yanked down, and in an upward thrust, aimed her metal object at his legs. He bucked and connected against her neck, the disorientation incredible. However, in her confusion she was sure of one thing . . . she'd cut meat.

Webb jerked. He kicked. He sank, his weight atop her

In the shadowy water, a force took hold of her arm. She attempted to wheel a punch, but the force took her other arm, pulling her up and out.

"Breathe, Callie."

Air surrounded her instead of water, but still, she'd forgotten to take it in. Then she felt the gravel and silt of the landing under her butt and legs. Someone held her arms. She fought to pull loose, but movement made her disorientation worse.

"Callie, Callie, shhhh, it's me."

Digging deep for the will to make sense of things, she opened her eyes. Mark looked down at her, his dark hair plastered to his forehead, his own wetness dripping on her. "It's over," he said.

She jerked up only for the world to sway. Nausea exploded within her, and she rolled to the side to let it spray across the shells and stones. When she wiped her mouth with the back of her hand, however, she smeared blood, and when the coppery flavor hit her tongue, she puked again until there was nothing but bile.

Mark slid himself under her and lifted her to an angle against his lap. Taking her hand, he turned it over. "Whatever you used, you've gouged yourself to the bone with it. And I'll be amazed if you don't have a concussion."

"Arthur?" She barely understood her own whisper.

Mark smiled, a bit pinched. "Bruised. Might need checking out, but my guess is he's fine. He'll live anyway."

"Webb." She didn't ask a question. She wanted to hear all was over, in whatever shape or manner that turned out to be. Caught, injured, cuffed. . . .

"Dead," he said.

Scowling sent jabs of pain through her brain, too sharp to speak for a moment which forced her lids shut.

"Callie!"

She opened her eyes. Took her a moment to remember what Mark had said. "Webb," she repeated. "He's dead. How?"

Had Raysor pounded the contractor in his attempt to flee? Had Mark shot him? Had he managed to drown? She'd take any or all of the above.

"Not to worry," he said, the manner in which he said it conflicting with his norm. She could tell he was protecting her.

She steadied herself against his leg, his gimp leg, and she hoped she wasn't hurting him. "I'm not worried. Why are you worried?"

Raysor showed up and attempted to lean over, past his ample girth. "How you feeling, Doll?"

The nickname made her smile. "Fine," was all she felt like saying. There was too much pain and dizziness to describe.

"See there?" Mark said, injecting some humor. "Stan calls her Chicklet. You call her Doll. Both of you make her grin when you do. I'm telling you, I need my own nickname for her."

She relaxed. She was wise enough to recognize she wasn't going anywhere but the hospital. Maybe they'd tell her what happened to Webb later. She could guess, but that made her head hurt, too.

Chapter 29

TWO WEEKS LATER, Callie stood in the back of the Edisto Town Council meeting in full daytime uniform, her hand still bandaged from the twenty stitches she'd incurred in her fight with Webb. She had to attend, to report the department's successes since the last board meeting. Statistics, mostly. Marie always prepared them, and Callie read them on the way to a meeting.

This time, however, she was leery about a coup. Brice would take some sort of shot at her, she was sure. He'd mouthed off about it too many times to too many people, which explained the bump in the number of attendees. She wasn't the only one standing against the wall in the small room, and the scents of the freshly showered clashed with those who slid in after a day in the sun.

How many damn times had he pulled this stunt? Six? Seven? It was like he used the threat of axing the police chief to raise ratings and improve attendance, always on the heels of a case, a death, or something Alex posted in the news.

Sophie had been her sidekick at past meetings, but tonight she ran El Marko's while its proprietor sat two rows from the front. After Steamboat Landing, Mark had been watching her closely.

Stan came to every meeting, and Callie often felt he did so to watch her perform. Tonight, Thomas sat groomed in jeans and a collared shirt, crisp and clean. Raysor asked her at quitting time if he ought to be there, and Callie had told him not to bother. He showed up anyway, still in uniform.

Callie's report held a few negatives this time, and they all knew it. Webb's death. Dud's death. The Myrtle Street fires. Minnie's death—the identification confirmed. Even tonight people still offered condolences for *Chelsea Morning's* loss as Callie walked in. She wouldn't talk about the negative news coverage but fully expected Brice to fill in whatever she chose to leave out of her presentation.

Surprisingly, Brice waited for her to recuperate to make a move, waiting for the scheduled monthly event instead of requesting anything interim. He'd threatened her innumerable times since she'd been chief of police, and he'd actually followed through on two impromptu, emergency meetings in addition to the regular sessions. Each of those times, residents and other law enforcement had come to her defense, one time an FBI agent capitalizing on the gathering to give her an award for solving a joint case. Brice had turned ten shades of red atop his customary alcoholic hue.

Tonight, Callie had her own surprise.

The meeting dragged with the discussion of committee vacancies, and there seemed to be a lot of them. Water and Sewer Committee, always a hot topic on the beach. The Town Hall Design Committee, the Planning Commission, and four slots were unexpectedly empty on the Construction Board of Appeals, its work a never-ending contested bucket of worms. Not Callie's concern until someone lost their mind or broke a law.

Next on the agenda were first readings of ordinance changes, second readings of amendments, and a lengthy discussion on how much tax revenue to make available to the Chamber of Commerce. Plus, this was the time of year they nailed down dates for a half dozen parades, festivals, and road races.

With the doors closed, as time dragged on, a stuffiness crept in and clung to the attendees, but she'd learned to be patient at these things a long time ago. The council routinely scheduled the police department's business toward the end of the agenda, partly because Callie had to stay the entire meeting anyway as a safety presence or deterrent against heated tempers slipping the leash.

A town councilwoman got particularly long-winded about the destruction of dunes on the three hundred block, feeling the need to pontificate in spite of a pending contract for renewal. Everyone welcomed the distraction when thirty minutes into things, Alexandra Hanson showed up, minus a camera person, and escorted her grandmother and Monty Bartow to seats behind Janet Wainwright and Arthur.

Almost seventy and living alone except for Alex's periodic visits, Mrs. Hanson had taken Monty in for the time being. Monty's bandages shined white, his hair neatly parted and clothes crisply ironed. Though the placement had been Callie's idea, she let Alex take the credit, the personal interest story making the evening news, aiding the young reporter's professional endeavors, and counteracting some of the negative rumors about Monty. The more positive Edisto looked the better. The less attention Callie received the better.

Callie hadn't been able to cement all the details of that God-forsaken week of fires and injury, but she would bet her badge on Webb having planted the uninscribed badge at the Myrtle Street fires. When Booker McPhee hadn't been able to pay Webb due to a financial crisis, Webb had decided to ensure his chances of compensation with a fire, banking on an insurance payout. He directed attention for the arson onto an easy target, Monty, never expecting anyone to question the culprit and certainly not believing Monty could talk his way out of a charge. Attempting to kill Monty had shown how desperate he'd grown seeing Callie not taking the bait, and that had started his undoing.

The original engraved badge remained missing. Monty hadn't asked for it, either. He'd lost interest in law enforcement. That part weighed heavily on Callie. Something told her she was no longer a hero in the man's eyes, even after she'd spent hours going over Alex's video footage to further clear him.

After Arthur's kidnapping, Janet fessed up that Webb had deeper financial problems than she'd admitted, confessing she'd hoped to ac-quire the houses once they were repaired and hadn't wanted to get in-volved with Callie's crime-solving. Nobody accused her of collaborating with Webb to force a sale, which wasn't her style, nor did she need the money. She'd been awful silent since Arthur came home from Steamboat Landing, and per Callie's read, Janet in her own muted way regretted not having cooperated sooner.

Thanks to Dud, bless him, Callie'd learned Webb had pulled the jewelry heists . . . at least one of them, and all three owners were reunited with their goods. Webb had hidden down the street from the Myrtle Street fire, distant from the crowds and chaos and, therefore, Alex's filming, and he'd lain in wait for opportunity. Whether he planned the thefts ahead of time or had a revelation to further his frame of Monty, he only had to slip behind Gerard, house to house, and wait for the homes to empty. Gerard finding no answer at Dud's house unexpectedly gave Webb the okay to enter.

Poor Gerard. He couldn't stop kicking himself for Webb, for Dudley, for his patrol car burning up.

At *Bikini Bottom*, Callie was ninety percent sure Webb had taken the engraved badge out of Monty's basket and inserted the stolen jewelry. Monty's recollection of the Ram insinuated Webb baited Monty to the dumpster, but Webb wasn't a natural-born murderer so he'd screwed up the attempt, and Monty's survival complicated the whole mess.

Callie had thought too long and too hard about the details and dribbles, the odds and possibilities every night since Steamboat. She felt spot on in her theories, not that anyone could prove her wrong or had any better explanations for the timeline of events. Not that it mattered with the likely culprit dead.

Minnie had lost her mind over the damage to her son and blamed Callie since she had no one else to blame. No doubt, Minnie wanted to set Callie's house on fire as payback but also to divert attention from Monty with someone else to blame. She too hadn't known how to be a good criminal. She hadn't planned on lighting herself up.

Ironically, the people who were supposed to die were Monty and Callie, both of whom happened to be the only ones who lived thanks to Webb and Minnie not knowing what the hell they were doing.

Smoke and fire would haunt Callie to her dying day. She'd dreamt about them every night since the incident.

She was grateful for the concussion, to be honest. She didn't remember the bloodiness of the creek, nor what happened to the sharp piece of a broken fluke anchor she'd found on the bottom. The anchor that had ripped into Webb's femoral artery and made him bleed out.

About the time Raysor had put a bullet in his head.

"Chief Morgan?"

She stiffened to attention, hoping that had been the first time he'd called her.

Brice peered over his reading glasses at her, almost eating the microphone to sound more ominous. "We're finally ready for your briefing. Afterwards, we have a matter to discuss in open forum." He gave a sweeping glance across the crowd. "Our apologies to the attendees for the long evening, but sometimes it takes time to run Edisto Beach."

Making her way up the center aisle, she stood at the pressboard podium and bent the mic lower. She hated podiums. Always too tall.

"As always, thanks for having me, Mr. LeGrand . . . council members." She smiled at the crowd and set her papers before her. She read off the routine items first . . . tickets, calls answered, domestics. At times in the past she would elaborate on a few of the calls, more for entertainment purpose than anything else, but tonight was not one of those nights. At the end of the statistics, she gave herself a breath and remained in place, informing everyone of the shift in subject.

"We might as well address the elephants in the room," she said, and a ripple rolled across the audience. This is what they'd been waiting for. The corner of Brice's mouth inched up in satisfaction. Let the show begin.

"Some of you are aware of recent criminal activities, but few know the real details." She gave a melancholy breath. "We do not have enough time tonight to tell you the intricacies, nor should we, but I can assure you that the danger is gone."

Grumblings traveled across the people.

"The casualties are these," she said, turning to quickly pan, no longer needing her notes.

"We had three fires at four different properties, and we can be ever grateful to Leon Hightower and his people for their service in containing them. All were deemed arson."

More rumblings.

She didn't include Brice's bucket fire in the mix.

"The first were *Shell Shack* and *Shark Shack* on Myrtle Street. Severe damage, but insurance will pay for renovations. *Bikini Bottom* was the second, involving a dumpster fire, also arson, and a person was injured." She glanced at Monty and smiled. He raised a wrapped hand as if cued, and a few chuckles lightened the atmosphere. He'd been embraced by a lot of folks since he lost his mother . . . since Webb died.

"Finally, *Chelsea Morning*. . . ." She paused, and the room quieted in understanding. "*Chelsea Morning* on Jungle Road was a complete loss. That arsonist died in the fire." She didn't explain that her bandage had nothing to do with the fire and everything to do with killing Webb. Justified or not, civilians struggled meeting killers, and if these people realized how many souls Callie had killed or been killed, or been affiliated with the killer who did the killing, they'd fear her being in the same room with them.

Also, these people had no need to learn the whys of these fires, neither Webb's insurance plan and attempted murder nor Minnie's misguided anger about the police department being responsible for the rumor-mongering toward Monty. Callie still wondered what she could've said differently to avoid falling so far from grace with Minnie. Callie thought she'd been the person most loyal to Monty, maybe with the exception of Thomas.

Her gaze strayed toward her deputy at the thought, and he smiled back, showing his support. God, she loved that kid. He was part of why tonight would be difficult.

"I'd like us to remember the loss of life," she said. "Minnie Bartow . . . so sorry, Monty," she said directly to him. "And Dudley Vaughn, what a dear." She gave a pause for that memory. "And Harbin Webb." She couldn't mention the two without the third. Damn that was hard.

The microphone exaggerated her sudden need to sigh, the delay causing a few to whisper to their neighbor. "Sorry," she said, when Mark did an eyebrow thing at her. "Regretfully, I must add that we are losing two officers. Officers Gerard Valentine and Cobb LaRoache have tendered resignations."

The council had no idea. Callie hadn't warned them. To tell one was to tell the others, and she hadn't wanted Brice to know in advance for fear of whom he'd blab to and how he'd blab it.

"We have two more weeks to enjoy Gerard and three more to appreciate LaRoache. When you see them, please thank them for their service and wish them luck."

The audience felt an applause in order, making her smile. She'd told the two officers not to appear at tonight's meeting, and they'd been grateful.

Stan and Mark knew ahead of time, and both gave solemn acknowledgement of how difficult a time she was having. Raysor hadn't heard any of this from Callie, but he didn't act surprised. No doubt the junior officers had asked him for advice, at least felt the need to give him a heads-up. Thomas apparently knew as well, from his lack of reaction.

She loved all these men for their unconditional endorsement.

"Chief Morgan."

She redirected her attention to the chair of the council. "Mr. LeGrand?"

"We, the council, commend you for bringing this crime spree to a conclusion. While we wish it could have been handled with less damage, less loss of both property and life . . . our condolences on your own loss, by the way. . . ."

She gave him a gracious nod.

He offered his own meek smile and continued. "But I had my own small fire, if you recall, that you determined wasn't a part of this rash of crimes."

She wasn't taking the bait. That would only bring Leon Hightower and his department into this and he didn't need that.

"How long have you been chief on Edisto Beach?" Brice asked.

"Two years," she said with a forced strength, thinking the two felt like ten.

A couple of the council members could no longer maintain eye contact with her, hinting at what was to come.

She folded the papers in front of her, giving them more attention than needed, then lengthened her spine, shoulders back. "Mr. LeGrand and the other honorable members of county council, I would first like to make a statement please."

"But Chief," Brice started, "first I must—"

"I assure you it can wait," she said. "Monty, come on up."

Confused, Monty looked to Mrs. Hanson who nodded it was okay for him to go forward. As he approached, Callie reached into the podium where she'd had Marie hide a bag.

"Monty Bartow," she said when he reached her. She took a second to slide him around so the audience could see his face, sharing a warm smile with him.

After a night of dry bureaucracy laced with smatterings of cynicism, the audience seemed to welcome a more lightheaded moment, and smiles covered the crowd.

"Monty, you're a true Edistonian," she said. "You've helped traffic, helped visitors, and most assuredly helped me and my department. We love having you as a part of this beach."

He beamed, which made everyone else beam. Callie unfolded the bag and slid out a plaque. "We wanted to commend you for all the work you've done in helping make Edisto a better place to live, visit, and enjoy."

His smile lit up the room, all the way into his crinkling eyes. She couldn't help herself . . . she gave him a hug. She let the applause carry for a moment or two, then motioned to them to let her speak. "We also thank you with this medal of service." And she pinned it on him.

The applause erupted again. Amidst it, she leaned close and spoke in his ear. "It's not a badge, but I believe it says a lot more about you, Monty. Thank you."

She'd never seen him happier. "Thank you, Chief."

The crowd enjoyed the moment on and on until Callie turned Monty toward Mrs. Hanson to return to his seat, and Brice held up palms for the noise to cease.

He'd been totally unaware, and his expression wasn't nearly as pleased as the rest. "Chief Morgan, I'd like to continue with another matter—"

"Hold on, Mr. LeGrand," she interrupted.

Like the sea bass he always claimed to fish for when he was drinking on his boat, his mouth opened and shut several times. "See here—"

"I resign effective immediately."

The air went stone dead still.

Then before the uproar started, she left her folded notes on the podium and strolled up the center aisle, hiding the fact she found it difficult to breathe. By the time she reached the double doors, the talking and shouting began, but she continued through. She didn't dare breathe until she found her way outdoors, because she wasn't quite sure how she'd react. She couldn't hear her feet on the gravel for the noise of her heart slamming into her chest.

"Callie!" She'd have guessed Mark made it out first.

"Callie!" And Stan second.

But she continued walking up Myrtle Street, through the shadows, the dim spots of each house guiding her toward Palmetto, each step taking her closer to the outgoing Atlantic tide. She'd walked to the meeting to start with, needing the time to sort her thoughts in preparation, just as she needed this time leaving to adjust to what she'd done.

Also, as she'd predicted . . . as she had hoped . . . her men took the hint, and nobody chased after her.

Thank God for that.

Chapter 30

CALLIE SPENT THE night at *Windswept*, slowly nudging herself for hours on Seabrook's red swing before making her way inside around three in the morning, to where she slept in his bed. She'd ignored twenty-one calls and texts by then.

Unfortunately, frenzied knocks woke her around eight a.m.

Ignoring the first raps, she dove under a pillow, yanking the bedspread over best she could, but the relentlessness of the visitor continued. She slid out, not giving a damn she had no robe and wore only a nightshirt that had happened to be in a suitcase at Mark's when her house went up in flames. She didn't care. She tired of being account-able anymore.

Opening the main door, she expected Stan or Mark. "Shouldn't you be teaching a yoga class?" she asked at the sight of Sophie.

"My off day," she said, yanking on the screen door, pouting when the latch held it shut.

Callie flipped it open, turned, and went to the kitchen to turn on the coffee.

"What in Hades have you done, Callie Jean Morgan?" Sophie said, her angry voice screechy around the edges.

"I resigned," Callie replied, having prepared her answers to this type of conversation which she expected a dozen times before the day was through. "Allow me my coffee before we launch into this, okay?"

But Sophie continued, this screech a couple decibels higher. "Have you at least told Jeb?"

"Can't even wait for my coffee," Callie murmured, watching the Keurig spit and sputter the last dribbles. Not answering, she took her cup to the porch. "Help yourself if you want one."

Ignoring coffee, Sophie beat her to the porch, and in understanding of how Callie embraced this house of Seabrook's, she took up residence on the red swing's end that gave her the better view of the water across Palmetto, so that her friend would have to face her. Callie assumed the other end of the swing.

To the passersby, they appeared two girlfriends escaping the world to gossip, one a half-naked woman dressed in a nightshirt and the other in yoga tights and an off-the-shoulder blouse. Not a bit odd in a coastal community. The tide was out, leaving a calmer impression of the beach. A fisherman and his wife crossed the road with a custom wagon filled with assorted poles and bait, ready to stake their claim on some sand before the tide returned.

Sophie kicked them into a wide sway, and then—being as short as Callie—folded her legs in the seat. "The guys are afraid to talk to you."

"So they sent you instead . . . nope, let me guess, you offered." The coffee was too hot to sip yet, the cup too hot to deal with other than rest it on the swing's arm and watch it to avoid a spill.

Sophie took her tone down to gossip level and repeated, "Have you told Jeb?"

"I was going to call him when I woke up, but you stepped ahead of the line." Callie'd kill for that coffee to cool. She lifted it anyway and took a scalding sip, blowing afterward, feeling silly getting that backward. "He'll be fine with it."

He'd never embraced law enforcement after losing a father and grandfather to the criminal element in Callie's world, and he'd insinuated more than a few times that she didn't have to work thanks to those same deaths leaving her financially set.

Oh, no, he wouldn't have a problem at all.

And if she'd told Jeb before the meeting yesterday, he'd have told his girlfriend, who'd have told her mother . . . the same woman sharing the swing with her now . . . and no telling how far that would've gone before last night's meeting ever got started.

The only person who'd known in advance had been Marie. She ran the department. She had to be informed. She also kept secrets. She'd cried.

After the Webb ordeal, once back from the ER, Callie'd stayed with Mark a few nights. She'd been fed and pampered. Stan and Sophie, even Janet and Arthur, visited her. She heard nothing from Brice . . . totally expected, and hadn't seen him until the meeting last night.

She found herself needing space to process recent events, analyze her shortcomings, second-guess her decisions, and after doing so, she felt lost as to where she needed to be. She couldn't shed the feeling of her own negligence to the beach, and with all the noise around her, it only festered.

So she'd spoken to Janet, who managed the empty *Windswept* house since Seabrook died. The family hadn't been able to part with it, and they rented it with a critical eye. No weekend affairs, preferring leases a month long or more. When she approached them, through Janet, they welcomed Callie's offer to rent it for six months, with the possibility of longer.

They'd learned early on how much Callie meant to Seabrook . . . and him to her.

Nobody claimed Dudley, which broke her heart. The evening she'd learned he'd wind up with little more than a simple cremation organized by county health, she'd sat on Seabrook's red swing and cried. His demise had pushed her in her decision to leave the department, but the last straw might have been a night at El Marko's.

Brice strode in and put the blame of all three deaths on her before an evening crowd. One would've thought the son of a bitch would know better than to air his opinions there, but Brice wasn't renowned for his mental prowess. Mark put him out to a round of applause.

Brice would never cease being corrosive or adversarial and would never go away, which she had to accept, but what pained her was the incessant pressure these islanders felt to take a side. Janet, Stan, and Mark had all run to her defense during this last case, almost running over her to do it. Not only did she hate people reacting this way, but she hated being saved, physically or mentally.

She wasn't sure if it took more strength to leave or stay as chief of police, but to put the town through what it had been put through this last month told her they needed the option of functioning without her. They now could decide how to replace her without having to oust her first.

Brice got what he wanted. Now let the town figure out how to deal with it.

She assumed responsibility for Dudley's remains, and his ashes were strewn in the bay one evening at sunset, amidst a small collection of boats. Probate would take time without heirs, so she'd thrown her name in the hat to manage that as well. An attempt at redemption maybe?

The necklace no longer needed for evidence, she'd parked it on its celadon display vase there at Seabrook's. Mike Seabrook would've liked that. Callie was ashamed to say she wasn't sure Mike knew Dud. Surely he had. Regardless, he'd approve of the addition of this vase and necklace on the living room credenza.

Guess she was starting a new collection of dead people memorabilia. Her other collection had burned in the fire. She'd lost her son's entire past. Her own graduations and police commendations. She'd never been a material girl, but she guessed some things did matter.

Fingers snapped in her face. "Damn, girl, you *are* messed up," Sophie said once Callie returned her attention. "I said I brought sage."

"Good for you." Callie wasn't bothering telling Sophie not to sage the house, the porch, whatever else she felt like purifying.

But Sophie didn't pull out her sage. Instead, she stared. Callie had drunk only half her coffee, but it had cooled, so she parked it on a small semi-circle weathered table against the wall beside her.

"Talk, Sophie. Get it all out of your system. You must have thirty people waiting for you to deliver some sort of news about me." Then she smiled at her friend.

Sophie leaned in, mysterious and slow. "Are you broken?"

The honest simplicity of the question touched Callie, and her smile warmed. This spoke to how fragile everyone considered her to be.

She couldn't hide like this for long. Intelligence told her that. And while she thought she'd given this exodus and new direction immense consideration, she could see that others could not relate. Truth was, she wasn't as strong as people thought she was. She was just stronger than most of them.

The question still hung in the air, though . . . *are you broken?*

"I'd like to see if I can be somebody without being law enforcement," she ultimately said.

Sophie backed off the leaning in. "What if people think—"

"I don't care what people think, Soph."

Sophie studied her. "Is this a vacation?"

"No."

"What if they want you back?"

Callie had prepared answers for a lot of expected questions. This one, however, she hadn't considered. "No answer for that one. Never considered that would be in Brice's game plan."

Sophie grimaced.

"Soph, tell me this. What plans do you have for your life? What if you get it wrong?"

"I'm not you," she said.

Callie laughed. "We agree on that. But what if a man comes along, for instance? Do you let him move in?"

"Only on the weekends. The weekdays are mine. And I will never marry. Don't want to jeopardize my money or my house. Plus, I need my *me* space to keep in touch with my spirit."

"Wow. That's pretty exact."

"I feel strongly about that. I want to be in control."

"No floating wherever fate, ghosts, and the universe's powers take you, huh?"

Sophie shook her head, her coral-lipsticked mouth pursed. "That's not how it works. Besides, like I said, you're not me. This beach needs all kinds of people. The yous . . . the mes . . . the idiots . . . the wise."

Callie wasn't asking her who fell in what category.

As nosey as this conversation was, Callie appreciated it. It cleared her head. It made her realize that as long as she lived on Edisto Beach, she was still part of the community. There was no escaping that fact. She might be a loner by nature, but she wasn't letting herself become a Dudley.

"We haven't spoken of your mother," Sophie said. "She got any opinions?"

Her adopted mother, she meant. Beverly, whom she now knew as her stepmother, and her biological father Lawton had raised her. *Chelsea Morning* had molded a slew of childhood memories for Callie. No telling what kind of memories for Beverly who'd looked the other way as Lawton continued seeing Callie's biological mother on Edisto.

"She said rebuild it," Callie said, her mother having seen the fire as a purge.

"That's it?"

"That's it."

Sophie scratched her hairline. "Doesn't anyone in your family get upset about anything?"

Callie unfolded herself and retrieved her cold coffee. "I need a shower. Tell everyone I'm still alive."

Traffic had picked up on the main road. A patrol car cruised by. Thomas. Callie wished he'd stop. He didn't, but he waved.

"Well, I'll spread the news best I can," Sophie said, noting where Callie's attention had gone.

With a chuckle, Callie slid over and squished her in a hug. "I'm sure you will."

Sophie left, a little reluctant, somewhat hesitant at not having collected straight answers. Inside, however, Callie found a fresh sage bundle resting on an abalone shell, small pink flowers entwined in the sage. Some of Sophie's best.

The visit had killed a couple hours of Callie's first day in her new life, but with no place to go, she took her time showering. She had no food in the house. Frankly, she hadn't had an appetite, but better now than ever to assume the role of civilian . . . and the stares, and the whispers.

She walked to Bi-Lo. Sweaty by the time she arrived, she paused to study the still tilted Island Ice Shack. A half dozen people walked around it, attempting to define the physics of righting it back on its foundation. *Wow, felt like ages ago.*

She grabbed a cart from under the store's overhang and shivered upon entering the store. While her civilian clothes helped disguise her, too many people spotted her up close once she arrived.

"Chief."

"Hey, Chief."

"Nice day, Chief."

Ignoring the expired title, she shopped, having to smile to at least one person per aisle. She filled up two bags of groceries, having to stop herself before spilling into three. And through it all, she never lost the smile needed for yet another greeting. Arms full, she resumed the mile-long walk back.

Sweat ran down her jaw and with the groceries, she couldn't reach a shoulder up to catch it. Other trickles itched her back.

It was almost noon. The sun blazed on broil.

A patrol car eased up to her, its passenger window rolling down. "Need a ride?"

She took Thomas up on the offer. The air-conditioning ranked up there with a gin and tonic. Bags at her feet, she clipped her seat belt then turned a vent on her. "Damn it's hot."

But he didn't immediately leave the curb.

"That was an obscene move dumping us like that."

"I couldn't tell one without telling everyone," she said. "Except Marie. And don't you fuss at her for not telling you, either."

But that didn't satisfy him in the least. She had to look away when he uttered, "What the hell, Chief?"

She could tell him she'd lost too much. She could say she tired of the continual undermining, backstabbing plays from council, but what police chief didn't have to deal with politics? What she had trouble saying was too many people had died on her watch, in her wake, and even at her hand. The best way for that to stop was for her to leave law enforcement before she destroyed herself.

But he was young and eager. He would see her rationale as selfish, exaggerated, and an easy problem to fix. Young people could always tackle the world and leave it a better place. She used to feel that way. And somehow, in this last case, she'd robbed Gerard and LaRoache of that zeal.

"Gerard and LaRoache," she said.

"They made mistakes anyone could've made. You wouldn't find me quitting over any of that."

"Someone died on each of their watches," she said. "LaRoache has stuck it out for a while carrying that death. That's a hellacious burden to bear. Not everyone has shoulders that wide."

"You do."

Not anymore, she almost said, but she didn't. "You do, too," she said. "You could run this place."

He shook his head double time. "No, ma'am. You're not making this about me. Today I don't need stroking. You do."

Bless him. "Stroking doesn't do it for me anymore, Thomas. And my shoulders are damn tired."

His jaw worked beneath the skin. "I'm not giving up on you yet," he said.

"And I love you for that."

Thomas drove on and soon pulled into the *Windswept* drive. "This," and he pointed up to the porch, "is not good for you."

"I have no house, Thomas."

"Not what I meant, and you know it." The kid sounded much older than his almost-thirty age. She really really loved this guy.

"Listen," she tried again. "Maybe I can join the ranks of Stan and Mark as someone on the sidelines the department could call on when needed." She left off that she'd first arrived on Edisto with that very plan in mind. Seabrook had convinced her she was better suited wearing a badge, then he'd maneuvered her into the chief's role because he didn't want it.

Thomas declined that option. "Nope. You're the real deal."

She scoffed. "Mark and Stan were the real deal, too."

He had no comeback. He was hurting.

She exited the vehicle before leaning in to recover her bags, seeking a more common conversation. "Want to come up?"

"Gotta work," he said.

"After work, then," she countered.

Marie's voice came over the radio. Callie listened. A domestic on Catherine Street, a few blocks down.

Thomas noted her listening, raised a brow in a silent message of *not your job anymore*, and left.

She stood in the drive holding her groceries, unable to ignore the sting.

Inside, to avoid the silence of the house, she returned phone calls and texts, deciding to hit the inquiries head on. Between her talks with Sophie and Thomas and the small questions in Bi-Lo, she felt she handled herself well. When someone told her to tackle *Chelsea Morning* with fervor, she shifted her purpose for leaving to that, rebuilding her home. She let them think it was only about the house.

By seven, she'd made most of the calls and walked away from Jeb's conversation with a double-down warning not to drink. "You lose your home, with someone dying inside in the process, Mom, and then you quit your job? The professionals say one life change at a time." After sighing to her, at her, for her, hell, she couldn't tell, he ended with, "Do I need to come home?"

She dodged the intention. "Our home is gone."

"You hear me, Mom. Do I?"

"No, sir." He did not need to babysit her. He would in a heartbeat. She couldn't take that atop of everything else. "You continue with your studies. I'll stay occupied with contractors and paint swatches."

"Love you," he said.

"Adore you," she replied.

"Promise you'll call if you need something. Please, promise."

Tears caught in her throat. "I promise."

She'd saved him to last to give him her all. Now she wanted that drink. She hadn't a drop in the house, and if she returned to the liquor store next door to Bi-Lo, word would spread.

Unless she drove to Walterboro. . . .

But her personal car had burned with the house. She had to ask for rides until she managed a way to get to Charleston to find a new vehicle.

She put that on her list . . . car hunt online.

She turned to her new laptop. Also, a contractor she toyed with hiring had told her to find a plan she liked and notify him soon before he got backed up with jobs. She leaned toward a new design rather than replicating the old, to go along with the changes she yearned for her life.

Yeah, that was good for a laugh. She had no idea what to do with her life now, and less how to design a house.

Looking up after imagining herself walking through the rooms of twenty-seven designs, she noted shadows on the floor where there'd been none. She'd lost track of time. This part of the year it could be almost nine and you'd still be able to read a book. She was right. Ten minutes till nine.

She'd weathered her first day.

The knock at the front door almost scared her off the sofa cushion. Peering from the bedroom window, in case she didn't want to answer, she groaned. She thought her day was over.

Chapter 31

"HEY," MARK SAID, brown bag in hand. He made a conscious effort to peer around, like there might be others in the house behind Callie.

"Come in," she said, holding the door.

"No ghosts?"

"No ghosts."

Making himself at home in the kitchen, his favorite room anywhere, he laid out an array of enchiladas, tacos, and tamales, with a tomatoey Spanish rice on the side. Without words, he set the dining room table and motioned for Callie to sit.

"This is nice," she said, pleased at the normalcy, tensed waiting for *the talk*. She lifted her fork, then chose to open the subject first to get it out of the way. She'd quit. She'd tired of Brice, the conflict . . . the death. "There was no way to forewarn people," she said, stirring the rice to savor the aroma. "Not without showing my hand to council."

He cut into his tamale. "So that was your motive, huh? To stun Brice . . . while hurting the rest of us?" He took a bite and chewed.

Stunned, she lay down her fork. "No, that was absolutely not my motive."

"Just saying. . . ."

"That's not me at all," she stammered. "I did not hurt the department. I left them with a clean slate. No open cases. Nothing but tickets to write. I took all scandal with me."

He continued cutting his food, very level in his demeanor. "You left them with a chasm, Chief. Them and us, your friends. And you dumped a heavy burden on Gerard and LaRoache who at least gave two weeks' notice."

"You've been here, what, less than a year? What would you have done if—"

"We're not talking me. This is about you."

She gave up trying to take a bite between words. "I'm tired of it being about me. This town is incessantly torn over me and what I uncover, who I put in jail, whose reputation I tarnish . . . who dies when I get involved. Anyone else in my shoes would've been seeing ghosts."

Mouth full, he rolled his eyes over the Seabrook interior, a mild wave with his hand holding a knife.

"Not funny," she said. "If I had a house, I wouldn't be here. And I told you, no ghosts."

"You could've been with me, Stan, Sophie. . . ."

She wanted peace, though. To be alone. To decide if her disappointment with herself was due to history, people skills, or simply being chief. She wasn't sure she could tell him that without sounding awfully pitiful. "Back to Gerard and LaRoache. They're a big part of why I left, but they can't know that. There was no convincing them to stay. Gerard feels responsible for Dudley Vaughn. LaRoache killed someone in the spring, his first and hopefully his last, to keep the man from killing me. Not catching Webb crossing the causeway with Arthur pushed his last button. I feel I let them down somehow. Maybe should've taught them better."

"Their shortcomings, not yours."

"My men, under my training. Under my watch. Do you know how many people I've lost in this department?"

Mark had scratched the scabs off multiple emotional wounds in bare minutes, and an anger began to light her up.

"Are you moving?" he asked.

The shift diffused the anger. "What? No, why would I move?"

He shrugged with his entire body, a sarcasm pouring out with it. "You quit, admittedly to escape ridicule. Yet you remain right here in the thick of things on Edisto Beach. All the people judging you are still here. Doesn't take a badge for them to keep doing it."

True, but—"Where else would I go?"

"No idea. I like it here."

"I have a house to rebuild."

"Sell the lot," he said.

"I don't want to sell the lot."

In the middle of his enchilada, he ceased eating. "And why would that be?"

She didn't want to say it.

Sliding his food away, he lowered elbows to his placemat to give her his all. "Answer the question."

"Because it's home," she whispered.

He pushed her plate out of the way, too, and motioned for her to give him her hands. "You lost hope," he said. "You just lost your way, honey."

"People died." Saying the words choked her. "People lost family. People lost reputations. Two lovely officers want to leave. Don't make me talk about the two officers who died before."

"Shit . . . happens, Callie. You of all people know that. You," and he shook her hands, his cradling hers from beneath. "You are this gifted, most remarkable person who's weathered more and weathered it better than anyone I've ever met. Without a doubt, you've paid a heavy toll. Your strength gave every single body in your department the power to do their job."

"But Brice."

She regretted how she'd tricked Brice about Webb, making him use his sleezy side to spread the word and flush out the contractor. "I baited Brice and stooped to his level. After that, Dudley died, Arthur got kidnapped, Webb. . . ." She didn't finish.

What kind of law enforcement did she represent?

"Webb was your training talking. That was survival."

She didn't want to talk about Webb anymore.

"Brice is jealous of your strength."

Nice words, but words were easy.

"You retreated here," he said, looking around the room. "Why is that?"

"That isn't fair," she said.

"Fair for who?"

"You. Listen, it's not that you compete against him. It's— "

"This conversation isn't about me, Callie. Answer the question."

The pure altruistic nature of him broke her defenses. He indeed was making this all about her.

"He believed in me," she said in a rush of breathy words. "Seabrook saw me like nobody ever has. He dragged me out of the dark, after Boston."

Mark's breath sounded full of empathy.

"I don't need pity," she said.

"And I don't give it," he replied, so matter of fact she was taken aback. "I've been there and more. One day I'll share, but not now. Callie,"—

and he released one hand so he could pat her other—"there is such a depth to you that you can't see even when others can. People love you here. There's already a campaign to win you back, did you know that?"

That news gobsmacked her.

"But we're not discussing that," he said. "You've resigned. Be a civilian. Don't wear that God-awful utility belt for a few weeks. Sleep until noon. Spend some time with a contractor. Let your mind rest. Let your body heal. Let your friends be there for you." He lifted a finger to reach over and wipe her cheek.

She was crying.

"You are Edisto Beach, Sunshine. Through and through. And everyone, even Brice to a teeny degree, needs you here."

She could not hold back the tears, and he wouldn't let loose of her hands so she could hide them. So head down on her arms, she sobbed.

He moved her outside to the red swing and held her until she no longer needed holding. She finally sat up and sniffled. "I can work for you at El Marko's."

Nodding, he added, "You can."

"I can do yoga with Sophie and take those trips to Charleston that Stan likes to make, maybe eat lunch with Jeb while we're there." She brushed the residual moisture off her chin with her shoulder. "Help plan parades, volunteer at the bookstore."

"Or decide you cannot part with that badge," he said.

But she didn't want to have that discussion. When she tallied her losses versus her wins, she still felt she'd terribly failed. Mark was telling her that the wins for others factored just as heavily into the equation. That she hadn't considered, and she'd take time to do so.

"I have to think about this," she said.

"You do," he replied.

His leg had kept the porch swinging. On Seabrook's porch, on Seabrook's swing, Callie looked at Mark not just as a visiting friend but through the veil of someone who might understand. Stan kept saying they needed to talk, kept saying they had matters to learn about each other . . . that would help each other. Mark possessed a deep well of his own. She yearned to see what hid down there that had modeled this man sitting against her.

"Want to stay here tonight?" she asked.

"Of course I do," he said, laying his head back, eyes closed. "I'll stay in the guest room, or on the sofa, this swing . . . or anywhere you like but not in that bedroom there." He pointed to the corner of the porch, toward Seabrook's bed on the other wide of the wall.

"And 'Sunshine' will do just fine for now," she said.

He opened his eyes, not sure of her meaning.

"The nickname," she said. "It's lovely when you say it, and I promise to smile."

The End

Acknowledgements

This book came together easier than most, but never does one take form without the skill and support of more than the author.

Thanks so much to Edisto Beach and Edisto Island for feeling the life's blood of these books and giving them credence. Especially thanks to Edisto Bookstore owner Karen Carter for being Ground Zero for this mystery series, making these books a traditional purchase for returning tourists.

Kudos to Deni Ashby for being an incredible friend and cheerleader. If you haven't taken a yoga class from her on Edisto, you haven't done yoga.

Love to my two grandsons who've grown just old enough to realize grandma might be a little famous as an author. ("Between one and five, she's a three," said the oldest to his brother. "When she becomes a five, she can buy us really big gifts.")

Blessings to The Coffee Shelf in Chapin, SC. Its staff has decided they are Ground Zero for middle South Carolina and all things C. Hope Clark, and the owner Jerry Caldwell is just incredible in his endorsement and support. Thanks for all my sugar-free Irish creme lattes with half pumps and whole milk.

Of course, Debra Dixon at Bell Bridge Books makes me look better than I am. We've shared a lot this past year.

Love to Fuji, whom I love like a sister, who has read everything I've written and sung my praises maybe a little louder than I deserve.

And finally, but most definitely not last, Gary makes sure I've written, edited, whatever is needed to keep the gears turning. Through COVID, through foot surgery, through thick and thin, he has learned that I am my best after having written a few good paragraphs on a page each day.

About the Author

C. HOPE CLARK holds a fascination with the mystery genre and is author of the *Carolina Slade Mystery Series*, and the *Craven County Mystery Series* as well as the *Edisto Island Series*, all three set in her home state of South Carolina. In her previous federal life, she performed administrative investigations and married the agent she met on a bribery investigation. She enjoys nothing more than editing her books on the back porch with him, overlooking the lake with bourbons in hand. She can be found either on the banks of Lake Murray or Edisto Beach with one or two dachshunds in her lap. Hope is also editor of the award-winning FundsforWriters.com.

C. Hope Clark

Website: chopeclark.com

Twitter: twitter.com/hopeclark

Facebook: facebook.com/chopeclark

Goodreads: goodreads.com/hopeclark

Bookbub: bookbub.com/authors/c-hope-clark

Editor, FundsforWriters: fundsforwriters.com

Made in the USA
Middletown, DE
11 May 2023

30407210R00165